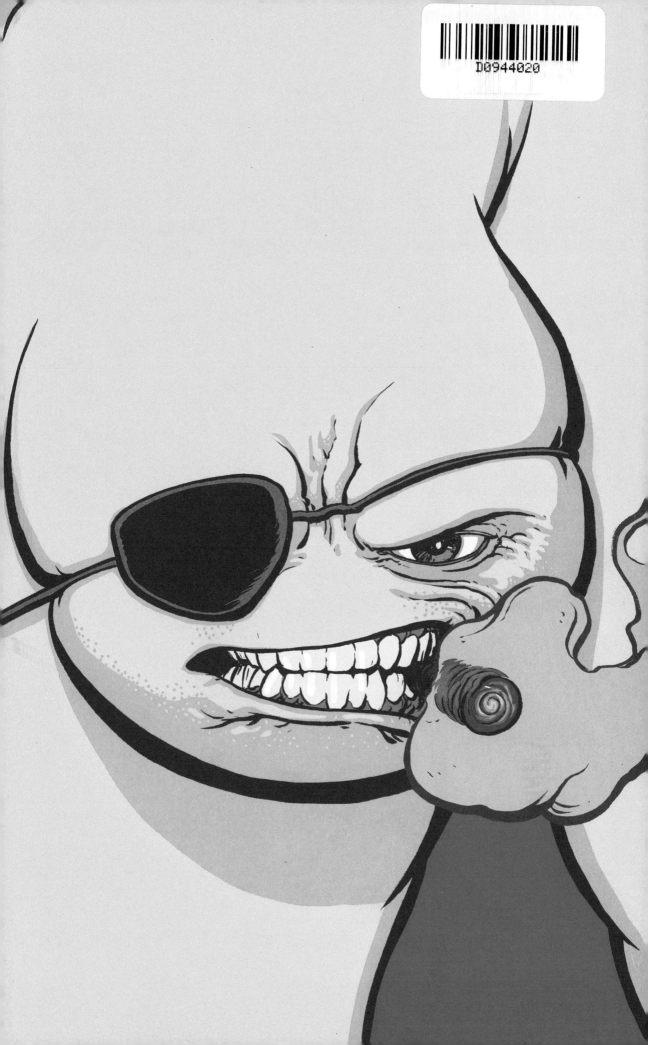

NIXON'S PALS

www.manofaction.tv

SCRIPT JOE CASEY

ART CHRIS BURNHAM

COLOR CARLOS BADILLA

LETTERING RUS WOOTON

GRAPHIC DESIGN SONIA HARRIS

COVER AND ENDPAGES COLOR NATHAN FAIRBAIRN

NIXON'S PALS CREATED BY JOE CASEY & CHRIS BURNHAM

IMAGE COMICS, INC

Robert Kirkman — Chief Operating Officer
Erik Larsen — Chief Financial Officer
Todd McFarlane — President
Marc Silvestri — Chief Executive Officer
Jim Valentino — Vice-President

Eric Stephenson — Publisher
Ron Richards — Director of Business Development
Jennifer de Guzman — Director of Trade Book Sales
Kat Salazar — Director of PR & Marketing
Corey Murphy — Director of Retail Sales
Jeremy Sullivan — Director of Digital Sales
Emilio Bautista — Sales Assistant
Branwyn Bigglestone — Senior Accounts Manager
Emily Miller — Accounts Manager
Jessica Ambriz — Administrative Assistant
David Brothers — Content Manager
Jonathan Chan — Production Manager
Drew Gill — Art Director
Meredith Wallace — Print Manager
Addison Duke — Production Artist
Vincent Kukua — Production Artist
Tricia Ramos — Production Assistant

www.imagecomics.com

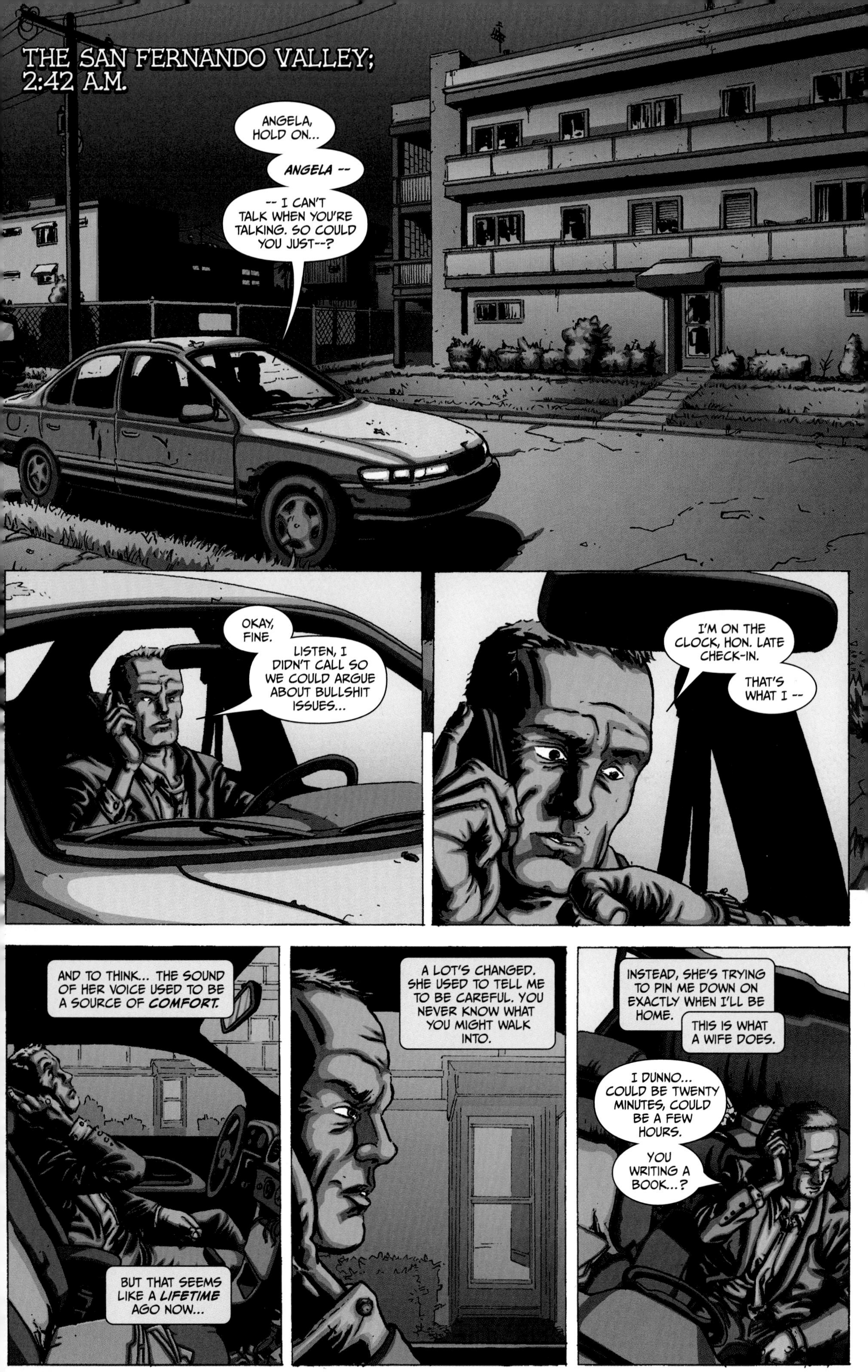
THE SAN FERNANDO VALLEY; 2:42 A.M.
ANGELA, HOLD ON...
ANGELA --
-- I CAN'T TALK WHEN YOU'RE TALKING. SO COULD YOU JUST--?
OKAY, FINE.
LISTEN, I DIDN'T CALL SO WE COULD ARGUE ABOUT BULLSHIT ISSUES...
I'M ON THE CLOCK, HON. LATE CHECK-IN.
THAT'S WHAT I --
AND TO THINK... THE SOUND OF HER VOICE USED TO BE A SOURCE OF COMFORT.
BUT THAT SEEMS LIKE A LIFETIME AGO NOW...
A LOT'S CHANGED. SHE USED TO TELL ME TO BE CAREFUL. YOU NEVER KNOW WHAT YOU MIGHT WALK INTO.
INSTEAD, SHE'S TRYING TO PIN ME DOWN ON EXACTLY WHEN I'LL BE HOME.
THIS IS WHAT A WIFE DOES.
I DUNNO... COULD BE TWENTY MINUTES, COULD BE A FEW HOURS.
YOU WRITING A BOOK...?

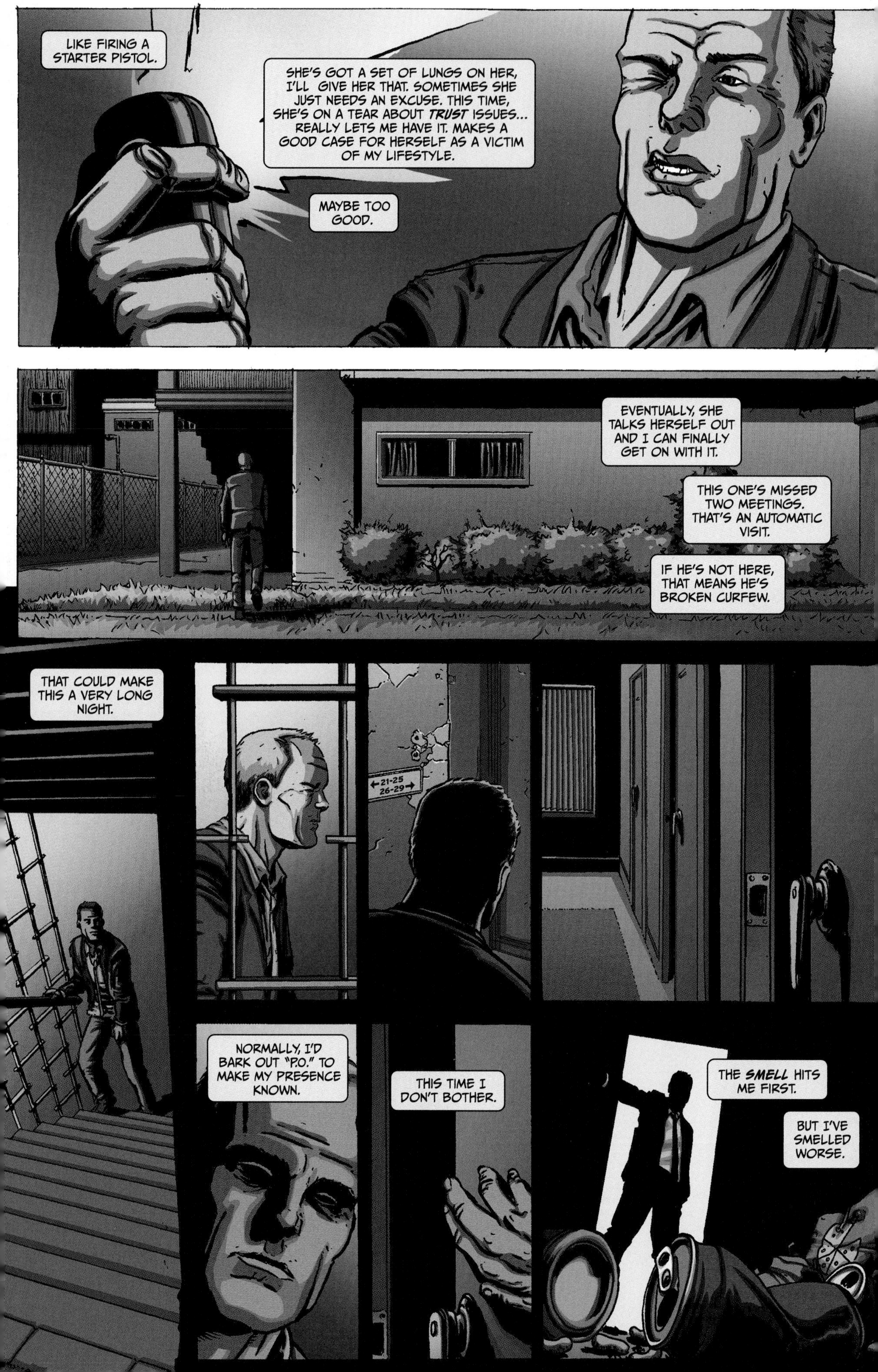
LIKE FIRING A STARTER PISTOL.
SHE'S GOT A SET OF LUNGS ON HER, I'LL GIVE HER THAT. SOMETIMES SHE JUST NEEDS AN EXCUSE. THIS TIME, SHE'S ON A TEAR ABOUT *TRUST* ISSUES... REALLY LETS ME HAVE IT. MAKES A GOOD CASE FOR HERSELF AS A VICTIM OF MY LIFESTYLE.
MAYBE TOO GOOD.
EVENTUALLY, SHE TALKS HERSELF OUT AND I CAN FINALLY GET ON WITH IT.
THIS ONE'S MISSED TWO MEETINGS. THAT'S AN AUTOMATIC VISIT.
IF HE'S NOT HERE, THAT MEANS HE'S BROKEN CURFEW.
THAT COULD MAKE THIS A VERY LONG NIGHT.
←21-25
26-29→
NORMALLY, I'D BARK OUT "P.O." TO MAKE MY PRESENCE KNOWN.
THIS TIME I DON'T BOTHER.
THE *SMELL* HITS ME FIRST.
BUT I'VE SMELLED WORSE.

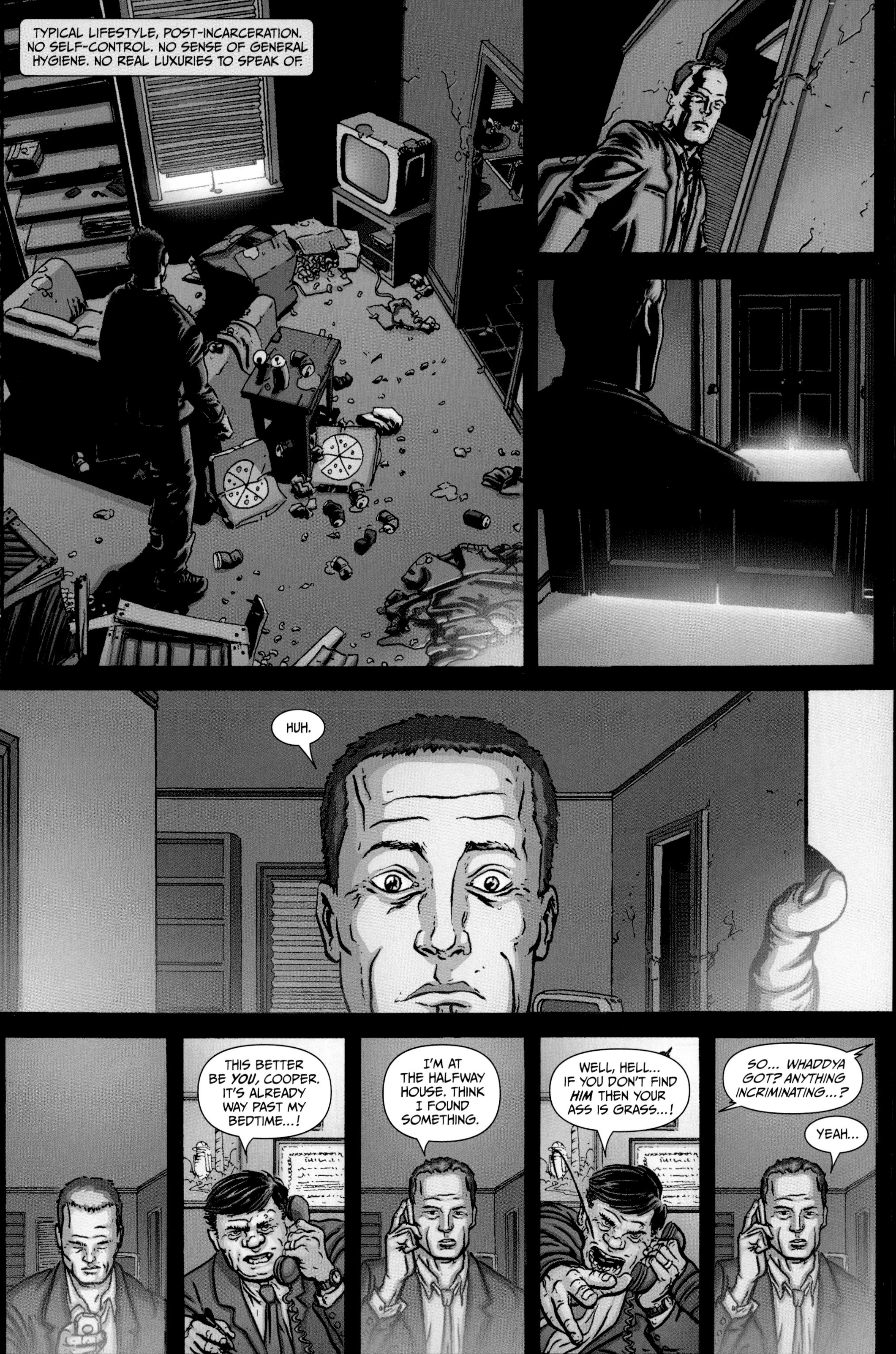
TYPICAL LIFESTYLE, POST-INCARCERATION. NO SELF-CONTROL. NO SENSE OF GENERAL HYGIENE. NO REAL LUXURIES TO SPEAK OF.
HUH.
THIS BETTER BE *YOU,* COOPER. IT'S ALREADY WAY PAST MY BEDTIME...!
I'M AT THE HALFWAY HOUSE. THINK I FOUND SOMETHING.
WELL, HELL... IF YOU DON'T FIND *HIM* THEN YOUR ASS IS GRASS...!
SO... WHADDYA GOT? ANYTHING INCRIMINATING...?
YEAH...

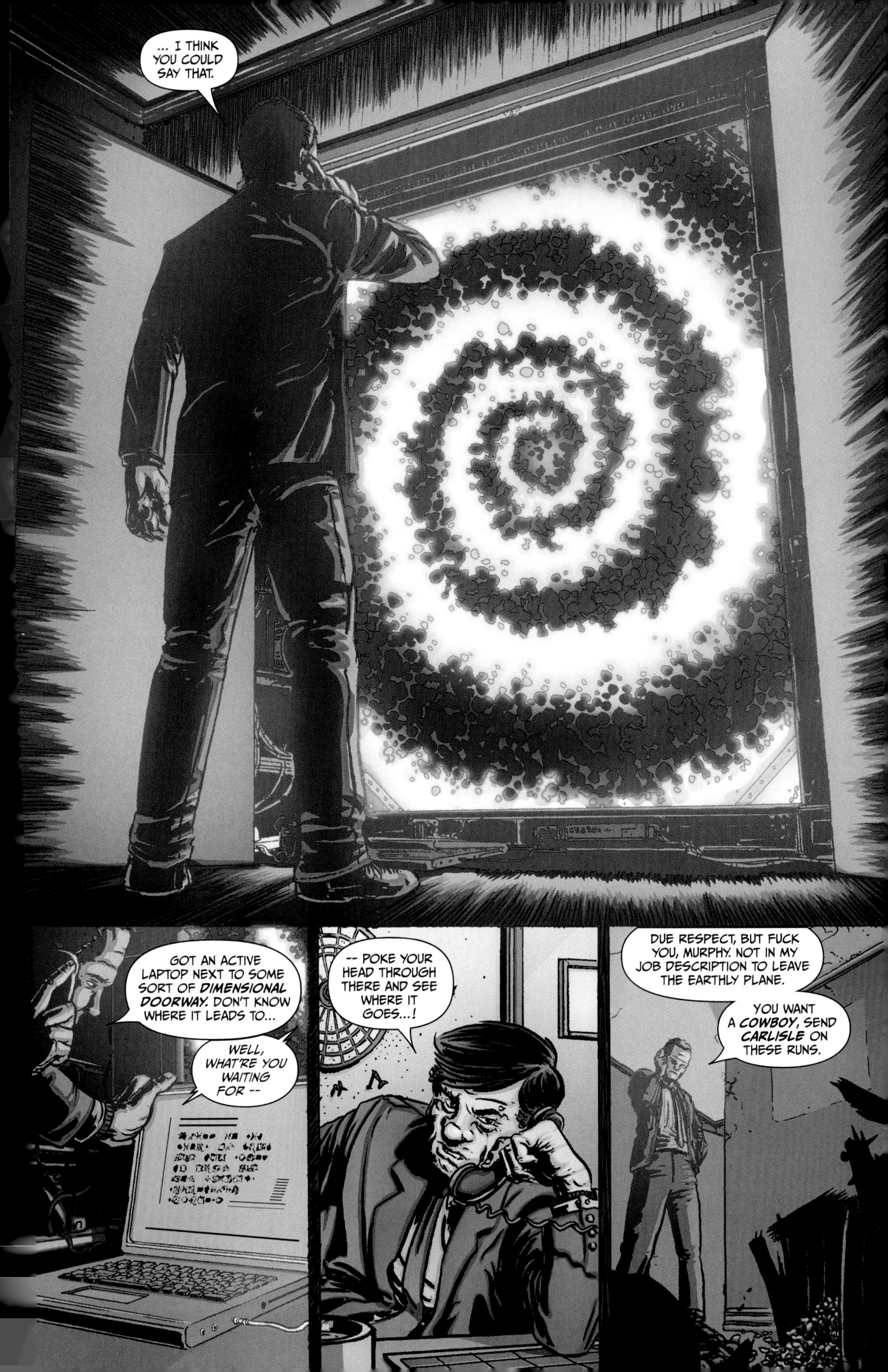
... I THINK YOU COULD SAY THAT.
GOT AN ACTIVE LAPTOP NEXT TO SOME SORT OF DIMENSIONAL DOORWAY. DON'T KNOW WHERE IT LEADS TO...
WELL, WHAT'RE YOU WAITING FOR --
-- POKE YOUR HEAD THROUGH THERE AND SEE WHERE IT GOES...!
DUE RESPECT, BUT FUCK YOU, MURPHY. NOT IN MY JOB DESCRIPTION TO LEAVE THE EARTHLY PLANE.
YOU WANT A COWBOY, SEND CARLISLE ON THESE RUNS.

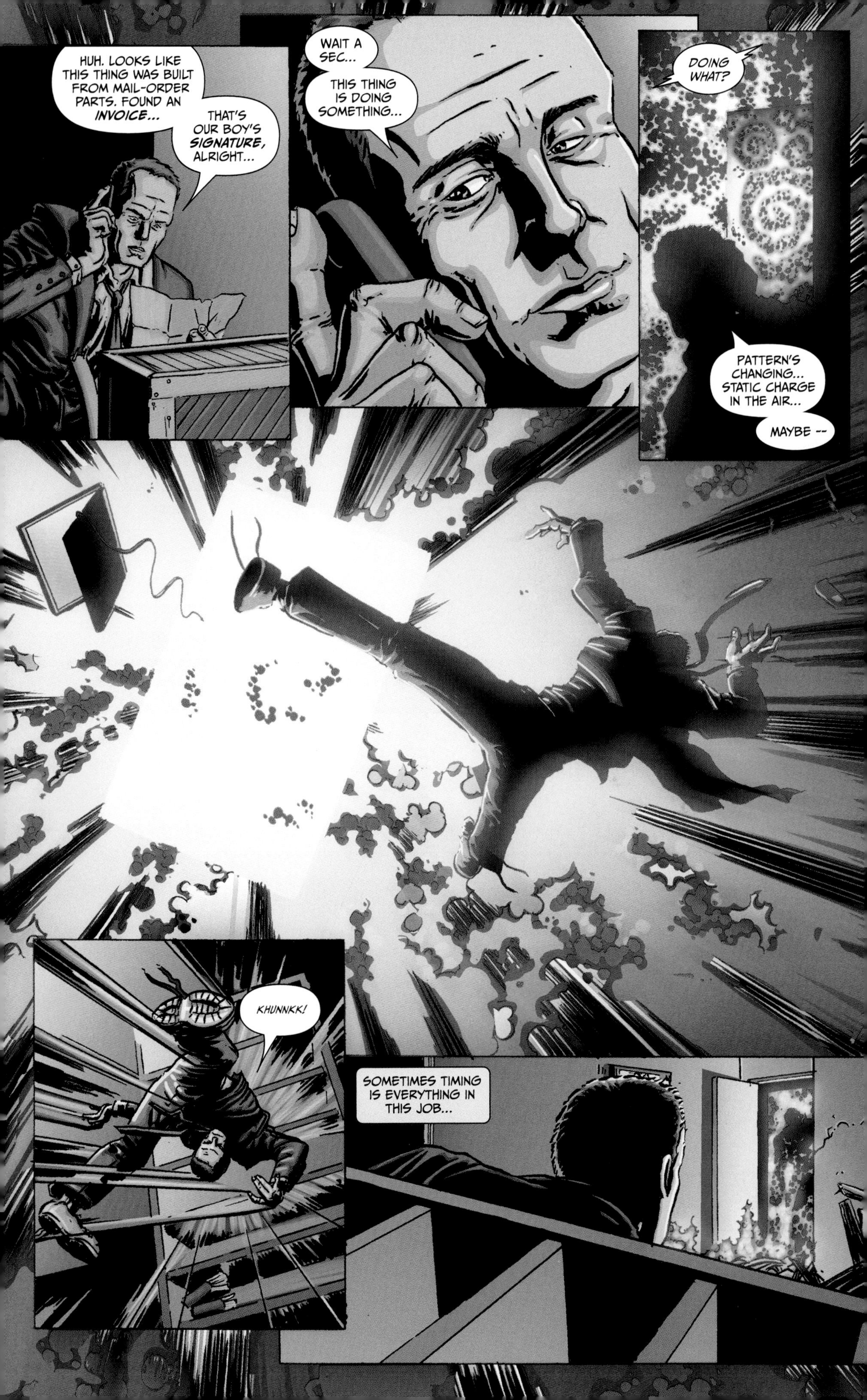
HUH. LOOKS LIKE THIS THING WAS BUILT FROM MAIL-ORDER PARTS. FOUND AN *INVOICE...*
THAT'S OUR BOY'S *SIGNATURE,* ALRIGHT...
WAIT A SEC...
THIS THING IS DOING SOMETHING...
DOING WHAT?
PATTERN'S CHANGING... STATIC CHARGE IN THE AIR...
MAYBE --
KHUNNKK!
SOMETIMES TIMING IS EVERYTHING IN THIS JOB...

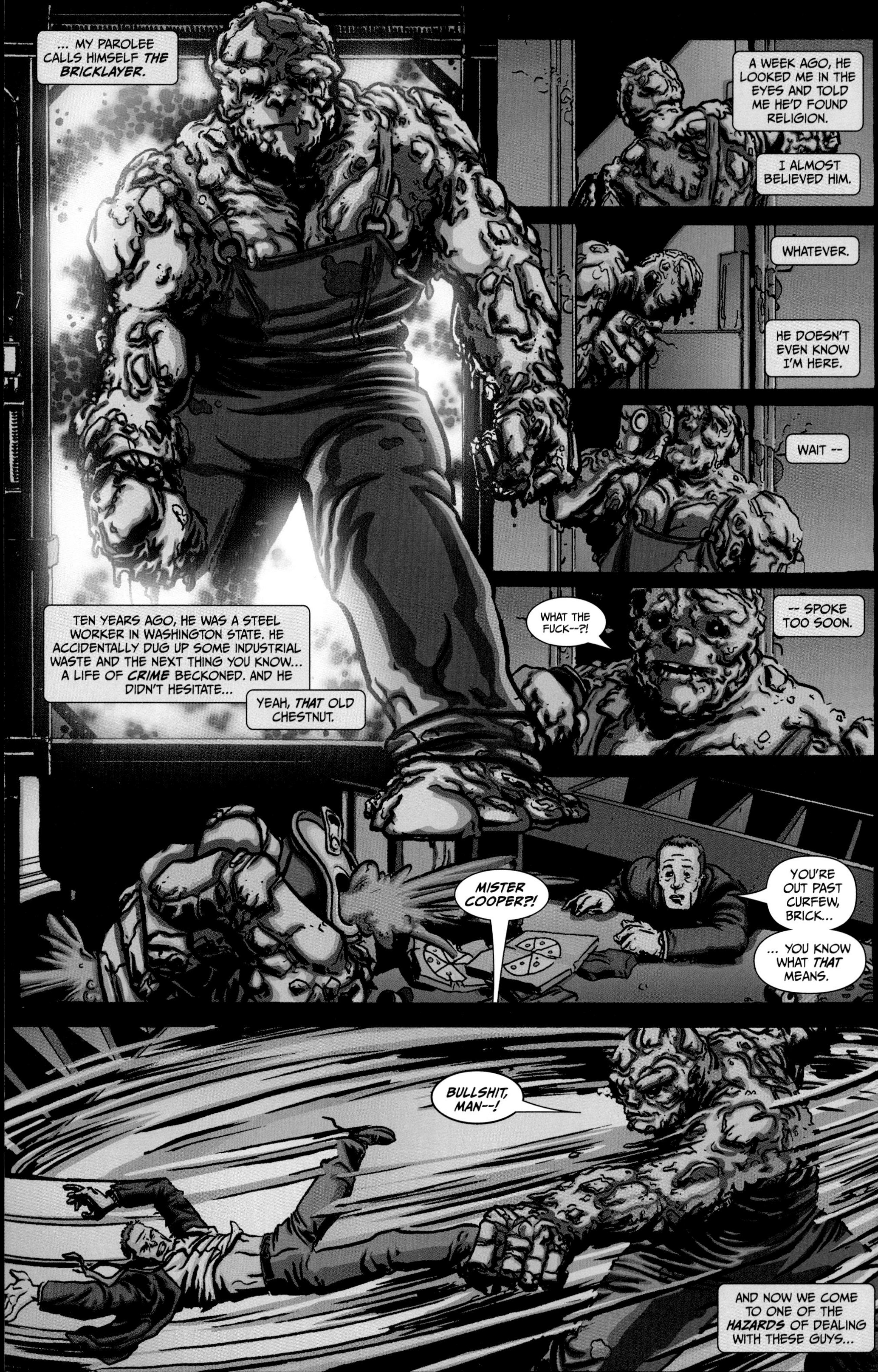
... MY PAROLEE CALLS HIMSELF *THE BRICKLAYER.*
A WEEK AGO, HE LOOKED ME IN THE EYES AND TOLD ME HE'D FOUND RELIGION.
I ALMOST BELIEVED HIM.
WHATEVER.
HE DOESN'T EVEN KNOW I'M HERE.
WAIT --
WHAT THE FUCK--?!
-- SPOKE TOO SOON.
TEN YEARS AGO, HE WAS A STEEL WORKER IN WASHINGTON STATE. HE ACCIDENTALLY DUG UP SOME INDUSTRIAL WASTE AND THE NEXT THING YOU KNOW... A LIFE OF *CRIME* BECKONED. AND HE DIDN'T HESITATE...
YEAH, *THAT* OLD CHESTNUT.
MISTER COOPER?!
YOU'RE OUT PAST CURFEW, BRICK...
... YOU KNOW WHAT *THAT* MEANS.
BULLSHIT, MAN--!
AND NOW WE COME TO ONE OF THE *HAZARDS* OF DEALING WITH THESE GUYS...

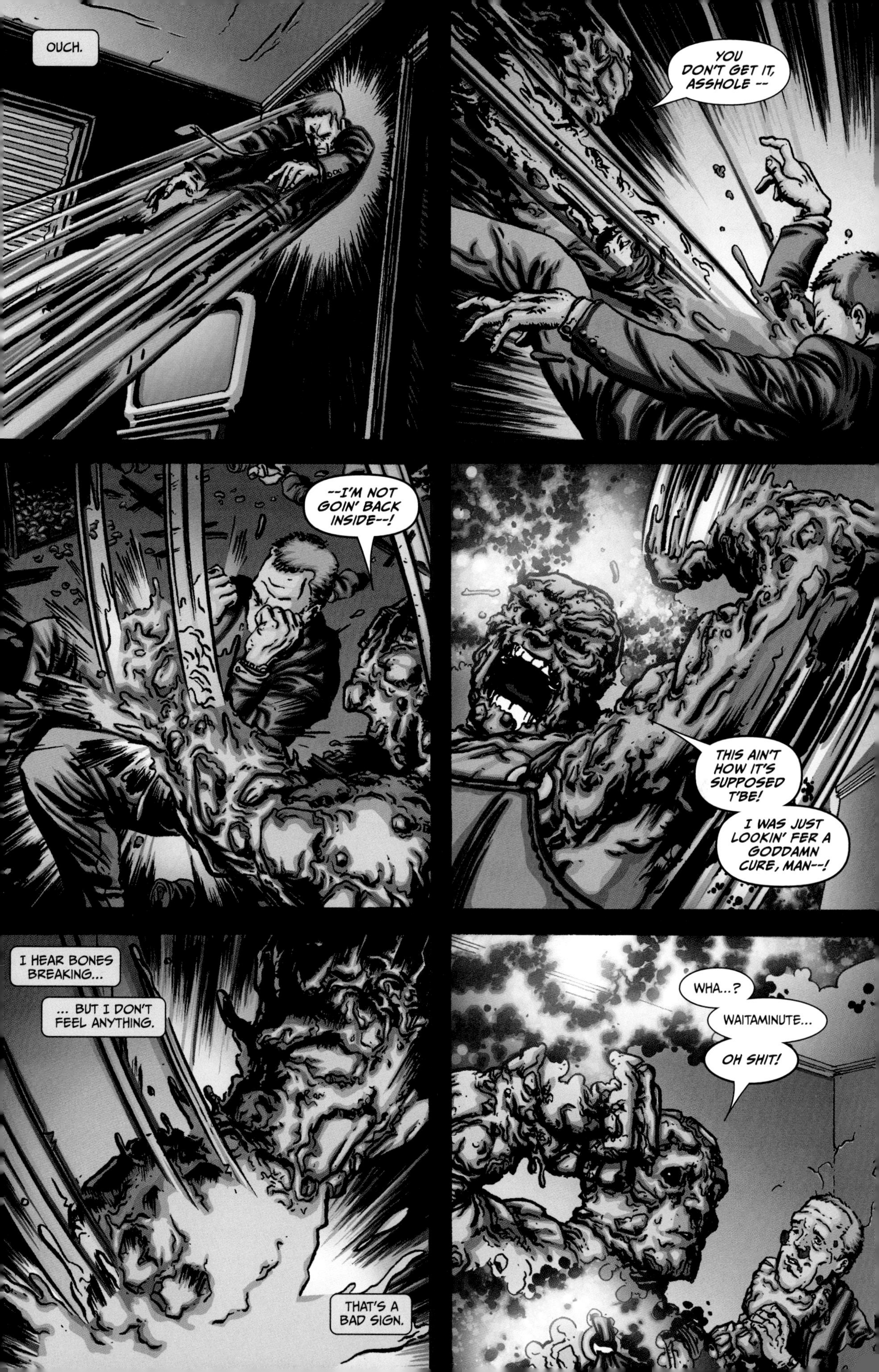
OUCH.
YOU DON'T GET IT, ASSHOLE --
--I'M NOT GOIN' BACK INSIDE--!
THIS AIN'T HOW IT'S SUPPOSED T'BE!
I WAS JUST LOOKIN' FER A GODDAMN CURE, MAN--!
I HEAR BONES BREAKING...
... BUT I DON'T FEEL ANYTHING.
THAT'S A BAD SIGN.
WHA...?
WAITAMINUTE...
OH SHIT!

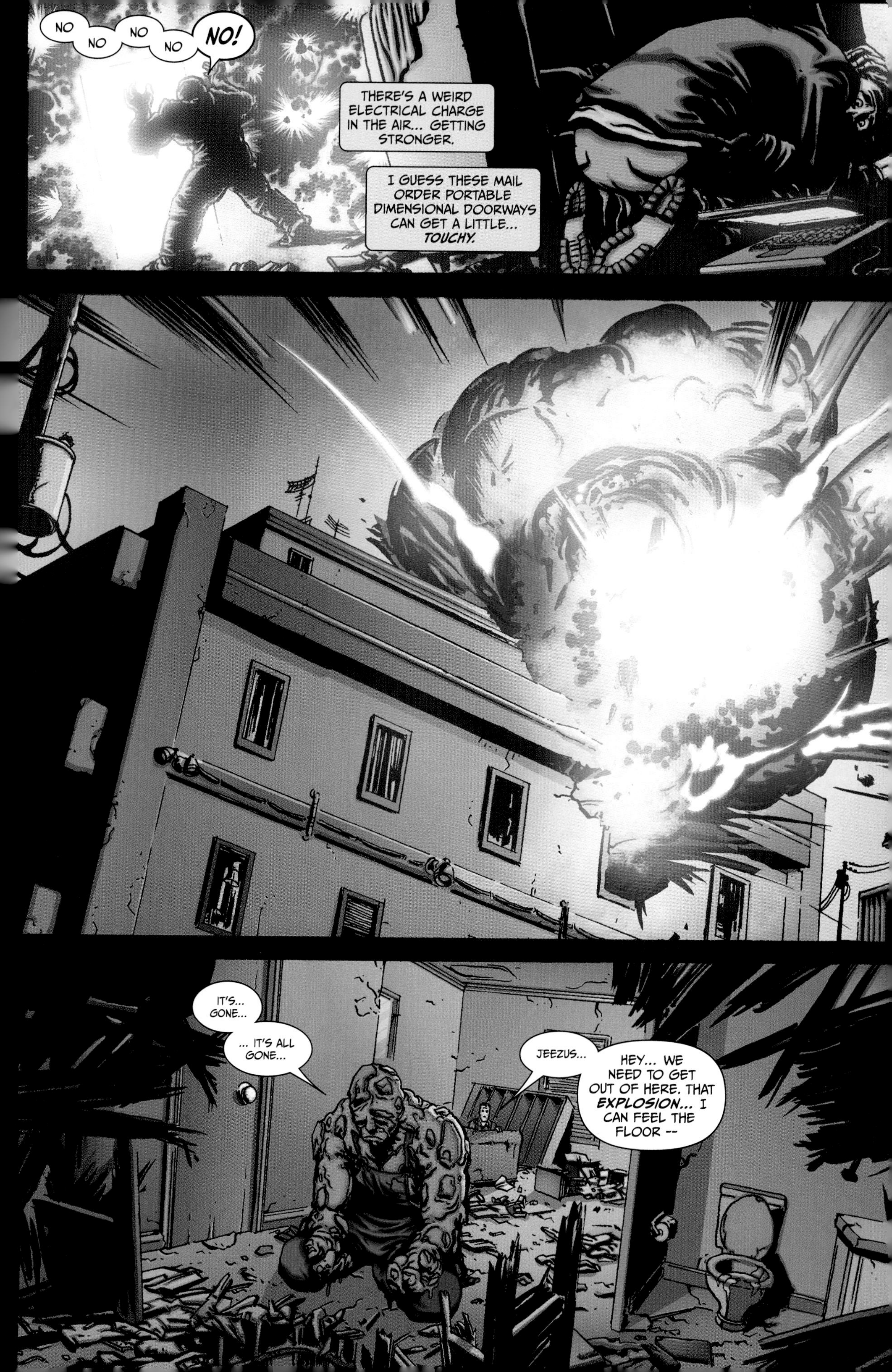
NO NO NO NO NO!
THERE'S A WEIRD ELECTRICAL CHARGE IN THE AIR... GETTING STRONGER.
I GUESS THESE MAIL ORDER PORTABLE DIMENSIONAL DOORWAYS CAN GET A LITTLE... TOUCHY.
IT'S... GONE...
... IT'S ALL GONE...
JEEZUS...
HEY... WE NEED TO GET OUT OF HERE. THAT EXPLOSION... I CAN FEEL THE FLOOR --

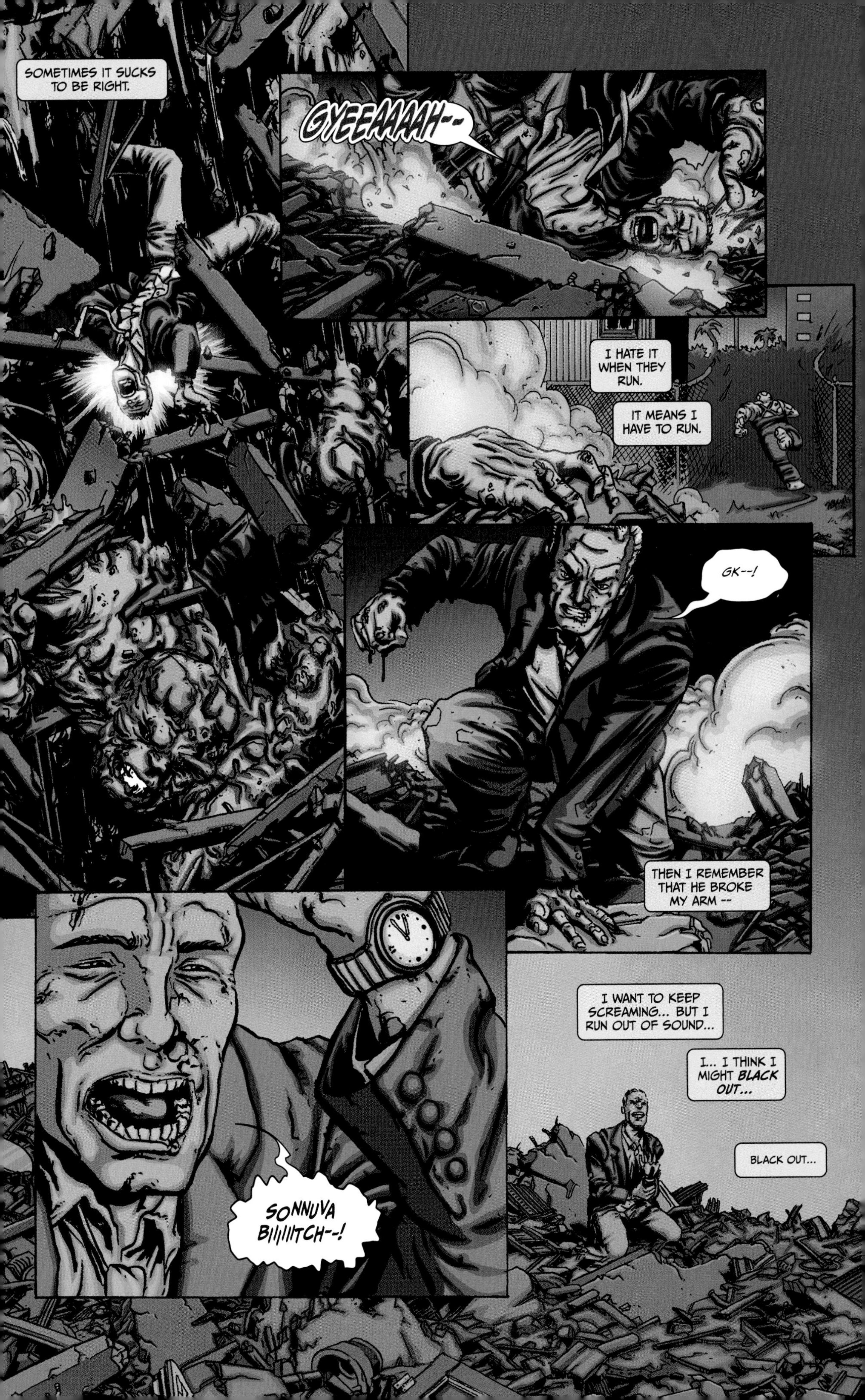
SOMETIMES IT SUCKS TO BE RIGHT.
GYEEAAAAH--
I HATE IT WHEN THEY RUN.
IT MEANS I HAVE TO RUN.
GK--!
THEN I REMEMBER THAT HE BROKE MY ARM --
SONNUVA BIIIIITCH--!
I WANT TO KEEP SCREAMING... BUT I RUN OUT OF SOUND...
I... I THINK I MIGHT BLACK OUT...
BLACK OUT...

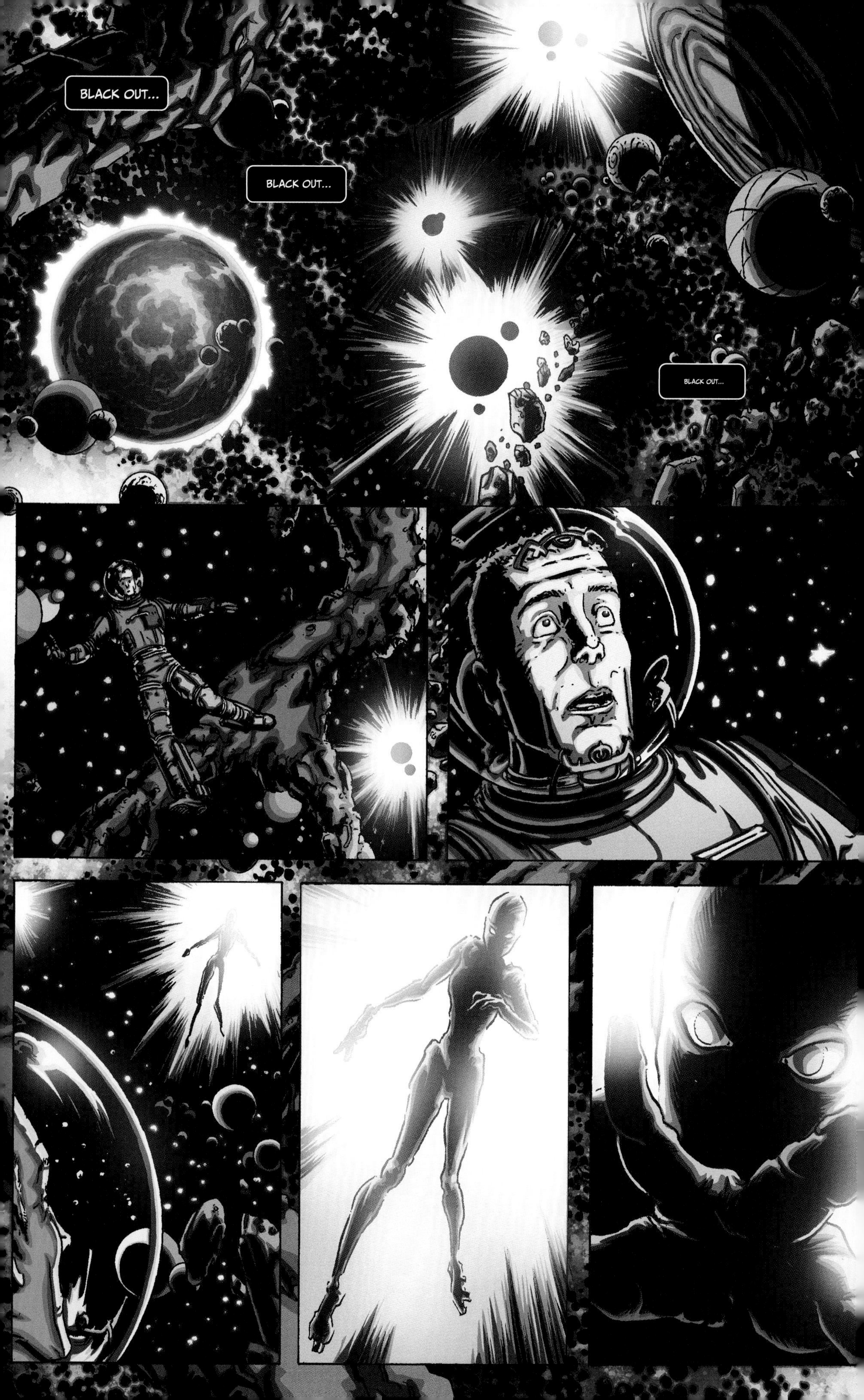
BLACK OUT...
BLACK OUT...
BLACK OUT...

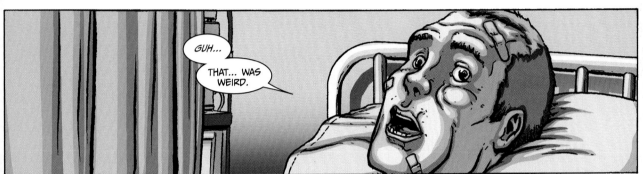

GUH...

THAT... WAS WEIRD.

I'VE HAD NIGHTMARES BEFORE... SHOWING UP NAKED IN HIGH SCHOOL ALGEBRA... DEAD RELATIVES COMING BACK TO FUCK WITH ME... TYPICAL STUFF...

... BUT NOTHING LIKE *THAT*. IT WAS... ALMOST TOO REAL.

WAIT A SEC... WHERE THE HELL *AM* I...?

HAVE A NICE NAP THERE...?

HOW... HOW'D I GET HERE...?

EMERGENCY VEHICLES FOUND YOU AT THE SCENE. SOME KIND OF GAS MAIN EXPLOSION IN VAN NUYS...

YOU GUYS HAVE FUN CUTTING UP MY SHIRT...?

HAD TO BE DONE. YOUR RADIUS WAS SNAPPED IN TWO.

DID YOU *LIVE* THERE OR --

NOT ME. ONE OF MY PAROLEES AT LARGE.

GODDAMMIT.

I ACTUALLY WENT TO SCHOOL FOR THIS.

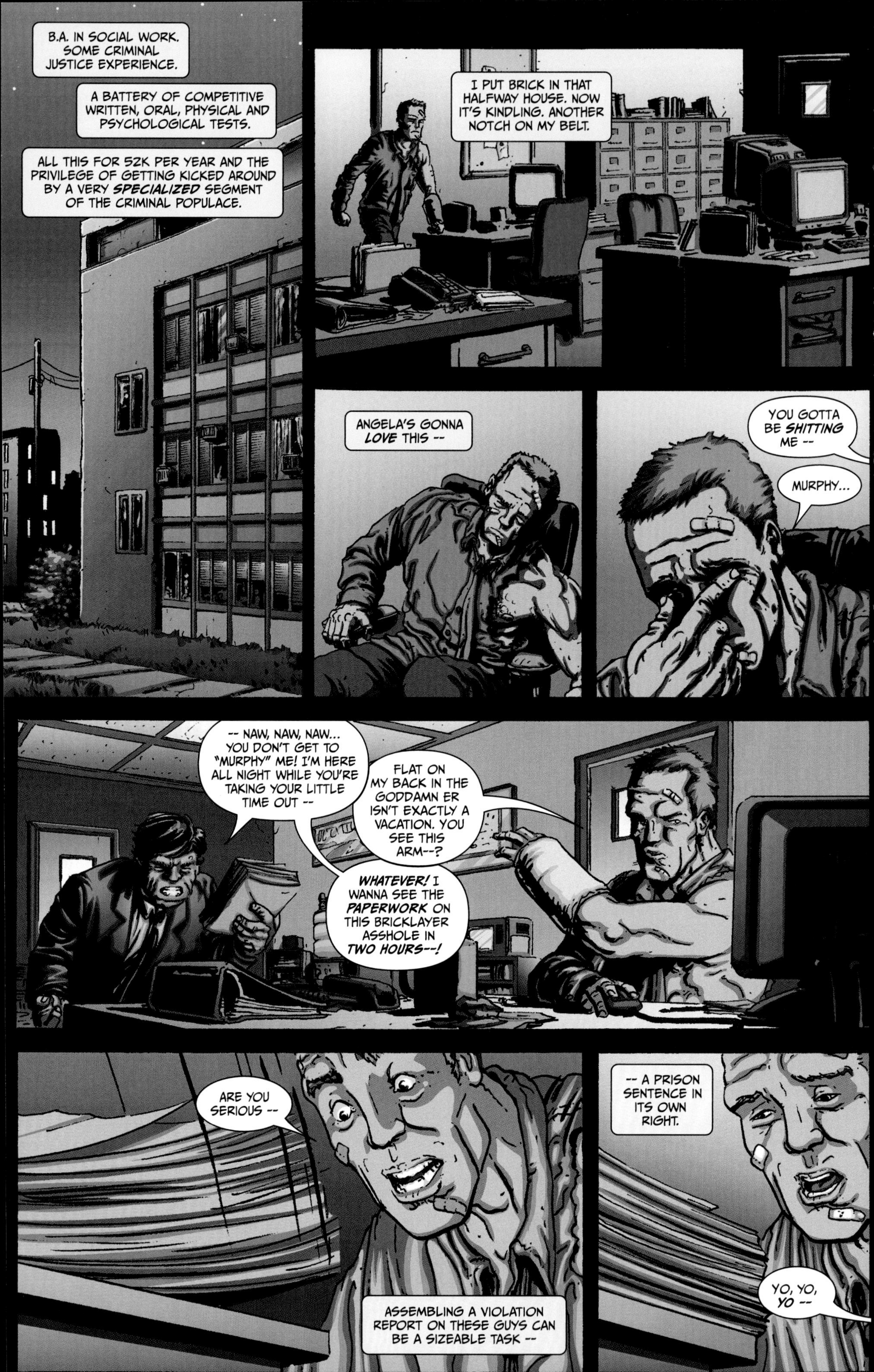
B.A. IN SOCIAL WORK. SOME CRIMINAL JUSTICE EXPERIENCE.
A BATTERY OF COMPETITIVE WRITTEN, ORAL, PHYSICAL AND PSYCHOLOGICAL TESTS.
ALL THIS FOR 52K PER YEAR AND THE PRIVILEGE OF GETTING KICKED AROUND BY A VERY *SPECIALIZED* SEGMENT OF THE CRIMINAL POPULACE.
I PUT BRICK IN THAT HALFWAY HOUSE. NOW IT'S KINDLING. ANOTHER NOTCH ON MY BELT.
ANGELA'S GONNA *LOVE* THIS --
YOU GOTTA BE *SHITTING* ME --
MURPHY...
-- NAW, NAW, NAW... YOU DON'T GET TO "MURPHY" ME! I'M HERE ALL NIGHT WHILE YOU'RE TAKING YOUR LITTLE TIME OUT --
FLAT ON MY BACK IN THE GODDAMN ER ISN'T EXACTLY A VACATION. YOU SEE THIS ARM--?
WHATEVER! I WANNA SEE THE *PAPERWORK* ON THIS BRICKLAYER ASSHOLE IN *TWO HOURS--!*
ARE YOU SERIOUS --
ASSEMBLING A VIOLATION REPORT ON THESE GUYS CAN BE A SIZEABLE TASK --
-- A PRISON SENTENCE IN ITS OWN RIGHT.
YO, YO, *YO* --

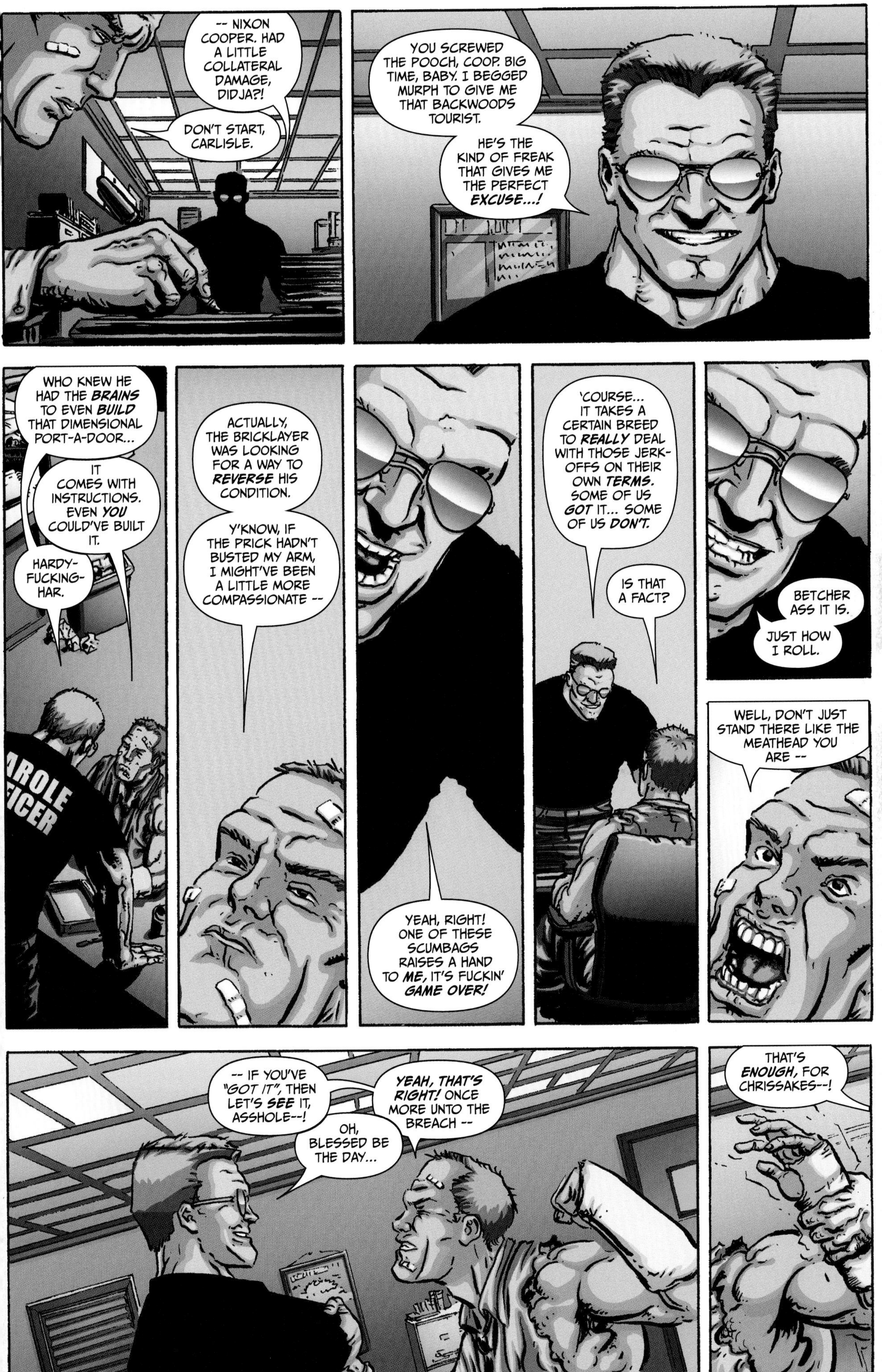
-- NIXON COOPER. HAD A LITTLE COLLATERAL DAMAGE, DIDJA?!
DON'T START, CARLISLE.
YOU SCREWED THE POOCH, COOP. BIG TIME, BABY. I BEGGED MURPH TO GIVE ME THAT BACKWOODS TOURIST.
HE'S THE KIND OF FREAK THAT GIVES ME THE PERFECT EXCUSE...!
WHO KNEW HE HAD THE BRAINS TO EVEN BUILD THAT DIMENSIONAL PORT-A-DOOR...
IT COMES WITH INSTRUCTIONS. EVEN YOU COULD'VE BUILT IT.
HARDY-FUCKING-HAR.
PAROLE OFFICER
ACTUALLY, THE BRICKLAYER WAS LOOKING FOR A WAY TO REVERSE HIS CONDITION.
Y'KNOW, IF THE PRICK HADN'T BUSTED MY ARM, I MIGHT'VE BEEN A LITTLE MORE COMPASSIONATE --
YEAH, RIGHT! ONE OF THESE SCUMBAGS RAISES A HAND TO ME, IT'S FUCKIN' GAME OVER!
'COURSE... IT TAKES A CERTAIN BREED TO REALLY DEAL WITH THOSE JERK-OFFS ON THEIR OWN TERMS. SOME OF US GOT IT... SOME OF US DON'T.
IS THAT A FACT?
BETCHER ASS IT IS.
JUST HOW I ROLL.
WELL, DON'T JUST STAND THERE LIKE THE MEATHEAD YOU ARE --
-- IF YOU'VE "GOT IT", THEN LET'S SEE IT, ASSHOLE--!
OH, BLESSED BE THE DAY...
YEAH, THAT'S RIGHT! ONCE MORE UNTO THE BREACH --
THAT'S ENOUGH, FOR CHRISSAKES--!

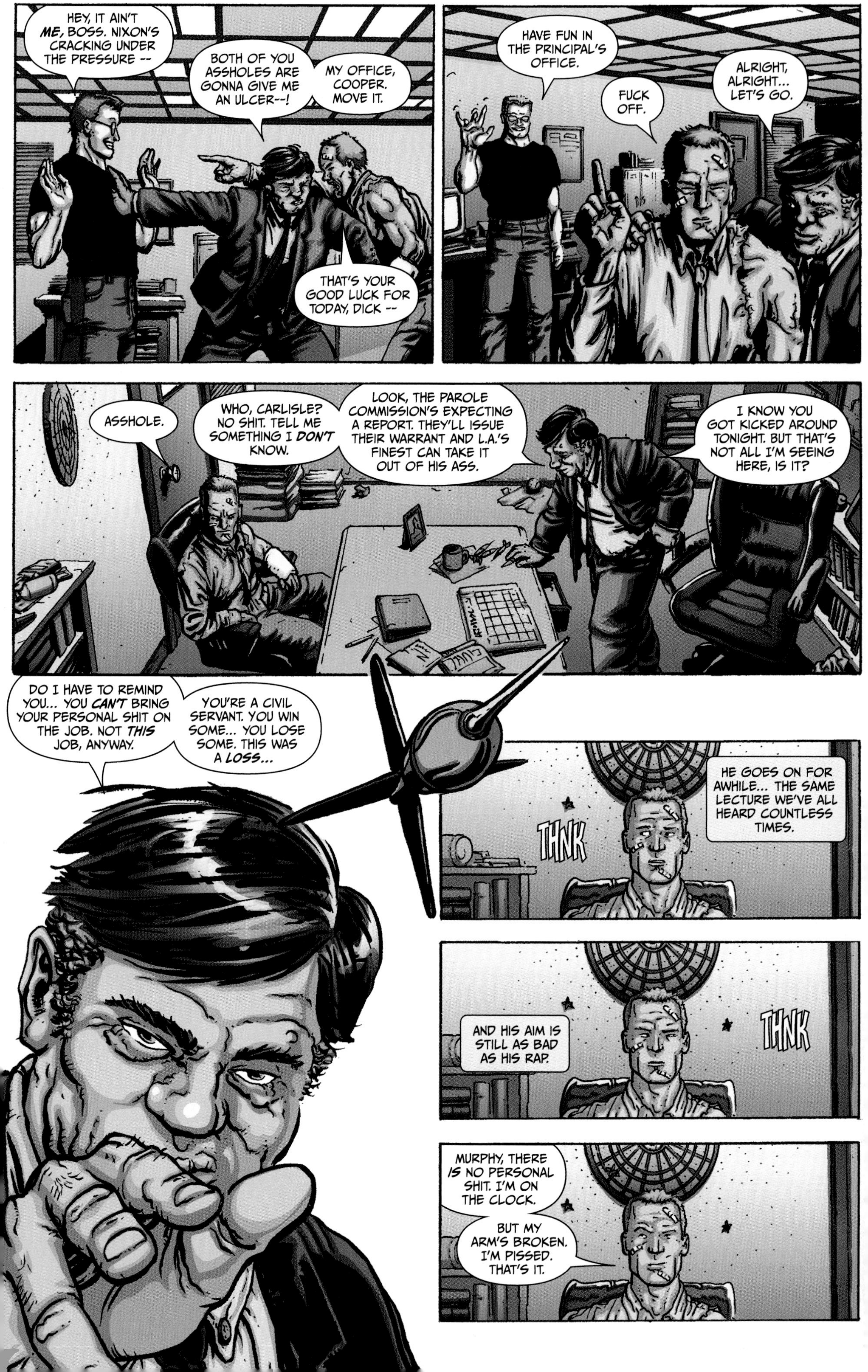
HEY, IT AIN'T *ME,* BOSS. NIXON'S CRACKING UNDER THE PRESSURE --
BOTH OF YOU ASSHOLES ARE GONNA GIVE ME AN ULCER--!
MY OFFICE, COOPER. MOVE IT.
THAT'S YOUR GOOD LUCK FOR TODAY, DICK --
HAVE FUN IN THE PRINCIPAL'S OFFICE.
FUCK OFF.
ALRIGHT, ALRIGHT... LET'S GO.
ASSHOLE.
WHO, CARLISLE? NO SHIT. TELL ME SOMETHING I *DON'T* KNOW.
LOOK, THE PAROLE COMMISSION'S EXPECTING A REPORT. THEY'LL ISSUE THEIR WARRANT AND L.A.'S FINEST CAN TAKE IT OUT OF HIS ASS.
I KNOW YOU GOT KICKED AROUND TONIGHT. BUT THAT'S NOT ALL I'M SEEING HERE, IS IT?
DO I HAVE TO REMIND YOU... YOU *CAN'T* BRING YOUR PERSONAL SHIT ON THE JOB. NOT *THIS* JOB, ANYWAY.
YOU'RE A CIVIL SERVANT. YOU WIN SOME... YOU LOSE SOME. THIS WAS A *LOSS...*
THNK
HE GOES ON FOR AWHILE... THE SAME LECTURE WE'VE ALL HEARD COUNTLESS TIMES.
AND HIS AIM IS STILL AS BAD AS HIS RAP.
THNK
MURPHY, THERE *IS* NO PERSONAL SHIT. I'M ON THE CLOCK.
BUT MY ARM'S BROKEN. I'M PISSED. THAT'S IT.

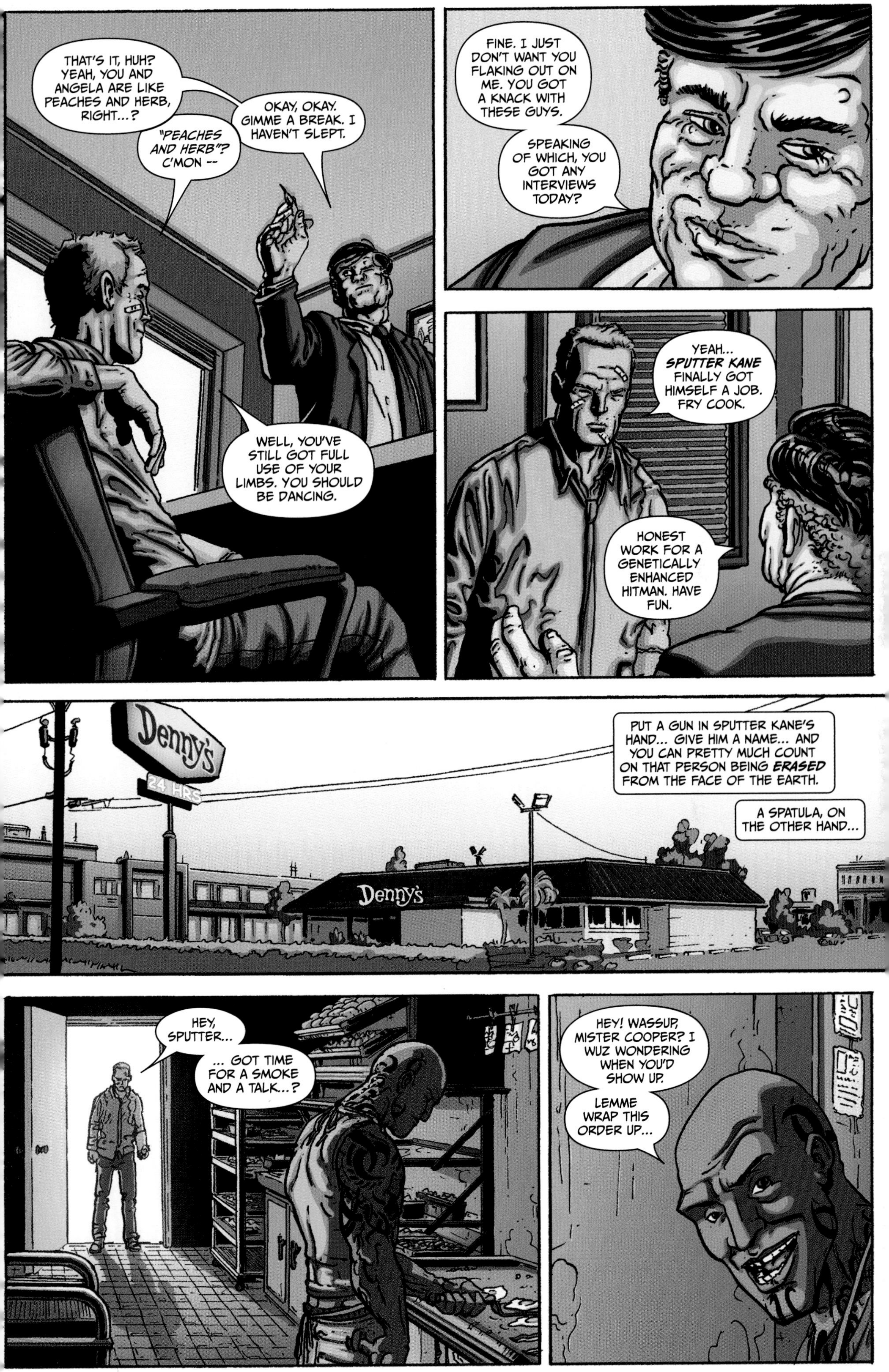
THAT'S IT, HUH? YEAH, YOU AND ANGELA ARE LIKE PEACHES AND HERB, RIGHT...?
OKAY, OKAY. GIMME A BREAK. I HAVEN'T SLEPT.
"PEACHES AND HERB"? C'MON --
WELL, YOU'VE STILL GOT FULL USE OF YOUR LIMBS. YOU SHOULD BE DANCING.
FINE. I JUST DON'T WANT YOU FLAKING OUT ON ME. YOU GOT A KNACK WITH THESE GUYS.
SPEAKING OF WHICH, YOU GOT ANY INTERVIEWS TODAY?
YEAH... SPUTTER KANE FINALLY GOT HIMSELF A JOB. FRY COOK.
HONEST WORK FOR A GENETICALLY ENHANCED HITMAN. HAVE FUN.
Denny's
24 HRS
Denny's
PUT A GUN IN SPUTTER KANE'S HAND... GIVE HIM A NAME... AND YOU CAN PRETTY MUCH COUNT ON THAT PERSON BEING ERASED FROM THE FACE OF THE EARTH.
A SPATULA, ON THE OTHER HAND...
HEY, SPUTTER...
... GOT TIME FOR A SMOKE AND A TALK...?
HEY! WASSUP, MISTER COOPER? I WUZ WONDERING WHEN YOU'D SHOW UP.
LEMME WRAP THIS ORDER UP...

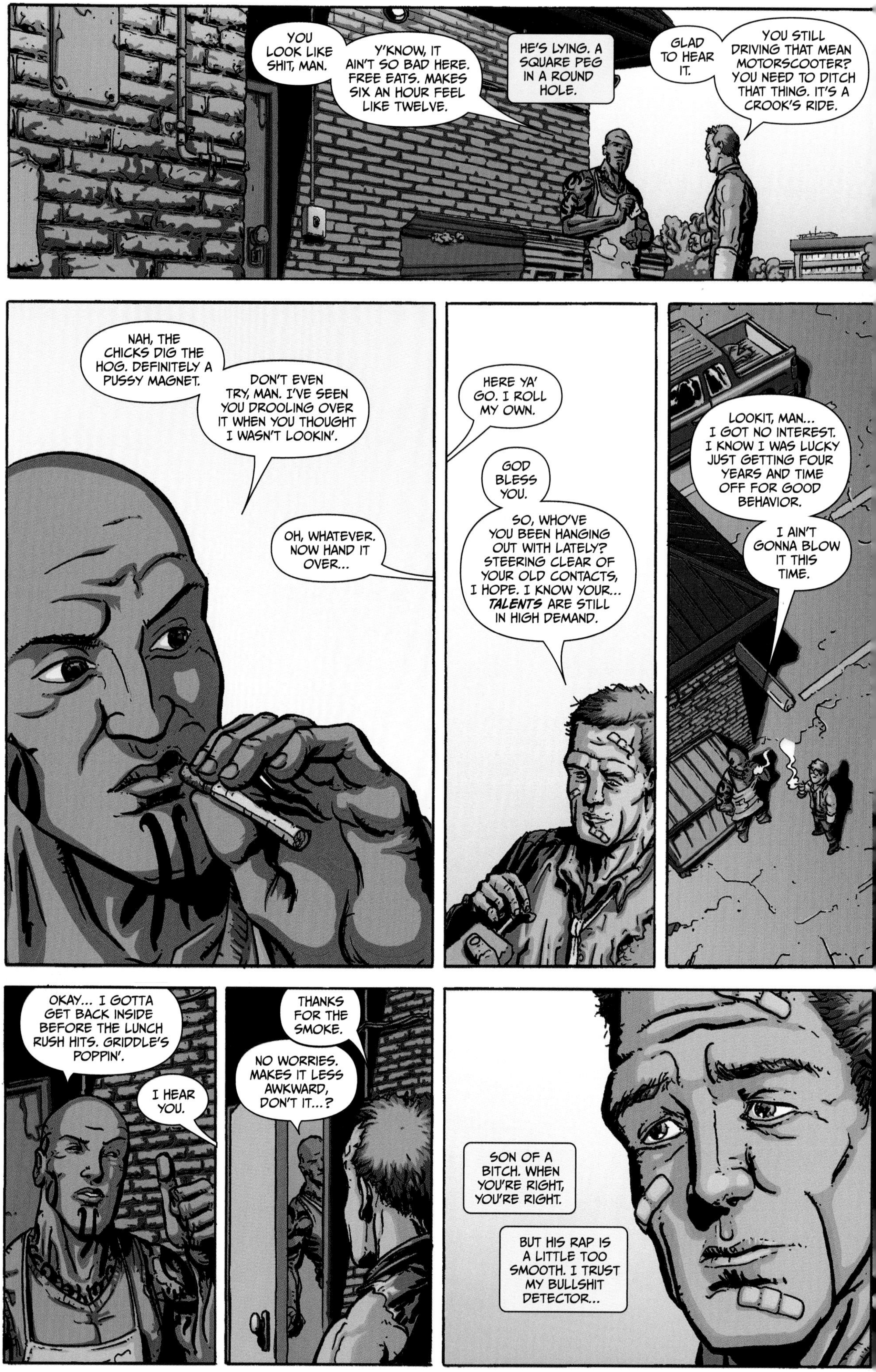
YOU LOOK LIKE SHIT, MAN.
Y'KNOW, IT AIN'T SO BAD HERE. FREE EATS. MAKES SIX AN HOUR FEEL LIKE TWELVE.
HE'S LYING. A SQUARE PEG IN A ROUND HOLE.
GLAD TO HEAR IT.
YOU STILL DRIVING THAT MEAN MOTORSCOOTER? YOU NEED TO DITCH THAT THING. IT'S A CROOK'S RIDE.
NAH, THE CHICKS DIG THE HOG. DEFINITELY A PUSSY MAGNET.
DON'T EVEN TRY, MAN. I'VE SEEN YOU DROOLING OVER IT WHEN YOU THOUGHT I WASN'T LOOKIN'.
OH, WHATEVER. NOW HAND IT OVER...
HERE YA' GO. I ROLL MY OWN.
GOD BLESS YOU.
SO, WHO'VE YOU BEEN HANGING OUT WITH LATELY? STEERING CLEAR OF YOUR OLD CONTACTS, I HOPE. I KNOW YOUR... *TALENTS* ARE STILL IN HIGH DEMAND.
LOOKIT, MAN... I GOT NO INTEREST. I KNOW I WAS LUCKY JUST GETTING FOUR YEARS AND TIME OFF FOR GOOD BEHAVIOR.
I AIN'T GONNA BLOW IT THIS TIME.
OKAY... I GOTTA GET BACK INSIDE BEFORE THE LUNCH RUSH HITS. GRIDDLE'S POPPIN'.
I HEAR YOU.
THANKS FOR THE SMOKE.
NO WORRIES. MAKES IT LESS AWKWARD, DON'T IT...?
SON OF A BITCH. WHEN YOU'RE RIGHT, YOU'RE RIGHT.
BUT HIS RAP IS A LITTLE TOO SMOOTH. I TRUST MY BULLSHIT DETECTOR...

... SINCE IT'S BEEN PINGING A *LOT* LATELY.

ESPECIALLY WHEN I WALK UP THE STEPS OF MY OWN FRONT PORCH.

SOMETIMES I DON'T KNOW IF THE DREAD'S *WAITING* FOR ME... OR IF I BRING IT *WITH* ME.

I MET ANGELA A FEW YEARS OUT OF COLLEGE. SHE THOUGHT I WAS A PROVIDER.

IN THAT RESPECT, I GUESS SHE COULD'VE DONE WORSE. NOT MUCH, BUT STILL...

THESE DAYS, WHENEVER I COME HOME AT ODD HOURS... THE DARKEST PARTS OF MY BRAIN CAN'T HELP BUT *WONDER*...

... WHAT I MIGHT FIND.

I DON'T TRY TO BE STEALTHY.

IT DOESN'T MATTER.

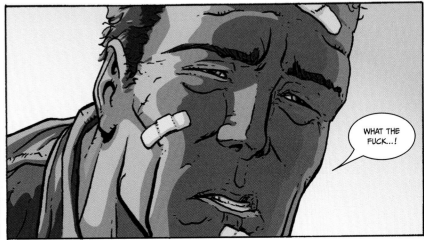

WHAT THE FUCK...!

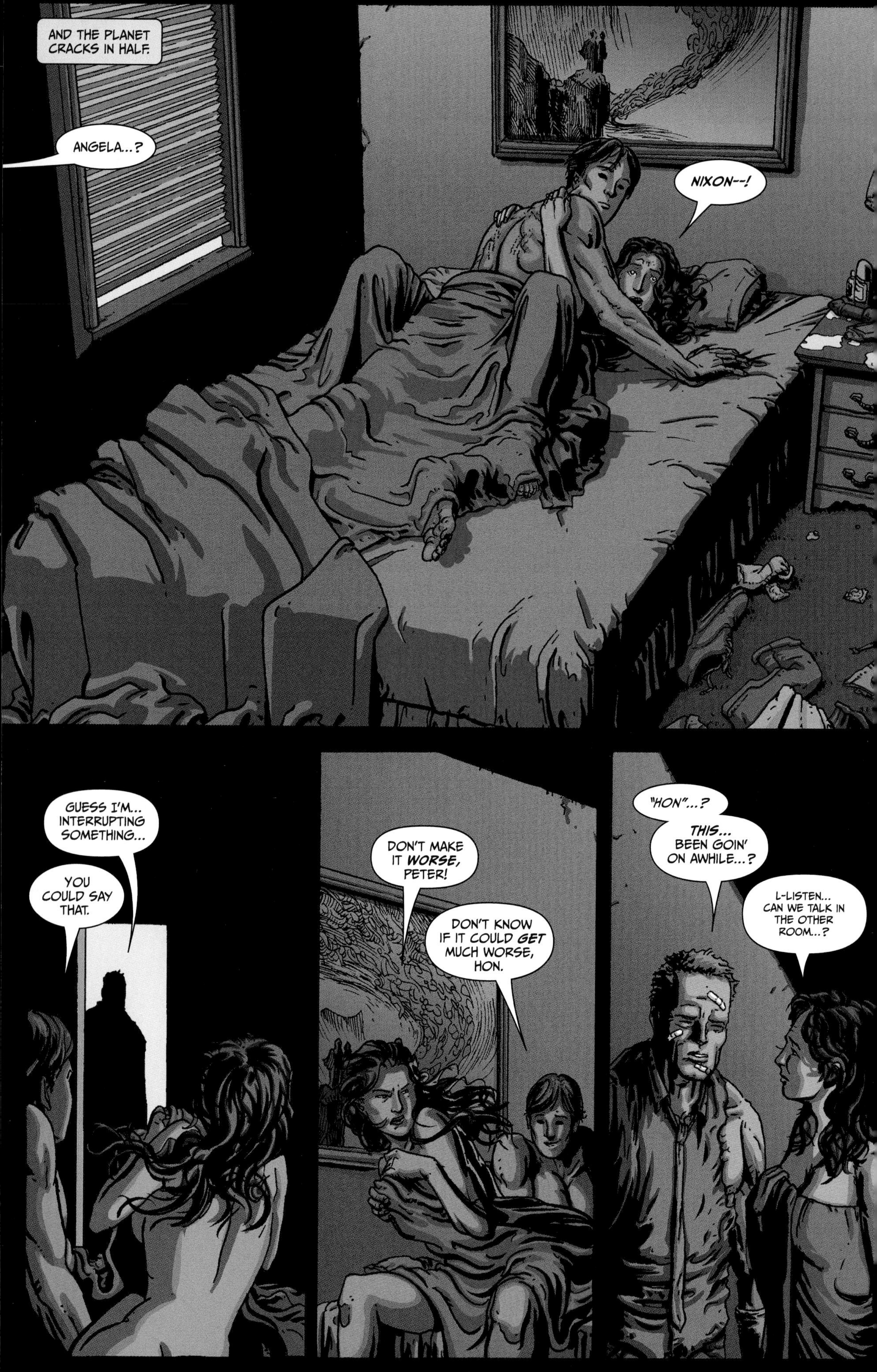
AND THE PLANET CRACKS IN HALF.
ANGELA...?
NIXON--!
GUESS I'M... INTERRUPTING SOMETHING...
YOU COULD SAY THAT.
DON'T MAKE IT *WORSE,* PETER!
DON'T KNOW IF IT COULD *GET* MUCH WORSE, HON.
"HON"...?
THIS... BEEN GOIN' ON AWHILE...?
L-LISTEN... CAN WE TALK IN THE OTHER ROOM...?

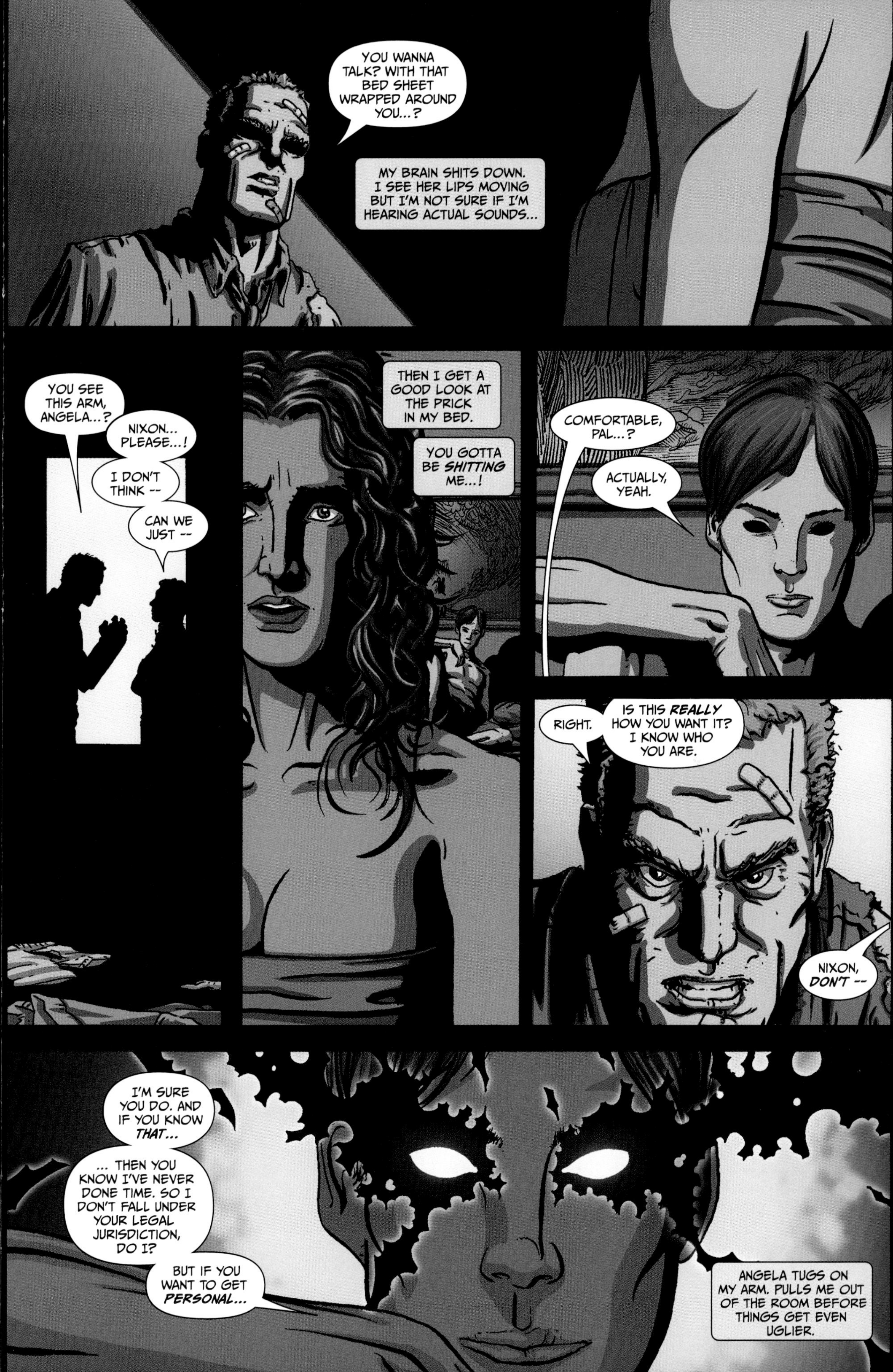
YOU WANNA TALK? WITH THAT BED SHEET WRAPPED AROUND YOU...?
MY BRAIN SHITS DOWN. I SEE HER LIPS MOVING BUT I'M NOT SURE IF I'M HEARING ACTUAL SOUNDS...
YOU SEE THIS ARM, ANGELA...?
NIXON... PLEASE...!
I DON'T THINK --
CAN WE JUST --
THEN I GET A GOOD LOOK AT THE PRICK IN MY BED.
YOU GOTTA BE SHITTING ME...!
COMFORTABLE, PAL...?
ACTUALLY, YEAH.
RIGHT.
IS THIS REALLY HOW YOU WANT IT? I KNOW WHO YOU ARE.
NIXON, DON'T --
I'M SURE YOU DO. AND IF YOU KNOW THAT...
... THEN YOU KNOW I'VE NEVER DONE TIME. SO I DON'T FALL UNDER YOUR LEGAL JURISDICTION, DO I?
BUT IF YOU WANT TO GET PERSONAL...
ANGELA TUGS ON MY ARM. PULLS ME OUT OF THE ROOM BEFORE THINGS GET EVEN UGLIER.

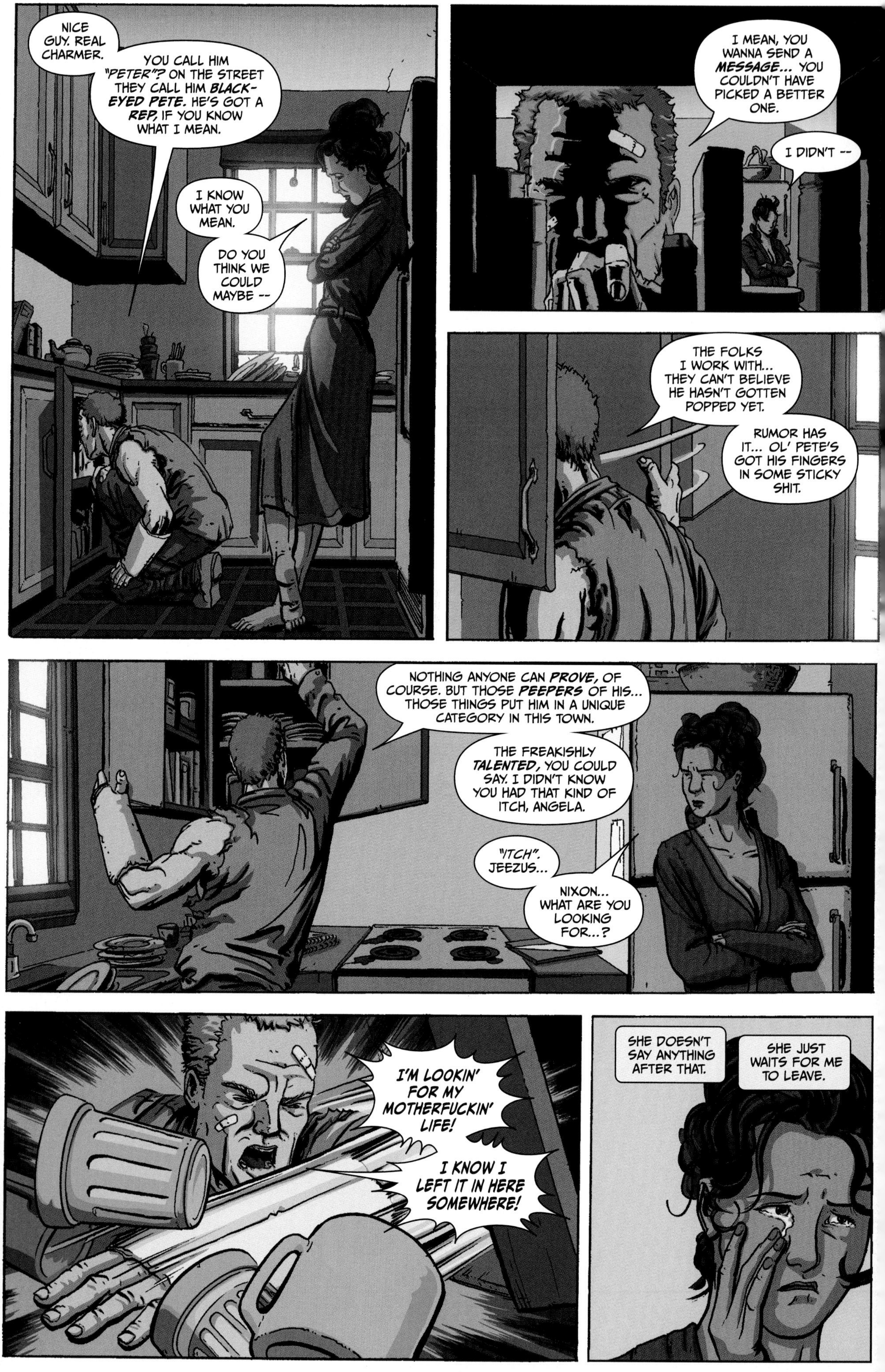
NICE GUY. REAL CHARMER.
YOU CALL HIM "PETER"? ON THE STREET THEY CALL HIM BLACK-EYED PETE. HE'S GOT A REP, IF YOU KNOW WHAT I MEAN.
I KNOW WHAT YOU MEAN.
DO YOU THINK WE COULD MAYBE --
I MEAN, YOU WANNA SEND A MESSAGE... YOU COULDN'T HAVE PICKED A BETTER ONE.
I DIDN'T --
THE FOLKS I WORK WITH... THEY CAN'T BELIEVE HE HASN'T GOTTEN POPPED YET.
RUMOR HAS IT... OL' PETE'S GOT HIS FINGERS IN SOME STICKY SHIT.
NOTHING ANYONE CAN PROVE, OF COURSE. BUT THOSE PEEPERS OF HIS... THOSE THINGS PUT HIM IN A UNIQUE CATEGORY IN THIS TOWN.
THE FREAKISHLY TALENTED, YOU COULD SAY. I DIDN'T KNOW YOU HAD THAT KIND OF ITCH, ANGELA.
"ITCH". JEEZUS...
NIXON... WHAT ARE YOU LOOKING FOR...?
I'M LOOKIN' FOR MY MOTHERFUCKIN' LIFE!
I KNOW I LEFT IT IN HERE SOMEWHERE!
SHE DOESN'T SAY ANYTHING AFTER THAT.
SHE JUST WAITS FOR ME TO LEAVE.

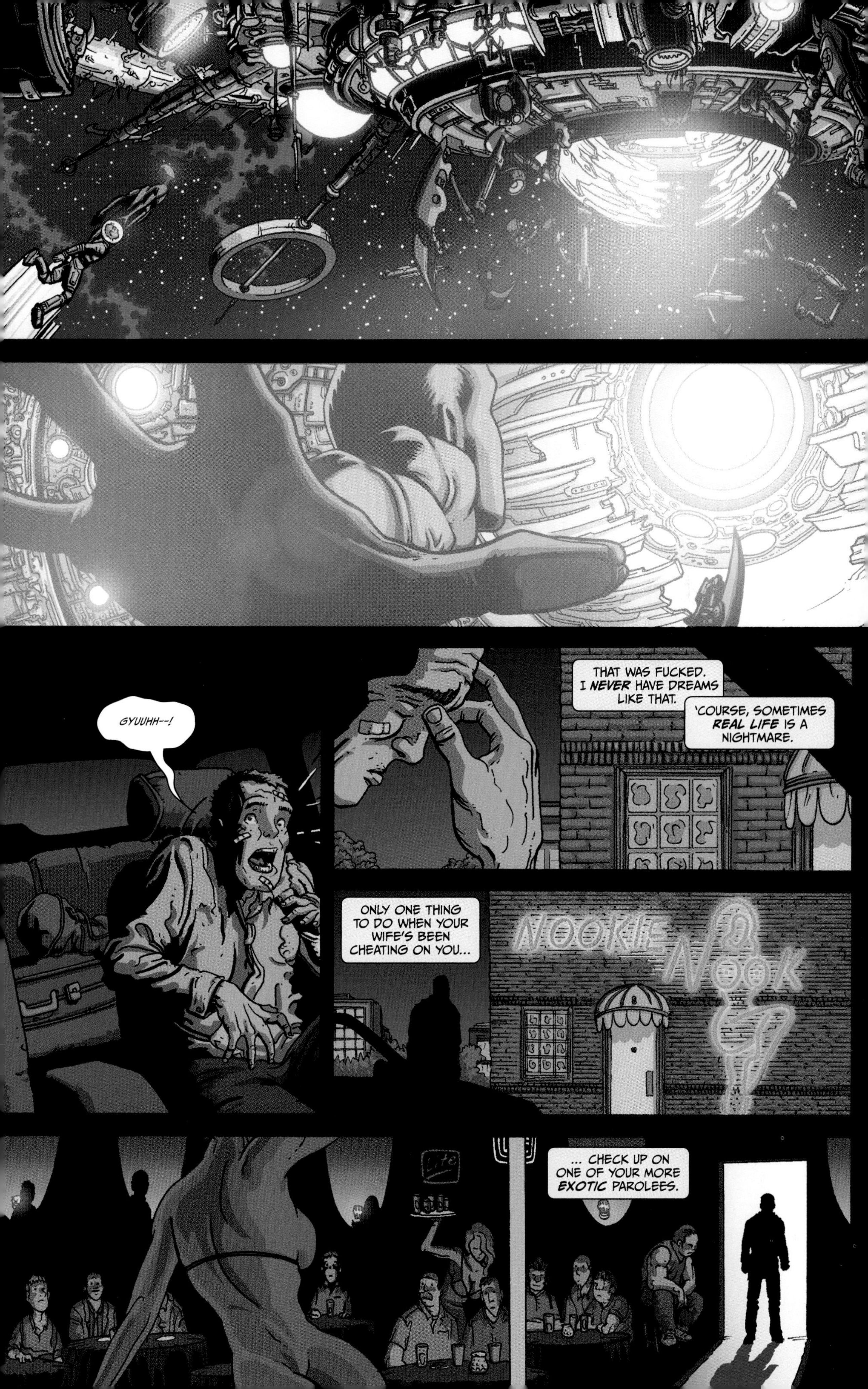
GYUUHH--!
THAT WAS FUCKED. I NEVER HAVE DREAMS LIKE THAT.
'COURSE, SOMETIMES REAL LIFE IS A NIGHTMARE.
ONLY ONE THING TO DO WHEN YOUR WIFE'S BEEN CHEATING ON YOU...
NOOKIE NOOK
... CHECK UP ON ONE OF YOUR MORE EXOTIC PAROLEES.

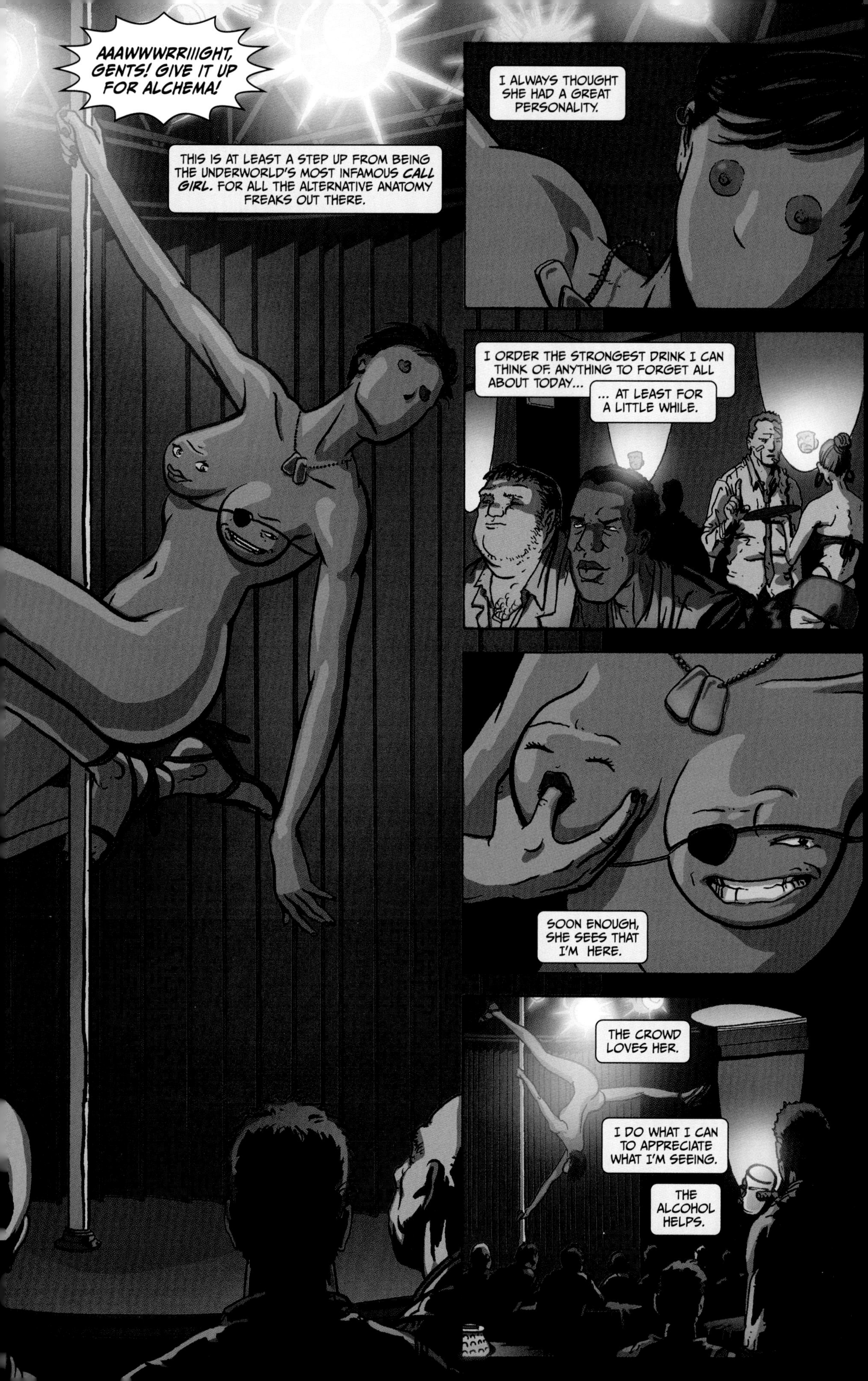
AAAWWWRRIIIGHT, GENTS! GIVE IT UP FOR ALCHEMA!
THIS IS AT LEAST A STEP UP FROM BEING THE UNDERWORLD'S MOST INFAMOUS CALL GIRL. FOR ALL THE ALTERNATIVE ANATOMY FREAKS OUT THERE.
I ALWAYS THOUGHT SHE HAD A GREAT PERSONALITY.
I ORDER THE STRONGEST DRINK I CAN THINK OF. ANYTHING TO FORGET ALL ABOUT TODAY...
... AT LEAST FOR A LITTLE WHILE.
SOON ENOUGH, SHE SEES THAT I'M HERE.
THE CROWD LOVES HER.
I DO WHAT I CAN TO APPRECIATE WHAT I'M SEEING.
THE ALCOHOL HELPS.

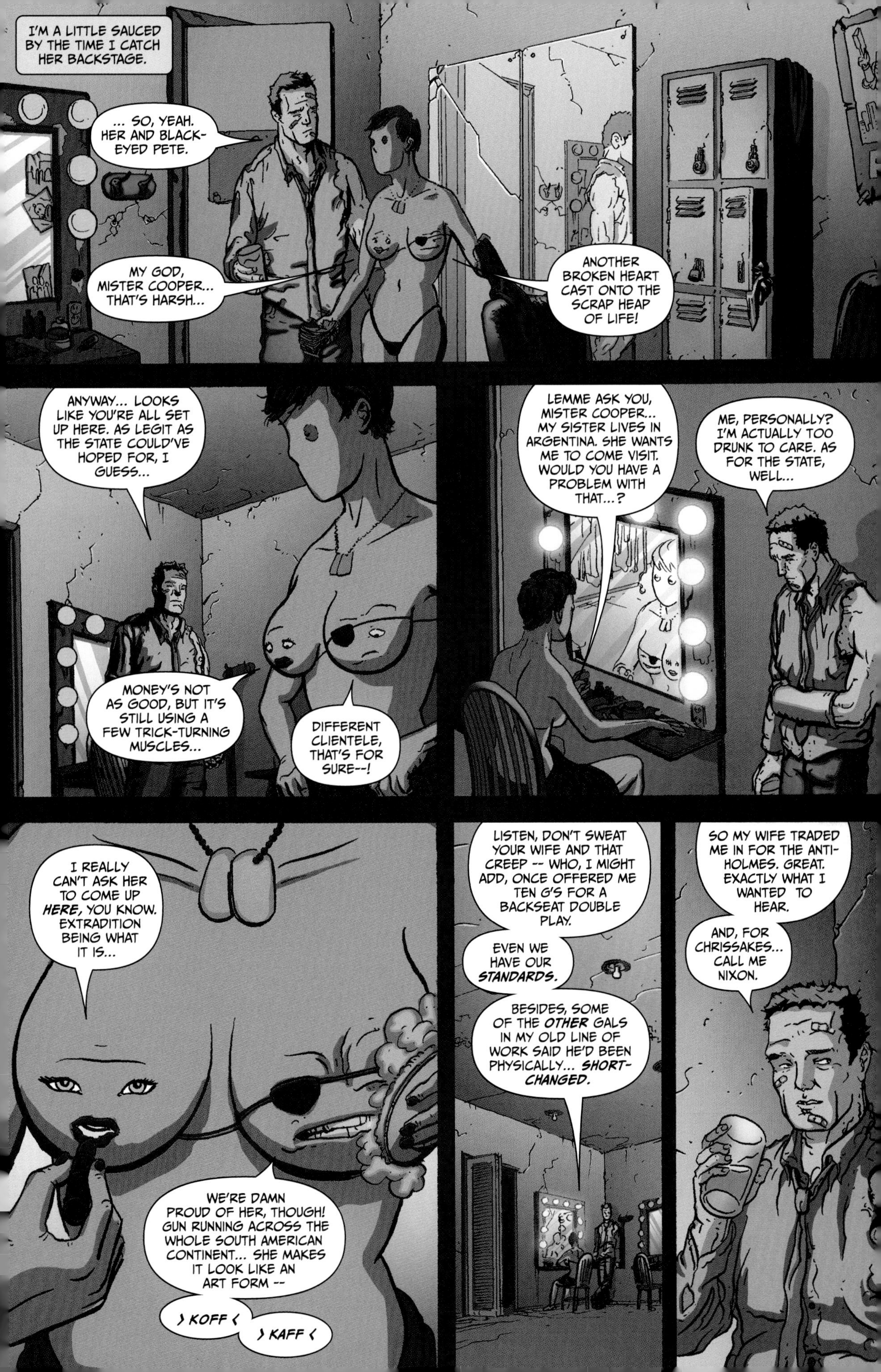
I'M A LITTLE SAUCED BY THE TIME I CATCH HER BACKSTAGE.
... SO, YEAH. HER AND BLACK-EYED PETE.
MY GOD, MISTER COOPER... THAT'S HARSH...
ANOTHER BROKEN HEART CAST ONTO THE SCRAP HEAP OF LIFE!
ANYWAY... LOOKS LIKE YOU'RE ALL SET UP HERE. AS LEGIT AS THE STATE COULD'VE HOPED FOR, I GUESS...
MONEY'S NOT AS GOOD, BUT IT'S STILL USING A FEW TRICK-TURNING MUSCLES...
DIFFERENT CLIENTELE, THAT'S FOR SURE--!
LEMME ASK YOU, MISTER COOPER... MY SISTER LIVES IN ARGENTINA. SHE WANTS ME TO COME VISIT. WOULD YOU HAVE A PROBLEM WITH THAT...?
ME, PERSONALLY? I'M ACTUALLY TOO DRUNK TO CARE. AS FOR THE STATE, WELL...
I REALLY CAN'T ASK HER TO COME UP *HERE*, YOU KNOW. EXTRADITION BEING WHAT IT IS...
WE'RE DAMN PROUD OF HER, THOUGH! GUN RUNNING ACROSS THE WHOLE SOUTH AMERICAN CONTINENT... SHE MAKES IT LOOK LIKE AN ART FORM --
› KOFF ‹
› KAFF ‹
LISTEN, DON'T SWEAT YOUR WIFE AND THAT CREEP -- WHO, I MIGHT ADD, ONCE OFFERED ME TEN G'S FOR A BACKSEAT DOUBLE PLAY.
EVEN WE HAVE OUR ***STANDARDS.***
BESIDES, SOME OF THE ***OTHER*** GALS IN MY OLD LINE OF WORK SAID HE'D BEEN PHYSICALLY... ***SHORT-CHANGED.***
SO MY WIFE TRADED ME IN FOR THE ANTI-HOLMES. GREAT. EXACTLY WHAT I WANTED TO HEAR.
AND, FOR CHRISSAKES... CALL ME NIXON.

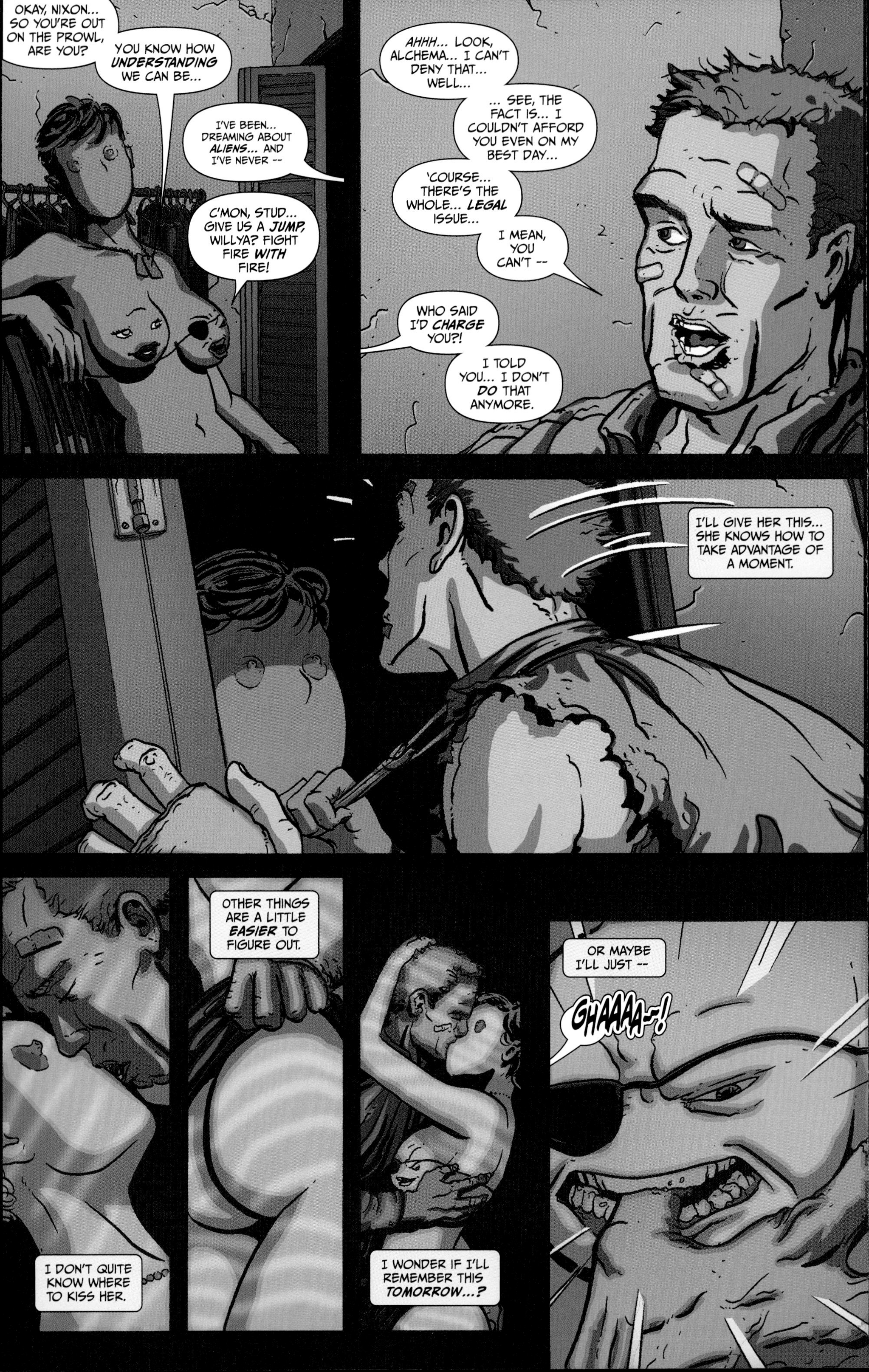
OKAY, NIXON... SO YOU'RE OUT ON THE PROWL, ARE YOU?
YOU KNOW HOW UNDERSTANDING WE CAN BE...
I'VE BEEN... DREAMING ABOUT ALIENS... AND I'VE NEVER --
C'MON, STUD... GIVE US A JUMP, WILLYA? FIGHT FIRE WITH FIRE!
AHHH... LOOK, ALCHEMA... I CAN'T DENY THAT... WELL...
... SEE, THE FACT IS... I COULDN'T AFFORD YOU EVEN ON MY BEST DAY...
'COURSE... THERE'S THE WHOLE... LEGAL ISSUE...
I MEAN, YOU CAN'T --
WHO SAID I'D CHARGE YOU?!
I TOLD YOU... I DON'T DO THAT ANYMORE.
I'LL GIVE HER THIS... SHE KNOWS HOW TO TAKE ADVANTAGE OF A MOMENT.
I DON'T QUITE KNOW WHERE TO KISS HER.
OTHER THINGS ARE A LITTLE EASIER TO FIGURE OUT.
I WONDER IF I'LL REMEMBER THIS TOMORROW...?
OR MAYBE I'LL JUST --
GHAAAA--!

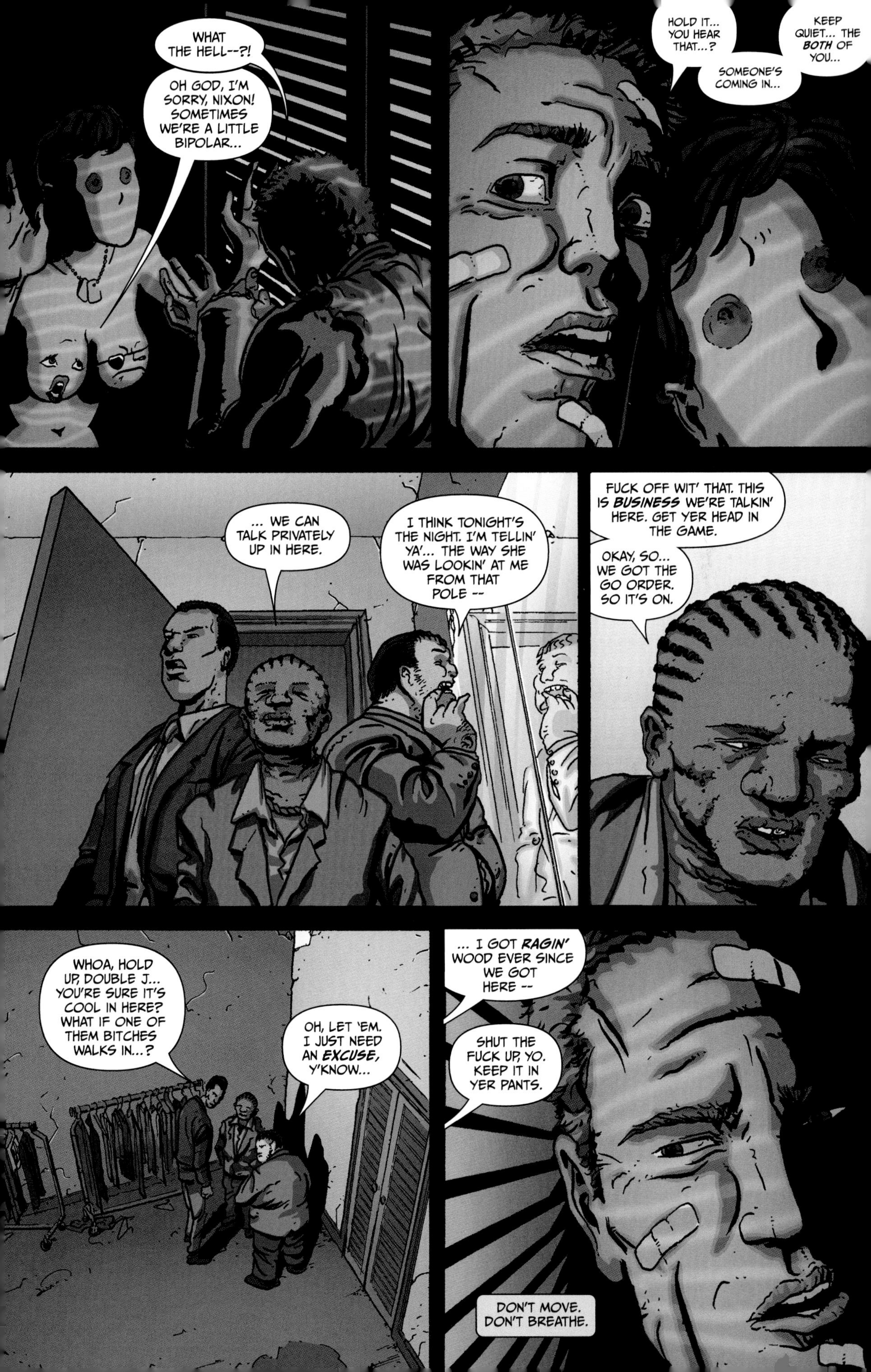
WHAT THE HELL--?!
OH GOD, I'M SORRY, NIXON! SOMETIMES WE'RE A LITTLE BIPOLAR...
HOLD IT... YOU HEAR THAT...?
SOMEONE'S COMING IN...
KEEP QUIET... THE *BOTH* OF YOU...
... WE CAN TALK PRIVATELY UP IN HERE.
I THINK TONIGHT'S THE NIGHT. I'M TELLIN' YA'... THE WAY SHE WAS LOOKIN' AT ME FROM THAT POLE --
FUCK OFF WIT' THAT. THIS IS ***BUSINESS*** WE'RE TALKIN' HERE. GET YER HEAD IN THE GAME.
OKAY, SO... WE GOT THE GO ORDER. SO IT'S ON.
WHOA, HOLD UP, DOUBLE J... YOU'RE SURE IT'S COOL IN HERE? WHAT IF ONE OF THEM BITCHES WALKS IN...?
OH, LET 'EM. I JUST NEED AN ***EXCUSE,*** Y'KNOW...
... I GOT ***RAGIN'*** WOOD EVER SINCE WE GOT HERE --
SHUT THE FUCK UP, YO. KEEP IT IN YER PANTS.
DON'T MOVE. DON'T BREATHE.

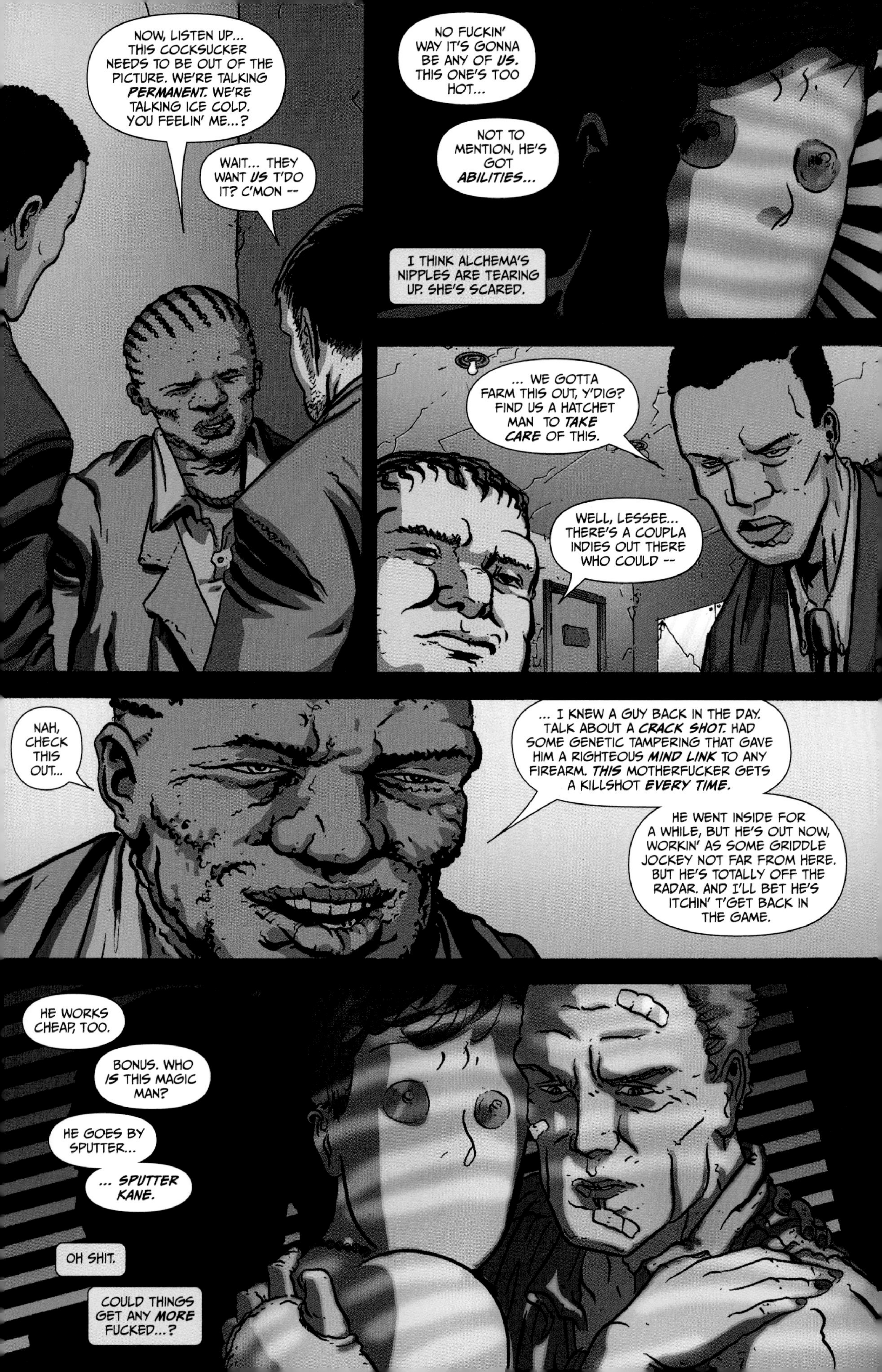
NOW, LISTEN UP... THIS COCKSUCKER NEEDS TO BE OUT OF THE PICTURE. WE'RE TALKING PERMANENT. WE'RE TALKING ICE COLD. YOU FEELIN' ME...?
WAIT... THEY WANT US T'DO IT? C'MON --
NO FUCKIN' WAY IT'S GONNA BE ANY OF US. THIS ONE'S TOO HOT...
NOT TO MENTION, HE'S GOT ABILITIES...
I THINK ALCHEMA'S NIPPLES ARE TEARING UP. SHE'S SCARED.
... WE GOTTA FARM THIS OUT, Y'DIG? FIND US A HATCHET MAN TO TAKE CARE OF THIS.
WELL, LESSEE... THERE'S A COUPLA INDIES OUT THERE WHO COULD --
NAH, CHECK THIS OUT...
... I KNEW A GUY BACK IN THE DAY. TALK ABOUT A CRACK SHOT. HAD SOME GENETIC TAMPERING THAT GAVE HIM A RIGHTEOUS MIND LINK TO ANY FIREARM. THIS MOTHERFUCKER GETS A KILLSHOT EVERY TIME.
HE WENT INSIDE FOR A WHILE, BUT HE'S OUT NOW, WORKIN' AS SOME GRIDDLE JOCKEY NOT FAR FROM HERE. BUT HE'S TOTALLY OFF THE RADAR. AND I'LL BET HE'S ITCHIN' T'GET BACK IN THE GAME.
HE WORKS CHEAP, TOO.
BONUS. WHO IS THIS MAGIC MAN?
HE GOES BY SPUTTER...
... SPUTTER KANE.
OH SHIT.
COULD THINGS GET ANY MORE FUCKED...?

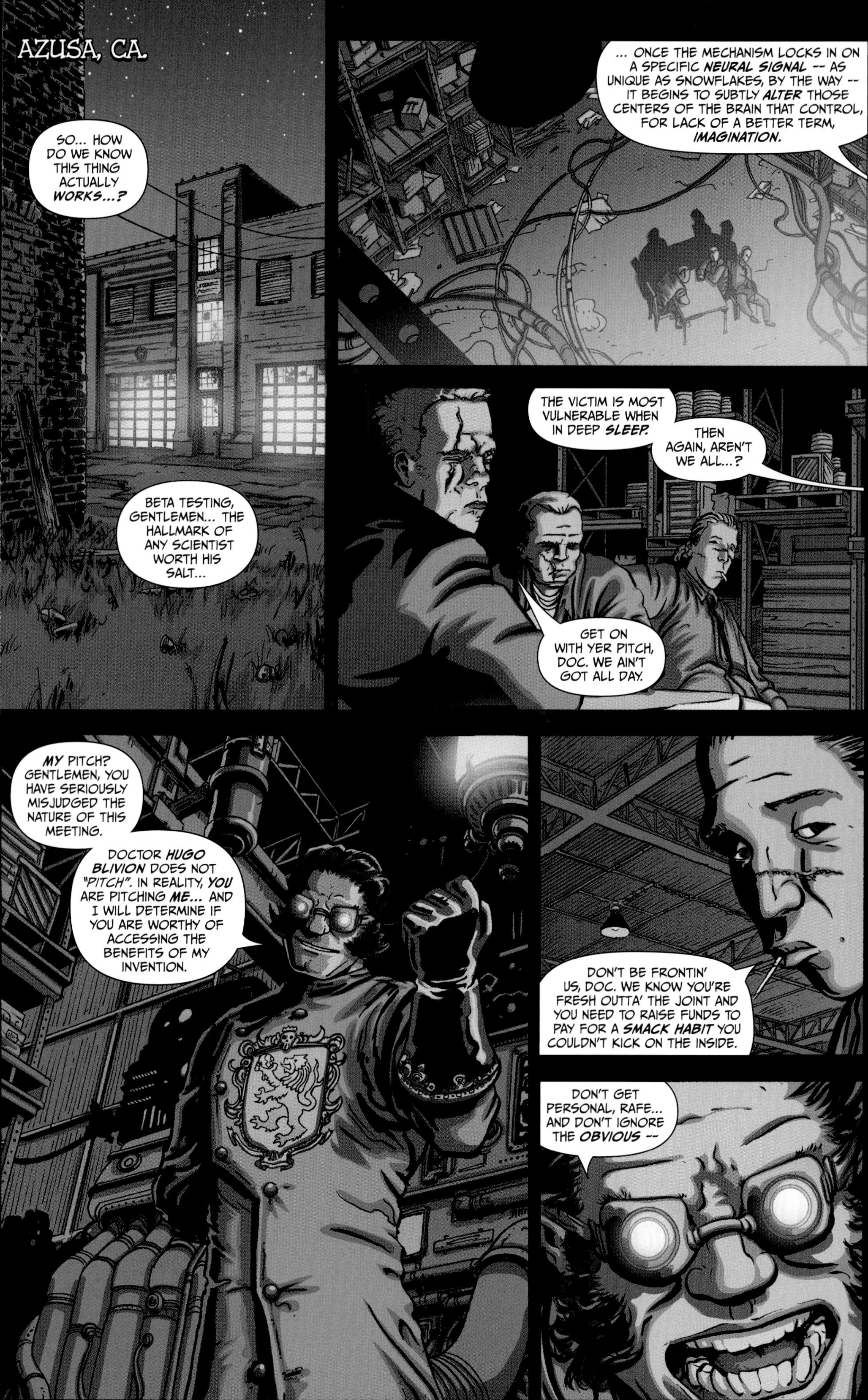
AZUSA, CA.
SO... HOW DO WE KNOW THIS THING ACTUALLY WORKS...?
BETA TESTING, GENTLEMEN... THE HALLMARK OF ANY SCIENTIST WORTH HIS SALT...
... ONCE THE MECHANISM LOCKS IN ON A SPECIFIC NEURAL SIGNAL -- AS UNIQUE AS SNOWFLAKES, BY THE WAY -- IT BEGINS TO SUBTLY ALTER THOSE CENTERS OF THE BRAIN THAT CONTROL, FOR LACK OF A BETTER TERM, IMAGINATION.
THE VICTIM IS MOST VULNERABLE WHEN IN DEEP SLEEP.
THEN AGAIN, AREN'T WE ALL...?
GET ON WITH YER PITCH, DOC. WE AIN'T GOT ALL DAY.
MY PITCH? GENTLEMEN, YOU HAVE SERIOUSLY MISJUDGED THE NATURE OF THIS MEETING.
DOCTOR HUGO BLIVION DOES NOT "PITCH". IN REALITY, YOU ARE PITCHING ME... AND I WILL DETERMINE IF YOU ARE WORTHY OF ACCESSING THE BENEFITS OF MY INVENTION.
DON'T BE FRONTIN' US, DOC. WE KNOW YOU'RE FRESH OUTTA' THE JOINT AND YOU NEED TO RAISE FUNDS TO PAY FOR A SMACK HABIT YOU COULDN'T KICK ON THE INSIDE.
DON'T GET PERSONAL, RAFE... AND DON'T IGNORE THE OBVIOUS --

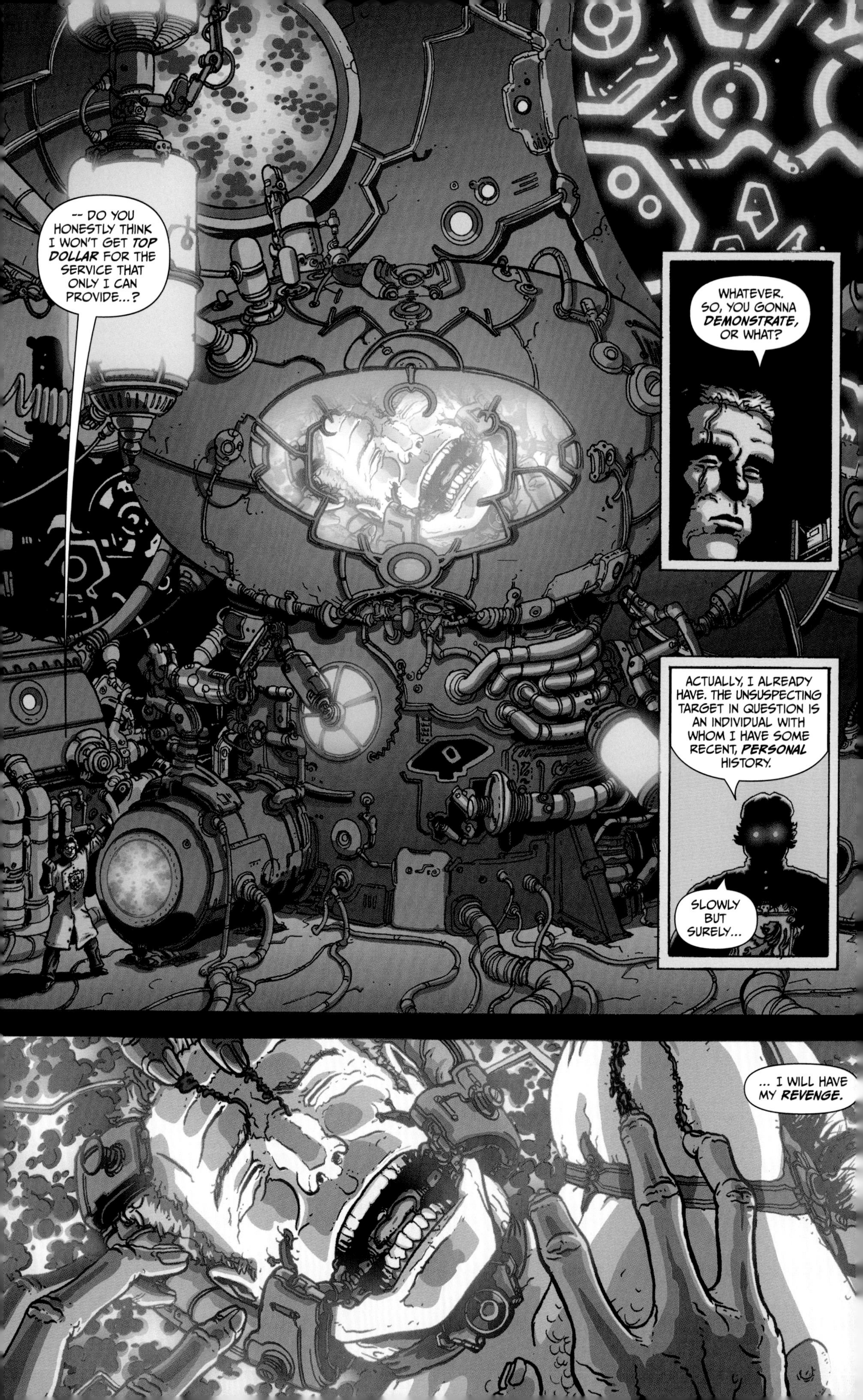
-- DO YOU HONESTLY THINK I WON'T GET TOP DOLLAR FOR THE SERVICE THAT ONLY I CAN PROVIDE...?
WHATEVER. SO, YOU GONNA DEMONSTRATE, OR WHAT?
ACTUALLY, I ALREADY HAVE. THE UNSUSPECTING TARGET IN QUESTION IS AN INDIVIDUAL WITH WHOM I HAVE SOME RECENT, PERSONAL HISTORY.
SLOWLY BUT SURELY...
... I WILL HAVE MY REVENGE.

HYUH~!

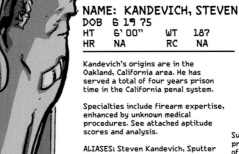

NAME: KANDEVICH, STEVEN
DOB 6 19 75
HT 6' 00"   WT 187
HR NA   RC NA

Kandevich's origins are in the Oakland, California area. He has served a total of four years prison time in the California penal system.

Specialties include firearm expertise, enhanced by unknown medical procedures. See attached aptitude scores and analysis.

ALIASES; Steven Kandevich, Sputter Kane

WEAPONS; prefers custom-made handguns, specifically calibrated to his psionic abilities.

WARNING; Should be considered armed and dangerous. DO NOT ATTEMPT TO APPREHEND WITHOUT SUPPORT!!

Subject has history of juvenile problems stemming from background of abuse and alcoholic parents. Parents divorce at age six months. Mother dead at age five.

OTHER CITATIONS; 4/28/94 5647-98 (drinking in public) misdemeanor conviction 25$ fine

3/6/96 78686-a (unregistered vehicle) misdemeanor conviction 24$ fine

JESUS. I'M REALLY GLAD NO ONE WAS HERE TO SEE THAT.

FALLING ASLEEP AT MY DESK IS *ONE* THING...

OH WELL, ENOUGH FUN AND GAMES...

SPUTTER'S FILE TELLS A PRETTY DEFINITIVE STORY. HE WAS PRACTICALLY BORN INTO THE LIFE.

HE WAS ALREADY A MARKSMAN... BEFORE HE SUBJECTED HIMSELF TO THE BLACK MARKET SCIENCE THAT RADICALLY ENHANCED THOSE ABILITIES.

A TRIGGERMAN LIKE THAT IS ALWAYS GOING TO BE ON THE SHORT LIST.

GETTING OFFERS HE CAN'T REFUSE.

THING IS, HE MIGHT'VE BEEN COVERING HIS ASS... BUT DEEP DOWN, I THINK HE'S A GOOD KID WHO REALLY DOES WANT *OUT.*

HE JUST NEEDS TO --

WELL, LOOKEE WHAT WE HAVE HERE...

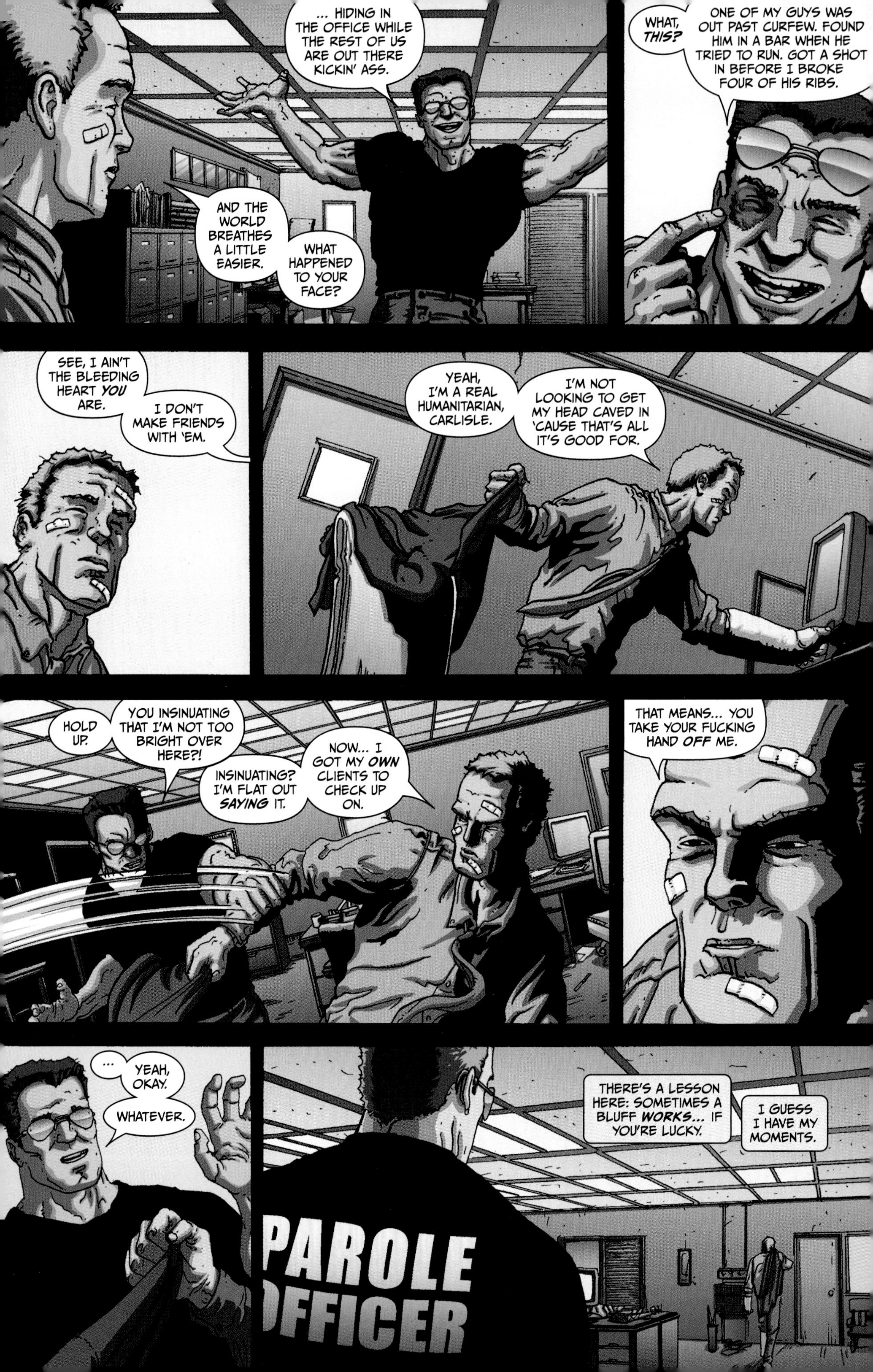
... HIDING IN THE OFFICE WHILE THE REST OF US ARE OUT THERE KICKIN' ASS.
AND THE WORLD BREATHES A LITTLE EASIER.
WHAT HAPPENED TO YOUR FACE?
WHAT, THIS?
ONE OF MY GUYS WAS OUT PAST CURFEW. FOUND HIM IN A BAR WHEN HE TRIED TO RUN. GOT A SHOT IN BEFORE I BROKE FOUR OF HIS RIBS.
SEE, I AIN'T THE BLEEDING HEART YOU ARE.
I DON'T MAKE FRIENDS WITH 'EM.
YEAH, I'M A REAL HUMANITARIAN, CARLISLE.
I'M NOT LOOKING TO GET MY HEAD CAVED IN 'CAUSE THAT'S ALL IT'S GOOD FOR.
HOLD UP.
YOU INSINUATING THAT I'M NOT TOO BRIGHT OVER HERE?!
INSINUATING? I'M FLAT OUT SAYING IT.
NOW... I GOT MY OWN CLIENTS TO CHECK UP ON.
THAT MEANS... YOU TAKE YOUR FUCKING HAND OFF ME.
...
YEAH, OKAY.
WHATEVER.
PAROLE OFFICER
THERE'S A LESSON HERE: SOMETIMES A BLUFF WORKS... IF YOU'RE LUCKY.
I GUESS I HAVE MY MOMENTS.

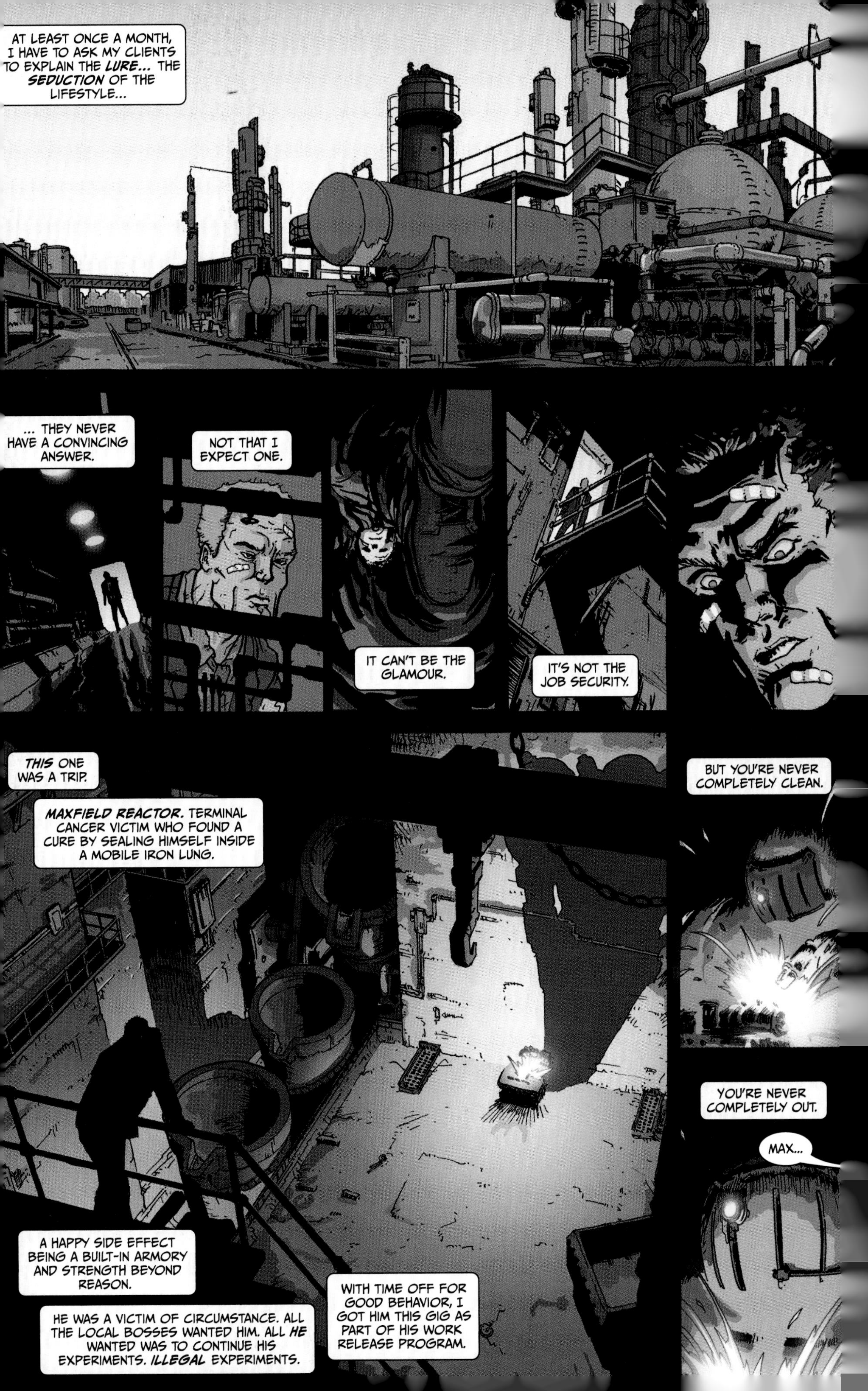
AT LEAST ONCE A MONTH, I HAVE TO ASK MY CLIENTS TO EXPLAIN THE LURE... THE SEDUCTION OF THE LIFESTYLE...
... THEY NEVER HAVE A CONVINCING ANSWER.
NOT THAT I EXPECT ONE.
IT CAN'T BE THE GLAMOUR.
IT'S NOT THE JOB SECURITY.
THIS ONE WAS A TRIP.
MAXFIELD REACTOR. TERMINAL CANCER VICTIM WHO FOUND A CURE BY SEALING HIMSELF INSIDE A MOBILE IRON LUNG.
A HAPPY SIDE EFFECT BEING A BUILT-IN ARMORY AND STRENGTH BEYOND REASON.
HE WAS A VICTIM OF CIRCUMSTANCE. ALL THE LOCAL BOSSES WANTED HIM. ALL HE WANTED WAS TO CONTINUE HIS EXPERIMENTS. ILLEGAL EXPERIMENTS.
WITH TIME OFF FOR GOOD BEHAVIOR, I GOT HIM THIS GIG AS PART OF HIS WORK RELEASE PROGRAM.
BUT YOU'RE NEVER COMPLETELY CLEAN.
YOU'RE NEVER COMPLETELY OUT.
MAX...

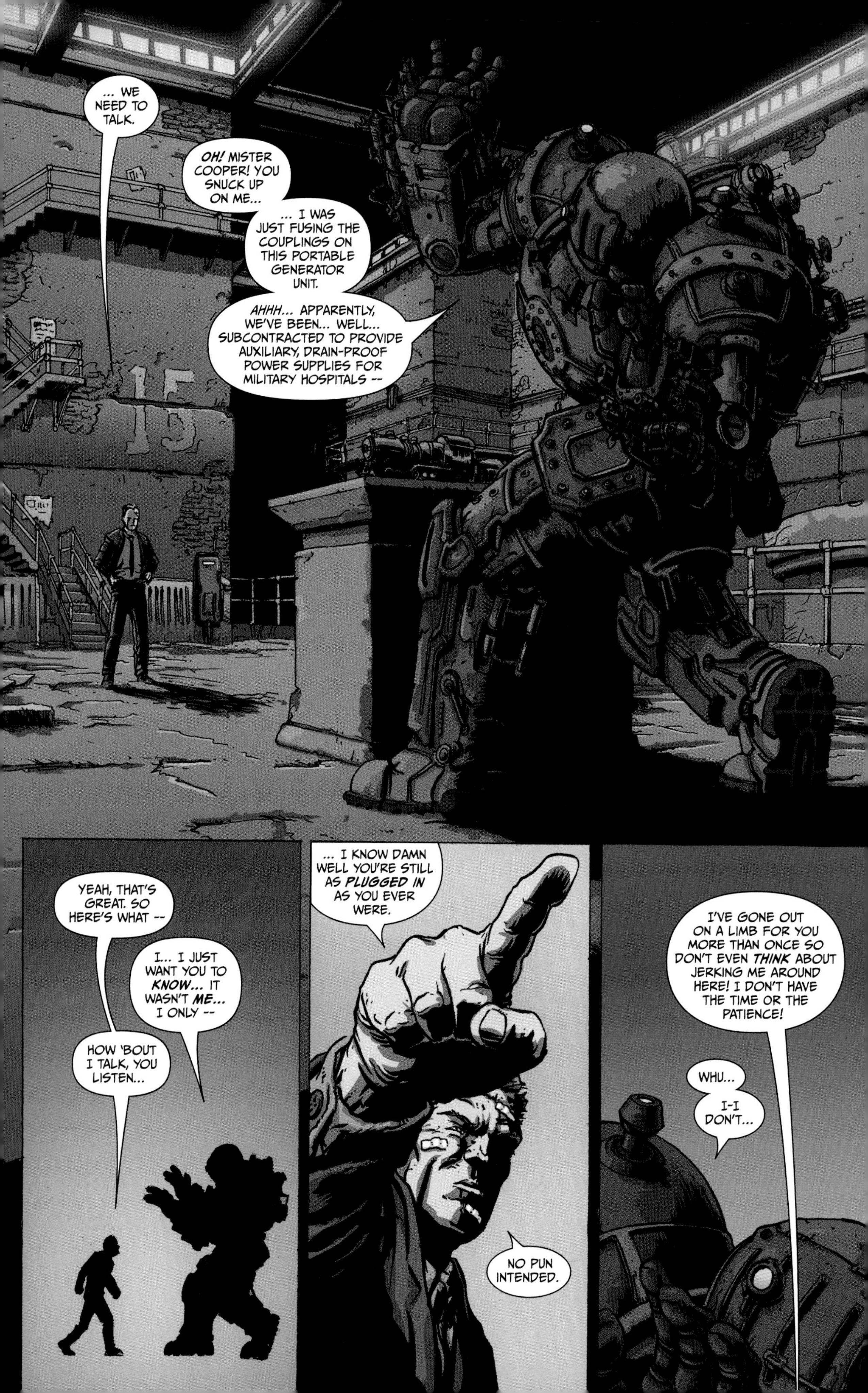
... WE NEED TO TALK.
OH! MISTER COOPER! YOU SNUCK UP ON ME...
... I WAS JUST FUSING THE COUPLINGS ON THIS PORTABLE GENERATOR UNIT.
AHHH... APPARENTLY, WE'VE BEEN... WELL... SUBCONTRACTED TO PROVIDE AUXILIARY, DRAIN-PROOF POWER SUPPLIES FOR MILITARY HOSPITALS --
15
YEAH, THAT'S GREAT. SO HERE'S WHAT --
I... I JUST WANT YOU TO KNOW... IT WASN'T ME... I ONLY --
HOW 'BOUT I TALK, YOU LISTEN...
... I KNOW DAMN WELL YOU'RE STILL AS PLUGGED IN AS YOU EVER WERE.
NO PUN INTENDED.
I'VE GONE OUT ON A LIMB FOR YOU MORE THAN ONCE SO DON'T EVEN THINK ABOUT JERKING ME AROUND HERE! I DON'T HAVE THE TIME OR THE PATIENCE!
WHU...
I-I DON'T...

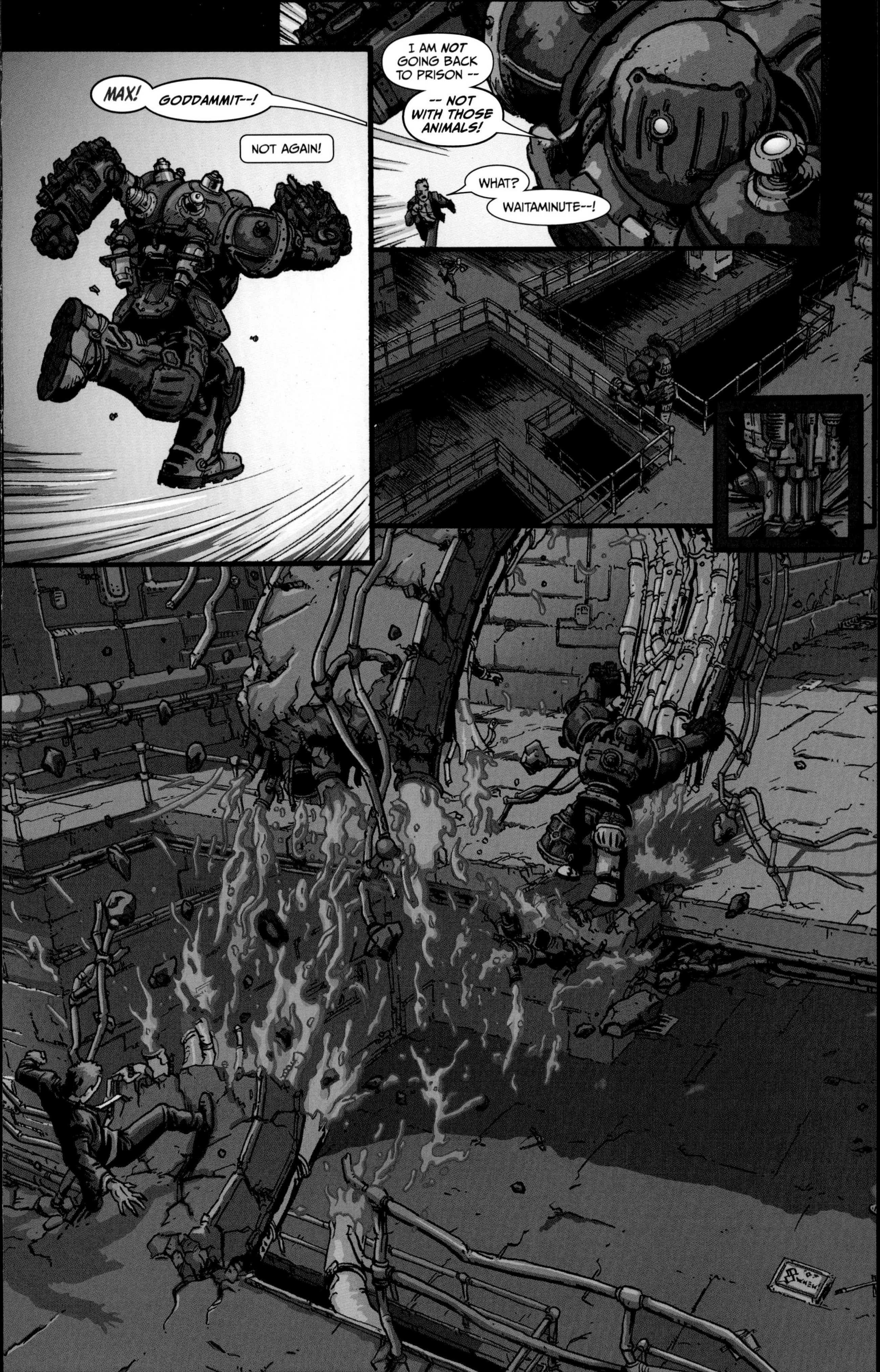
MAX!
GODDAMMIT--!
NOT AGAIN!
I AM NOT GOING BACK TO PRISON --
-- NOT WITH THOSE ANIMALS!
WHAT?
WAITAMINUTE--!

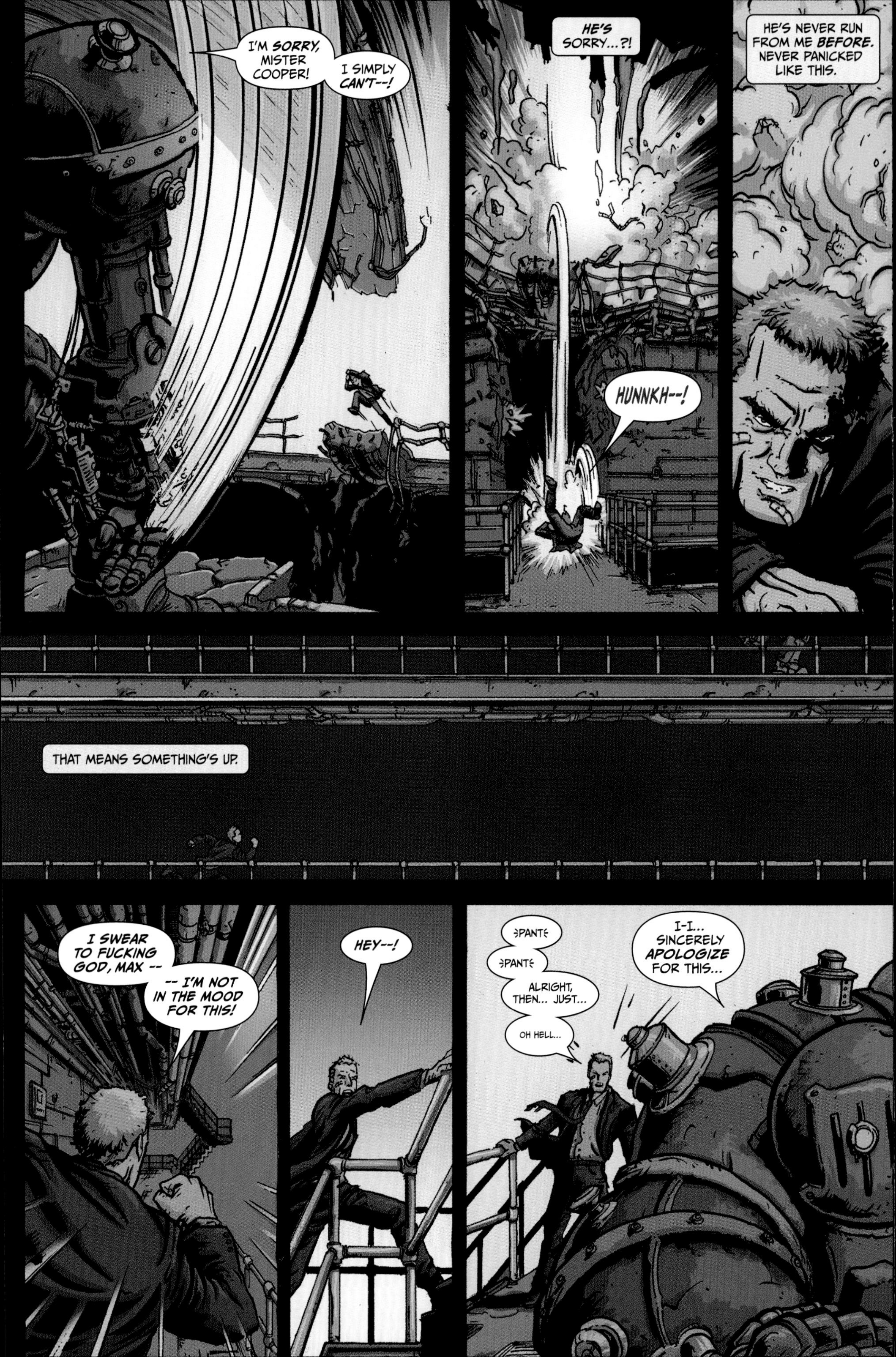

I'M SORRY, MISTER COOPER!
I SIMPLY CAN'T--!
HE'S SORRY...?!
HE'S NEVER RUN FROM ME BEFORE. NEVER PANICKED LIKE THIS.
HUNNKH--!
THAT MEANS SOMETHING'S UP.
I SWEAR TO FUCKING GOD, MAX --
-- I'M NOT IN THE MOOD FOR THIS!
HEY--!
PANT
PANT
ALRIGHT, THEN... JUST...
OH HELL...
I-I... SINCERELY APOLOGIZE FOR THIS...

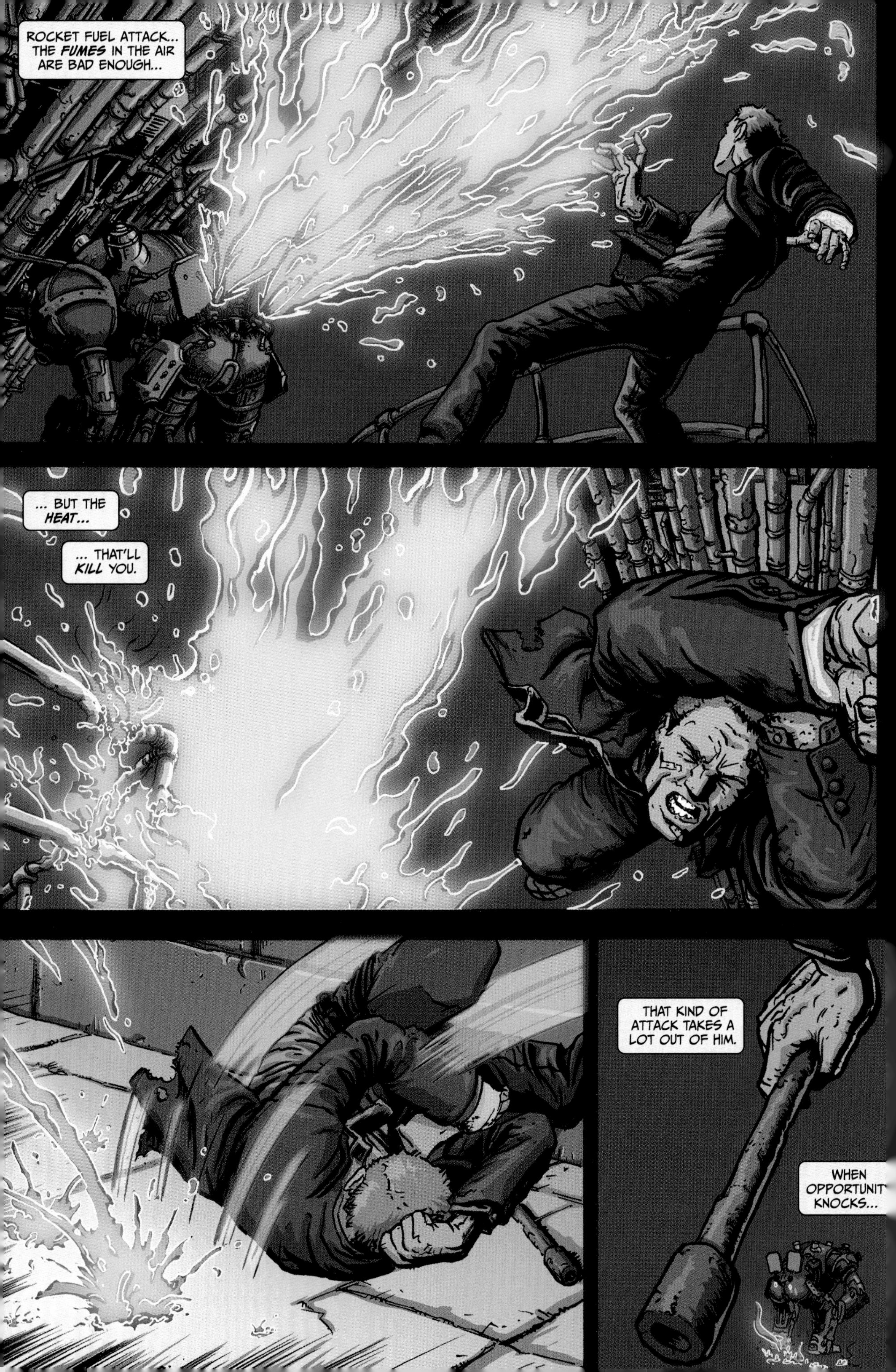
ROCKET FUEL ATTACK... THE FUMES IN THE AIR ARE BAD ENOUGH...
... BUT THE HEAT...
... THAT'LL KILL YOU.
THAT KIND OF ATTACK TAKES A LOT OUT OF HIM.
WHEN OPPORTUNITY KNOCKS...

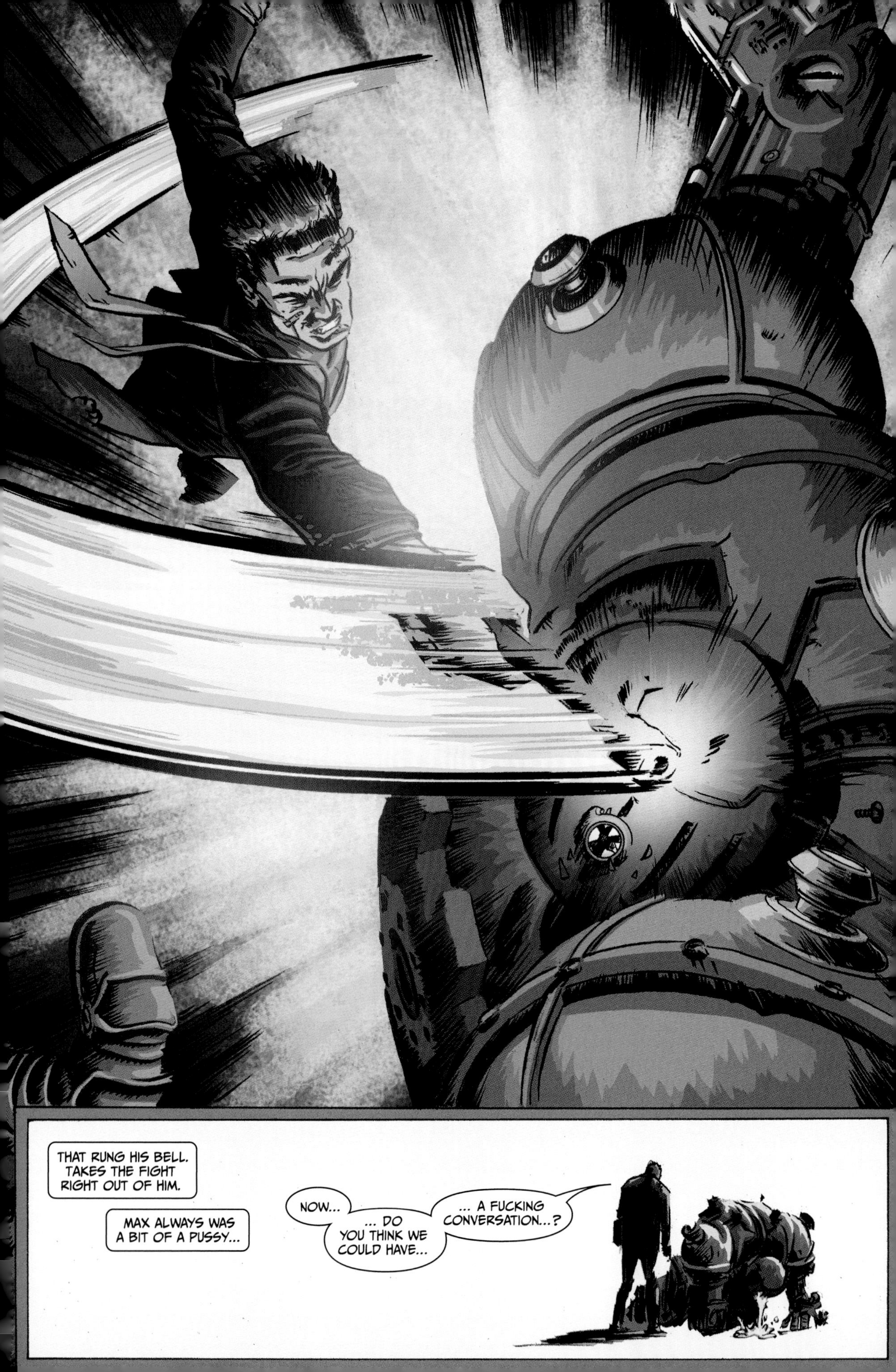
THAT RUNG HIS BELL. TAKES THE FIGHT RIGHT OUT OF HIM.
MAX ALWAYS WAS A BIT OF A PUSSY...
NOW...
... DO YOU THINK WE COULD HAVE...
... A FUCKING CONVERSATION...?

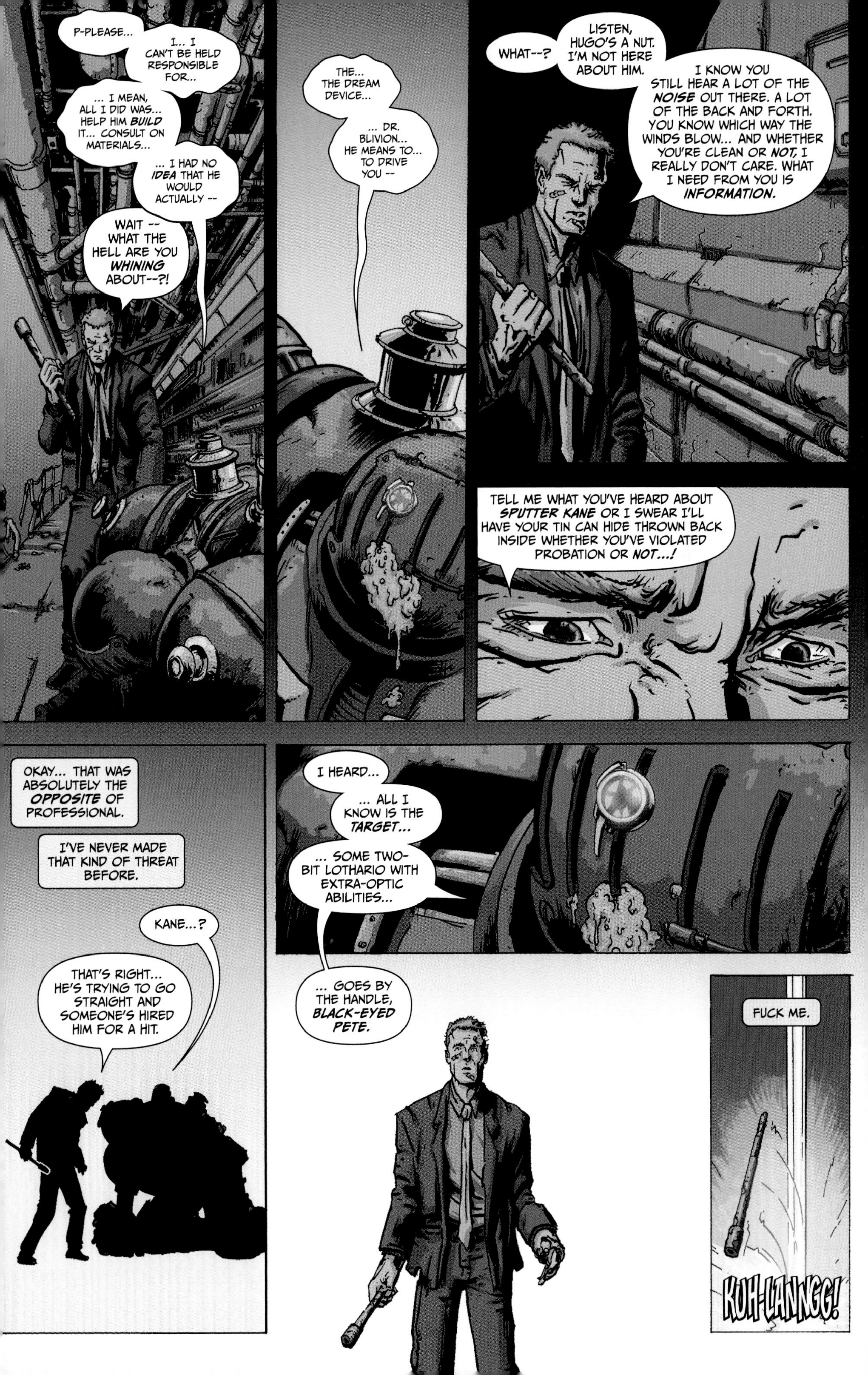

P-PLEASE...
I... I CAN'T BE HELD RESPONSIBLE FOR...
... I MEAN, ALL I DID WAS... HELP HIM BUILD IT... CONSULT ON MATERIALS...
... I HAD NO IDEA THAT HE WOULD ACTUALLY --
WAIT -- WHAT THE HELL ARE YOU WHINING ABOUT--?!
THE... THE DREAM DEVICE...
... DR. BLIVION... HE MEANS TO... TO DRIVE YOU --
WHAT--?
LISTEN, HUGO'S A NUT. I'M NOT HERE ABOUT HIM.
I KNOW YOU STILL HEAR A LOT OF THE NOISE OUT THERE. A LOT OF THE BACK AND FORTH. YOU KNOW WHICH WAY THE WINDS BLOW... AND WHETHER YOU'RE CLEAN OR NOT, I REALLY DON'T CARE. WHAT I NEED FROM YOU IS INFORMATION.
TELL ME WHAT YOU'VE HEARD ABOUT SPUTTER KANE OR I SWEAR I'LL HAVE YOUR TIN CAN HIDE THROWN BACK INSIDE WHETHER YOU'VE VIOLATED PROBATION OR NOT...!
OKAY... THAT WAS ABSOLUTELY THE OPPOSITE OF PROFESSIONAL.
I'VE NEVER MADE THAT KIND OF THREAT BEFORE.
KANE...?
THAT'S RIGHT... HE'S TRYING TO GO STRAIGHT AND SOMEONE'S HIRED HIM FOR A HIT.
I HEARD...
... ALL I KNOW IS THE TARGET...
... SOME TWO-BIT LOTHARIO WITH EXTRA-OPTIC ABILITIES...
... GOES BY THE HANDLE, BLACK-EYED PETE.
FUCK ME.
KUH-LANNGG!

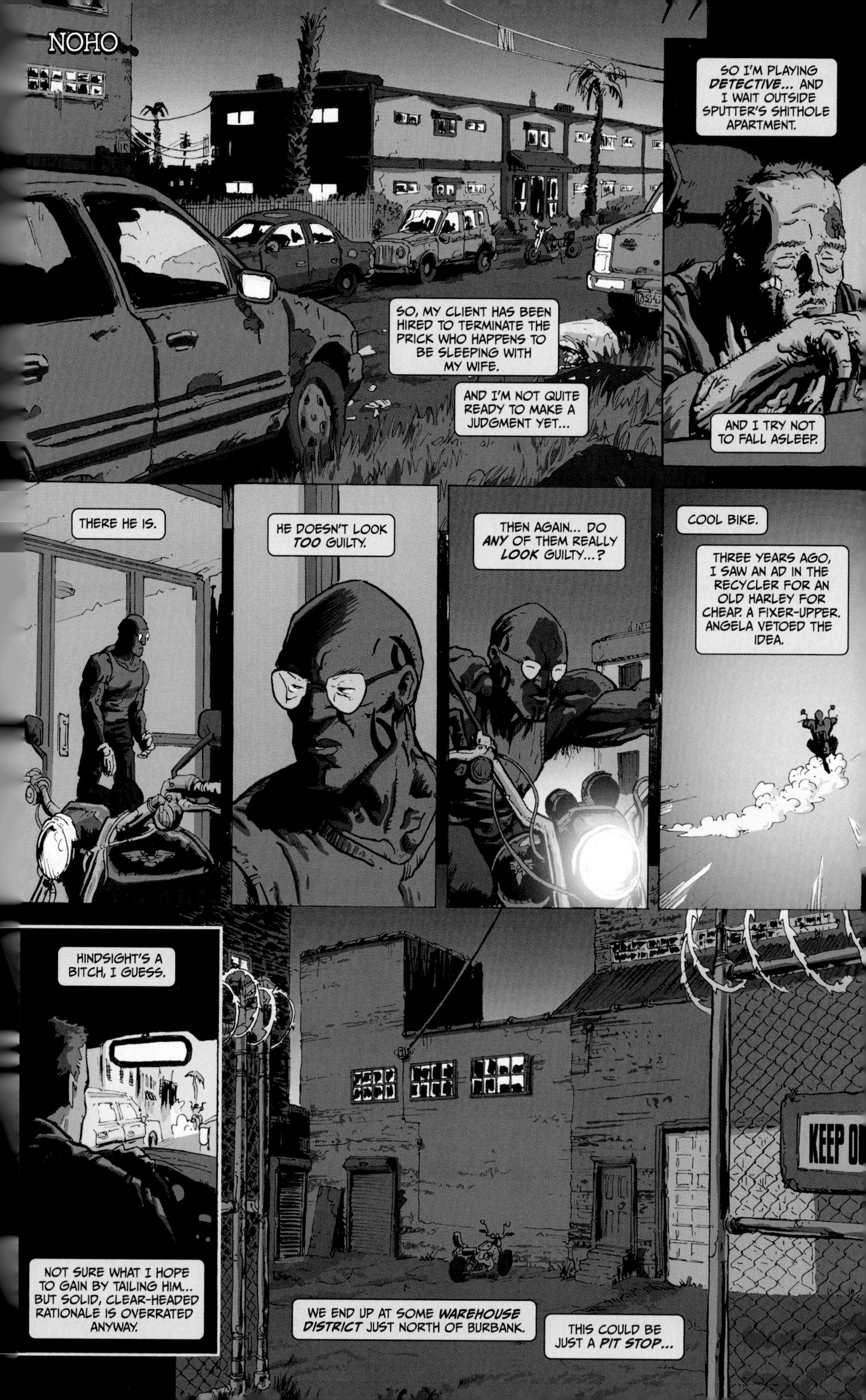
NOHO
SO, MY CLIENT HAS BEEN HIRED TO TERMINATE THE PRICK WHO HAPPENS TO BE SLEEPING WITH MY WIFE.
AND I'M NOT QUITE READY TO MAKE A JUDGMENT YET...
SO I'M PLAYING DETECTIVE... AND I WAIT OUTSIDE SPUTTER'S SHITHOLE APARTMENT.
AND I TRY NOT TO FALL ASLEEP.
THERE HE IS.
HE DOESN'T LOOK TOO GUILTY.
THEN AGAIN... DO ANY OF THEM REALLY LOOK GUILTY...?
COOL BIKE.
THREE YEARS AGO, I SAW AN AD IN THE RECYCLER FOR AN OLD HARLEY FOR CHEAP. A FIXER-UPPER. ANGELA VETOED THE IDEA.
HINDSIGHT'S A BITCH, I GUESS.
NOT SURE WHAT I HOPE TO GAIN BY TAILING HIM... BUT SOLID, CLEAR-HEADED RATIONALE IS OVERRATED ANYWAY.
WE END UP AT SOME WAREHOUSE DISTRICT JUST NORTH OF BURBANK.
THIS COULD BE JUST A PIT STOP...
KEEP O

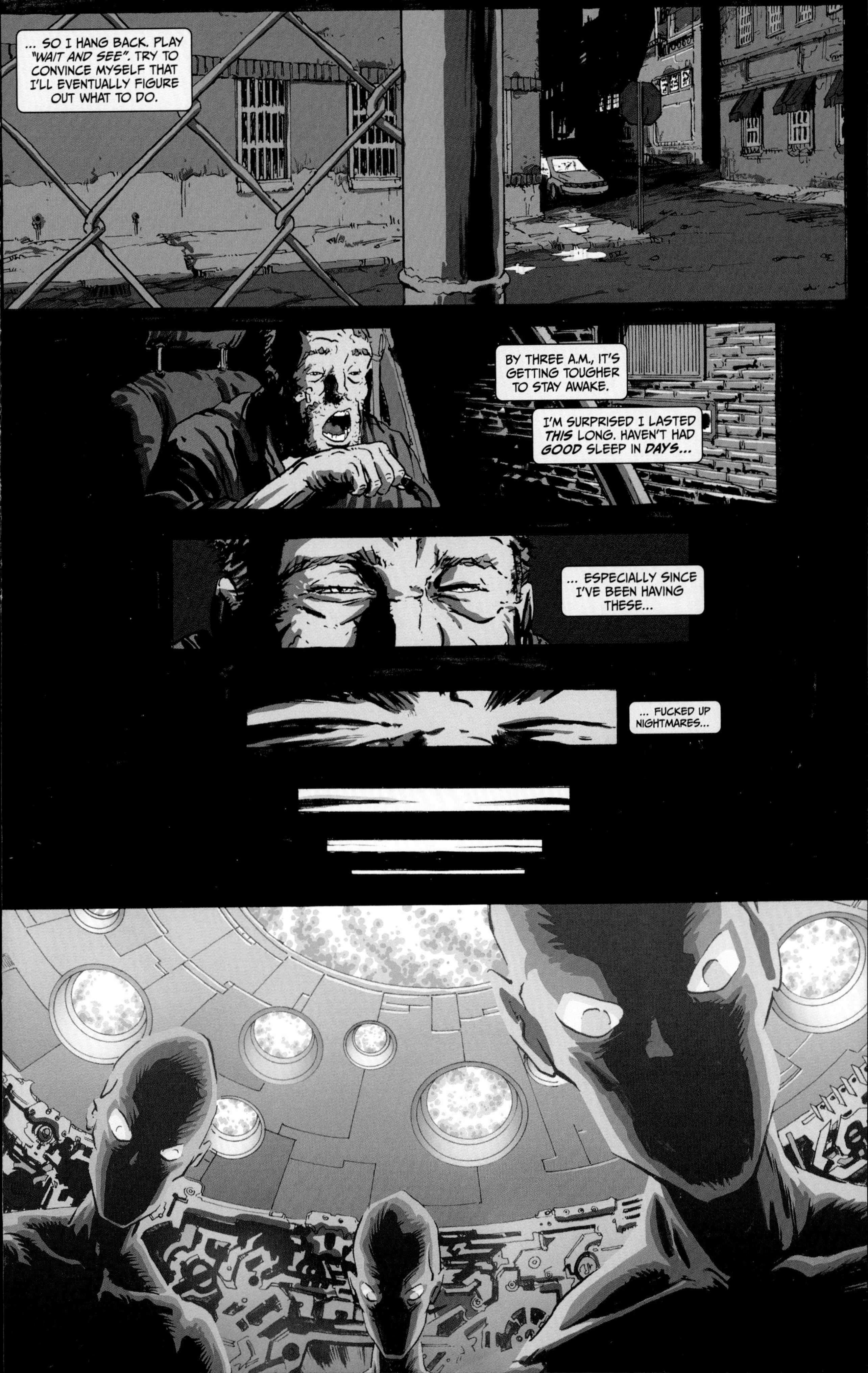

... SO I HANG BACK. PLAY "WAIT AND SEE". TRY TO CONVINCE MYSELF THAT I'LL EVENTUALLY FIGURE OUT WHAT TO DO.
BY THREE A.M., IT'S GETTING TOUGHER TO STAY AWAKE.
I'M SURPRISED I LASTED THIS LONG. HAVEN'T HAD GOOD SLEEP IN DAYS...
... ESPECIALLY SINCE I'VE BEEN HAVING THESE...
... FUCKED UP NIGHTMARES...

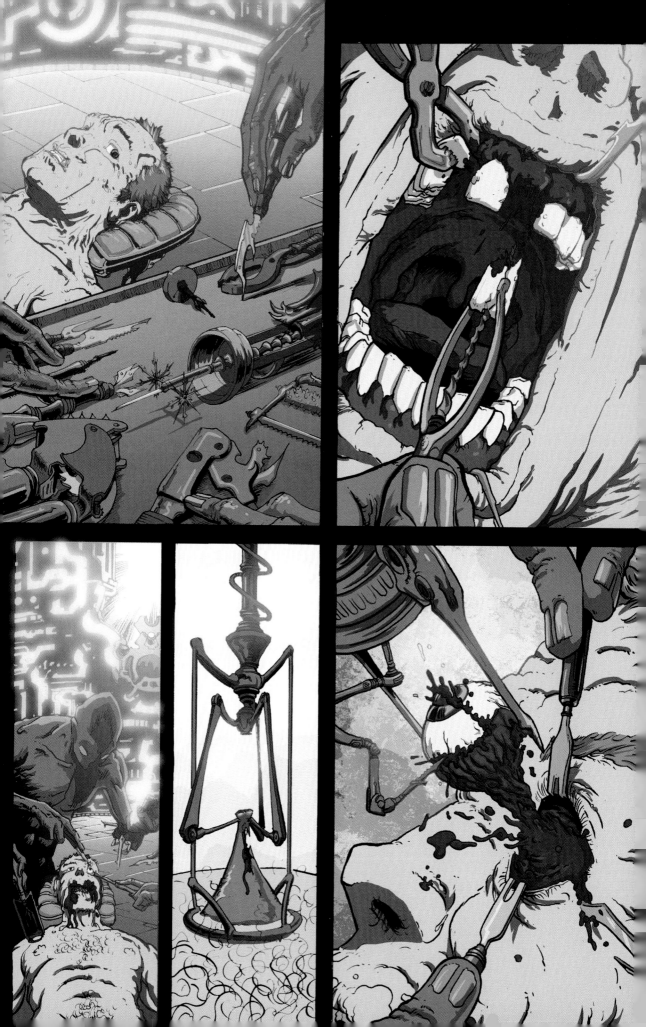

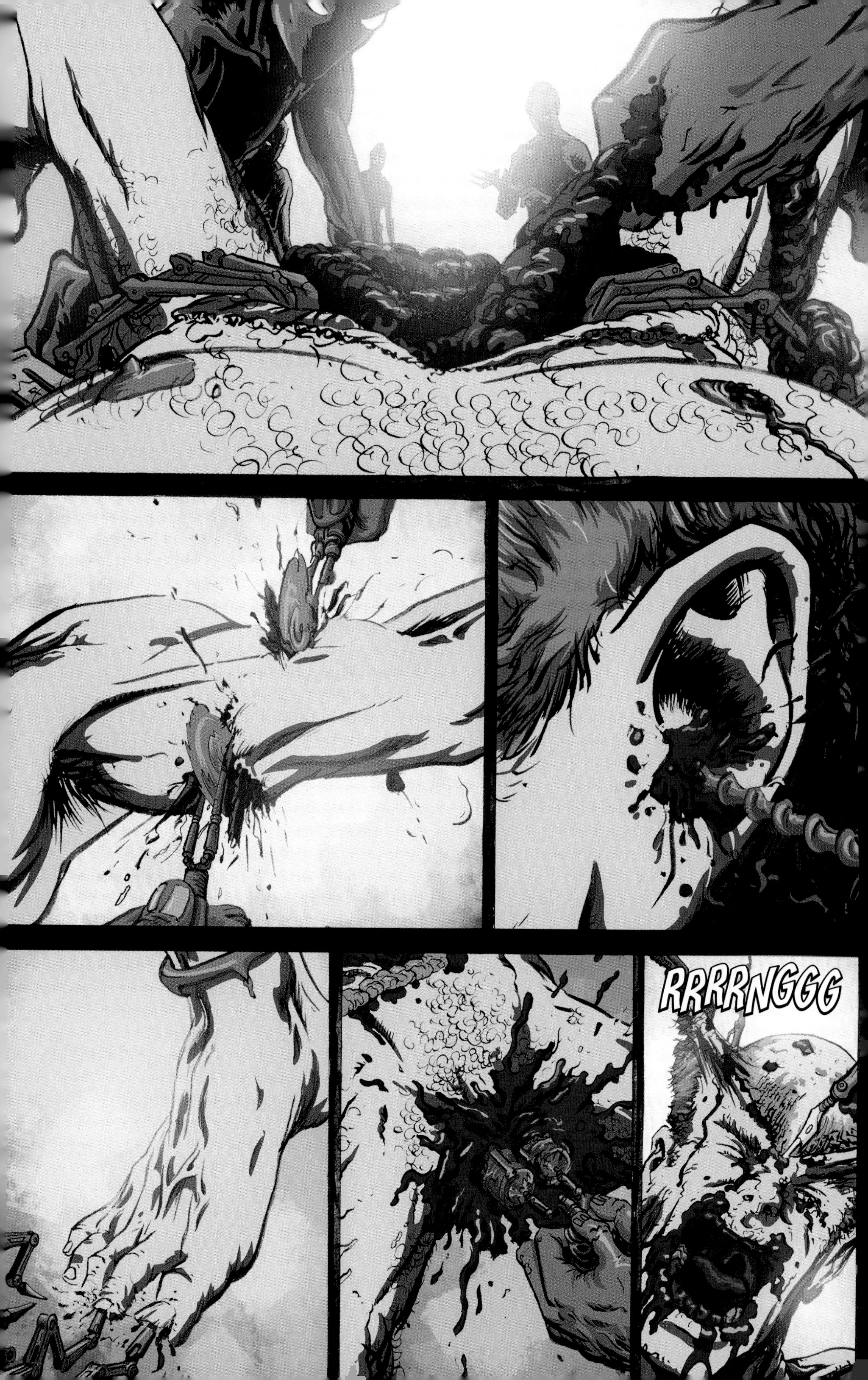
RRRRNGGG

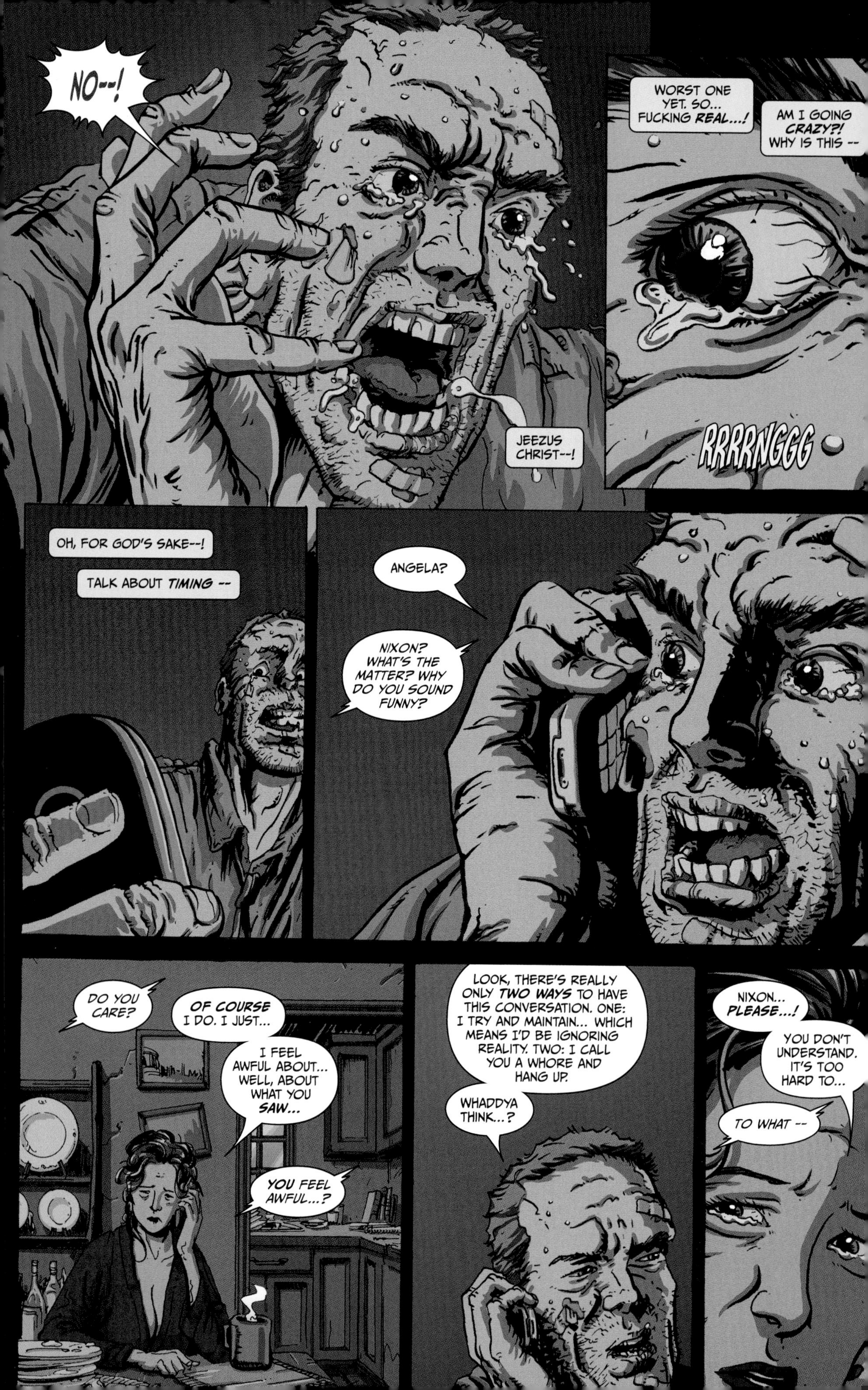

NO--!
JEEZUS CHRIST--!
WORST ONE YET. SO... FUCKING REAL...!
AM I GOING CRAZY?! WHY IS THIS --
RRRRNGGG
OH, FOR GOD'S SAKE--!
TALK ABOUT TIMING --
ANGELA?
NIXON? WHAT'S THE MATTER? WHY DO YOU SOUND FUNNY?
DO YOU CARE?
OF COURSE I DO. I JUST...
I FEEL AWFUL ABOUT... WELL, ABOUT WHAT YOU SAW...
YOU FEEL AWFUL...?
LOOK, THERE'S REALLY ONLY TWO WAYS TO HAVE THIS CONVERSATION. ONE: I TRY AND MAINTAIN... WHICH MEANS I'D BE IGNORING REALITY. TWO: I CALL YOU A WHORE AND HANG UP.
WHADDYA THINK...?
NIXON... PLEASE...!
YOU DON'T UNDERSTAND. IT'S TOO HARD TO...
TO WHAT --

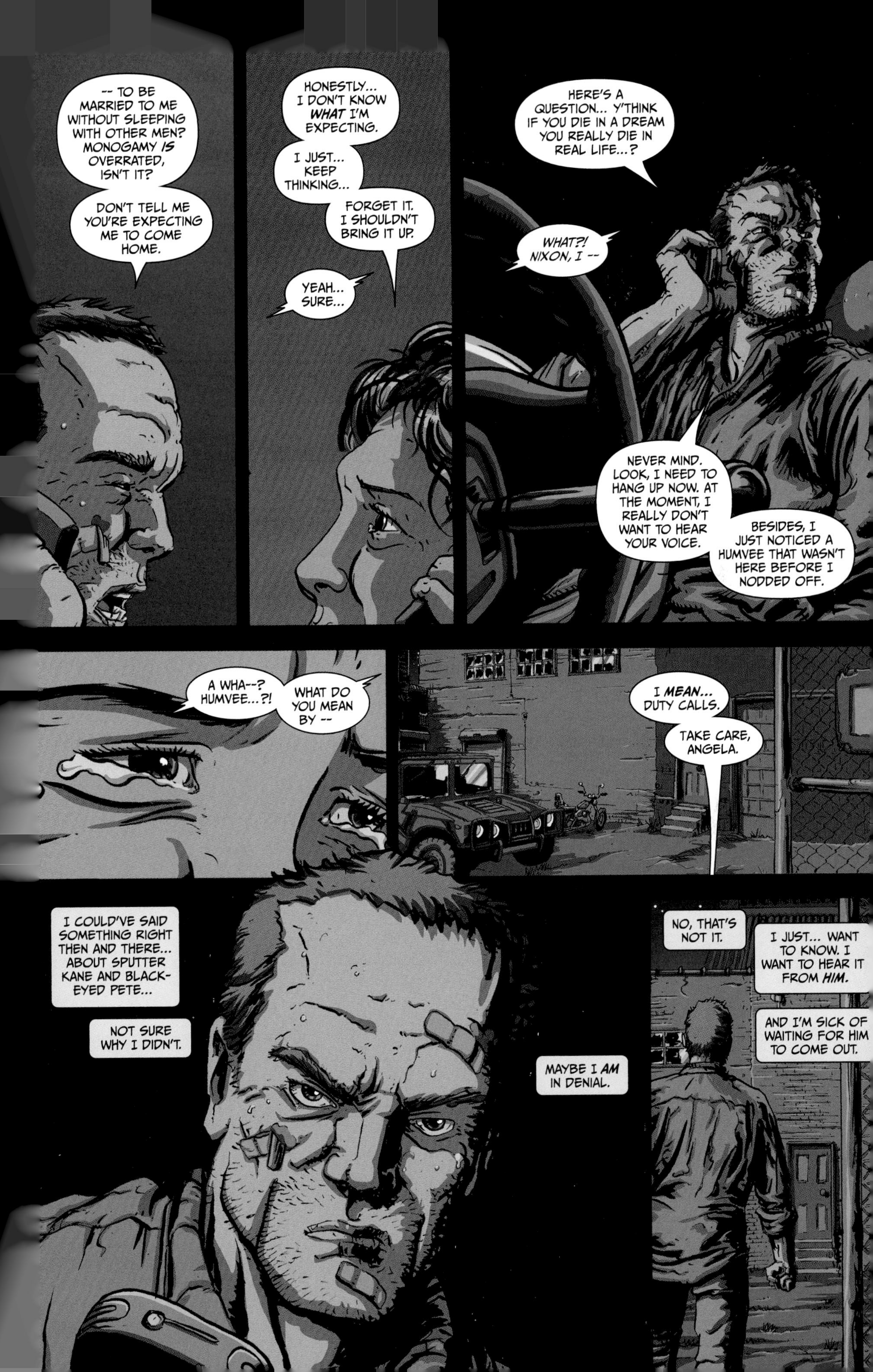
-- TO BE MARRIED TO ME WITHOUT SLEEPING WITH OTHER MEN? MONOGAMY *IS* OVERRATED, ISN'T IT?
DON'T TELL ME YOU'RE EXPECTING ME TO COME HOME.
HONESTLY... I DON'T KNOW *WHAT* I'M EXPECTING.
I JUST... KEEP THINKING...
FORGET IT. I SHOULDN'T BRING IT UP.
YEAH... SURE...
HERE'S A QUESTION... Y'THINK IF YOU DIE IN A DREAM YOU REALLY DIE IN REAL LIFE...?
WHAT?! NIXON, I --
NEVER MIND. LOOK, I NEED TO HANG UP NOW. AT THE MOMENT, I REALLY DON'T WANT TO HEAR YOUR VOICE.
BESIDES, I JUST NOTICED A HUMVEE THAT WASN'T HERE BEFORE I NODDED OFF.
A WHA--? HUMVEE...?!
WHAT DO YOU MEAN BY --
I *MEAN...* DUTY CALLS.
TAKE CARE, ANGELA.
I COULD'VE SAID SOMETHING RIGHT THEN AND THERE... ABOUT SPUTTER KANE AND BLACK-EYED PETE...
NOT SURE WHY I DIDN'T.
MAYBE I *AM* IN DENIAL.
NO, THAT'S NOT IT.
I JUST... WANT TO KNOW. I WANT TO HEAR IT FROM *HIM.*
AND I'M SICK OF WAITING FOR HIM TO COME OUT.

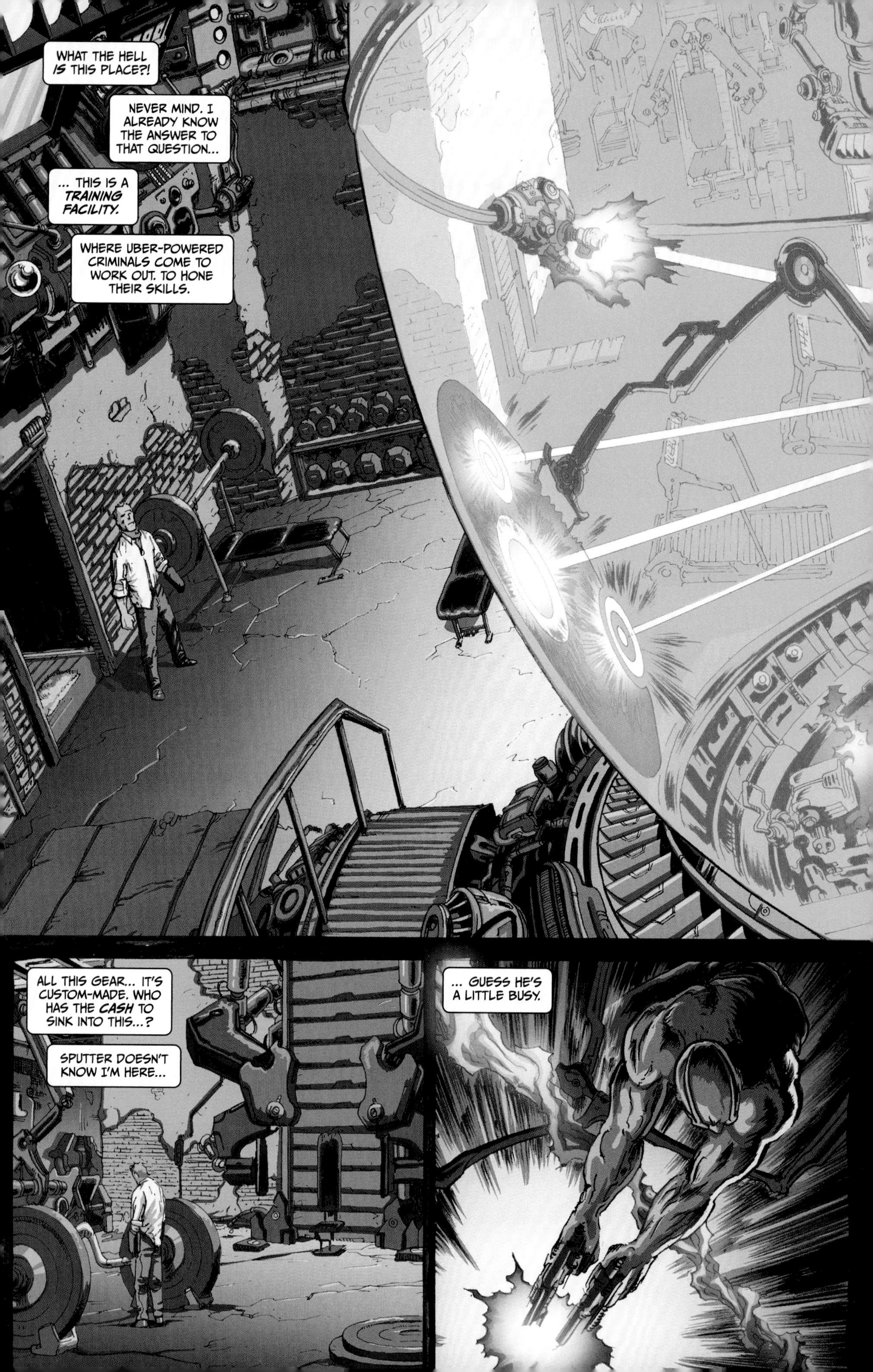
WHAT THE HELL *IS* THIS PLACE?!
NEVER MIND. I ALREADY KNOW THE ANSWER TO THAT QUESTION...
... THIS IS A *TRAINING FACILITY.*
WHERE UBER-POWERED CRIMINALS COME TO WORK OUT. TO HONE THEIR SKILLS.
ALL THIS GEAR... IT'S CUSTOM-MADE. WHO HAS THE *CASH* TO SINK INTO THIS...?
SPUTTER DOESN'T KNOW I'M HERE...
... GUESS HE'S A LITTLE BUSY.

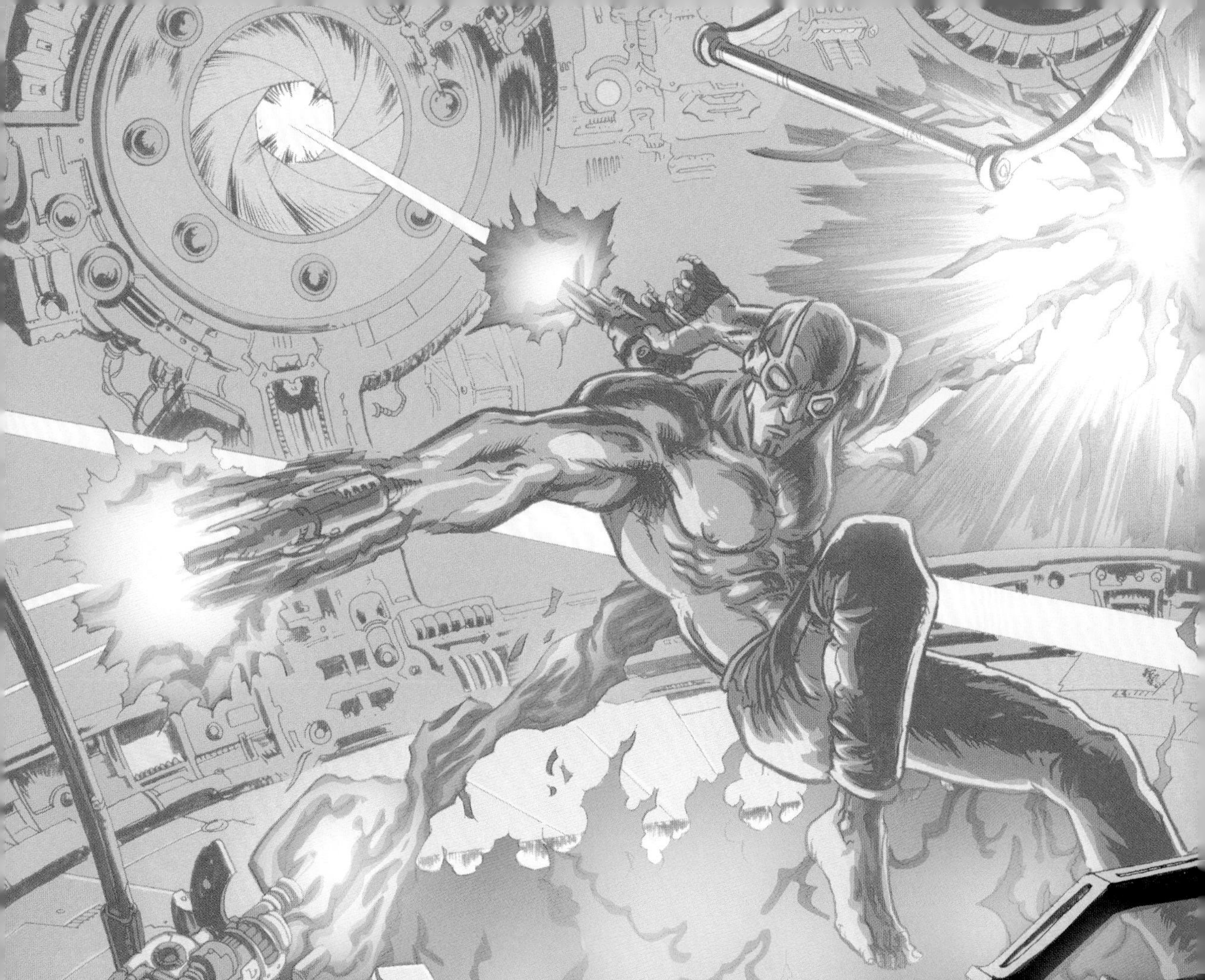

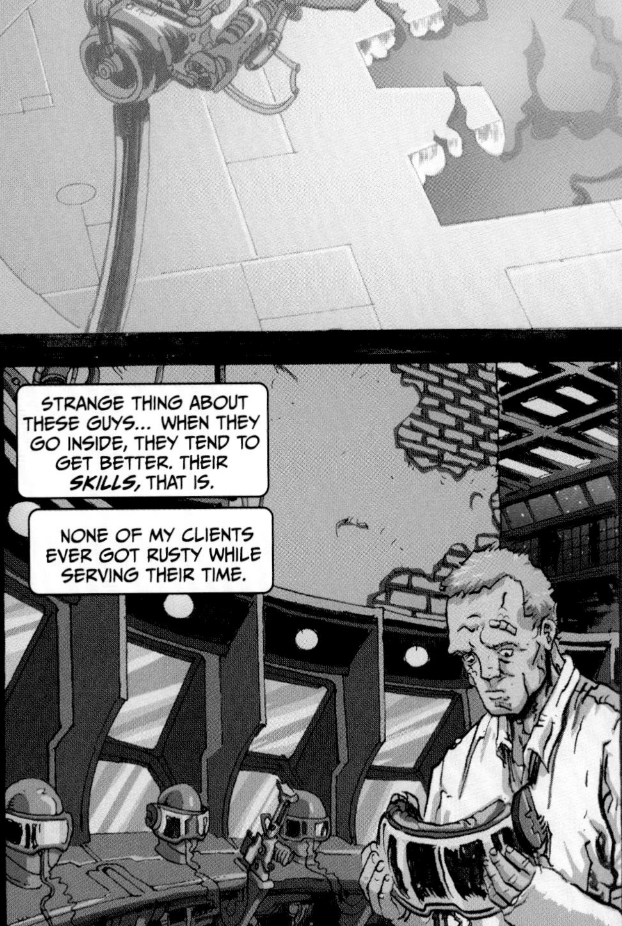
STRANGE THING ABOUT THESE GUYS... WHEN THEY GO INSIDE, THEY TEND TO GET BETTER. THEIR *SKILLS,* THAT IS.
NONE OF MY CLIENTS EVER GOT RUSTY WHILE SERVING THEIR TIME.

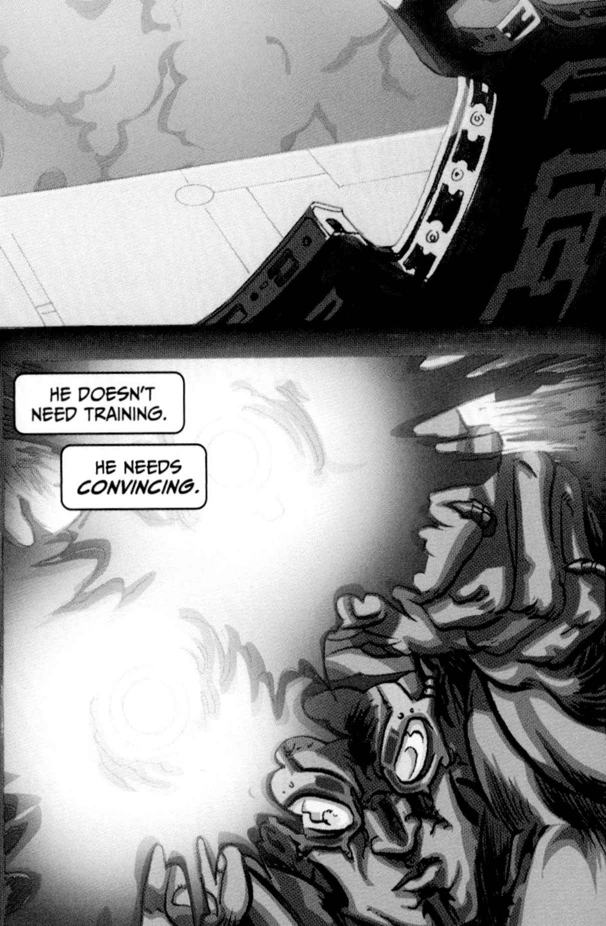
HE DOESN'T NEED TRAINING.
HE NEEDS *CONVINCING.*

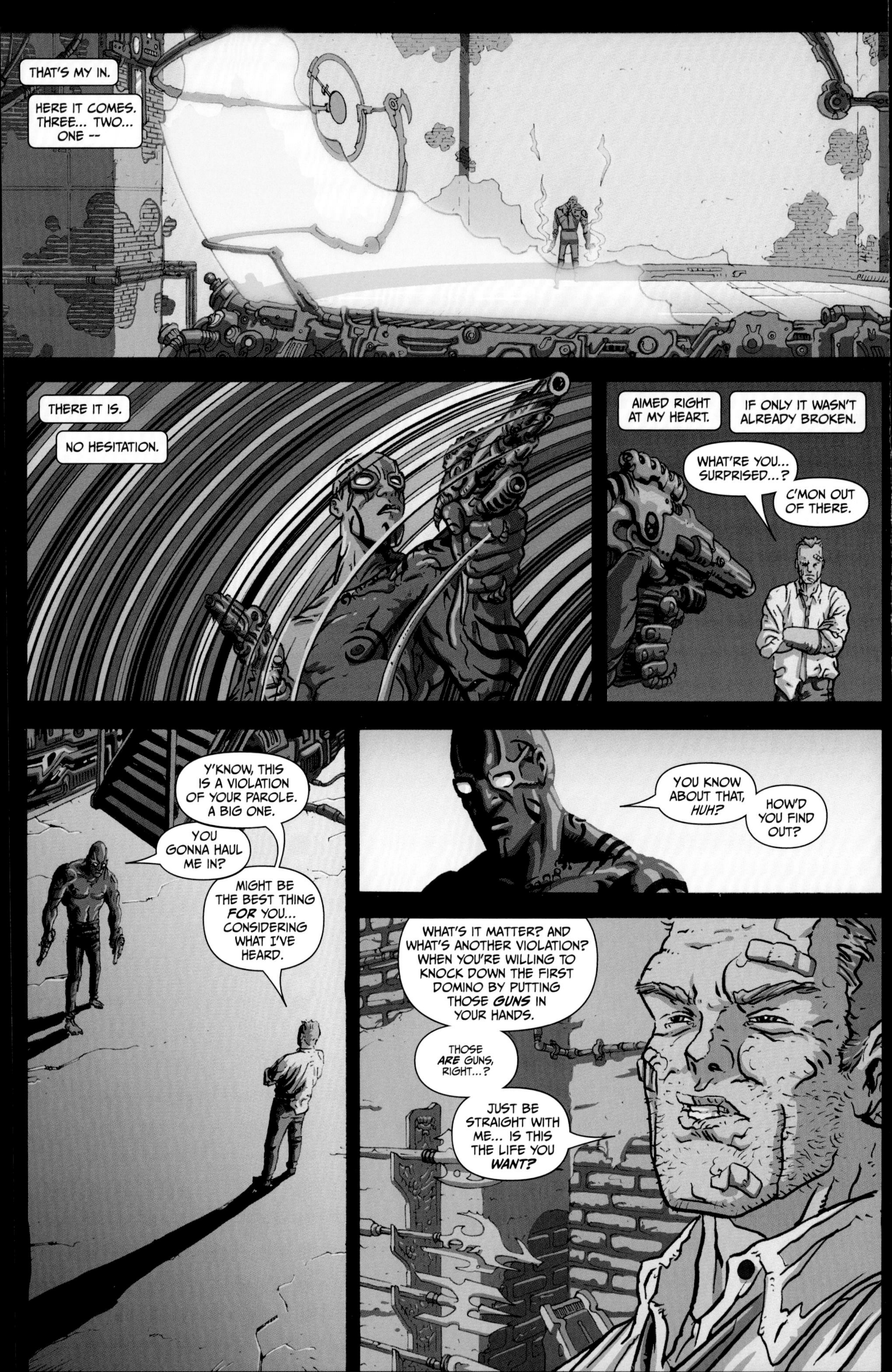
THAT'S MY IN.
HERE IT COMES. THREE... TWO... ONE --
THERE IT IS.
NO HESITATION.
AIMED RIGHT AT MY HEART.
IF ONLY IT WASN'T ALREADY BROKEN.
WHAT'RE YOU... SURPRISED...?
C'MON OUT OF THERE.
Y'KNOW, THIS IS A VIOLATION OF YOUR PAROLE. A BIG ONE.
YOU GONNA HAUL ME IN?
MIGHT BE THE BEST THING FOR YOU... CONSIDERING WHAT I'VE HEARD.
YOU KNOW ABOUT THAT, HUH?
HOW'D YOU FIND OUT?
WHAT'S IT MATTER? AND WHAT'S ANOTHER VIOLATION? WHEN YOU'RE WILLING TO KNOCK DOWN THE FIRST DOMINO BY PUTTING THOSE GUNS IN YOUR HANDS.
THOSE ARE GUNS, RIGHT...?
JUST BE STRAIGHT WITH ME... IS THIS THE LIFE YOU WANT?

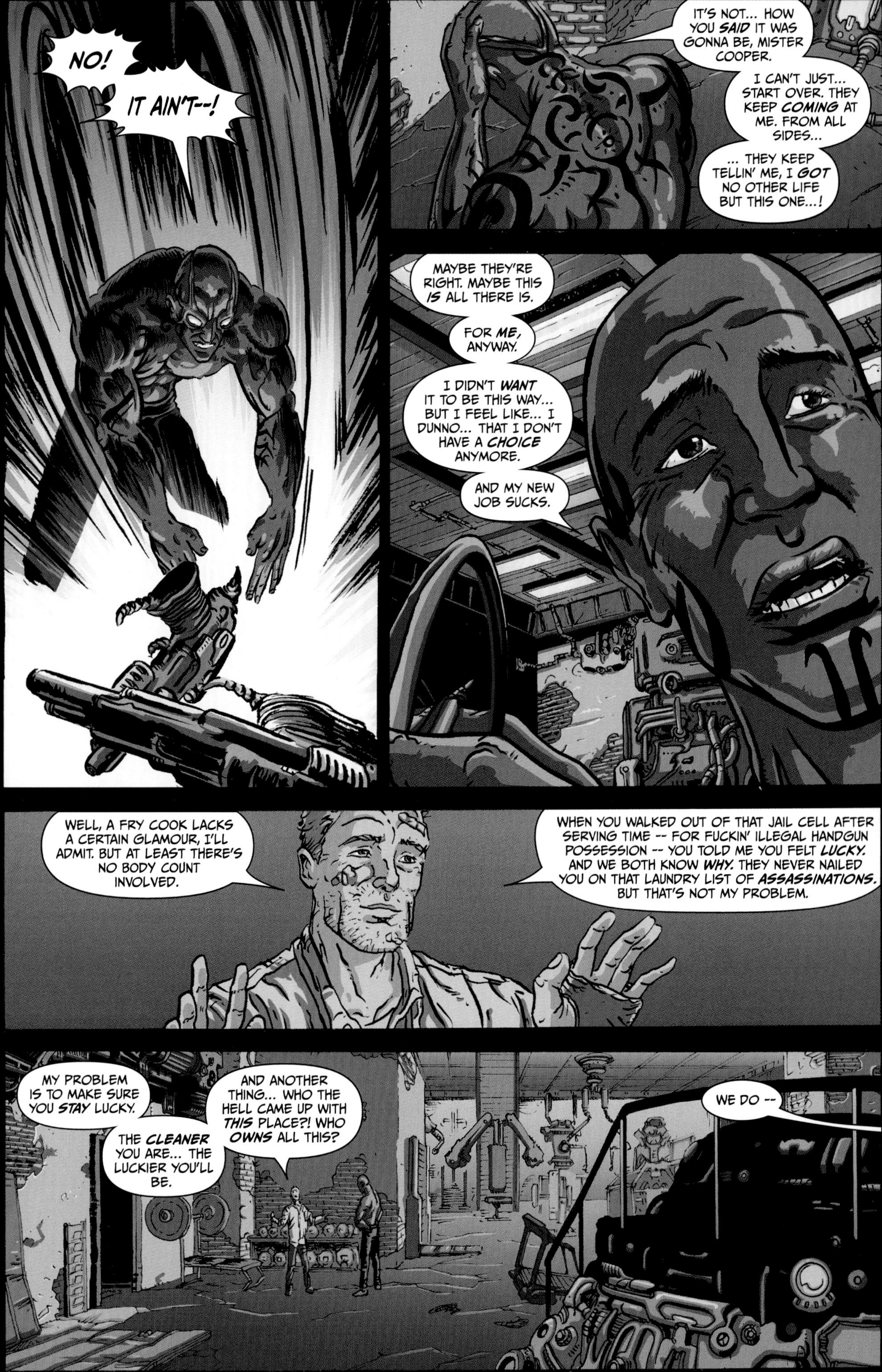
NO!
IT AIN'T--!
IT'S NOT... HOW YOU SAID IT WAS GONNA BE, MISTER COOPER.
I CAN'T JUST... START OVER. THEY KEEP COMING AT ME. FROM ALL SIDES...
... THEY KEEP TELLIN' ME, I GOT NO OTHER LIFE BUT THIS ONE...!
MAYBE THEY'RE RIGHT. MAYBE THIS IS ALL THERE IS.
FOR ME, ANYWAY.
I DIDN'T WANT IT TO BE THIS WAY... BUT I FEEL LIKE... I DUNNO... THAT I DON'T HAVE A CHOICE ANYMORE.
AND MY NEW JOB SUCKS.
WELL, A FRY COOK LACKS A CERTAIN GLAMOUR, I'LL ADMIT. BUT AT LEAST THERE'S NO BODY COUNT INVOLVED.
WHEN YOU WALKED OUT OF THAT JAIL CELL AFTER SERVING TIME -- FOR FUCKIN' ILLEGAL HANDGUN POSSESSION -- YOU TOLD ME YOU FELT LUCKY. AND WE BOTH KNOW WHY. THEY NEVER NAILED YOU ON THAT LAUNDRY LIST OF ASSASSINATIONS. BUT THAT'S NOT MY PROBLEM.
MY PROBLEM IS TO MAKE SURE YOU STAY LUCKY.
THE CLEANER YOU ARE... THE LUCKIER YOU'LL BE.
AND ANOTHER THING... WHO THE HELL CAME UP WITH THIS PLACE?! WHO OWNS ALL THIS?
WE DO --

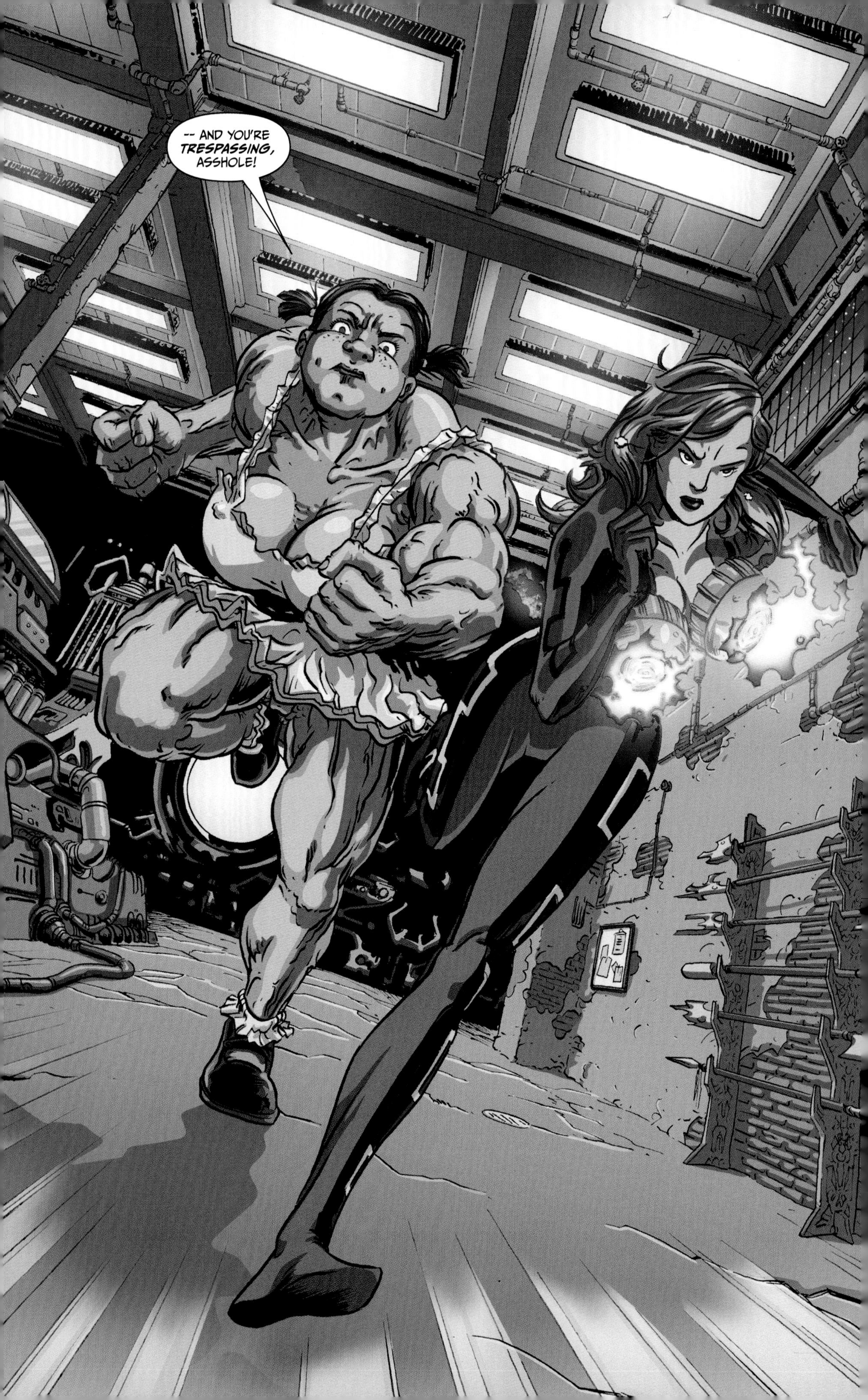
-- AND YOU'RE *TRESPASSING*, ASSHOLE!

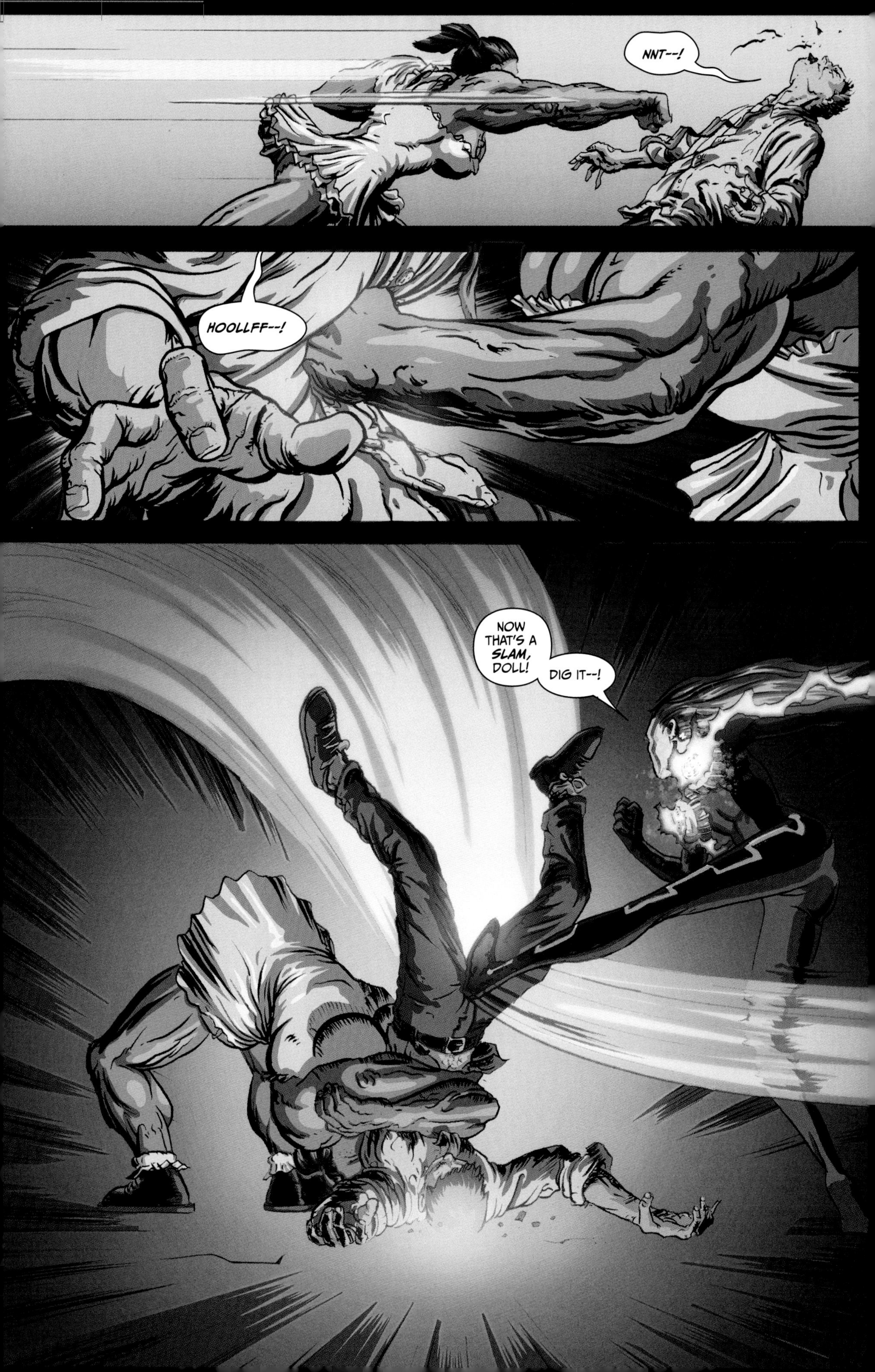
NNT--!
HOOLLFF--!
NOW THAT'S A SLAM, DOLL!
DIG IT--!

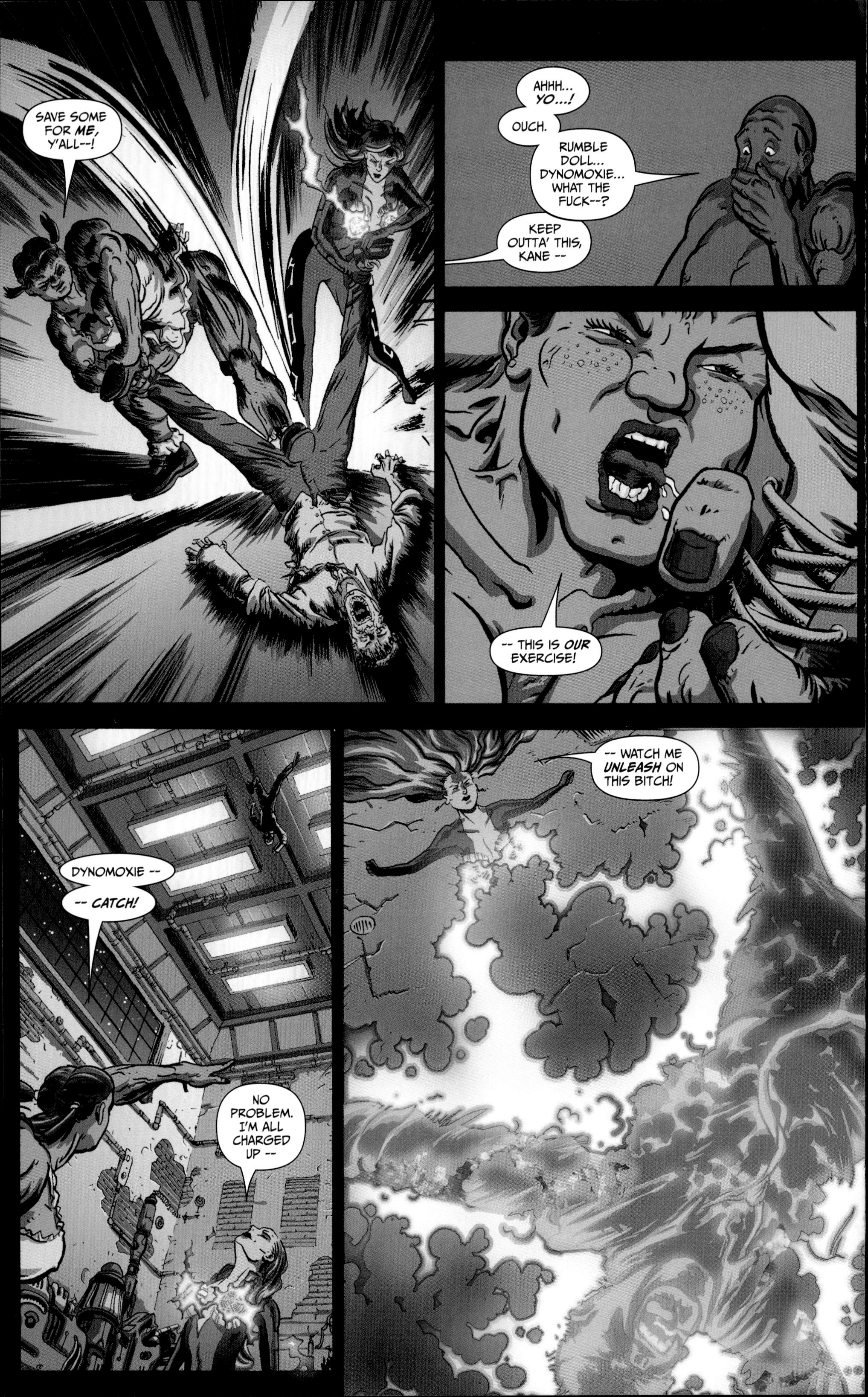
SAVE SOME FOR ME, Y'ALL--!
AHHH... YO...!
OUCH.
RUMBLE DOLL... DYNOMOXIE... WHAT THE FUCK--?
KEEP OUTTA' THIS, KANE --
-- THIS IS OUR EXERCISE!
DYNOMOXIE --
-- CATCH!
NO PROBLEM. I'M ALL CHARGED UP --
-- WATCH ME UNLEASH ON THIS BITCH!

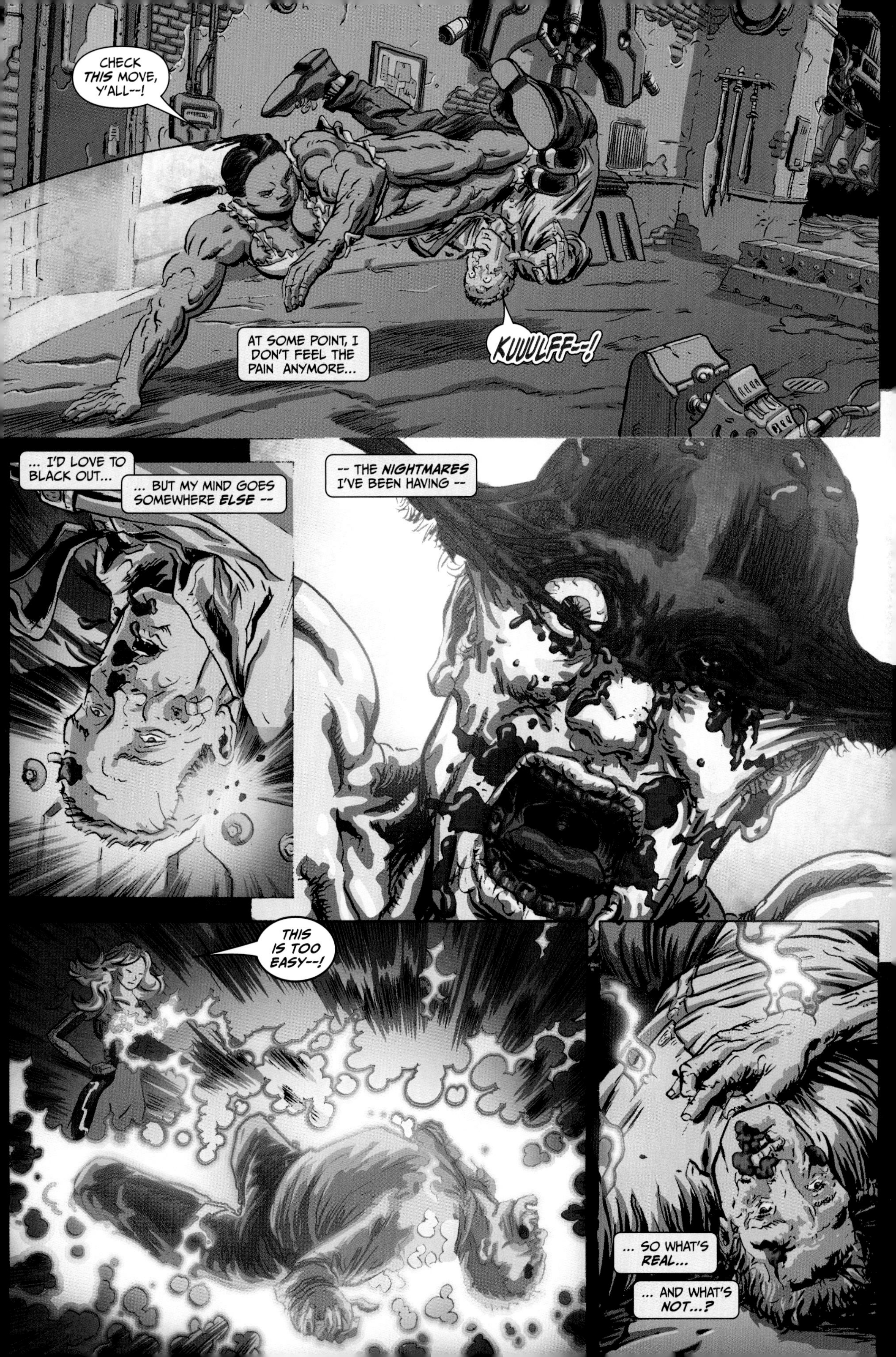
CHECK *THIS* MOVE, Y'ALL--!
AT SOME POINT, I DON'T FEEL THE PAIN ANYMORE...
KUUULFF--!
... I'D LOVE TO BLACK OUT...
... BUT MY MIND GOES SOMEWHERE *ELSE* --
-- THE *NIGHTMARES* I'VE BEEN HAVING --
THIS IS TOO EASY--!
... SO WHAT'S *REAL*...
... AND WHAT'S *NOT*...?

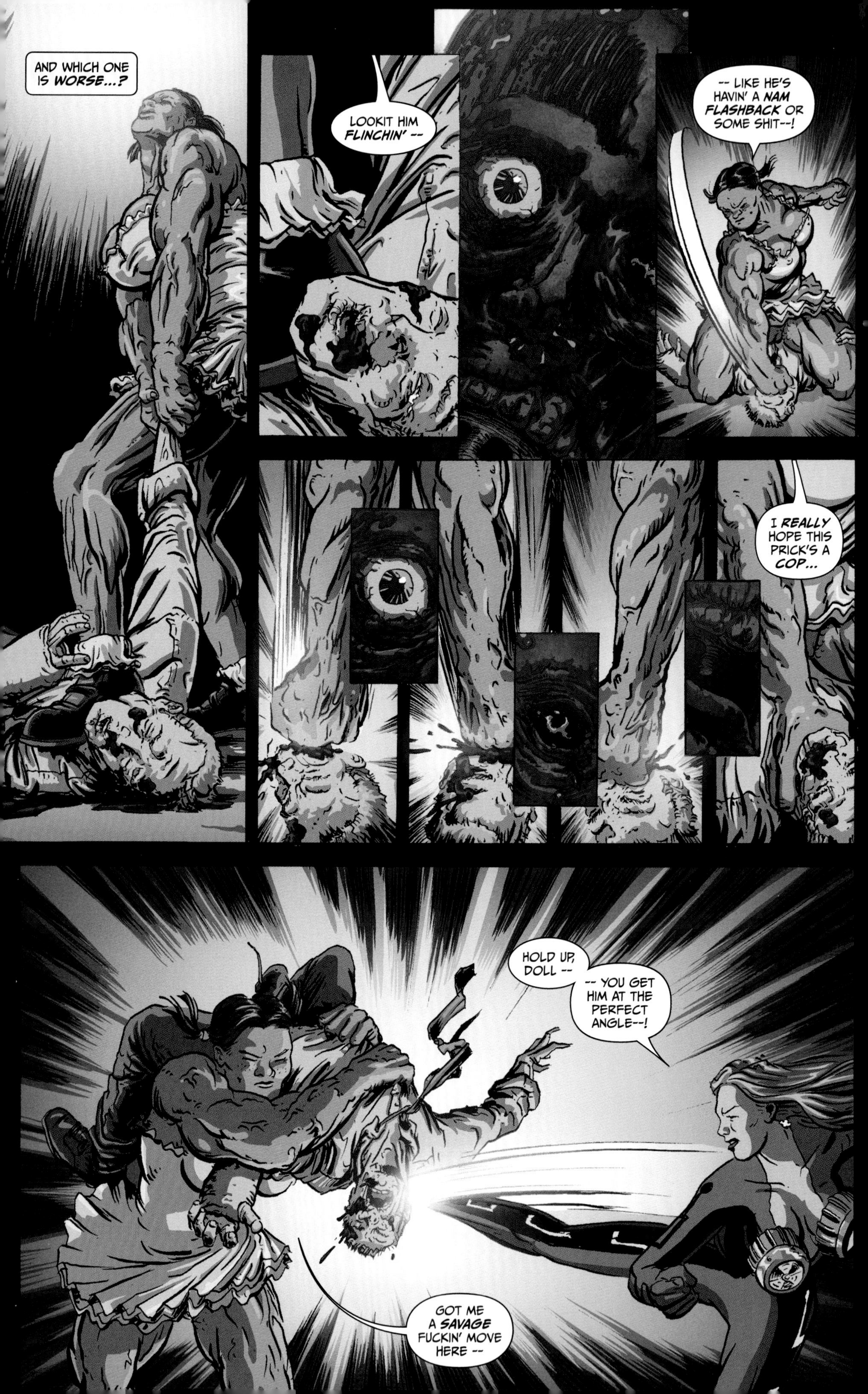
AND WHICH ONE IS WORSE...?
LOOKIT HIM FLINCHIN' --
-- LIKE HE'S HAVIN' A NAM FLASHBACK OR SOME SHIT--!
I REALLY HOPE THIS PRICK'S A COP...
HOLD UP, DOLL --
-- YOU GET HIM AT THE PERFECT ANGLE--!
GOT ME A SAVAGE FUCKIN' MOVE HERE --

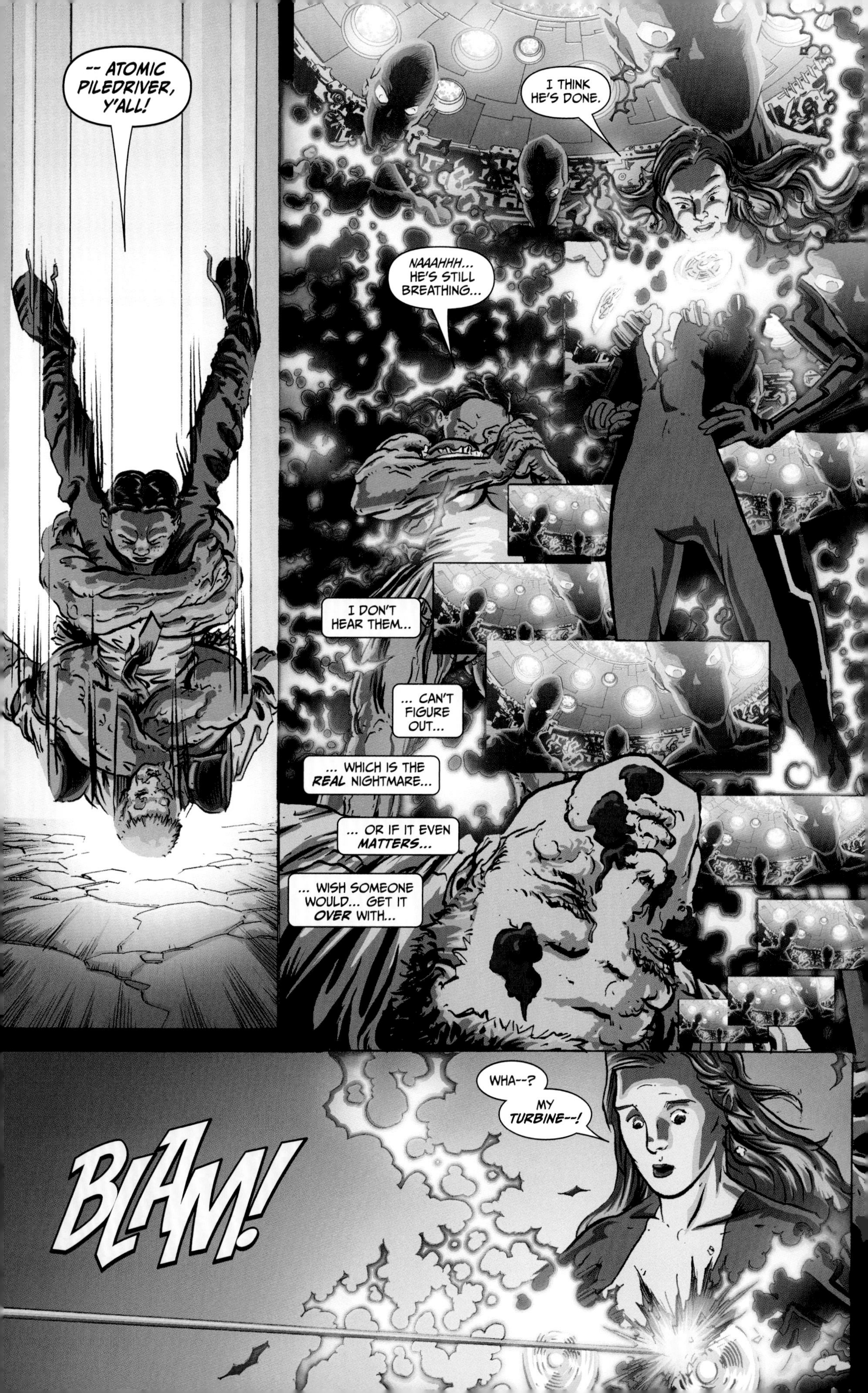
-- ATOMIC PILEDRIVER, Y'ALL!
I THINK HE'S DONE.
NAAAHHH... HE'S STILL BREATHING...
I DON'T HEAR THEM...
... CAN'T FIGURE OUT...
... WHICH IS THE REAL NIGHTMARE...
... OR IF IT EVEN MATTERS...
... WISH SOMEONE WOULD... GET IT OVER WITH...
WHA--?
MY TURBINE--!
BLAM!

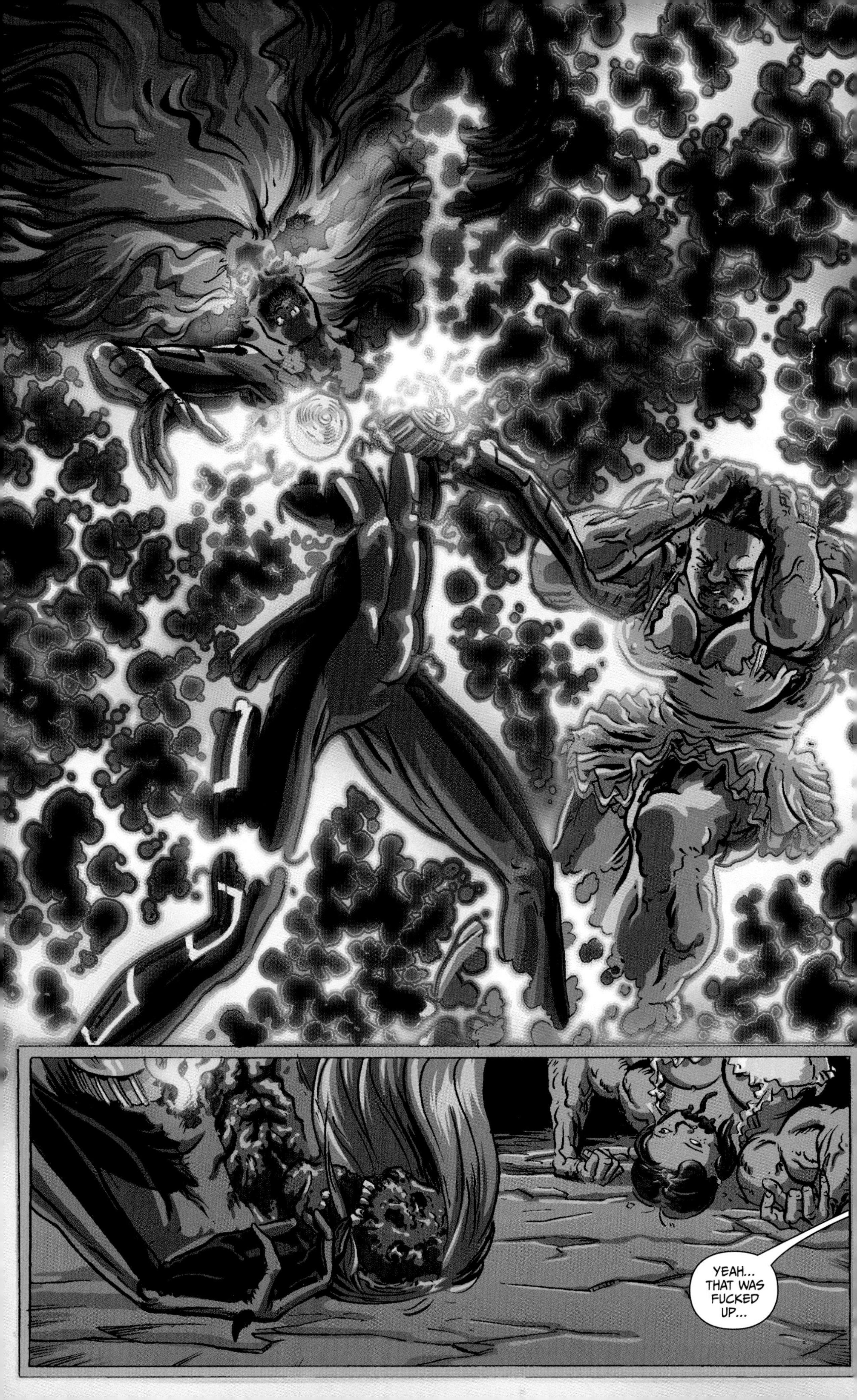
YEAH... THAT WAS FUCKED UP...

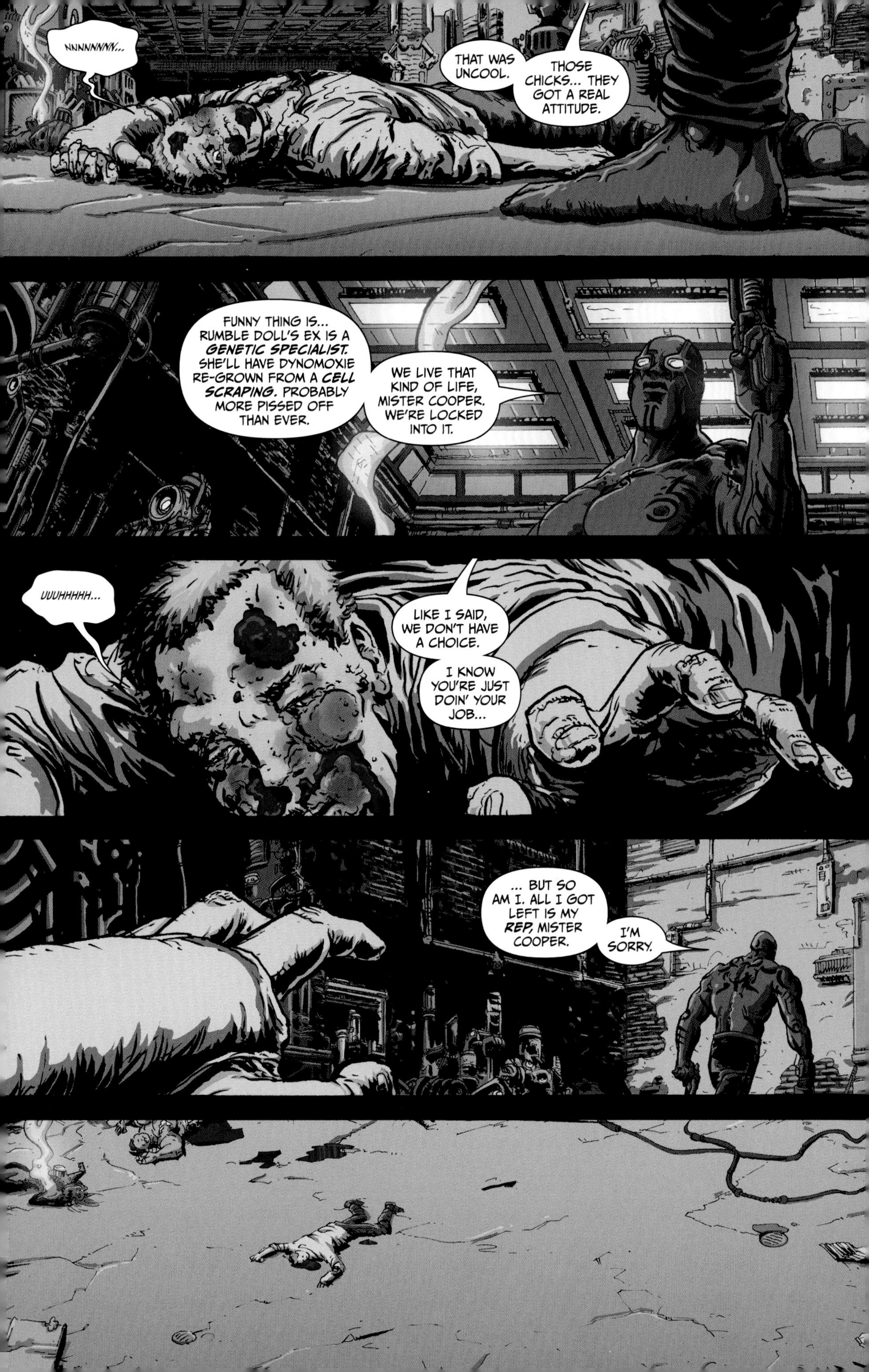
NNNNNNNN...
THAT WAS UNCOOL.
THOSE CHICKS... THEY GOT A REAL ATTITUDE.
FUNNY THING IS... RUMBLE DOLL'S EX IS A GENETIC SPECIALIST. SHE'LL HAVE DYNOMOXIE RE-GROWN FROM A CELL SCRAPING. PROBABLY MORE PISSED OFF THAN EVER.
WE LIVE THAT KIND OF LIFE, MISTER COOPER. WE'RE LOCKED INTO IT.
UUUHHHHH...
LIKE I SAID, WE DON'T HAVE A CHOICE.
I KNOW YOU'RE JUST DOIN' YOUR JOB...
... BUT SO AM I. ALL I GOT LEFT IS MY REP, MISTER COOPER.
I'M SORRY.

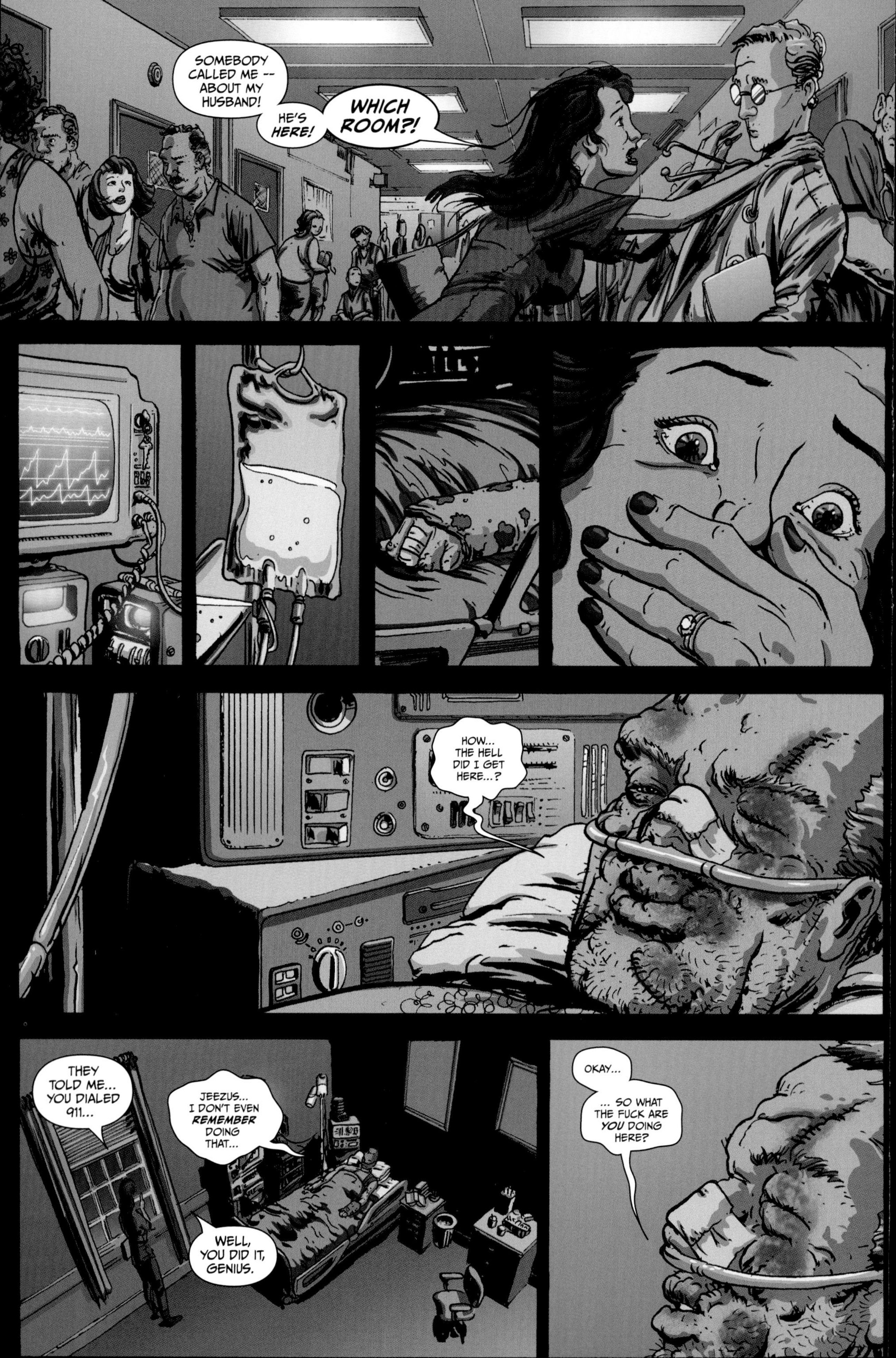

SOMEBODY CALLED ME -- ABOUT MY HUSBAND!
HE'S *HERE!*
WHICH ROOM?!
HOW... THE HELL DID I GET HERE...?
THEY TOLD ME... YOU DIALED 911...
JEEZUS... I DON'T EVEN *REMEMBER* DOING THAT...
WELL, YOU DID IT, GENIUS.
OKAY...
... SO WHAT THE FUCK ARE *YOU* DOING HERE?

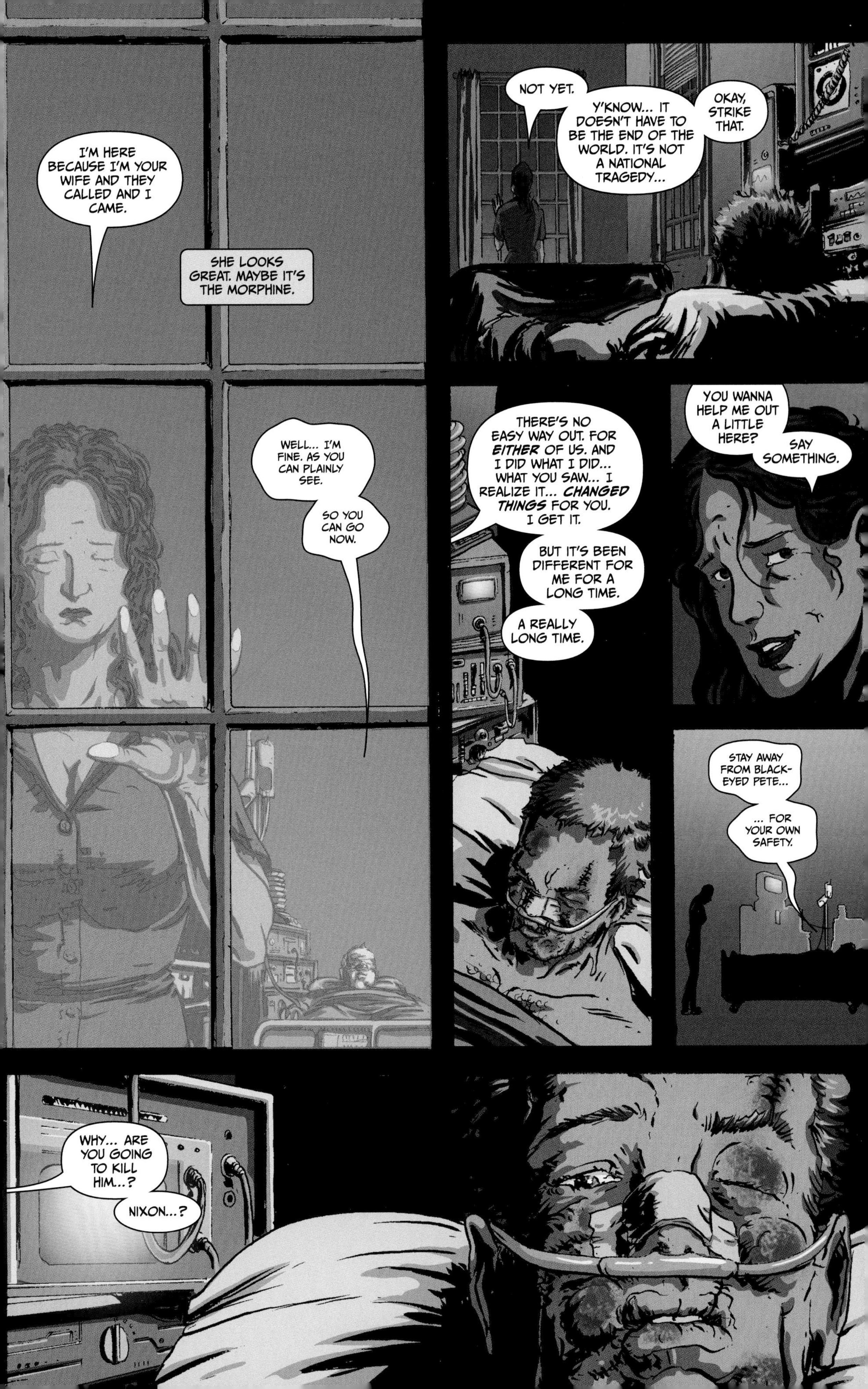
I'M HERE BECAUSE I'M YOUR WIFE AND THEY CALLED AND I CAME.
SHE LOOKS GREAT. MAYBE IT'S THE MORPHINE.
NOT YET.
Y'KNOW... IT DOESN'T HAVE TO BE THE END OF THE WORLD. IT'S NOT A NATIONAL TRAGEDY...
OKAY, STRIKE THAT.
WELL... I'M FINE. AS YOU CAN PLAINLY SEE.
SO YOU CAN GO NOW.
THERE'S NO EASY WAY OUT. FOR EITHER OF US. AND I DID WHAT I DID... WHAT YOU SAW... I REALIZE IT... CHANGED THINGS FOR YOU. I GET IT.
BUT IT'S BEEN DIFFERENT FOR ME FOR A LONG TIME.
A REALLY LONG TIME.
YOU WANNA HELP ME OUT A LITTLE HERE?
SAY SOMETHING.
STAY AWAY FROM BLACK-EYED PETE...
... FOR YOUR OWN SAFETY.
WHY... ARE YOU GOING TO KILL HIM...?
NIXON...?

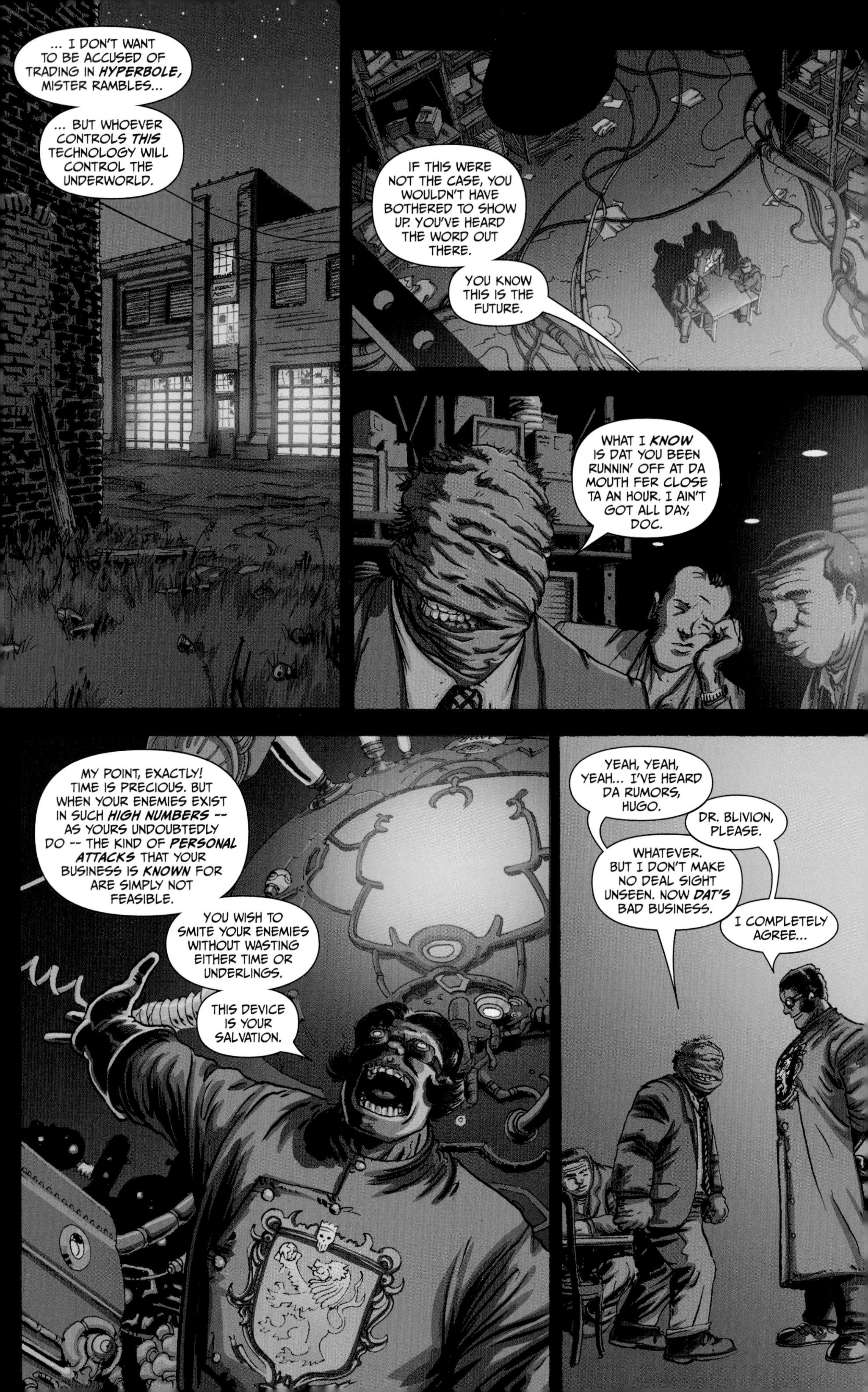
... I DON'T WANT TO BE ACCUSED OF TRADING IN *HYPERBOLE,* MISTER RAMBLES...
... BUT WHOEVER CONTROLS *THIS* TECHNOLOGY WILL CONTROL THE UNDERWORLD.
IF THIS WERE NOT THE CASE, YOU WOULDN'T HAVE BOTHERED TO SHOW UP. YOU'VE HEARD THE WORD OUT THERE.
YOU KNOW THIS IS THE FUTURE.
WHAT I *KNOW* IS DAT YOU BEEN RUNNIN' OFF AT DA MOUTH FER CLOSE TA AN HOUR. I AIN'T GOT ALL DAY, DOC.
MY POINT, EXACTLY! TIME IS PRECIOUS. BUT WHEN YOUR ENEMIES EXIST IN SUCH *HIGH NUMBERS* -- AS YOURS UNDOUBTEDLY DO -- THE KIND OF *PERSONAL ATTACKS* THAT YOUR BUSINESS IS *KNOWN* FOR ARE SIMPLY NOT FEASIBLE.
YOU WISH TO SMITE YOUR ENEMIES WITHOUT WASTING EITHER TIME OR UNDERLINGS.
THIS DEVICE IS YOUR SALVATION.
YEAH, YEAH, YEAH... I'VE HEARD DA RUMORS, HUGO.
DR. BLIVION, PLEASE.
WHATEVER. BUT I DON'T MAKE NO DEAL SIGHT UNSEEN. NOW *DAT'S* BAD BUSINESS.
I COMPLETELY AGREE...

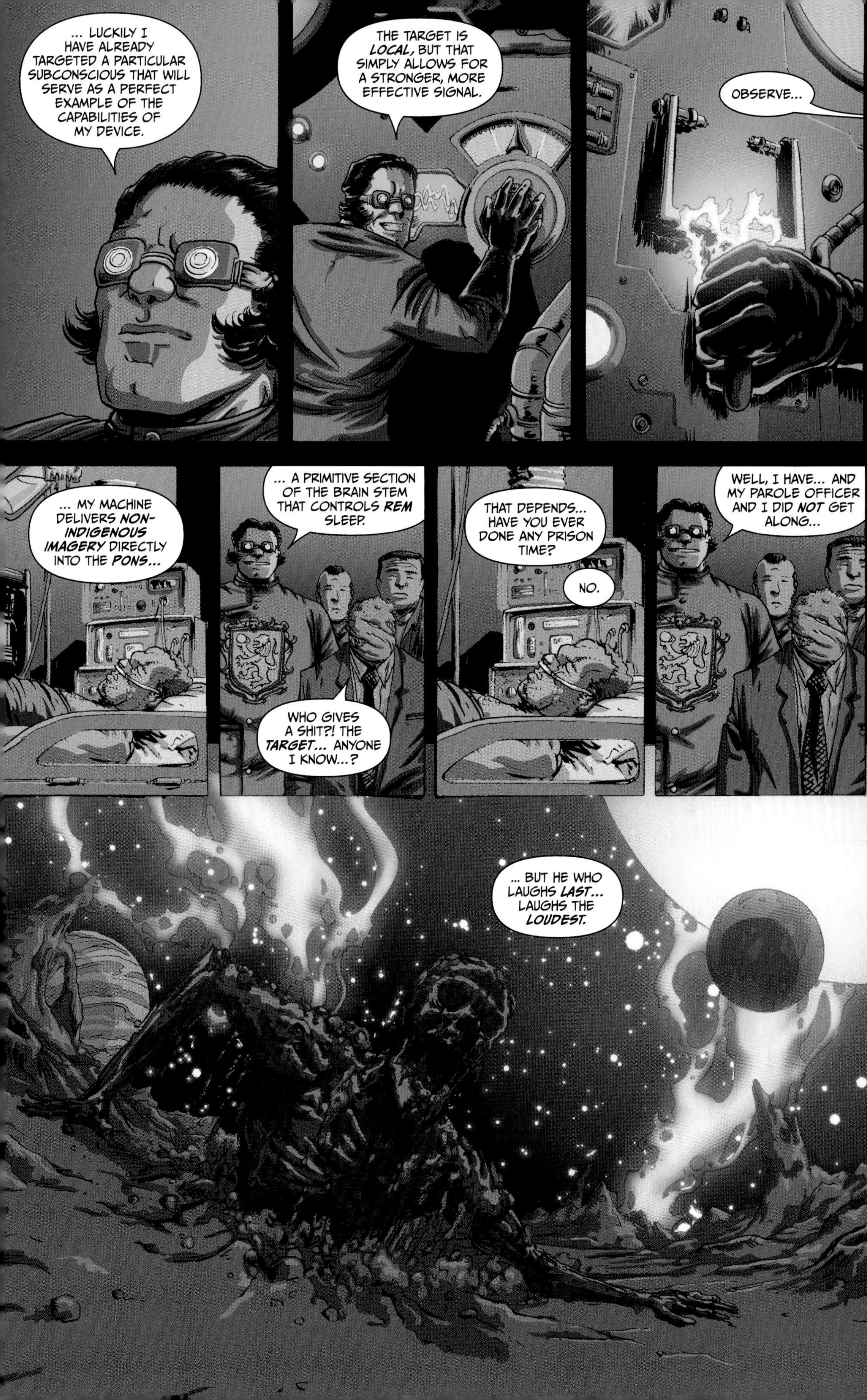
... LUCKILY I HAVE ALREADY TARGETED A PARTICULAR SUBCONSCIOUS THAT WILL SERVE AS A PERFECT EXAMPLE OF THE CAPABILITIES OF MY DEVICE.
THE TARGET IS LOCAL, BUT THAT SIMPLY ALLOWS FOR A STRONGER, MORE EFFECTIVE SIGNAL.
OBSERVE...
... MY MACHINE DELIVERS NON-INDIGENOUS IMAGERY DIRECTLY INTO THE PONS...
... A PRIMITIVE SECTION OF THE BRAIN STEM THAT CONTROLS REM SLEEP.
WHO GIVES A SHIT?! THE TARGET... ANYONE I KNOW...?
THAT DEPENDS... HAVE YOU EVER DONE ANY PRISON TIME?
NO.
WELL, I HAVE... AND MY PAROLE OFFICER AND I DID NOT GET ALONG...
... BUT HE WHO LAUGHS LAST... LAUGHS THE LOUDEST.

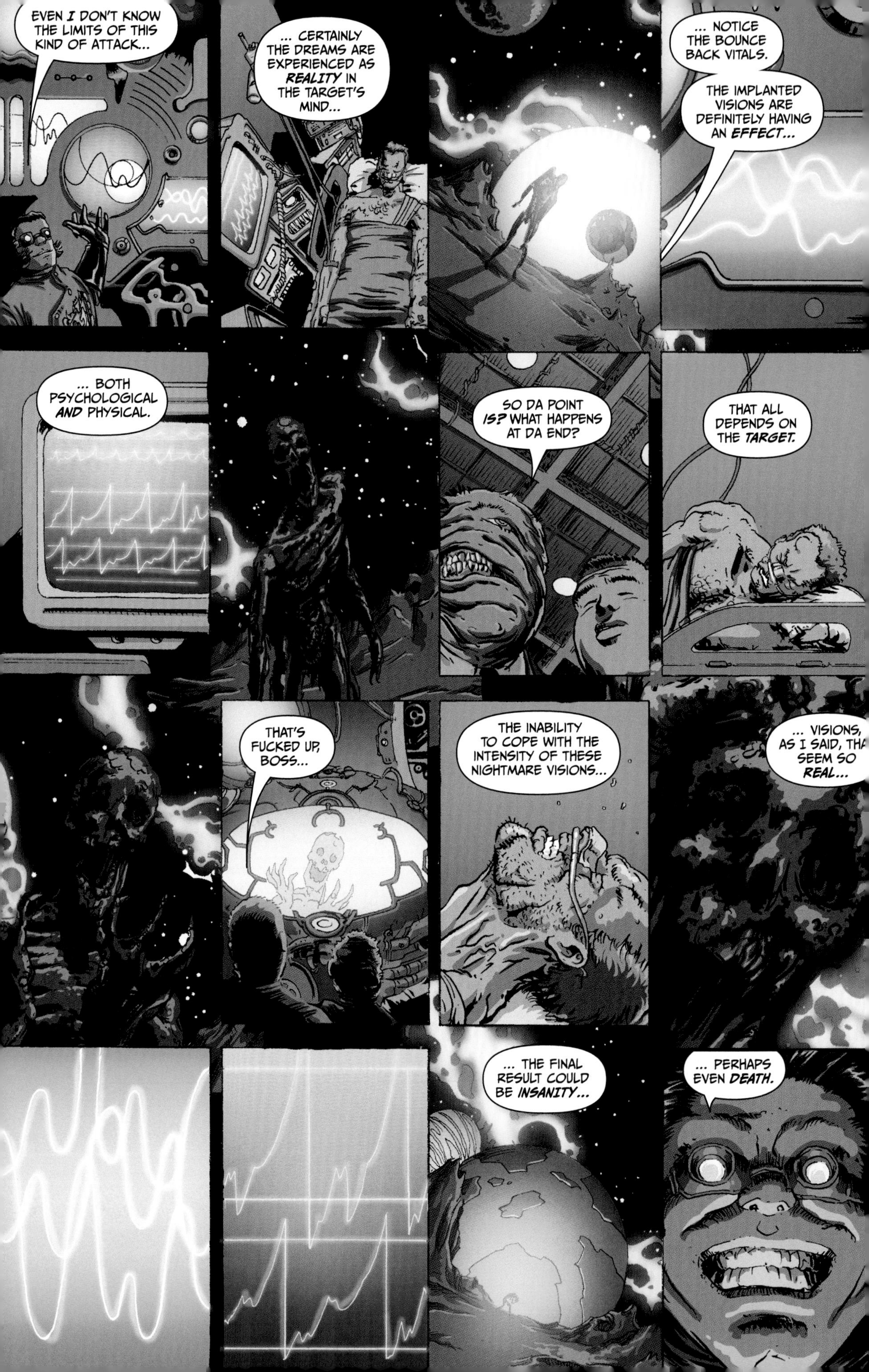
EVEN I DON'T KNOW THE LIMITS OF THIS KIND OF ATTACK...
... CERTAINLY THE DREAMS ARE EXPERIENCED AS REALITY IN THE TARGET'S MIND...
... NOTICE THE BOUNCE BACK VITALS.
THE IMPLANTED VISIONS ARE DEFINITELY HAVING AN EFFECT...
... BOTH PSYCHOLOGICAL AND PHYSICAL.
SO DA POINT IS? WHAT HAPPENS AT DA END?
THAT ALL DEPENDS ON THE TARGET.
THAT'S FUCKED UP, BOSS...
THE INABILITY TO COPE WITH THE INTENSITY OF THESE NIGHTMARE VISIONS...
... VISIONS, AS I SAID, THA SEEM SO REAL...
... THE FINAL RESULT COULD BE INSANITY...
... PERHAPS EVEN DEATH.

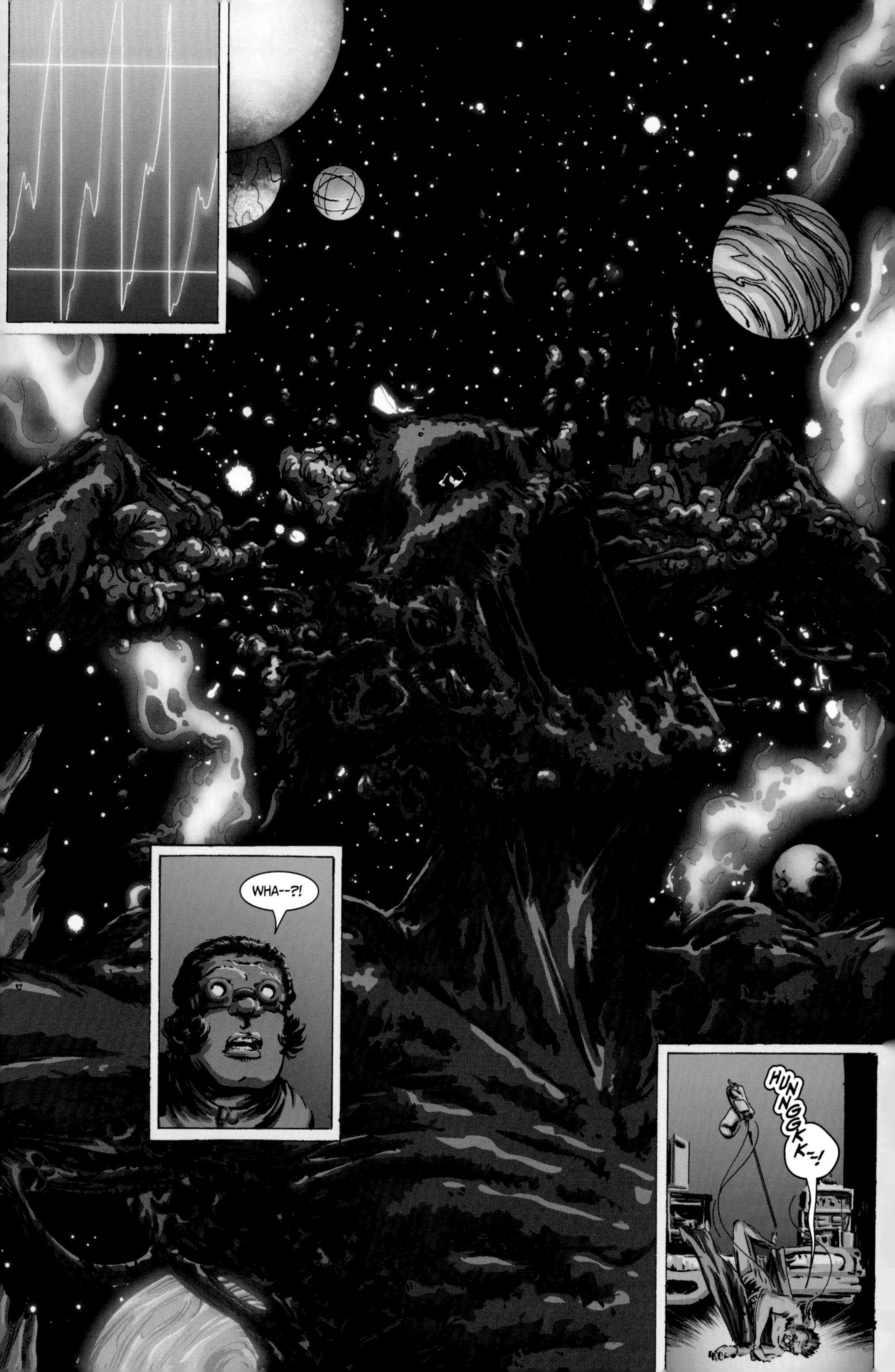
WHA--?!
HUNNGGKK--!

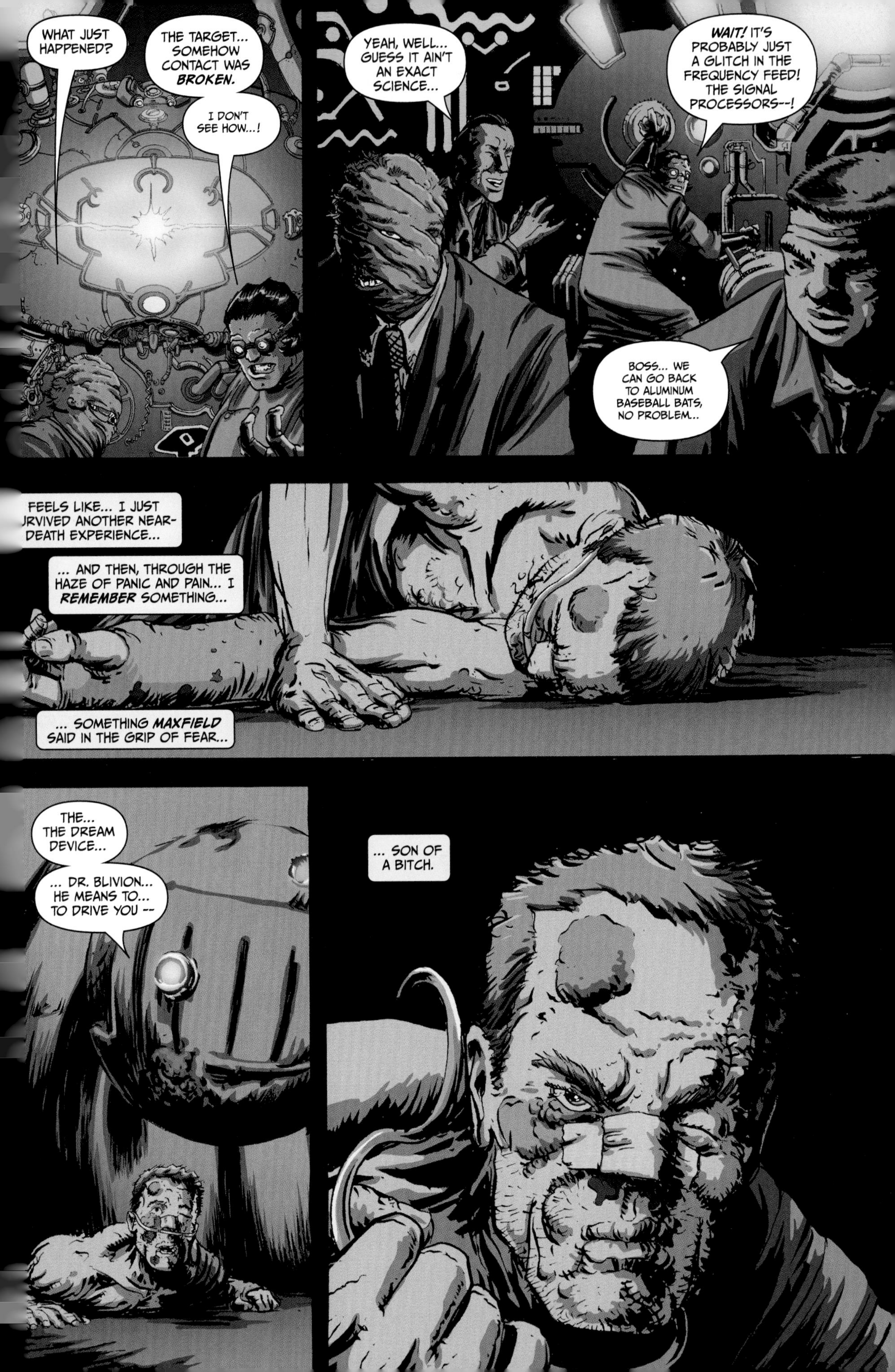
WHAT JUST HAPPENED?
THE TARGET... SOMEHOW CONTACT WAS **BROKEN.**
I DON'T SEE HOW...!
YEAH, WELL... GUESS IT AIN'T AN EXACT SCIENCE...
WAIT! IT'S PROBABLY JUST A GLITCH IN THE FREQUENCY FEED! THE SIGNAL PROCESSORS--!
BOSS... WE CAN GO BACK TO ALUMINUM BASEBALL BATS, NO PROBLEM...
FEELS LIKE... I JUST URVIVED ANOTHER NEAR-DEATH EXPERIENCE...
... AND THEN, THROUGH THE HAZE OF PANIC AND PAIN... I **REMEMBER** SOMETHING...
... SOMETHING **MAXFIELD** SAID IN THE GRIP OF FEAR...
THE... THE DREAM DEVICE...
... DR. BLIVION... HE MEANS TO... TO DRIVE YOU --
... SON OF A BITCH.

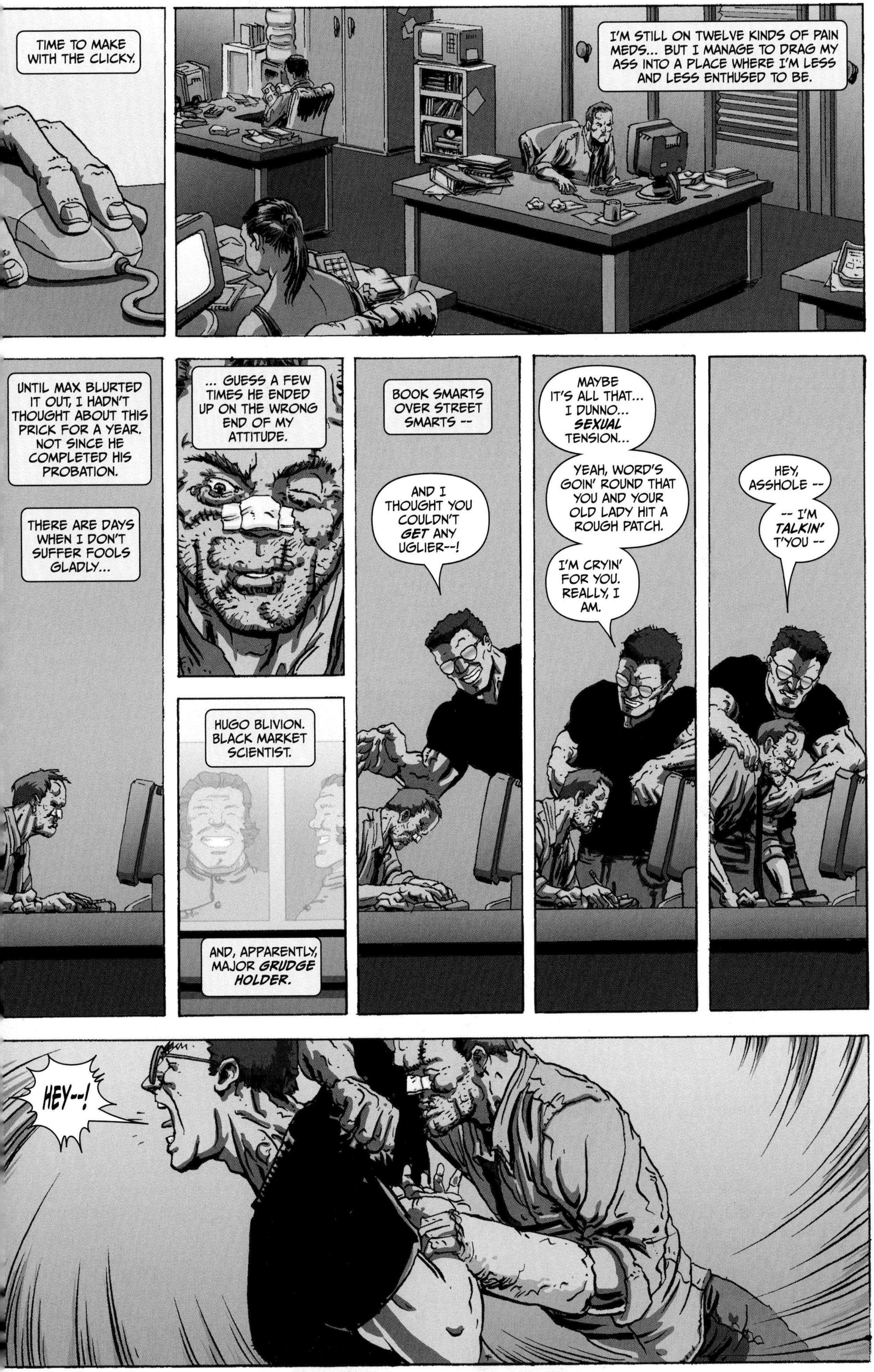
TIME TO MAKE WITH THE CLICKY.
I'M STILL ON TWELVE KINDS OF PAIN MEDS... BUT I MANAGE TO DRAG MY ASS INTO A PLACE WHERE I'M LESS AND LESS ENTHUSED TO BE.
UNTIL MAX BLURTED IT OUT, I HADN'T THOUGHT ABOUT THIS PRICK FOR A YEAR. NOT SINCE HE COMPLETED HIS PROBATION.
THERE ARE DAYS WHEN I DON'T SUFFER FOOLS GLADLY...
... GUESS A FEW TIMES HE ENDED UP ON THE WRONG END OF MY ATTITUDE.
HUGO BLIVION. BLACK MARKET SCIENTIST.
AND, APPARENTLY, MAJOR *GRUDGE HOLDER.*
BOOK SMARTS OVER STREET SMARTS --
AND I THOUGHT YOU COULDN'T *GET* ANY UGLIER--!
MAYBE IT'S ALL THAT... I DUNNO... *SEXUAL* TENSION...
YEAH, WORD'S GOIN' ROUND THAT YOU AND YOUR OLD LADY HIT A ROUGH PATCH.
I'M CRYIN' FOR YOU. REALLY, I AM.
HEY, ASSHOLE --
-- I'M *TALKIN'* T'YOU --
HEY--!

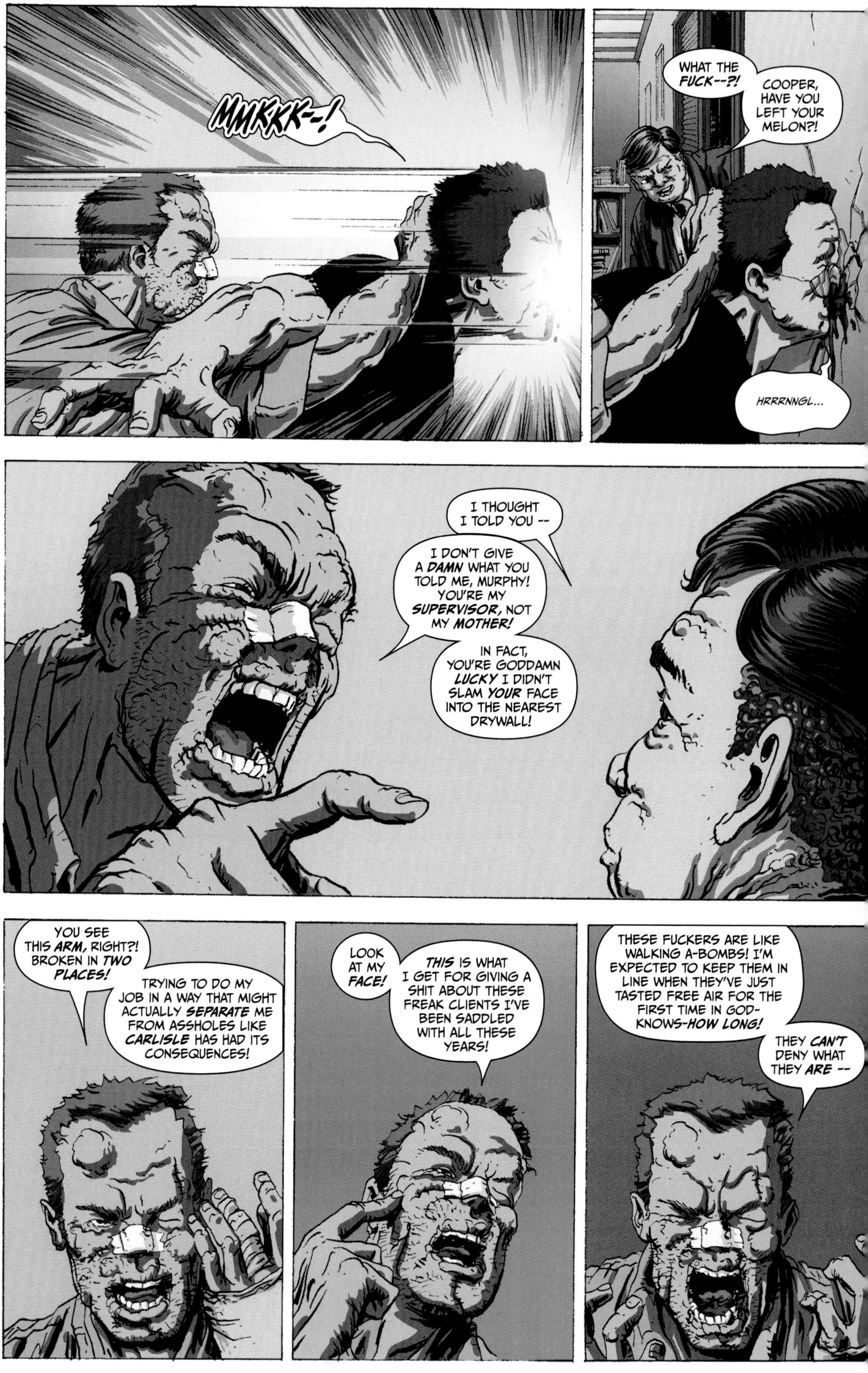
MMKKK--!
WHAT THE FUCK--?!
COOPER, HAVE YOU LEFT YOUR MELON?!
HRRRNNGL...
I THOUGHT I TOLD YOU --
I DON'T GIVE A DAMN WHAT YOU TOLD ME, MURPHY! YOU'RE MY SUPERVISOR, NOT MY MOTHER!
IN FACT, YOU'RE GODDAMN LUCKY I DIDN'T SLAM YOUR FACE INTO THE NEAREST DRYWALL!
YOU SEE THIS ARM, RIGHT?! BROKEN IN TWO PLACES!
TRYING TO DO MY JOB IN A WAY THAT MIGHT ACTUALLY SEPARATE ME FROM ASSHOLES LIKE CARLISLE HAS HAD ITS CONSEQUENCES!
LOOK AT MY FACE!
THIS IS WHAT I GET FOR GIVING A SHIT ABOUT THESE FREAK CLIENTS I'VE BEEN SADDLED WITH ALL THESE YEARS!
THESE FUCKERS ARE LIKE WALKING A-BOMBS! I'M EXPECTED TO KEEP THEM IN LINE WHEN THEY'VE JUST TASTED FREE AIR FOR THE FIRST TIME IN GOD-KNOWS-HOW LONG!
THEY CAN'T DENY WHAT THEY ARE --

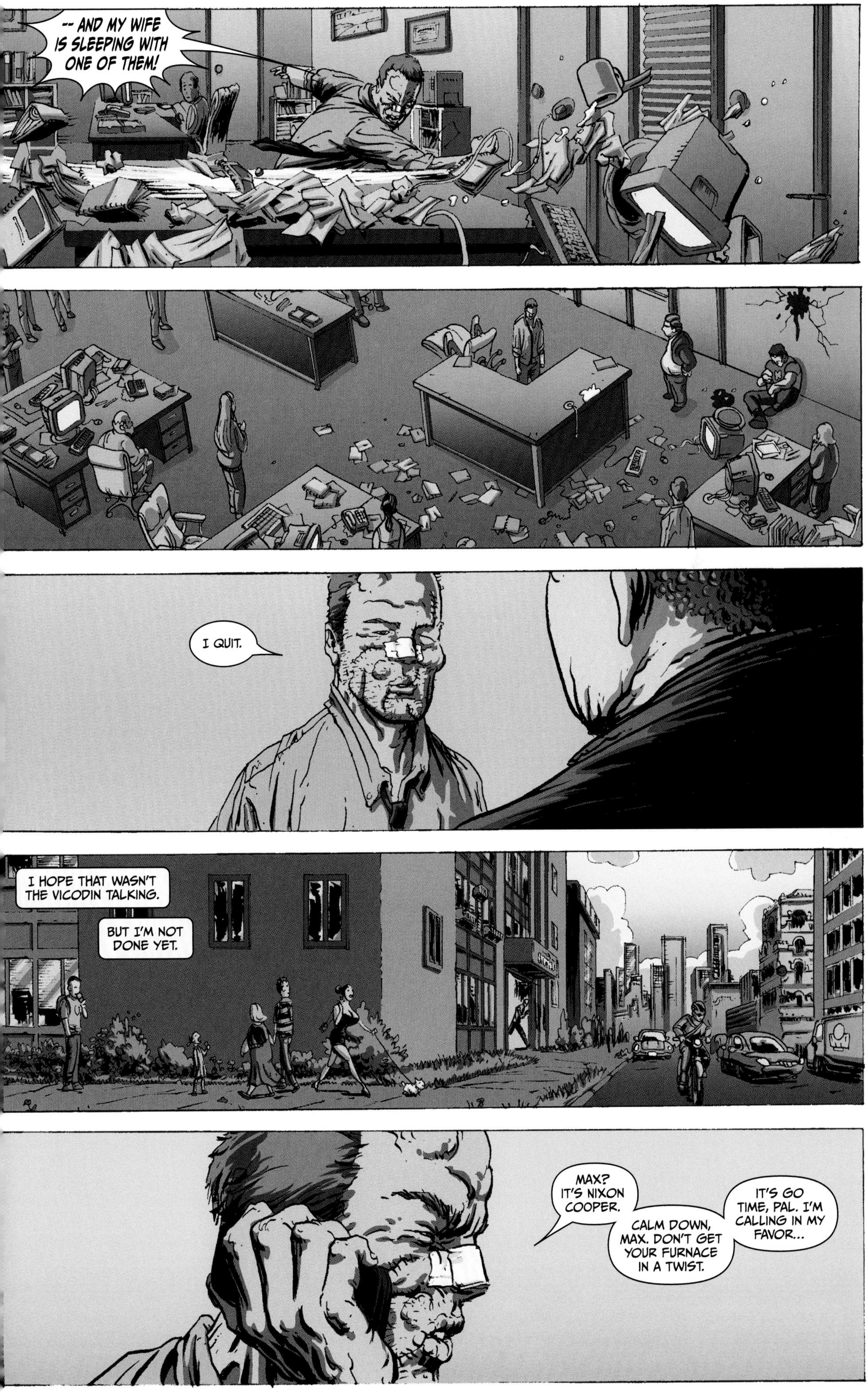
-- AND MY WIFE IS SLEEPING WITH ONE OF THEM!
I QUIT.
I HOPE THAT WASN'T THE VICODIN TALKING.
BUT I'M NOT DONE YET.
MAX? IT'S NIXON COOPER.
CALM DOWN, MAX. DON'T GET YOUR FURNACE IN A TWIST.
IT'S GO TIME, PAL. I'M CALLING IN MY FAVOR...

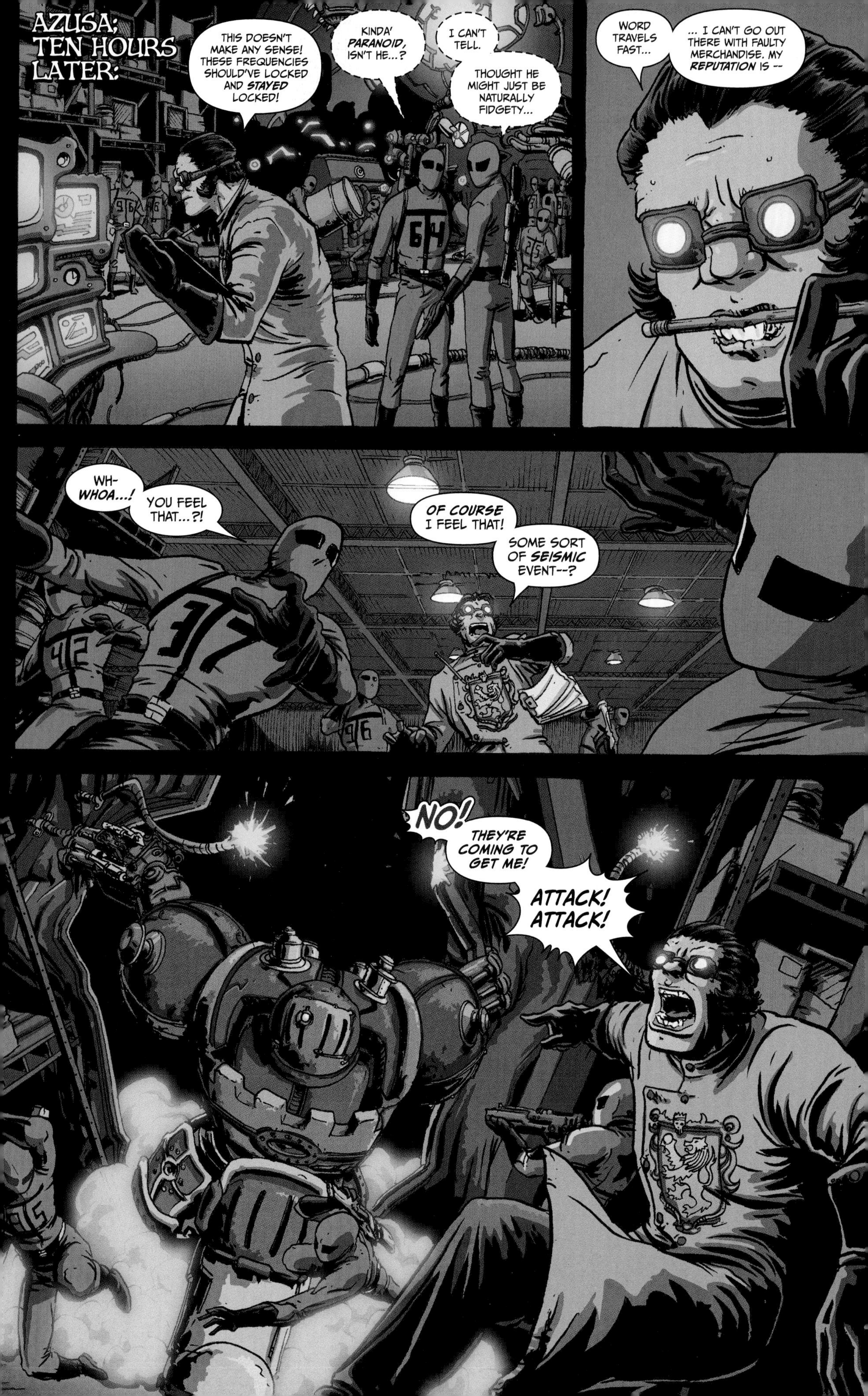
AZUSA; TEN HOURS LATER:
THIS DOESN'T MAKE ANY SENSE! THESE FREQUENCIES SHOULD'VE LOCKED AND STAYED LOCKED!
KINDA' PARANOID, ISN'T HE...?
I CAN'T TELL.
THOUGHT HE MIGHT JUST BE NATURALLY FIDGETY...
WORD TRAVELS FAST...
... I CAN'T GO OUT THERE WITH FAULTY MERCHANDISE. MY REPUTATION IS --
WH- WHOA...!
YOU FEEL THAT...?!
OF COURSE I FEEL THAT!
SOME SORT OF SEISMIC EVENT--?
NO!
THEY'RE COMING TO GET ME!
ATTACK! ATTACK!

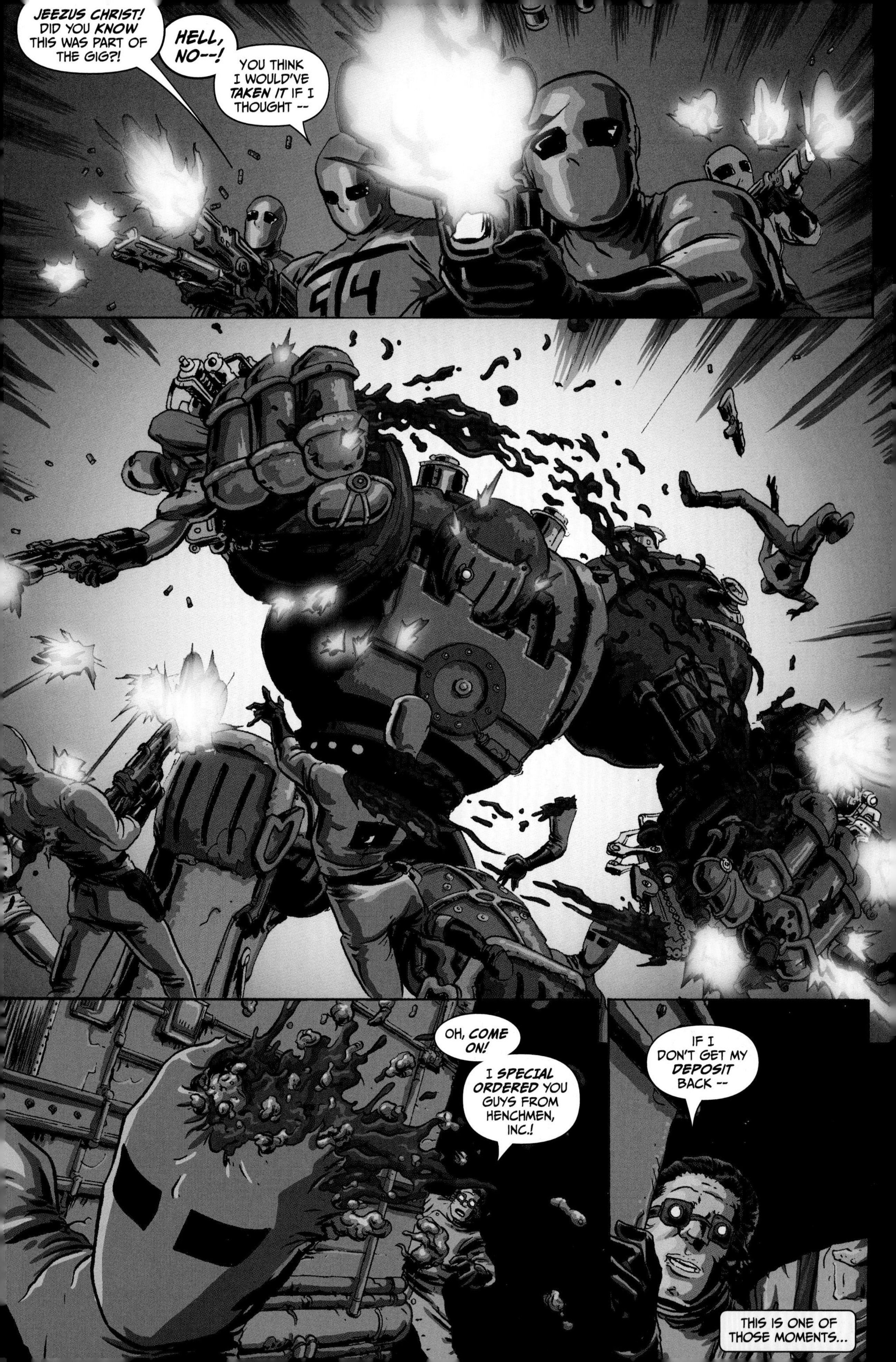

JEEZUS CHRIST! DID YOU KNOW THIS WAS PART OF THE GIG?!
HELL, NO--!
YOU THINK I WOULD'VE TAKEN IT IF I THOUGHT --
OH, COME ON!
I SPECIAL ORDERED YOU GUYS FROM HENCHMEN, INC.!
IF I DON'T GET MY DEPOSIT BACK --
THIS IS ONE OF THOSE MOMENTS...

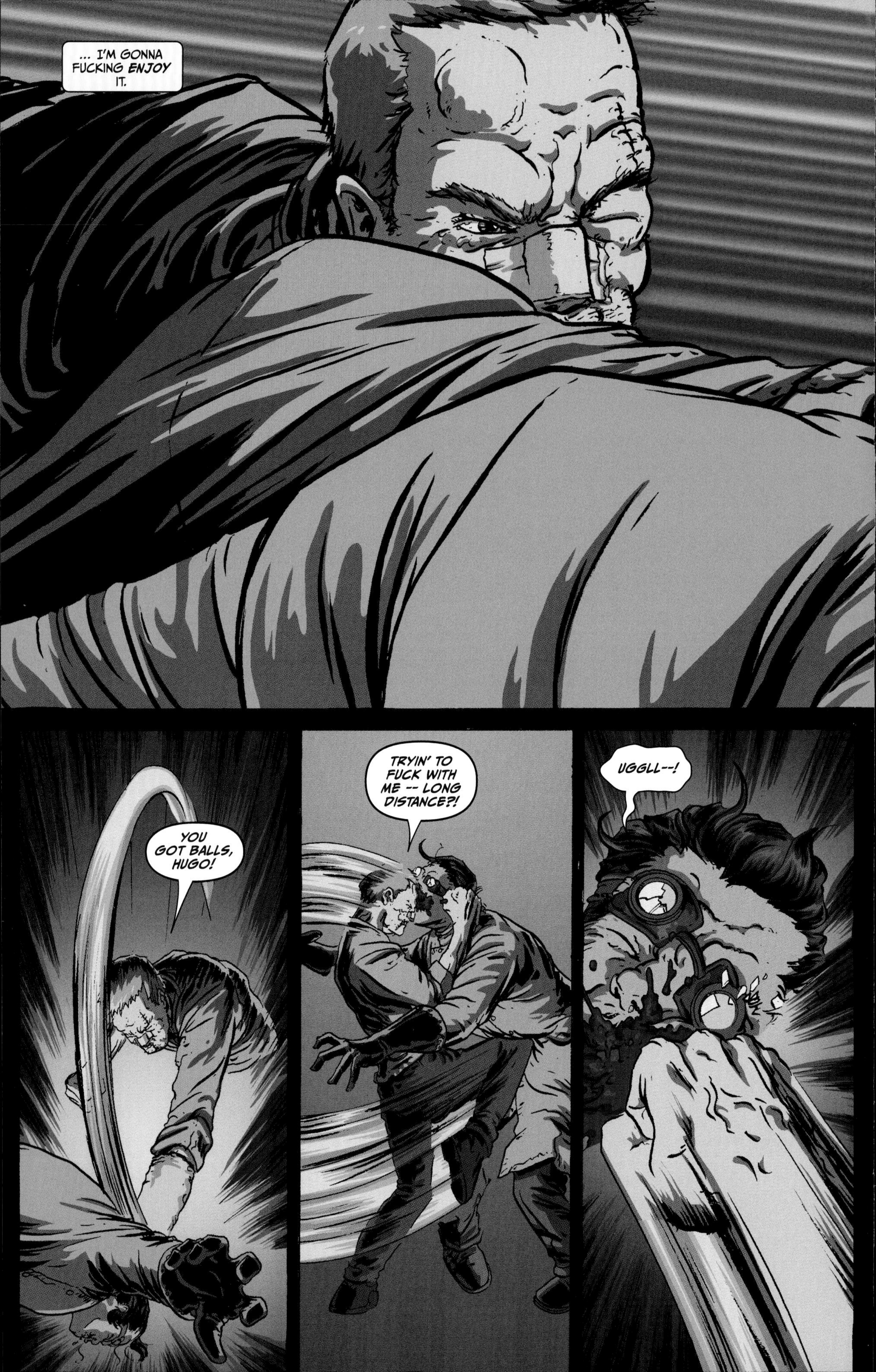
... I'M GONNA FUCKING ENJOY IT.
YOU GOT BALLS, HUGO!
TRYIN' TO FUCK WITH ME -- LONG DISTANCE?!
UGGLL--!

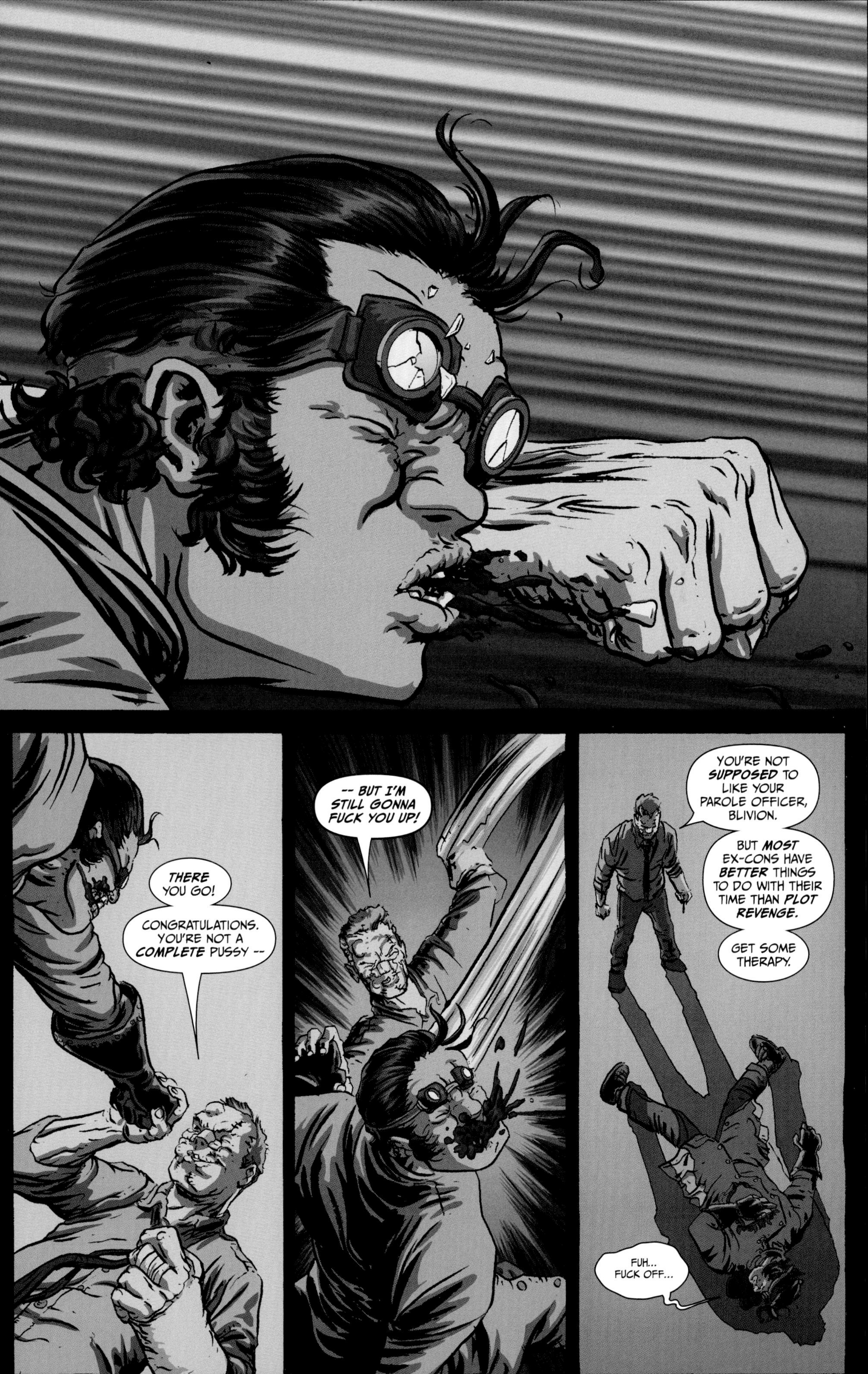
THERE YOU GO!
CONGRATULATIONS. YOU'RE NOT A COMPLETE PUSSY --
-- BUT I'M STILL GONNA FUCK YOU UP!
YOU'RE NOT SUPPOSED TO LIKE YOUR PAROLE OFFICER, BLIVION.
BUT MOST EX-CONS HAVE BETTER THINGS TO DO WITH THEIR TIME THAN PLOT REVENGE.
GET SOME THERAPY.
FUH... FUCK OFF...

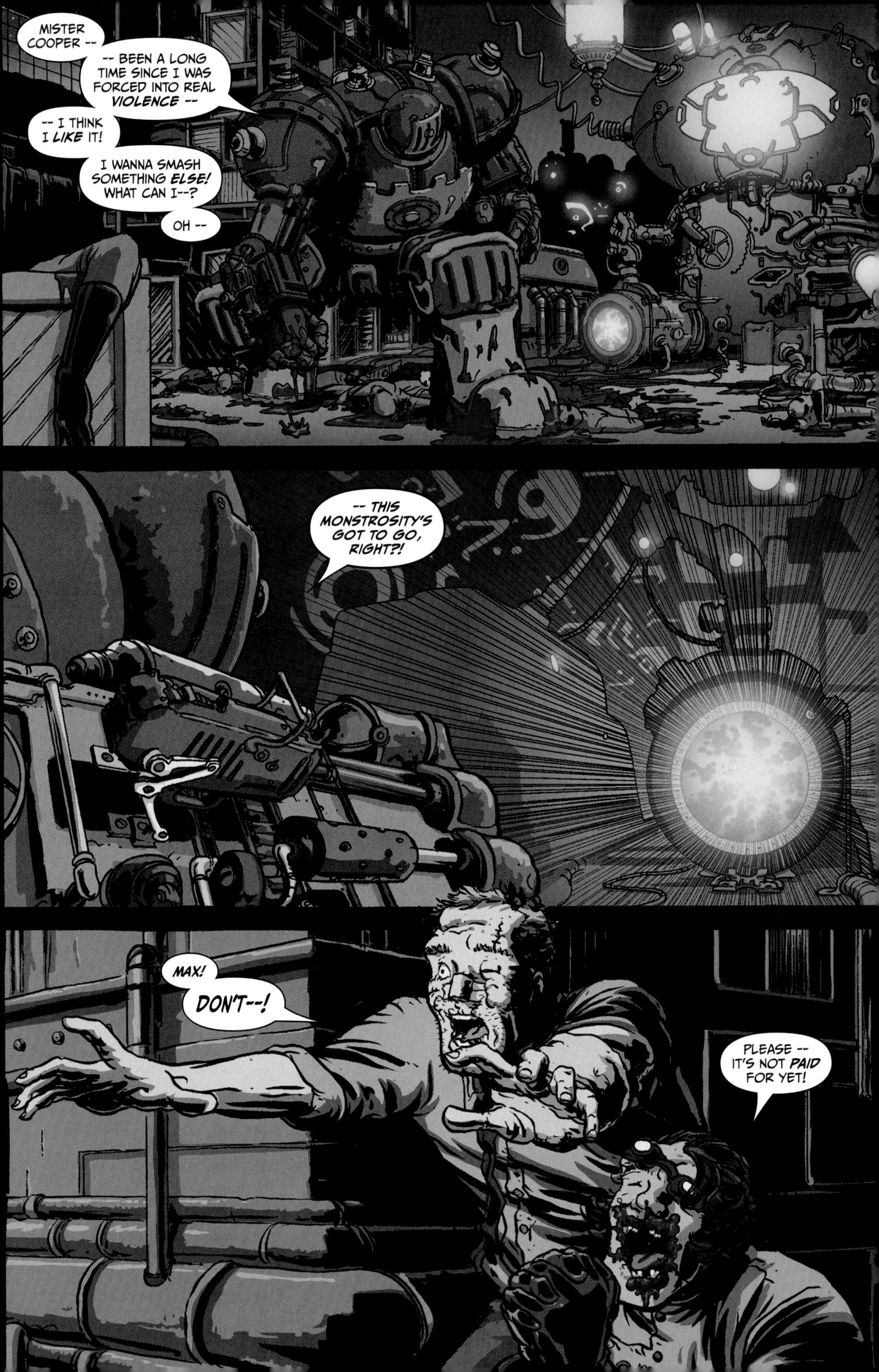
MISTER COOPER --
-- BEEN A LONG TIME SINCE I WAS FORCED INTO REAL *VIOLENCE* --
-- I THINK I *LIKE* IT!
I WANNA SMASH SOMETHING *ELSE!* WHAT CAN I--?
OH --
-- THIS MONSTROSITY'S GOT TO GO, RIGHT?!
MAX!
DON'T--!
PLEASE -- IT'S NOT *PAID* FOR YET!

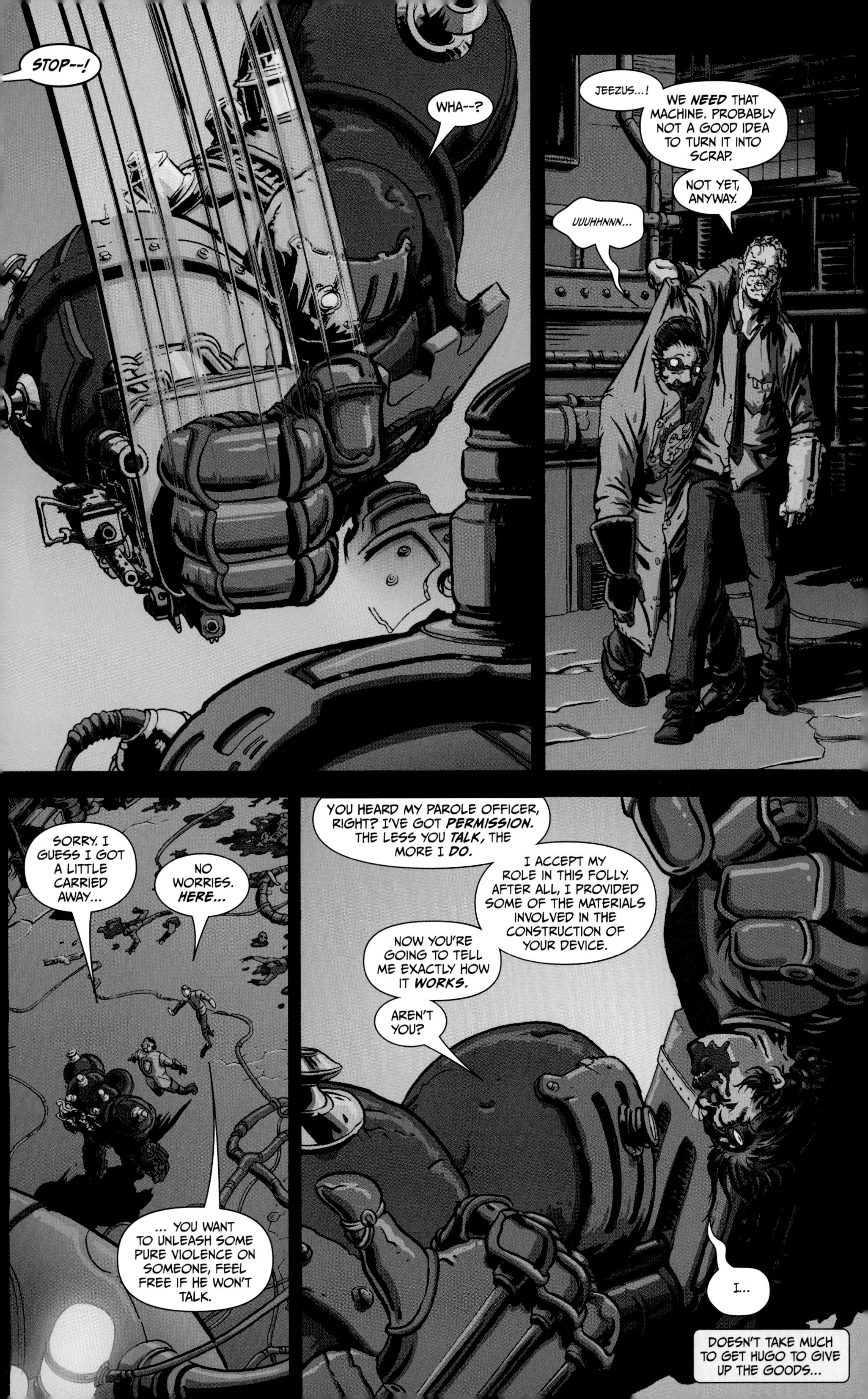
STOP--!
WHA--?
JEEZUS...!
WE NEED THAT MACHINE. PROBABLY NOT A GOOD IDEA TO TURN IT INTO SCRAP.
NOT YET, ANYWAY.
UUUHHNNN...
SORRY. I GUESS I GOT A LITTLE CARRIED AWAY...
NO WORRIES. HERE...
... YOU WANT TO UNLEASH SOME PURE VIOLENCE ON SOMEONE, FEEL FREE IF HE WON'T TALK.
YOU HEARD MY PAROLE OFFICER, RIGHT? I'VE GOT PERMISSION. THE LESS YOU TALK, THE MORE I DO.
I ACCEPT MY ROLE IN THIS FOLLY. AFTER ALL, I PROVIDED SOME OF THE MATERIALS INVOLVED IN THE CONSTRUCTION OF YOUR DEVICE.
NOW YOU'RE GOING TO TELL ME EXACTLY HOW IT WORKS.
AREN'T YOU?
I...
DOESN'T TAKE MUCH TO GET HUGO TO GIVE UP THE GOODS...

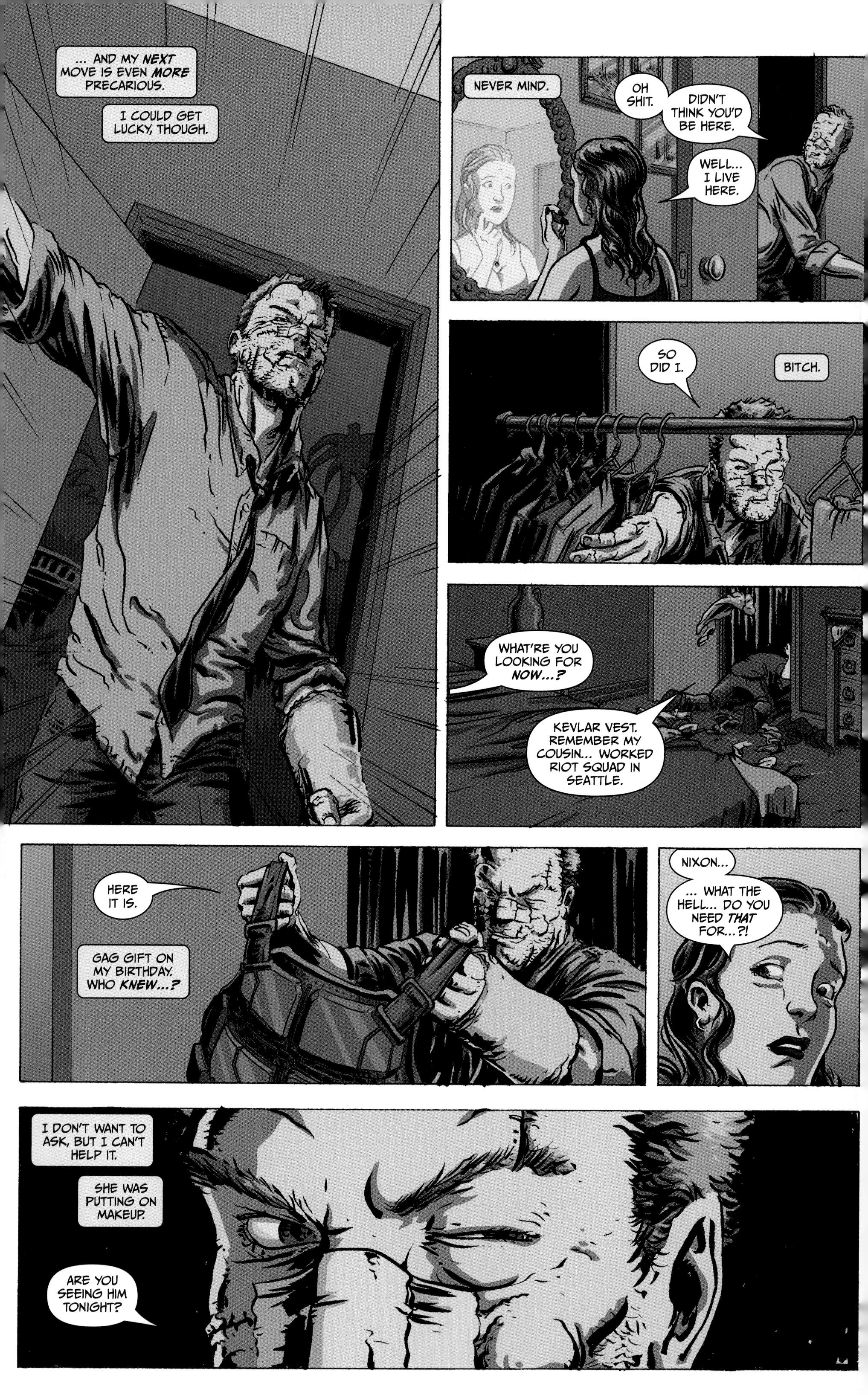
... AND MY NEXT MOVE IS EVEN MORE PRECARIOUS.
I COULD GET LUCKY, THOUGH.
NEVER MIND.
OH SHIT.
DIDN'T THINK YOU'D BE HERE.
WELL... I LIVE HERE.
SO DID I.
BITCH.
WHAT'RE YOU LOOKING FOR NOW...?
KEVLAR VEST. REMEMBER MY COUSIN... WORKED RIOT SQUAD IN SEATTLE.
HERE IT IS.
GAG GIFT ON MY BIRTHDAY. WHO KNEW...?
NIXON...
... WHAT THE HELL... DO YOU NEED THAT FOR...?!
I DON'T WANT TO ASK, BUT I CAN'T HELP IT.
SHE WAS PUTTING ON MAKEUP.
ARE YOU SEEING HIM TONIGHT?

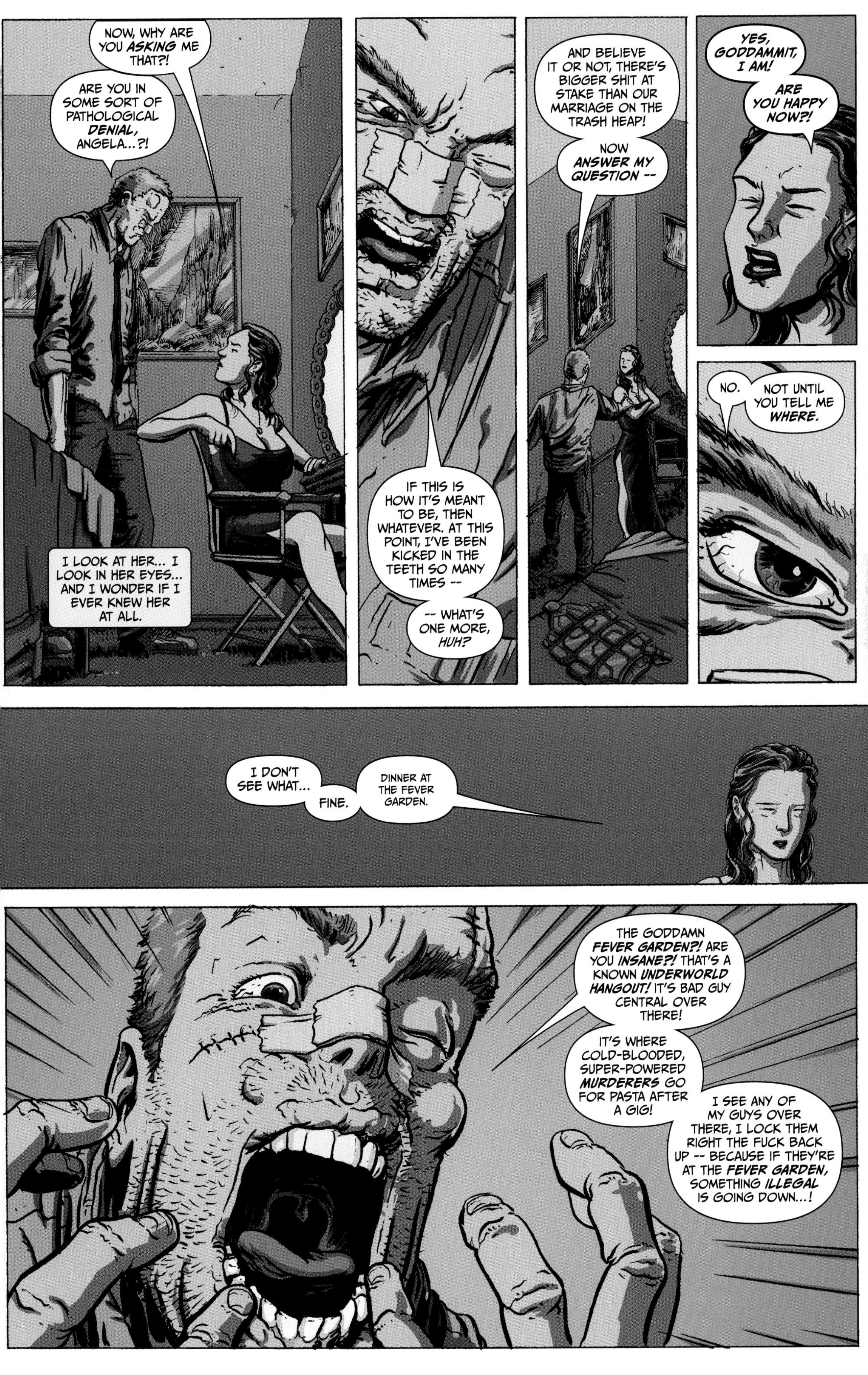
ARE YOU IN SOME SORT OF PATHOLOGICAL DENIAL, ANGELA...?!
NOW, WHY ARE YOU ASKING ME THAT?!
I LOOK AT HER... I LOOK IN HER EYES... AND I WONDER IF I EVER KNEW HER AT ALL.
IF THIS IS HOW IT'S MEANT TO BE, THEN WHATEVER. AT THIS POINT, I'VE BEEN KICKED IN THE TEETH SO MANY TIMES --
-- WHAT'S ONE MORE, HUH?
AND BELIEVE IT OR NOT, THERE'S BIGGER SHIT AT STAKE THAN OUR MARRIAGE ON THE TRASH HEAP!
NOW ANSWER MY QUESTION --
YES, GODDAMMIT, I AM!
ARE YOU HAPPY NOW?!
NO.
NOT UNTIL YOU TELL ME WHERE.
I DON'T SEE WHAT...
FINE.
DINNER AT THE FEVER GARDEN.
THE GODDAMN FEVER GARDEN?! ARE YOU INSANE?! THAT'S A KNOWN UNDERWORLD HANGOUT! IT'S BAD GUY CENTRAL OVER THERE!
IT'S WHERE COLD-BLOODED, SUPER-POWERED MURDERERS GO FOR PASTA AFTER A GIG!
I SEE ANY OF MY GUYS OVER THERE, I LOCK THEM RIGHT THE FUCK BACK UP -- BECAUSE IF THEY'RE AT THE FEVER GARDEN, SOMETHING ILLEGAL IS GOING DOWN...!

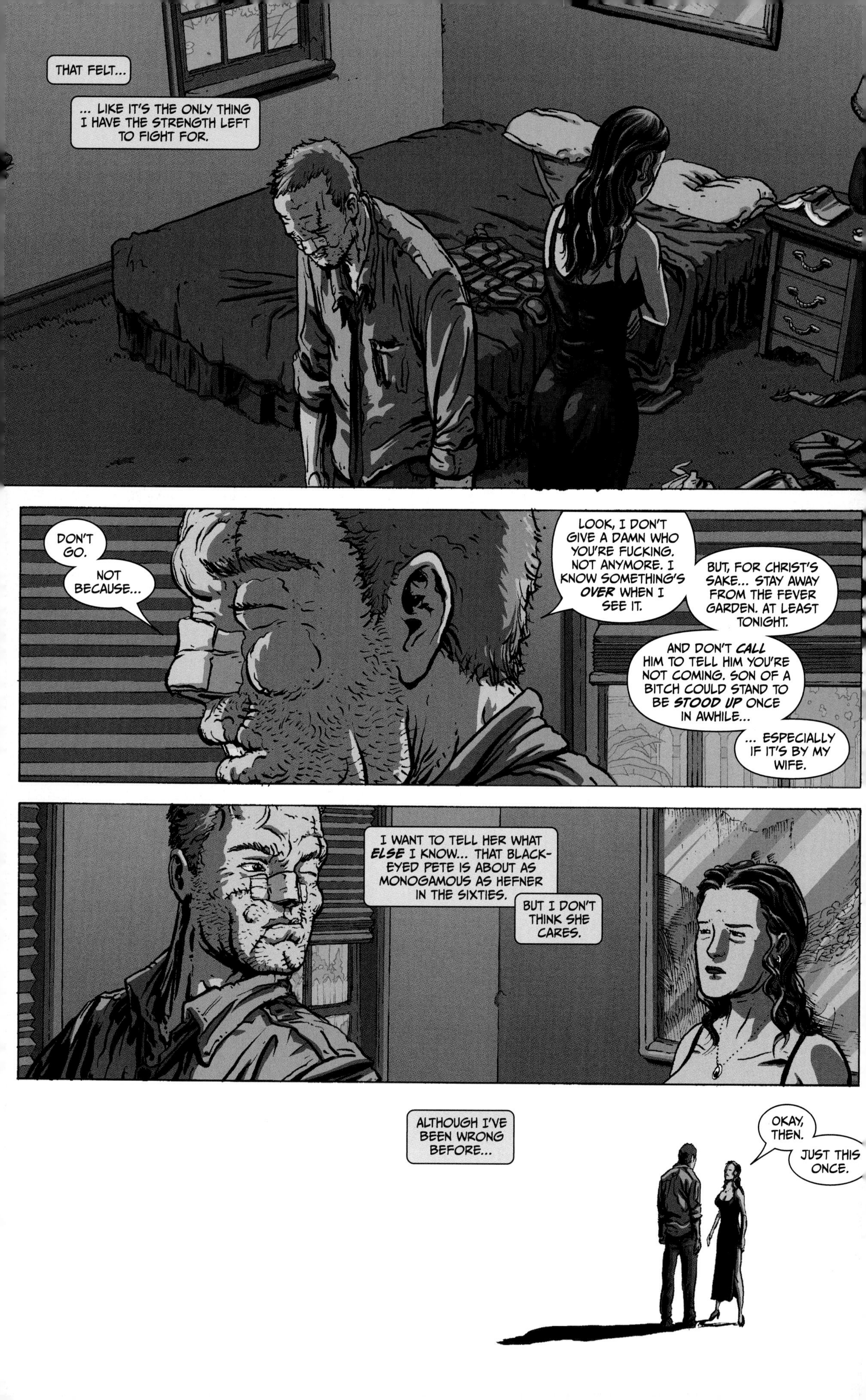
THAT FELT...
... LIKE IT'S THE ONLY THING I HAVE THE STRENGTH LEFT TO FIGHT FOR.
DON'T GO.
NOT BECAUSE...
LOOK, I DON'T GIVE A DAMN WHO YOU'RE FUCKING. NOT ANYMORE. I KNOW SOMETHING'S *OVER* WHEN I SEE IT.
BUT, FOR CHRIST'S SAKE... STAY AWAY FROM THE FEVER GARDEN. AT LEAST TONIGHT.
AND DON'T *CALL* HIM TO TELL HIM YOU'RE NOT COMING. SON OF A BITCH COULD STAND TO BE *STOOD UP* ONCE IN AWHILE...
... ESPECIALLY IF IT'S BY MY WIFE.
I WANT TO TELL HER WHAT *ELSE* I KNOW... THAT BLACK-EYED PETE IS ABOUT AS MONOGAMOUS AS HEFNER IN THE SIXTIES.
BUT I DON'T THINK SHE CARES.
ALTHOUGH I'VE BEEN WRONG BEFORE...
OKAY, THEN.
JUST THIS ONCE.

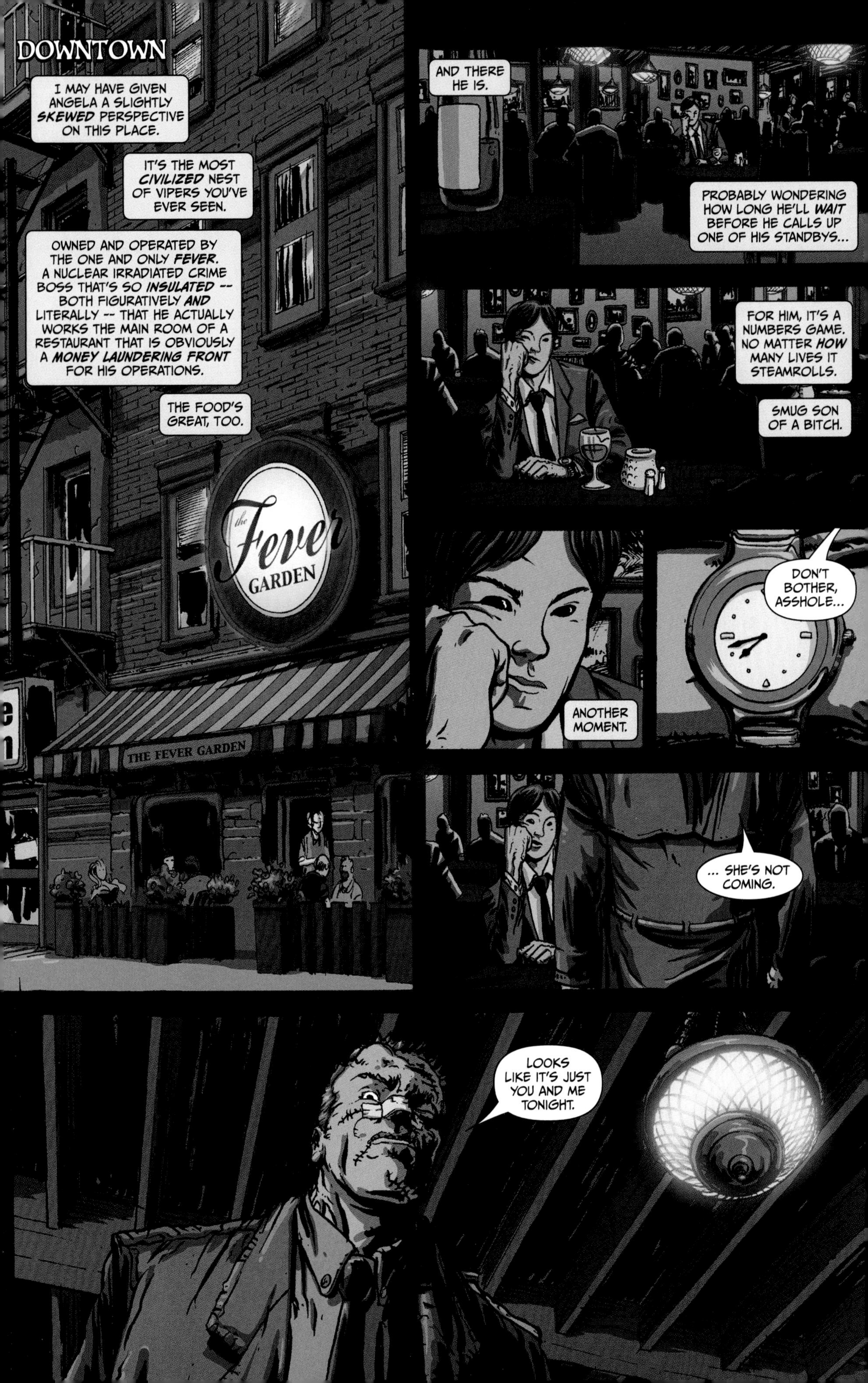
DOWNTOWN
I MAY HAVE GIVEN ANGELA A SLIGHTLY SKEWED PERSPECTIVE ON THIS PLACE.
IT'S THE MOST CIVILIZED NEST OF VIPERS YOU'VE EVER SEEN.
OWNED AND OPERATED BY THE ONE AND ONLY FEVER. A NUCLEAR IRRADIATED CRIME BOSS THAT'S SO INSULATED -- BOTH FIGURATIVELY AND LITERALLY -- THAT HE ACTUALLY WORKS THE MAIN ROOM OF A RESTAURANT THAT IS OBVIOUSLY A MONEY LAUNDERING FRONT FOR HIS OPERATIONS.
THE FOOD'S GREAT, TOO.
the Fever GARDEN
THE FEVER GARDEN
AND THERE HE IS.
PROBABLY WONDERING HOW LONG HE'LL WAIT BEFORE HE CALLS UP ONE OF HIS STANDBYS...
FOR HIM, IT'S A NUMBERS GAME. NO MATTER HOW MANY LIVES IT STEAMROLLS.
SMUG SON OF A BITCH.
ANOTHER MOMENT.
DON'T BOTHER, ASSHOLE...
... SHE'S NOT COMING.
LOOKS LIKE IT'S JUST YOU AND ME TONIGHT.

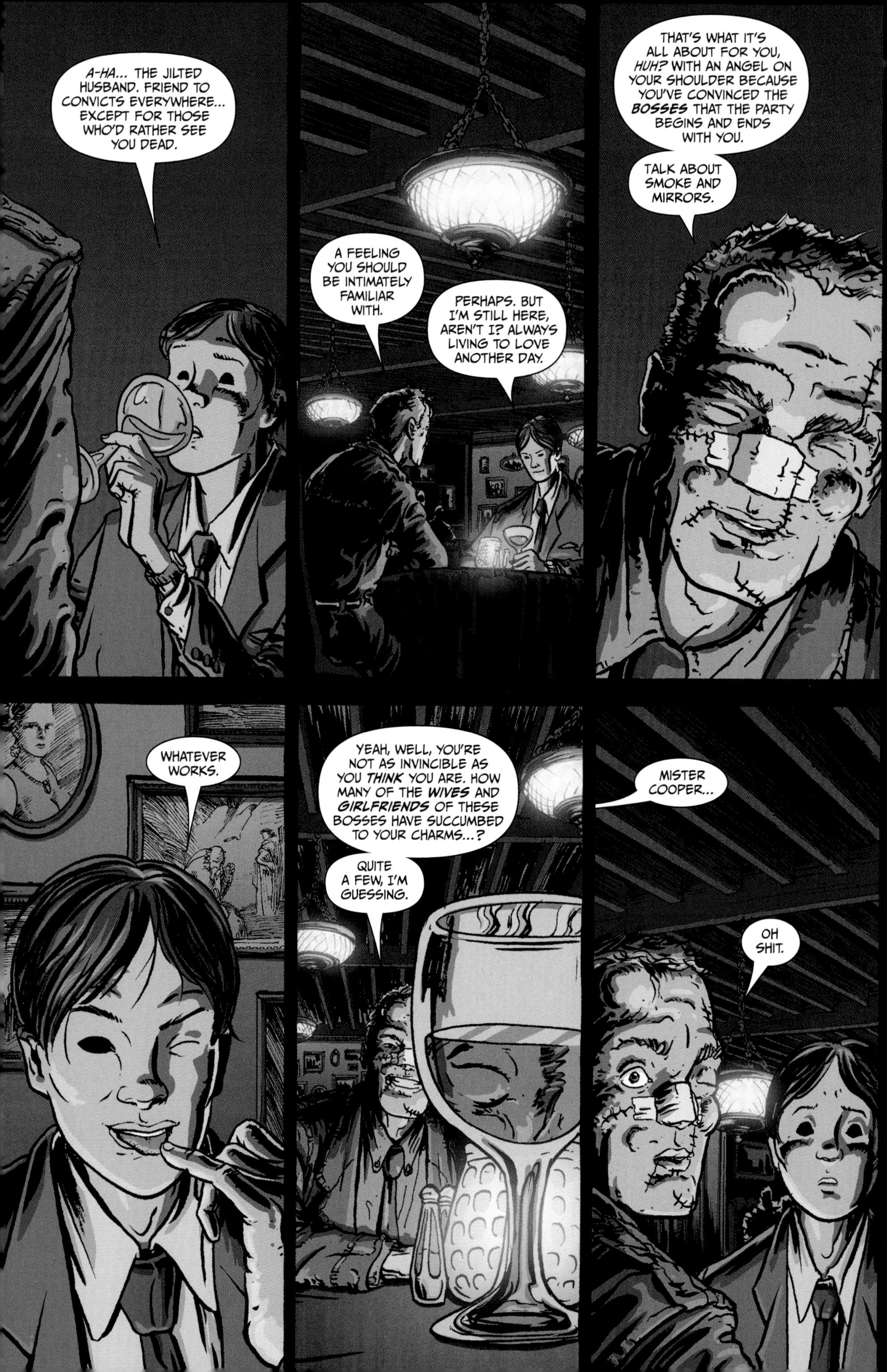
A-HA... THE JILTED HUSBAND. FRIEND TO CONVICTS EVERYWHERE... EXCEPT FOR THOSE WHO'D RATHER SEE YOU DEAD.
A FEELING YOU SHOULD BE INTIMATELY FAMILIAR WITH.
PERHAPS. BUT I'M STILL HERE, AREN'T I? ALWAYS LIVING TO LOVE ANOTHER DAY.
THAT'S WHAT IT'S ALL ABOUT FOR YOU, HUH? WITH AN ANGEL ON YOUR SHOULDER BECAUSE YOU'VE CONVINCED THE BOSSES THAT THE PARTY BEGINS AND ENDS WITH YOU.
TALK ABOUT SMOKE AND MIRRORS.
WHATEVER WORKS.
YEAH, WELL, YOU'RE NOT AS INVINCIBLE AS YOU THINK YOU ARE. HOW MANY OF THE WIVES AND GIRLFRIENDS OF THESE BOSSES HAVE SUCCUMBED TO YOUR CHARMS...?
QUITE A FEW, I'M GUESSING.
MISTER COOPER...
OH SHIT.

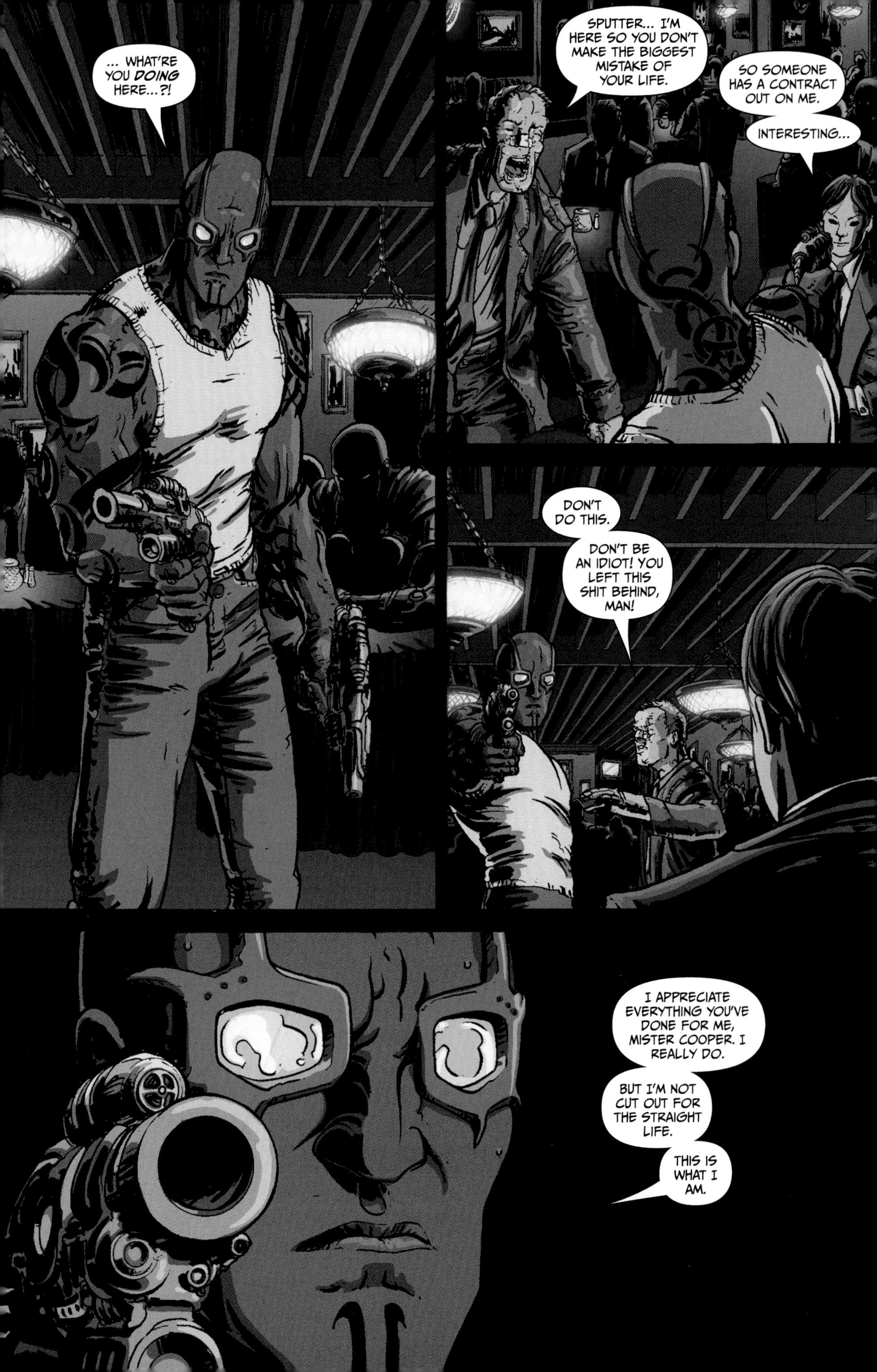
... WHAT'RE YOU DOING HERE...?!
SPUTTER... I'M HERE SO YOU DON'T MAKE THE BIGGEST MISTAKE OF YOUR LIFE.
SO SOMEONE HAS A CONTRACT OUT ON ME.
INTERESTING...
DON'T DO THIS.
DON'T BE AN IDIOT! YOU LEFT THIS SHIT BEHIND, MAN!
I APPRECIATE EVERYTHING YOU'VE DONE FOR ME, MISTER COOPER. I REALLY DO.
BUT I'M NOT CUT OUT FOR THE STRAIGHT LIFE.
THIS IS WHAT I AM.

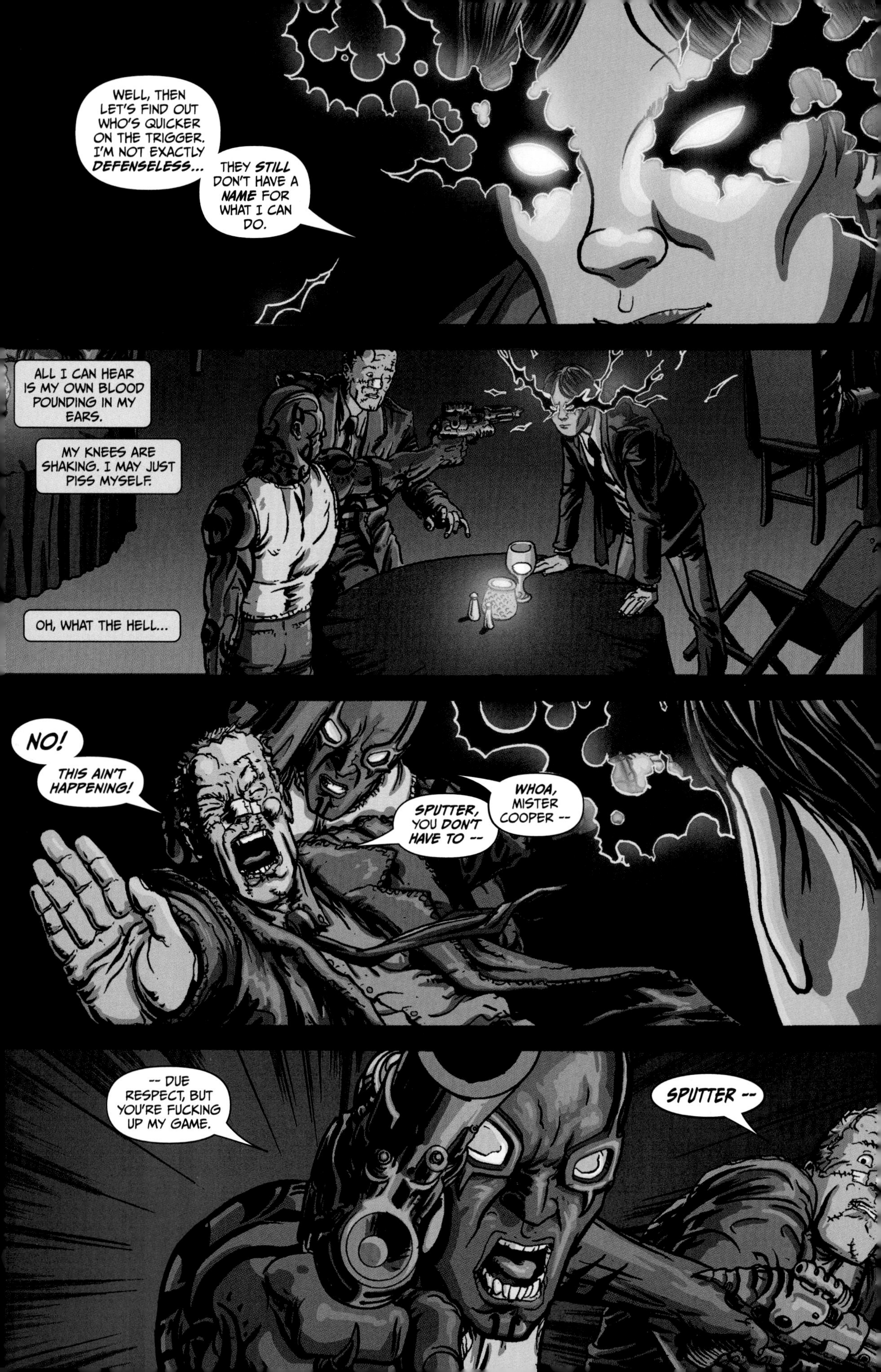
WELL, THEN LET'S FIND OUT WHO'S QUICKER ON THE TRIGGER. I'M NOT EXACTLY *DEFENSELESS*...
THEY *STILL* DON'T HAVE A *NAME* FOR WHAT I CAN DO.
ALL I CAN HEAR IS MY OWN BLOOD POUNDING IN MY EARS.
MY KNEES ARE SHAKING. I MAY JUST PISS MYSELF.
OH, WHAT THE HELL...
NO!
THIS AIN'T HAPPENING!
WHOA, MISTER COOPER --
SPUTTER, YOU *DON'T HAVE TO* --
-- DUE RESPECT, BUT YOU'RE FUCKING UP MY GAME.
SPUTTER --

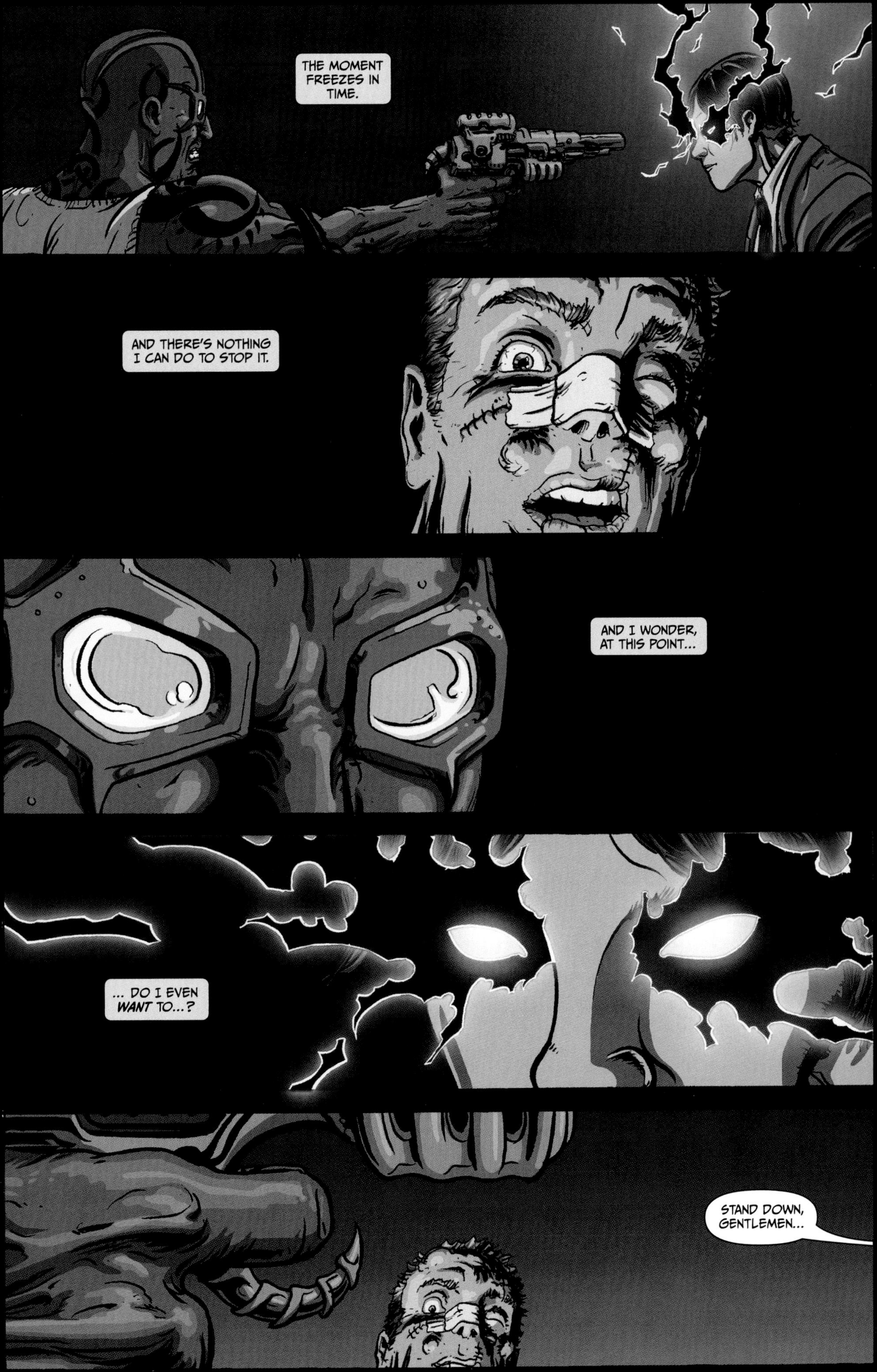
THE MOMENT FREEZES IN TIME.
AND THERE'S NOTHING I CAN DO TO STOP IT.
AND I WONDER, AT THIS POINT...
... DO I EVEN *WANT* TO...?
STAND DOWN, GENTLEMEN...

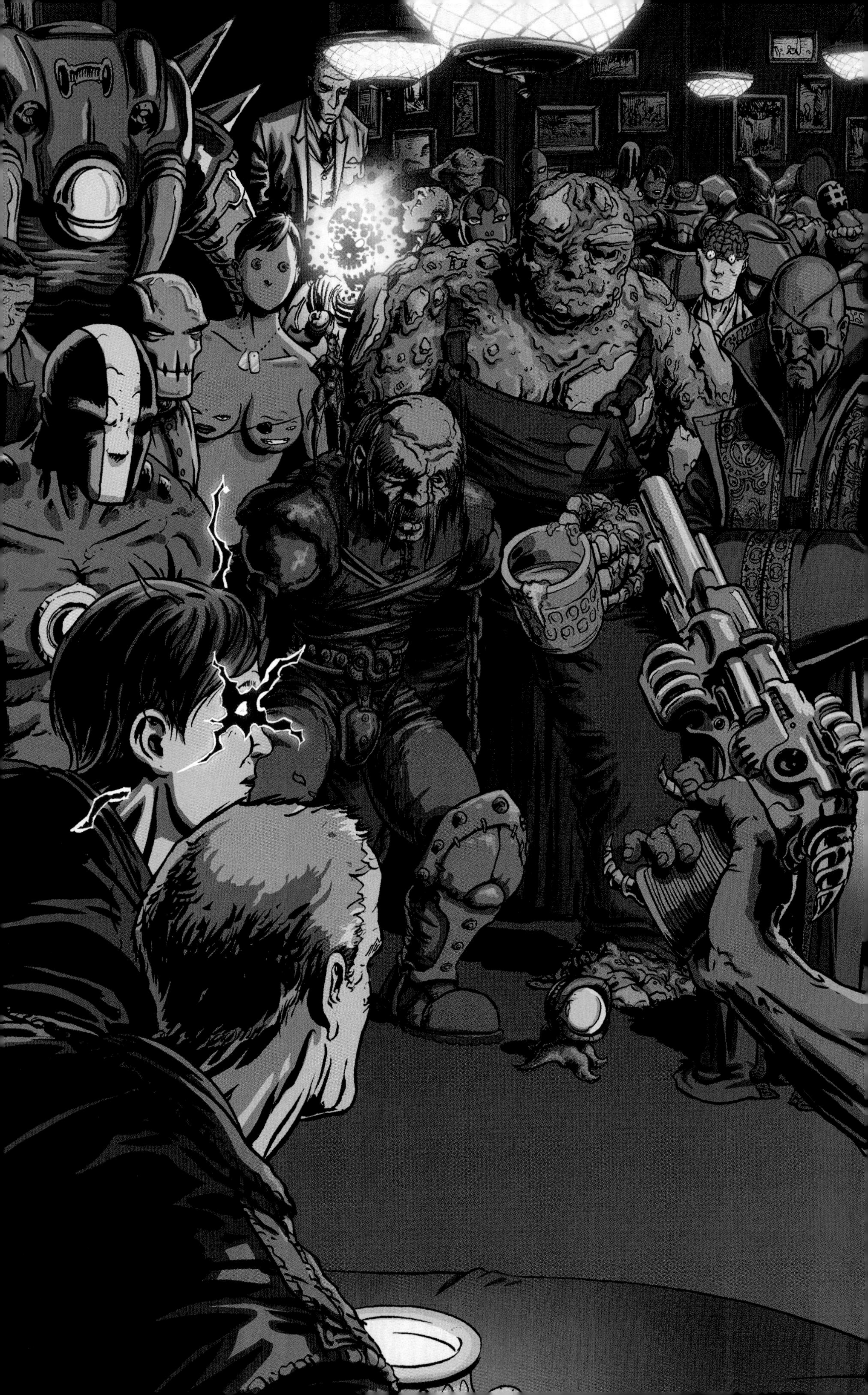

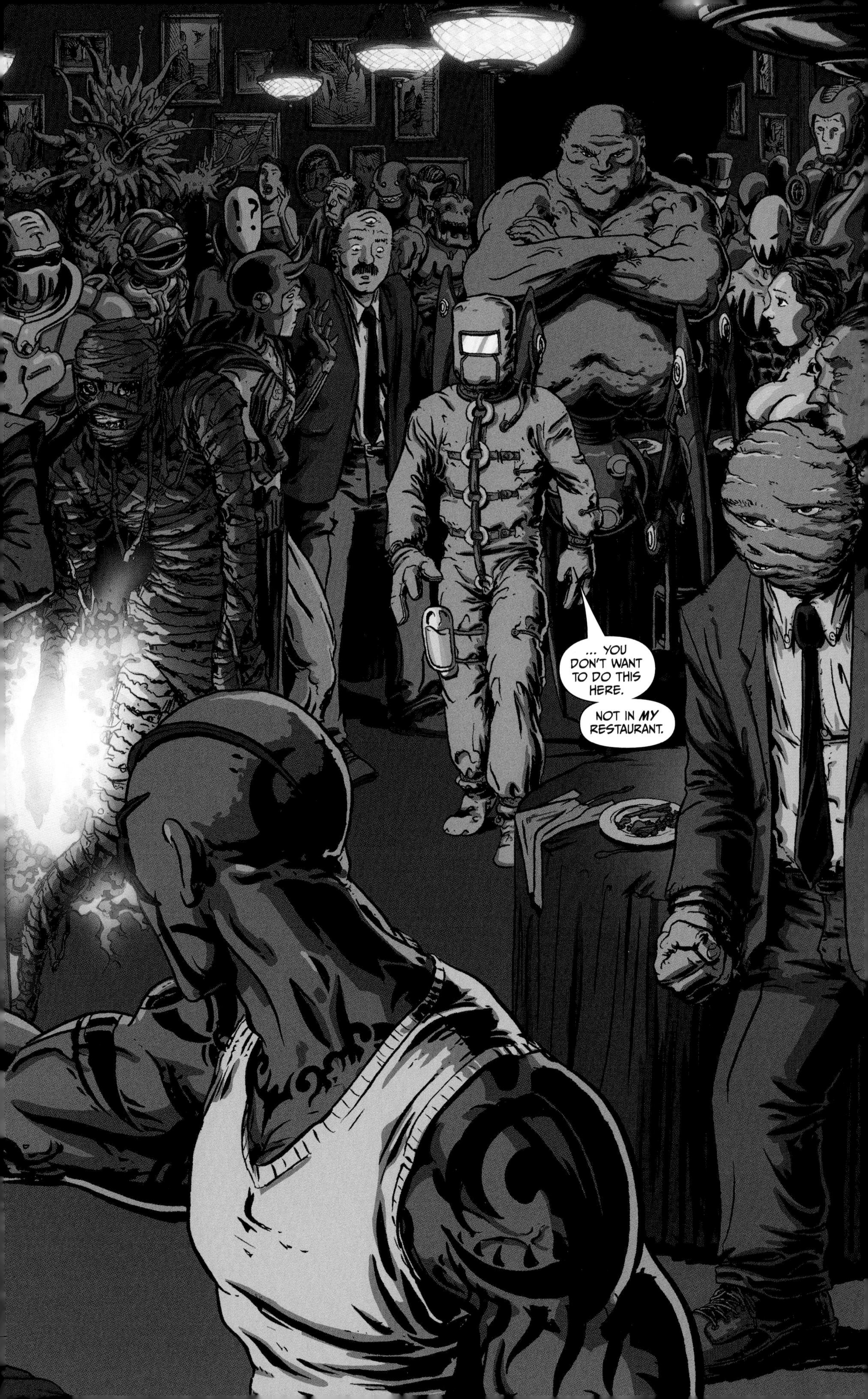
... YOU DON'T WANT TO DO THIS HERE.
NOT IN *MY* RESTAURANT.

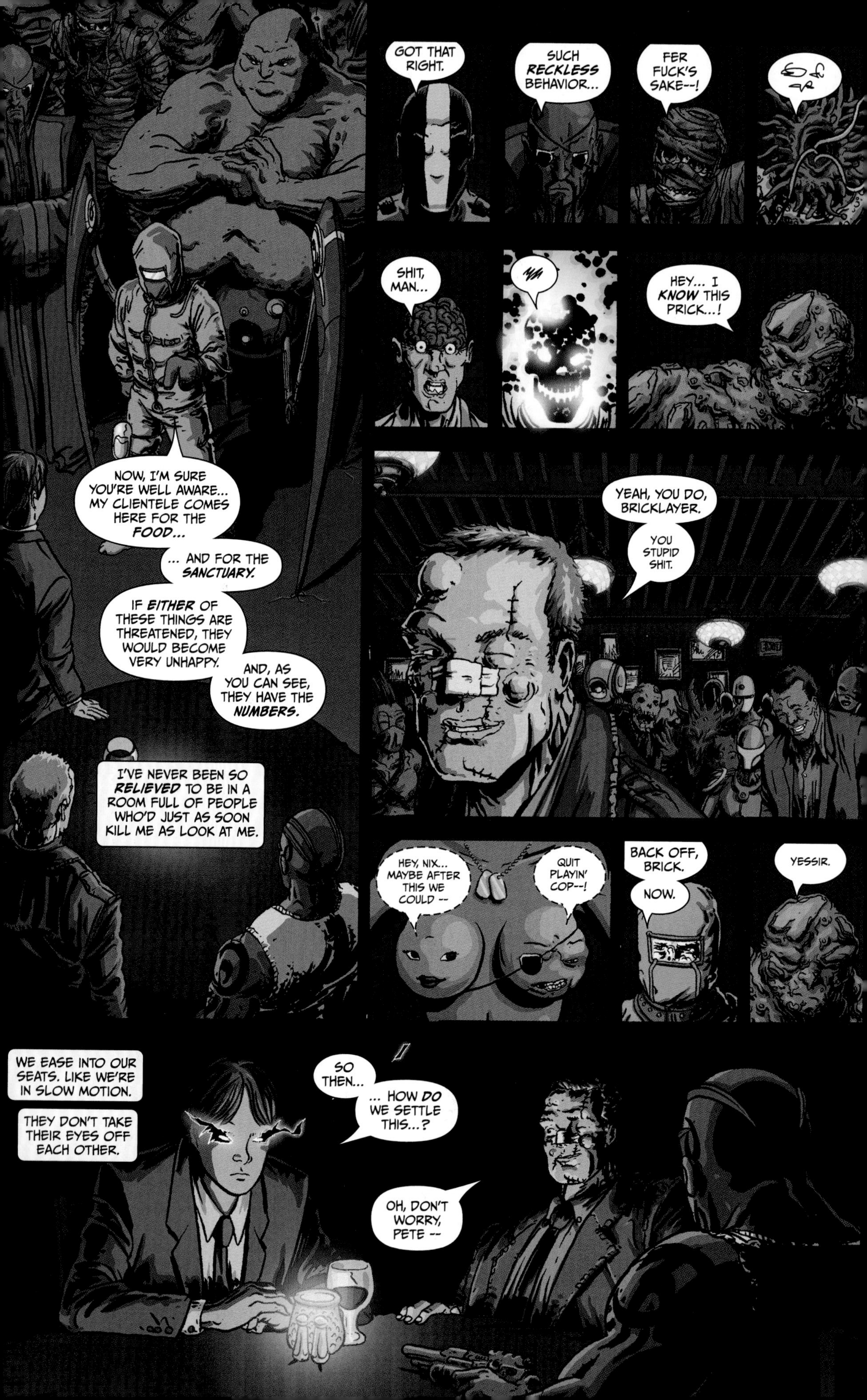

NOW, I'M SURE YOU'RE WELL AWARE... MY CLIENTELE COMES HERE FOR THE FOOD...
... AND FOR THE SANCTUARY.
IF EITHER OF THESE THINGS ARE THREATENED, THEY WOULD BECOME VERY UNHAPPY.
AND, AS YOU CAN SEE, THEY HAVE THE NUMBERS.
I'VE NEVER BEEN SO RELIEVED TO BE IN A ROOM FULL OF PEOPLE WHO'D JUST AS SOON KILL ME AS LOOK AT ME.
GOT THAT RIGHT.
SUCH RECKLESS BEHAVIOR...
FER FUCK'S SAKE--!
SHIT, MAN...
HEY... I KNOW THIS PRICK...!
YEAH, YOU DO, BRICKLAYER.
YOU STUPID SHIT.
HEY, NIX... MAYBE AFTER THIS WE COULD --
QUIT PLAYIN' COP--!
BACK OFF, BRICK.
NOW.
YESSIR.
WE EASE INTO OUR SEATS. LIKE WE'RE IN SLOW MOTION.
THEY DON'T TAKE THEIR EYES OFF EACH OTHER.
SO THEN...
... HOW DO WE SETTLE THIS...?
OH, DON'T WORRY, PETE --

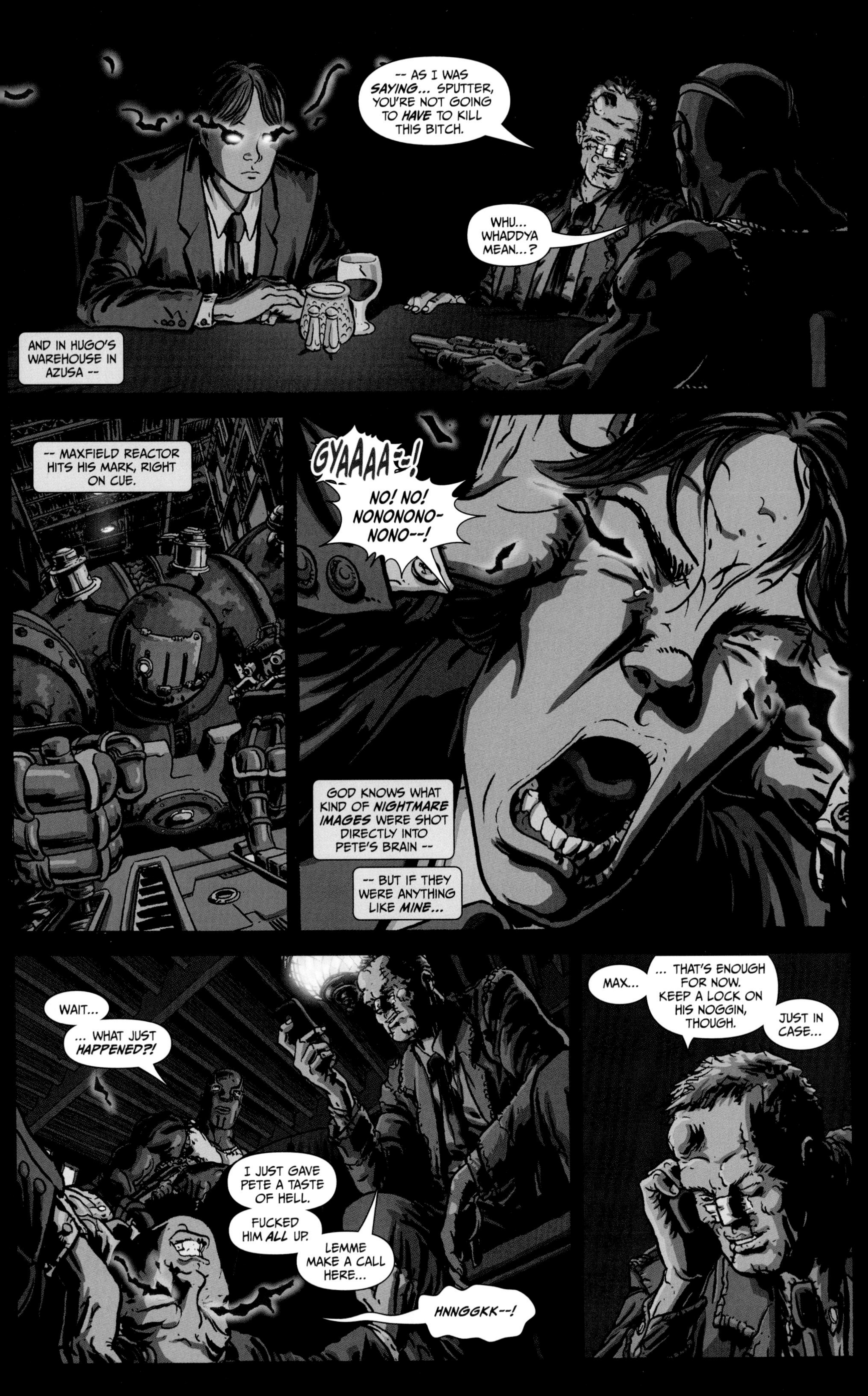
-- AS I WAS SAYING... SPUTTER, YOU'RE NOT GOING TO HAVE TO KILL THIS BITCH.
WHU... WHADDYA MEAN...?
AND IN HUGO'S WAREHOUSE IN AZUSA --
-- MAXFIELD REACTOR HITS HIS MARK, RIGHT ON CUE.
GYAAAA--!
NO! NO! NONONONO-NONO--!
GOD KNOWS WHAT KIND OF NIGHTMARE IMAGES WERE SHOT DIRECTLY INTO PETE'S BRAIN --
-- BUT IF THEY WERE ANYTHING LIKE MINE...
WAIT...
... WHAT JUST HAPPENED?!
I JUST GAVE PETE A TASTE OF HELL.
FUCKED HIM ALL UP.
LEMME MAKE A CALL HERE...
HNNGGKK--!
MAX...
... THAT'S ENOUGH FOR NOW. KEEP A LOCK ON HIS NOGGIN, THOUGH.
JUST IN CASE...

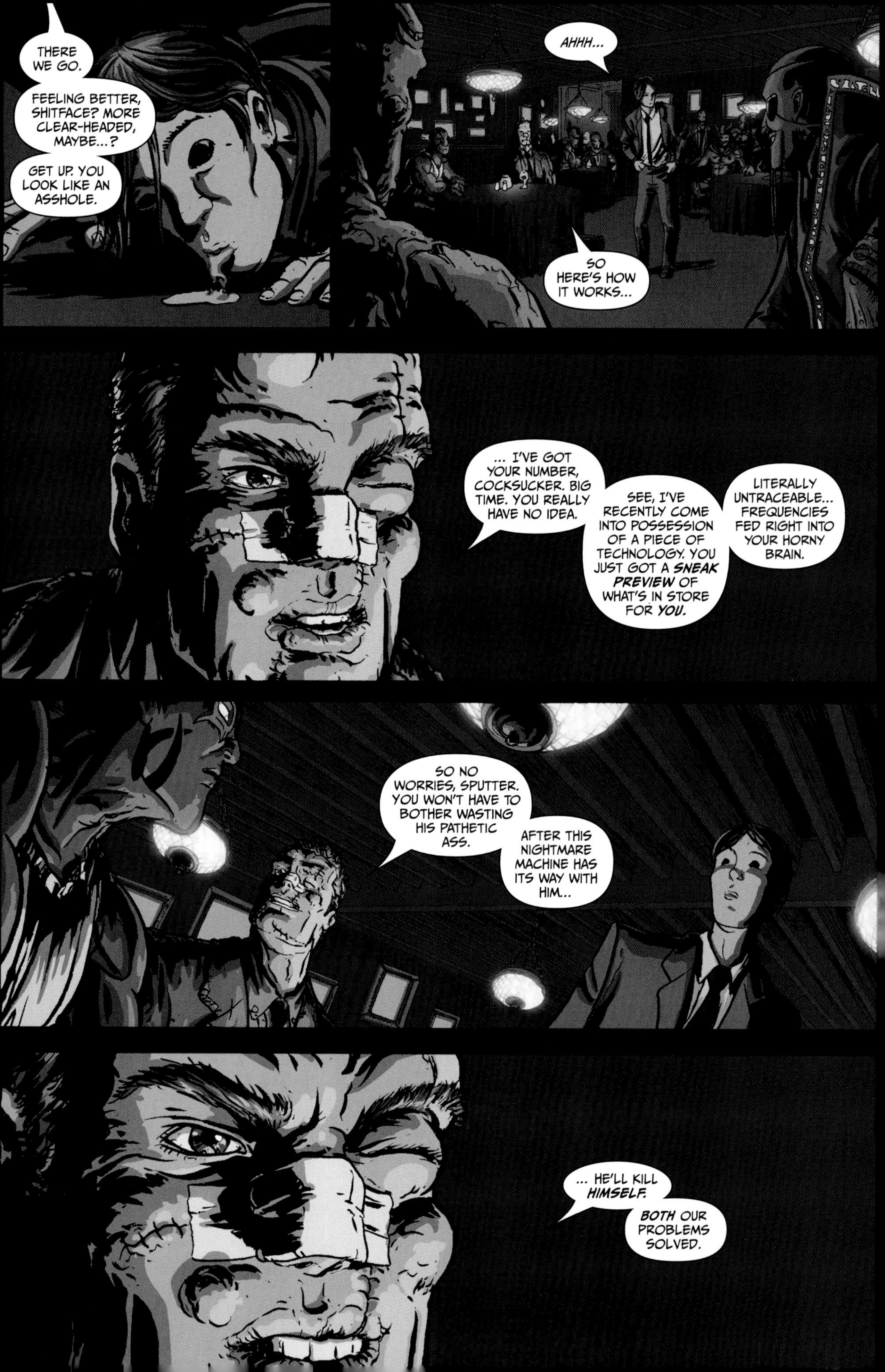
THERE WE GO.
FEELING BETTER, SHITFACE? MORE CLEAR-HEADED, MAYBE...?
GET UP. YOU LOOK LIKE AN ASSHOLE.
AHHH...
SO HERE'S HOW IT WORKS...
... I'VE GOT YOUR NUMBER, COCKSUCKER. BIG TIME. YOU REALLY HAVE NO IDEA.
SEE, I'VE RECENTLY COME INTO POSSESSION OF A PIECE OF TECHNOLOGY. YOU JUST GOT A SNEAK PREVIEW OF WHAT'S IN STORE FOR YOU.
LITERALLY UNTRACEABLE... FREQUENCIES FED RIGHT INTO YOUR HORNY BRAIN.
SO NO WORRIES, SPUTTER. YOU WON'T HAVE TO BOTHER WASTING HIS PATHETIC ASS.
AFTER THIS NIGHTMARE MACHINE HAS ITS WAY WITH HIM...
... HE'LL KILL HIMSELF.
BOTH OUR PROBLEMS SOLVED.

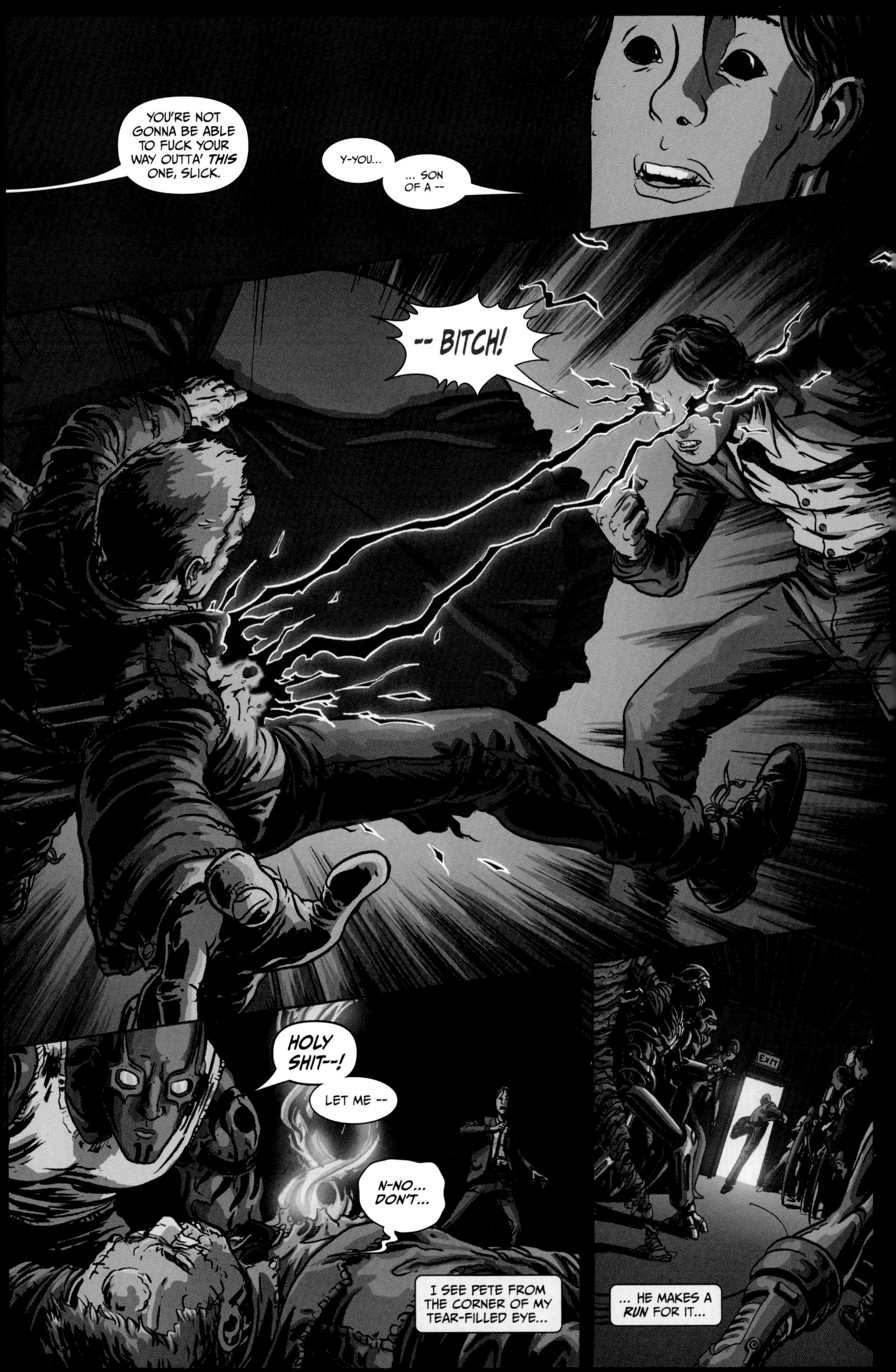
YOU'RE NOT GONNA BE ABLE TO FUCK YOUR WAY OUTTA' *THIS* ONE, SLICK.
Y-YOU...
... SON OF A --
-- BITCH!
HOLY SHIT--!
LET ME --
N-NO... DON'T...
I SEE PETE FROM THE CORNER OF MY TEAR-FILLED EYE...
EXIT
... HE MAKES A *RUN* FOR IT...

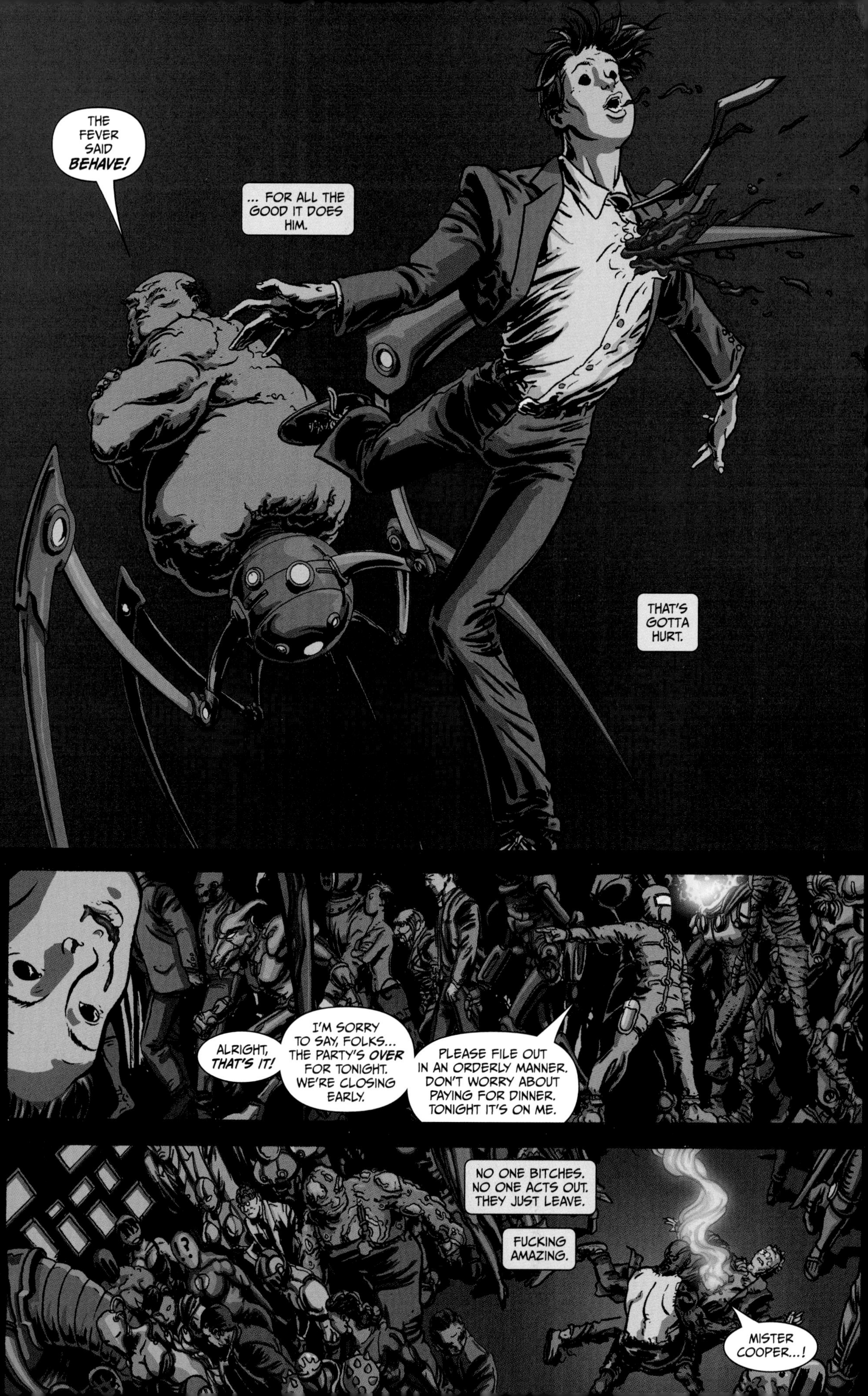
THE FEVER SAID **BEHAVE!**
... FOR ALL THE GOOD IT DOES HIM.
THAT'S GOTTA HURT.
ALRIGHT, **THAT'S IT!**
I'M SORRY TO SAY, FOLKS... THE PARTY'S **OVER** FOR TONIGHT. WE'RE CLOSING EARLY.
PLEASE FILE OUT IN AN ORDERLY MANNER. DON'T WORRY ABOUT PAYING FOR DINNER. TONIGHT IT'S ON ME.
NO ONE BITCHES. NO ONE ACTS OUT. THEY JUST LEAVE.
FUCKING AMAZING.
MISTER COOPER...!

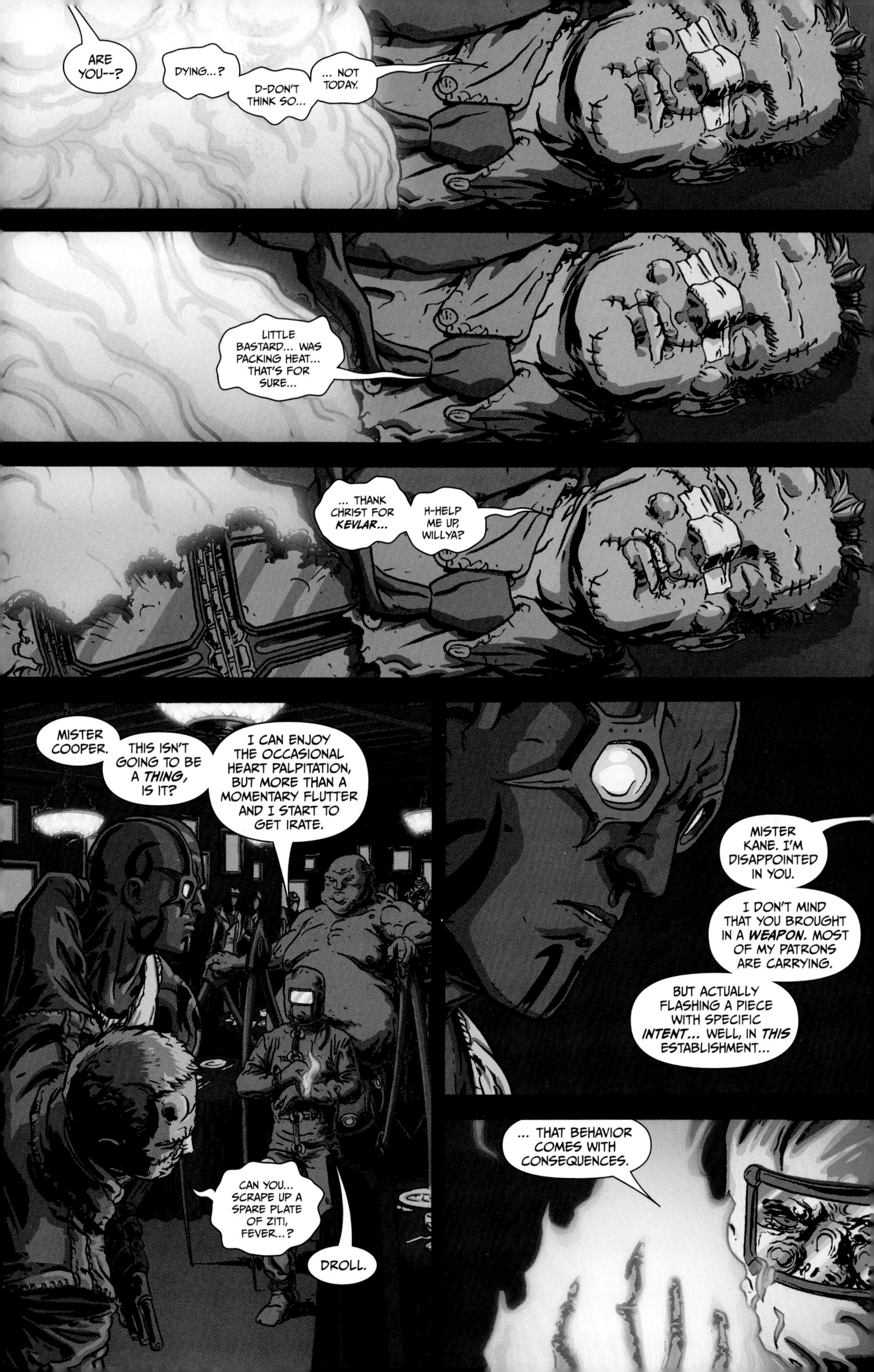
ARE YOU--?
DYING...?
D-DON'T THINK SO...
... NOT TODAY.
LITTLE BASTARD... WAS PACKING HEAT... THAT'S FOR SURE...
... THANK CHRIST FOR KEVLAR...
H-HELP ME UP, WILLYA?
MISTER COOPER.
THIS ISN'T GOING TO BE A THING, IS IT?
I CAN ENJOY THE OCCASIONAL HEART PALPITATION, BUT MORE THAN A MOMENTARY FLUTTER AND I START TO GET IRATE.
CAN YOU... SCRAPE UP A SPARE PLATE OF ZITI, FEVER...?
DROLL.
MISTER KANE. I'M DISAPPOINTED IN YOU.
I DON'T MIND THAT YOU BROUGHT IN A WEAPON. MOST OF MY PATRONS ARE CARRYING.
BUT ACTUALLY FLASHING A PIECE WITH SPECIFIC INTENT... WELL, IN THIS ESTABLISHMENT...
... THAT BEHAVIOR COMES WITH CONSEQUENCES.

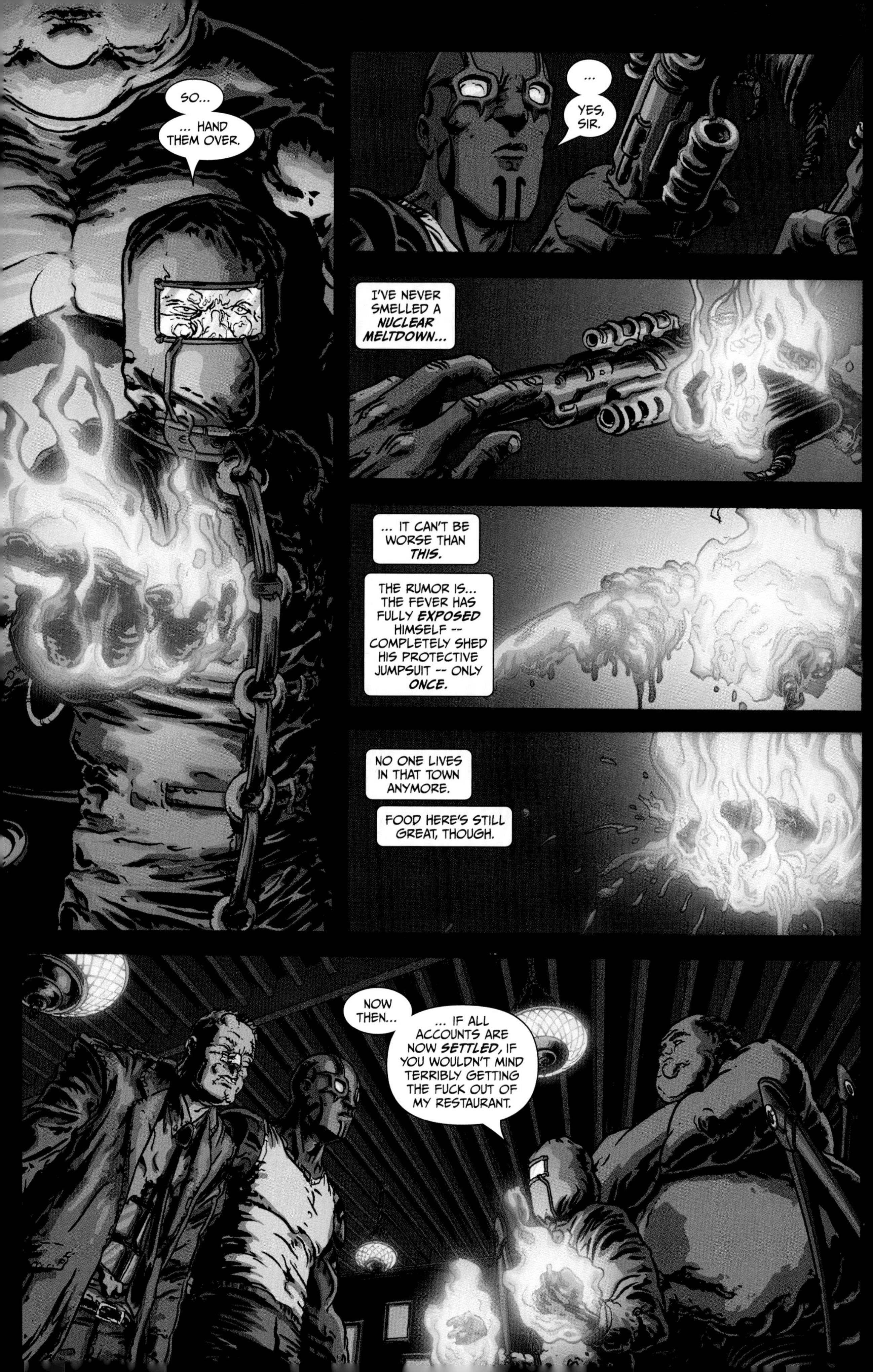
SO...
... HAND THEM OVER.
...
YES, SIR.
I'VE NEVER SMELLED A NUCLEAR MELTDOWN...
... IT CAN'T BE WORSE THAN THIS.
THE RUMOR IS... THE FEVER HAS FULLY EXPOSED HIMSELF -- COMPLETELY SHED HIS PROTECTIVE JUMPSUIT -- ONLY ONCE.
NO ONE LIVES IN THAT TOWN ANYMORE.
FOOD HERE'S STILL GREAT, THOUGH.
NOW THEN...
... IF ALL ACCOUNTS ARE NOW SETTLED, IF YOU WOULDN'T MIND TERRIBLY GETTING THE FUCK OUT OF MY RESTAURANT.

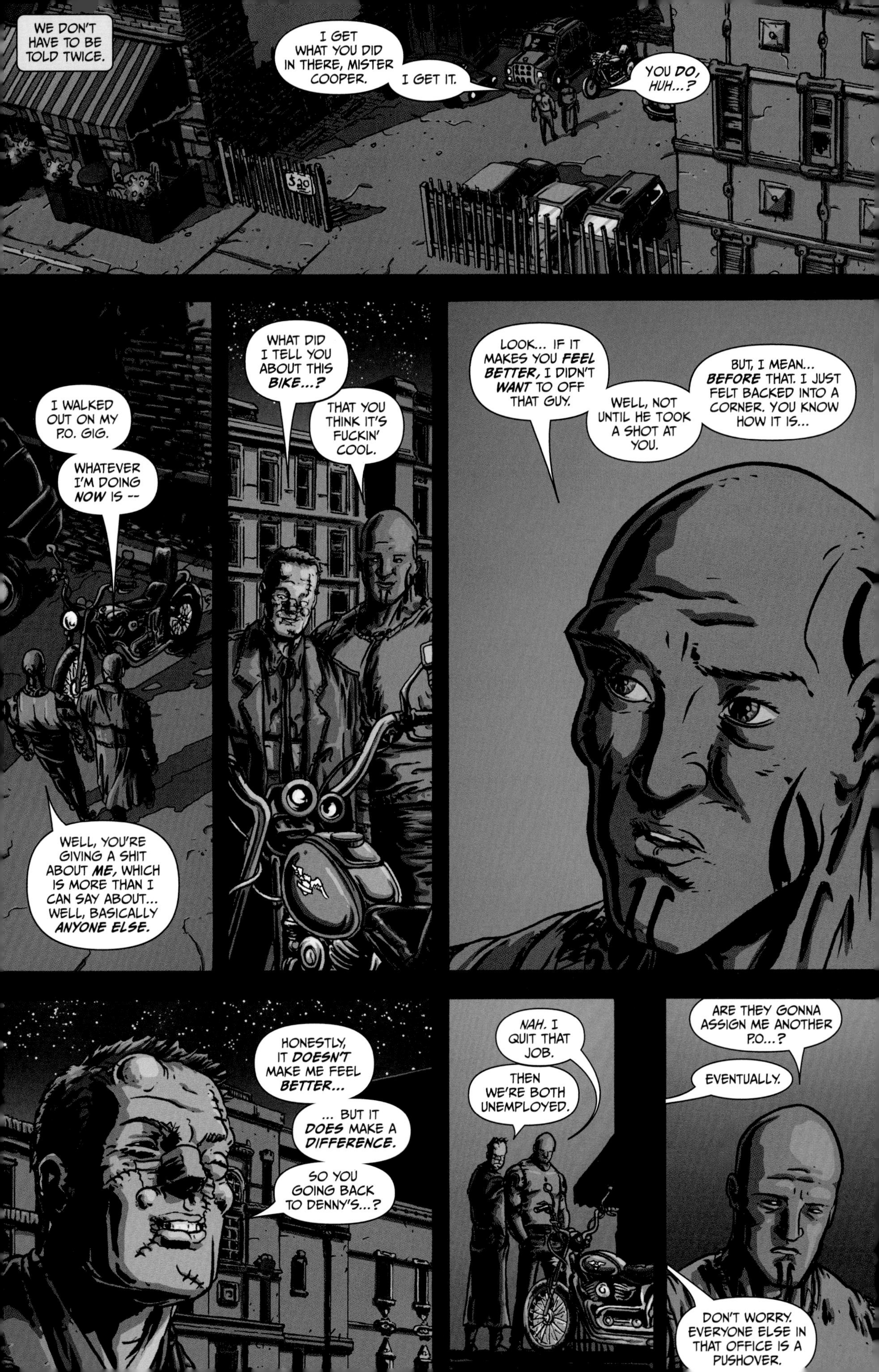
WE DON'T HAVE TO BE TOLD TWICE.
I GET WHAT YOU DID IN THERE, MISTER COOPER.
I GET IT.
YOU DO, HUH...?
$20
I WALKED OUT ON MY P.O. GIG.
WHATEVER I'M DOING NOW IS --
WELL, YOU'RE GIVING A SHIT ABOUT ME, WHICH IS MORE THAN I CAN SAY ABOUT... WELL, BASICALLY ANYONE ELSE.
WHAT DID I TELL YOU ABOUT THIS BIKE...?
THAT YOU THINK IT'S FUCKIN' COOL.
LOOK... IF IT MAKES YOU FEEL BETTER, I DIDN'T WANT TO OFF THAT GUY.
WELL, NOT UNTIL HE TOOK A SHOT AT YOU.
BUT, I MEAN... BEFORE THAT. I JUST FELT BACKED INTO A CORNER. YOU KNOW HOW IT IS...
HONESTLY, IT DOESN'T MAKE ME FEEL BETTER...
... BUT IT DOES MAKE A DIFFERENCE.
SO YOU GOING BACK TO DENNY'S...?
NAH. I QUIT THAT JOB.
THEN WE'RE BOTH UNEMPLOYED.
ARE THEY GONNA ASSIGN ME ANOTHER P.O...?
EVENTUALLY.
DON'T WORRY. EVERYONE ELSE IN THAT OFFICE IS A PUSHOVER.

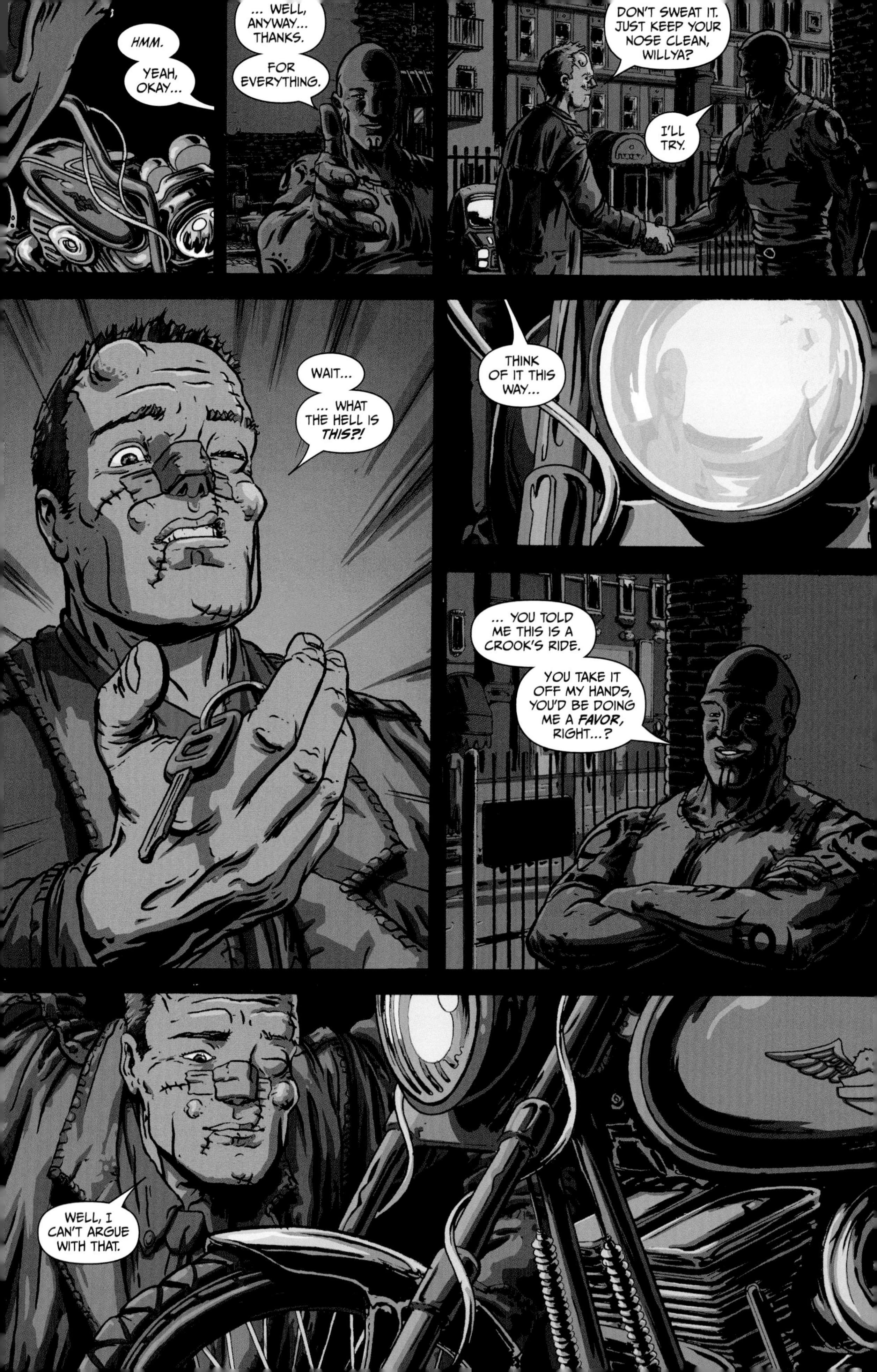
HMM.
YEAH, OKAY...
... WELL, ANYWAY... THANKS.
FOR EVERYTHING.
DON'T SWEAT IT. JUST KEEP YOUR NOSE CLEAN, WILLYA?
I'LL TRY.
WAIT...
... WHAT THE HELL IS *THIS?!*
THINK OF IT THIS WAY...
... YOU TOLD ME THIS IS A CROOK'S RIDE.
YOU TAKE IT OFF MY HANDS, YOU'D BE DOING ME A *FAVOR,* RIGHT...?
WELL, I CAN'T ARGUE WITH THAT.

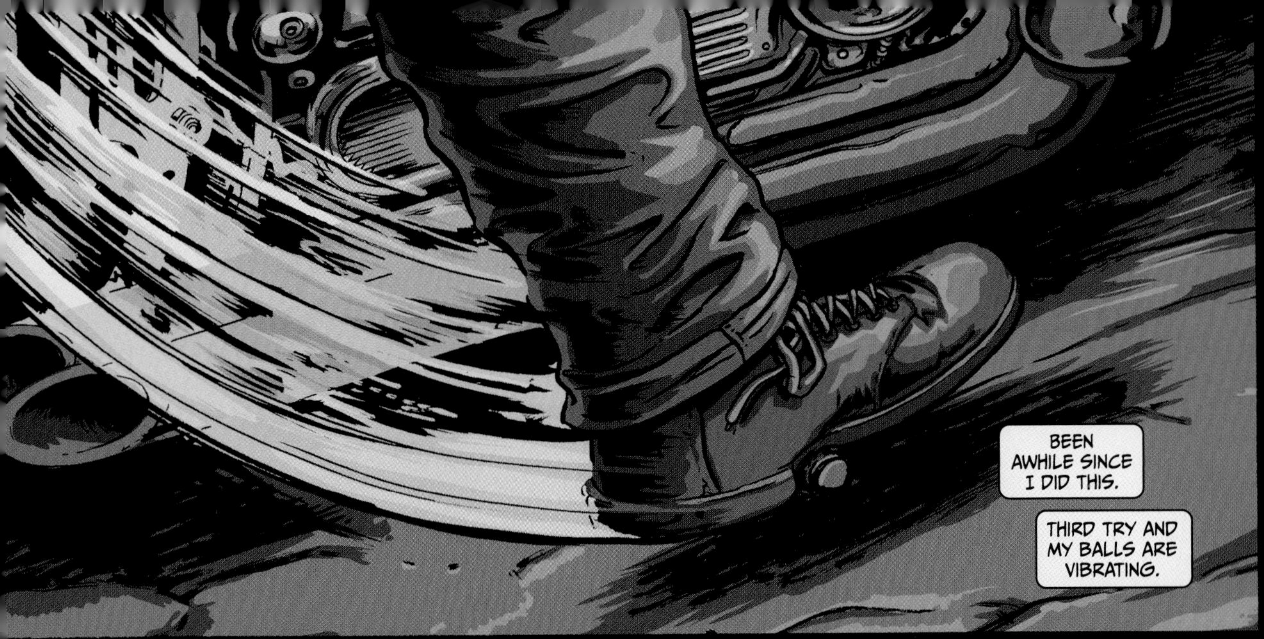
BEEN AWHILE SINCE I DID THIS.
THIRD TRY AND MY BALLS ARE VIBRATING.

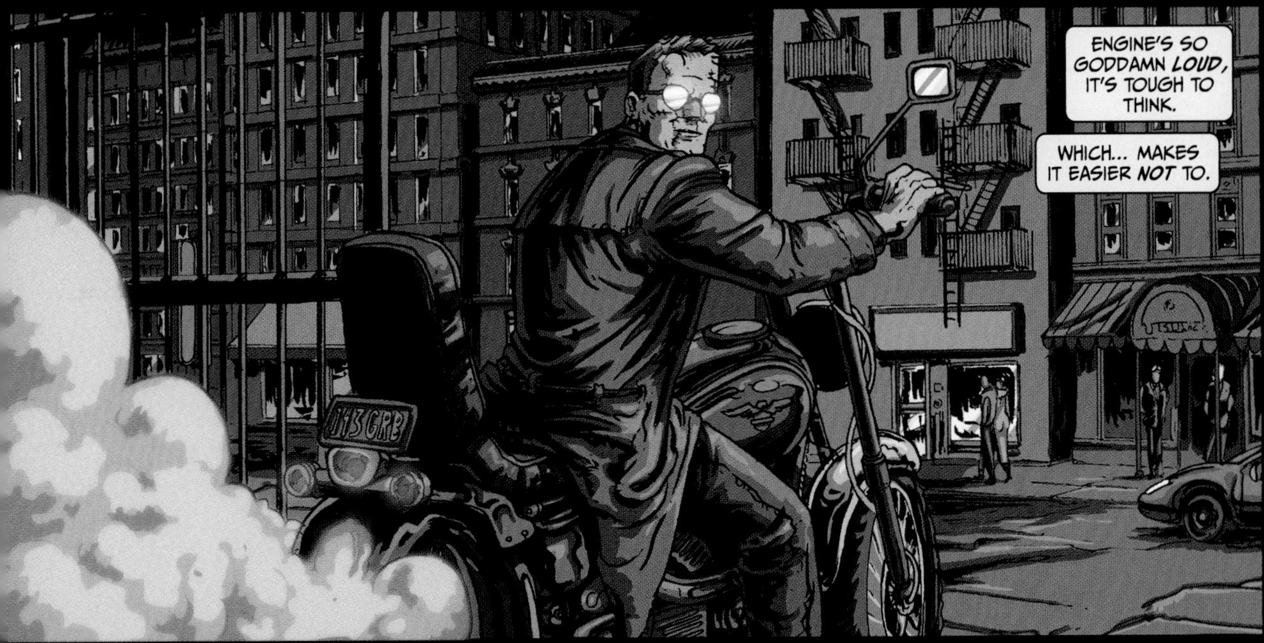
ENGINE'S SO GODDAMN *LOUD*, IT'S TOUGH TO THINK.
WHICH... MAKES IT EASIER *NOT* TO.

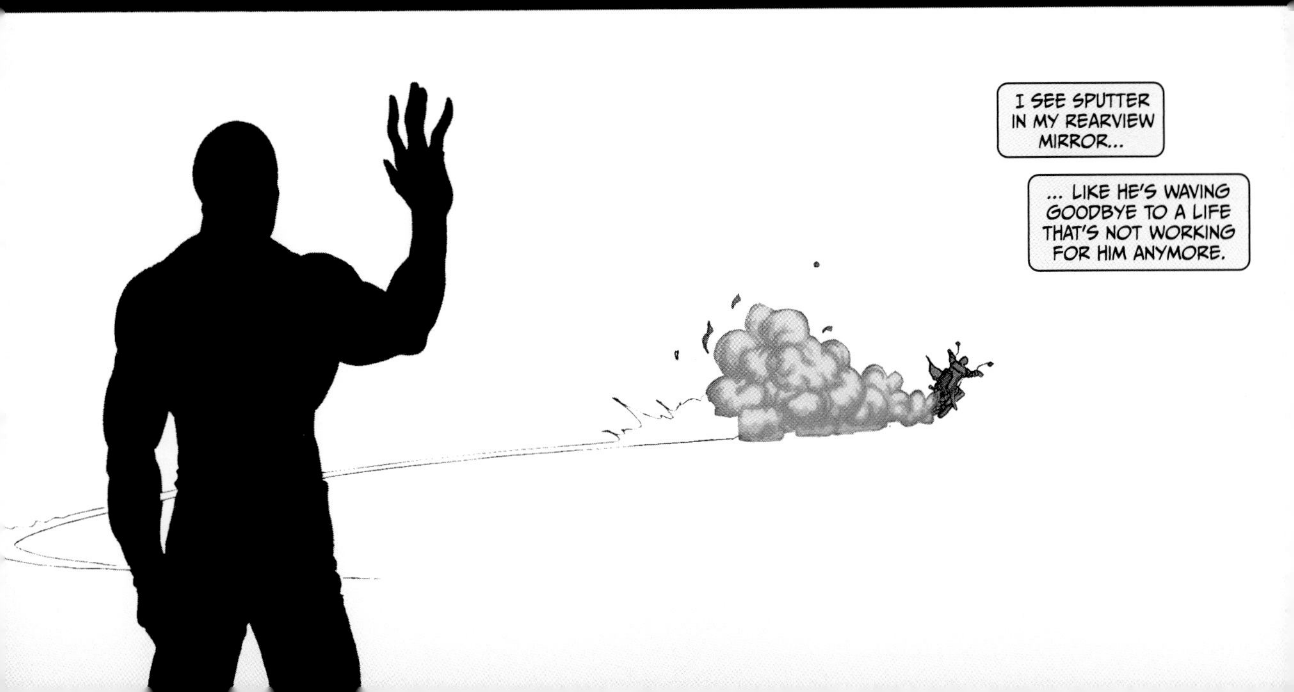
I SEE SPUTTER IN MY REARVIEW MIRROR...
... LIKE HE'S WAVING GOODBYE TO A LIFE THAT'S NOT WORKING FOR HIM ANYMORE.

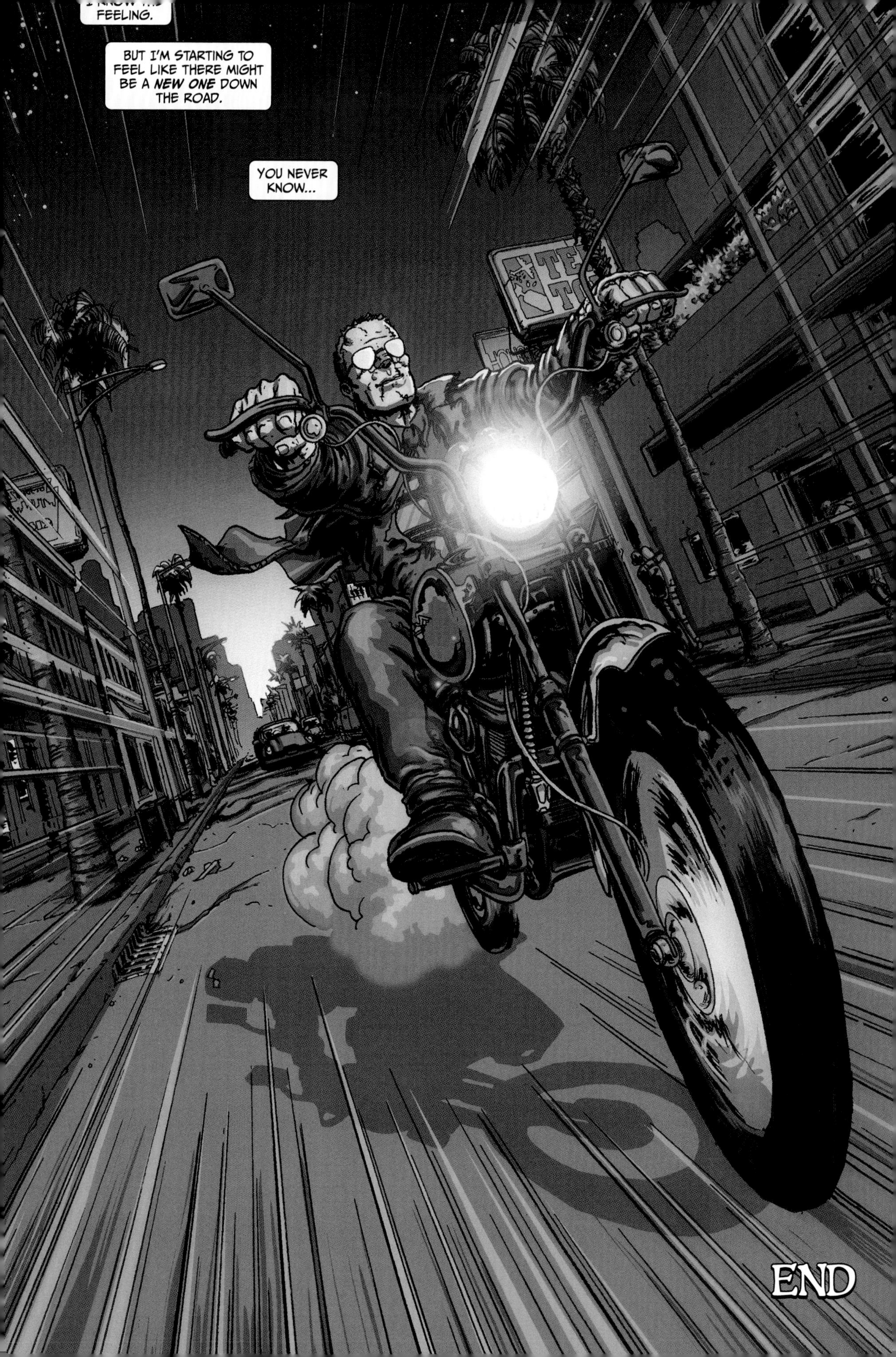
FEELING.
BUT I'M STARTING TO FEEL LIKE THERE MIGHT BE A *NEW ONE* DOWN THE ROAD.
YOU NEVER KNOW...
END

JOE CASEY

Dedicated in loving memory to **Christy McGee Vernon** (1970-2006).

Employed by the State of Tennessee Office of Criminal Justice, she was an invaluable resource while doing research for this book. More than that, she was a good friend at a specific time in my life when good friends were all that really mattered. This book wouldn't exist without her.

CHRIS BURNHAM

This one's for **Noah**, who is almost old enough to read it, and **Bea**, who is way too young.

ACKNOWLEDGEMENTS

PINUPS

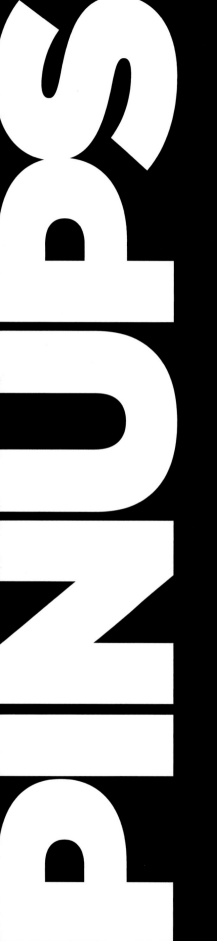

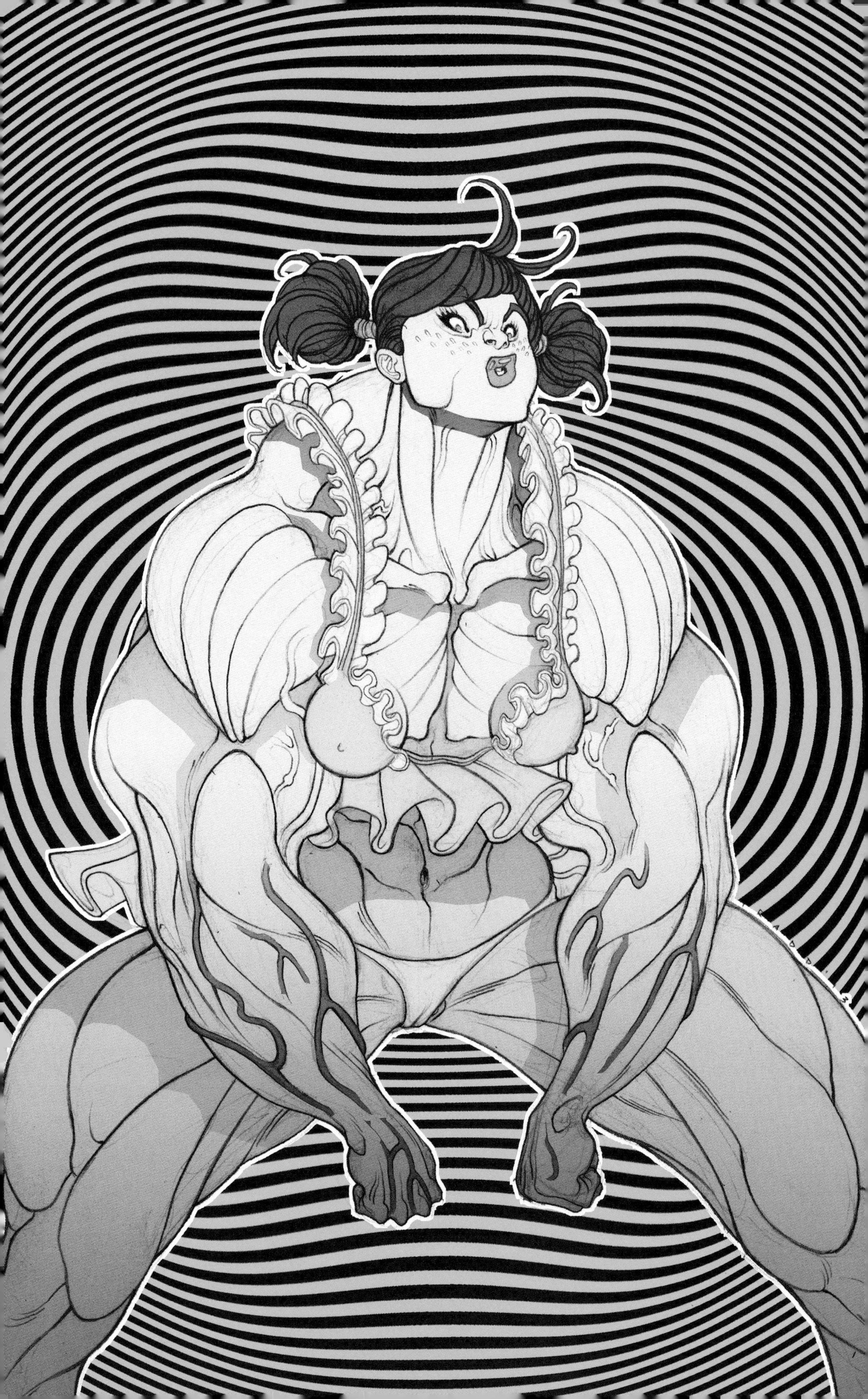

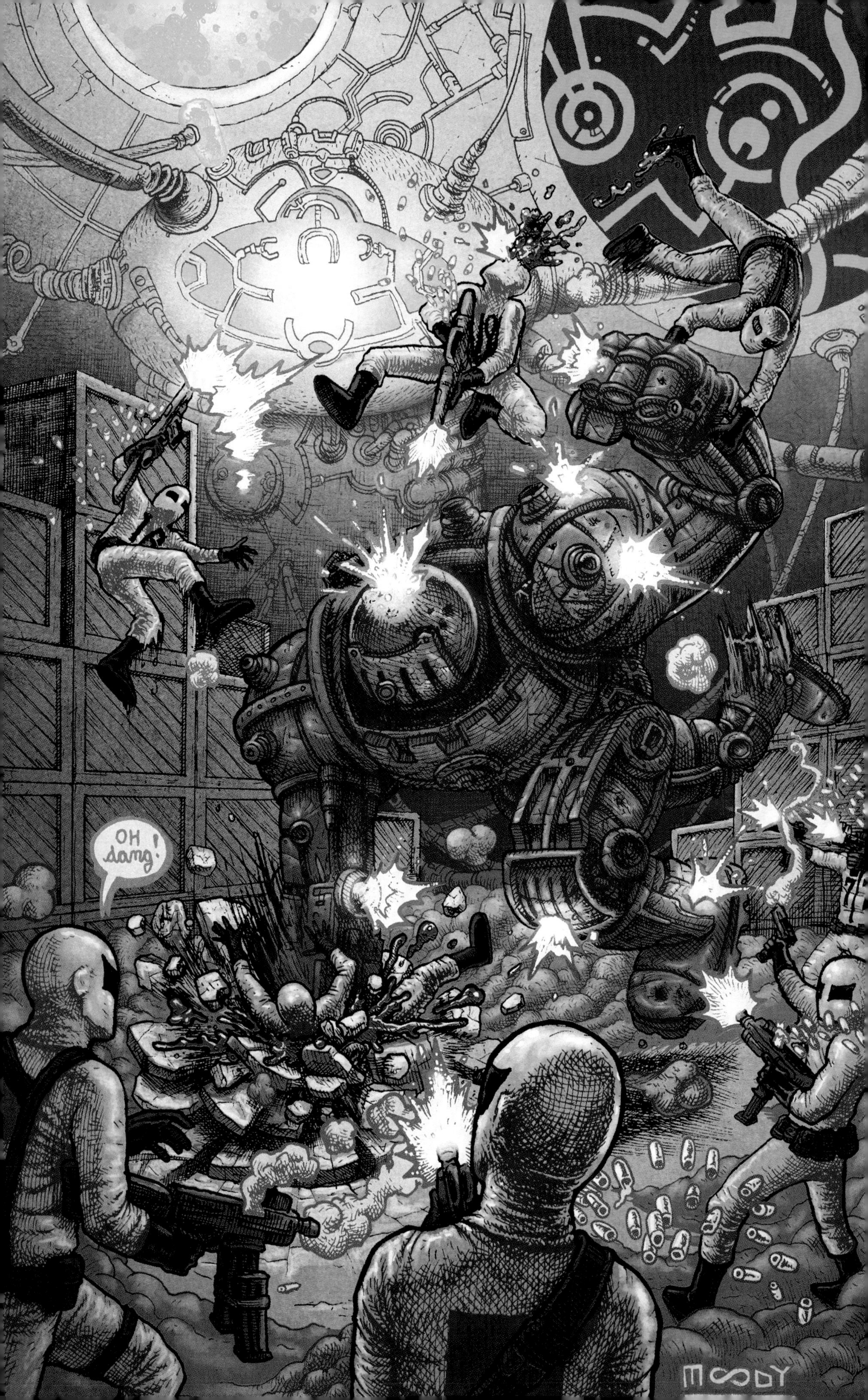
OH dang!
MOODY

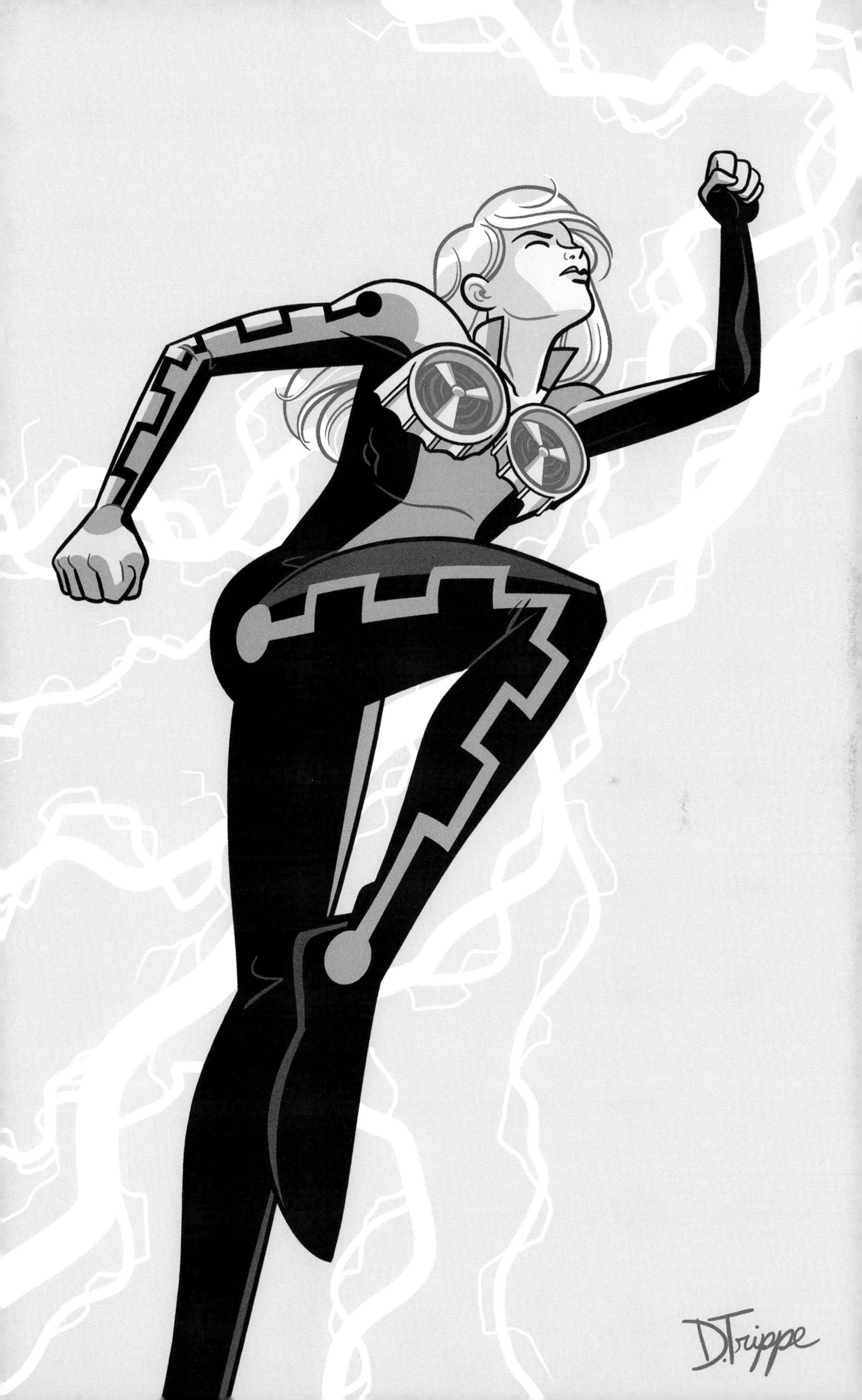
D.Trippe

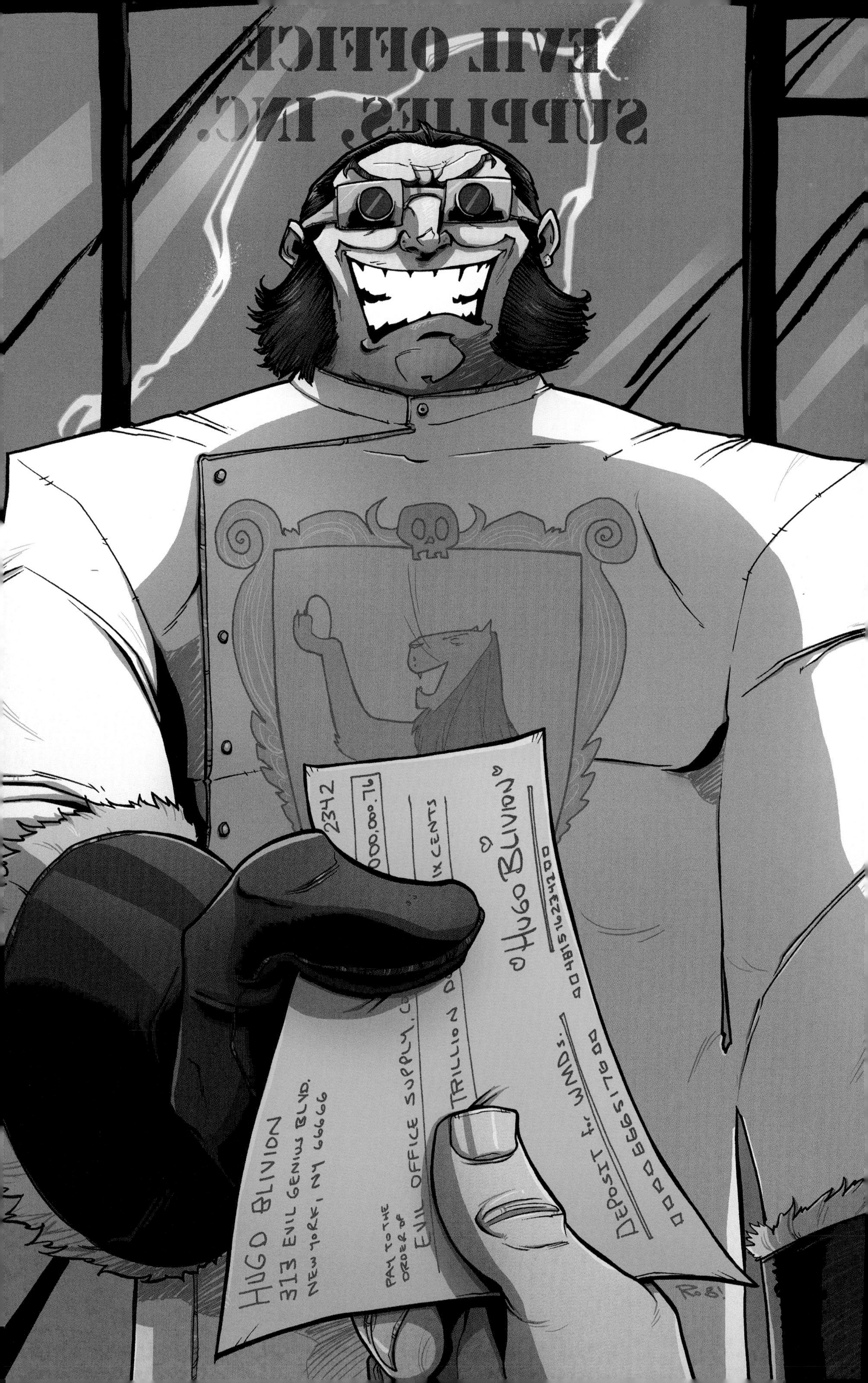

EVIL OFFICE
SUPPLIES, INC.
2342
HUGO BLIVION
313 EVIL GENIUS BLVD.
NEW YORK, NY 66666
PAY TO THE ORDER OF
OFFICE SUPPLY,
TRILLION
DEPOSIT for WMDs:
Hugo Blivion

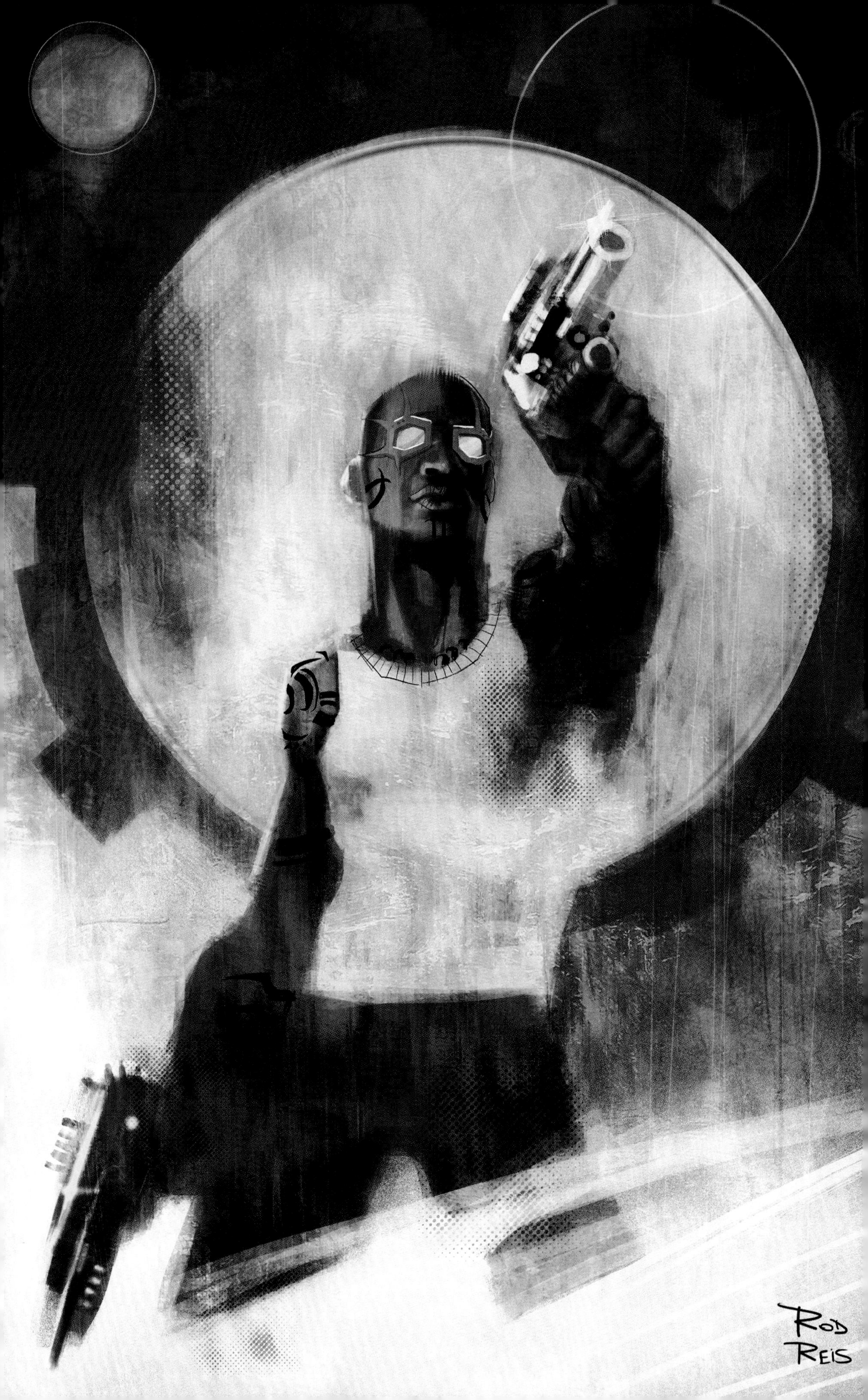
ROD
REIS

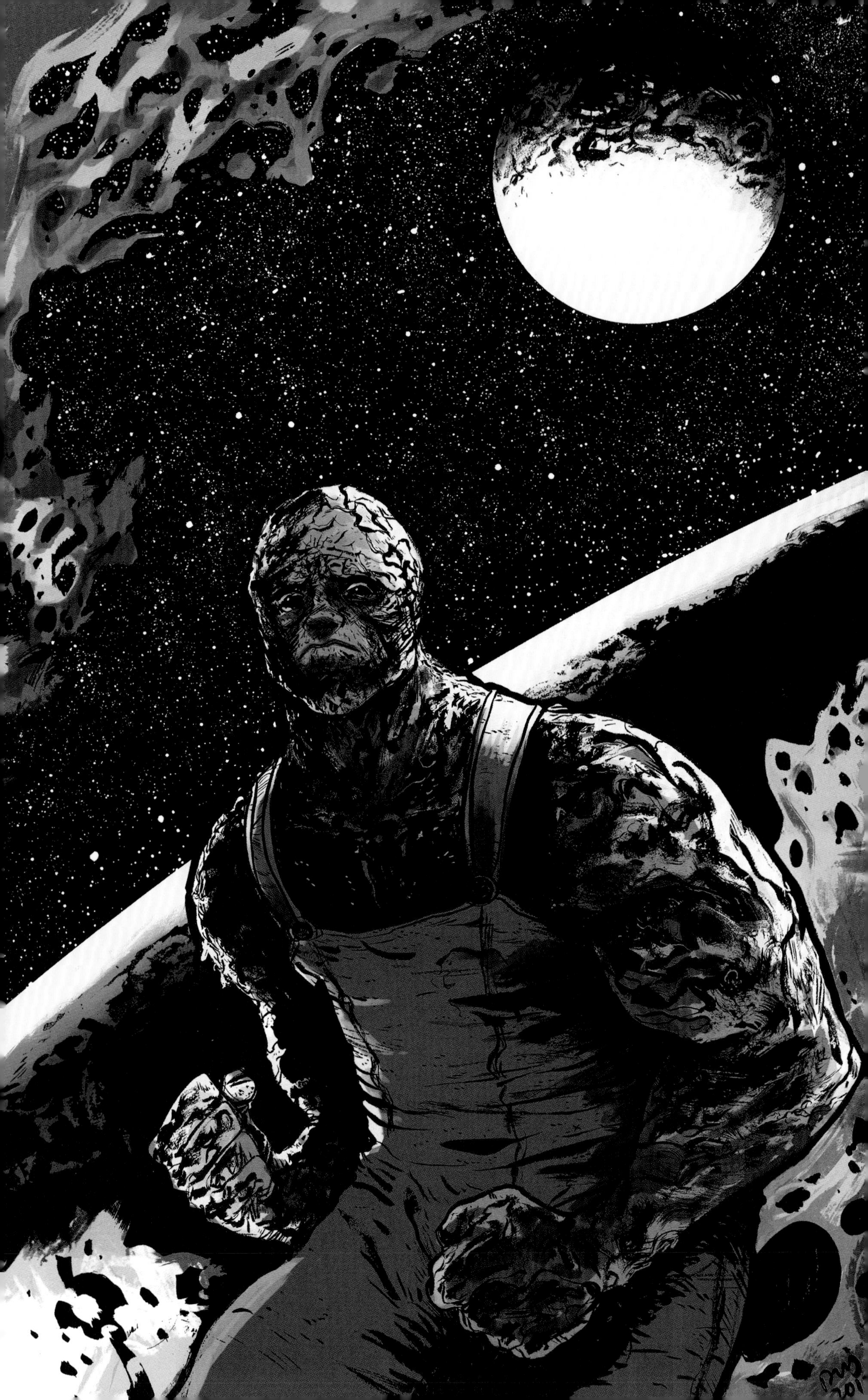

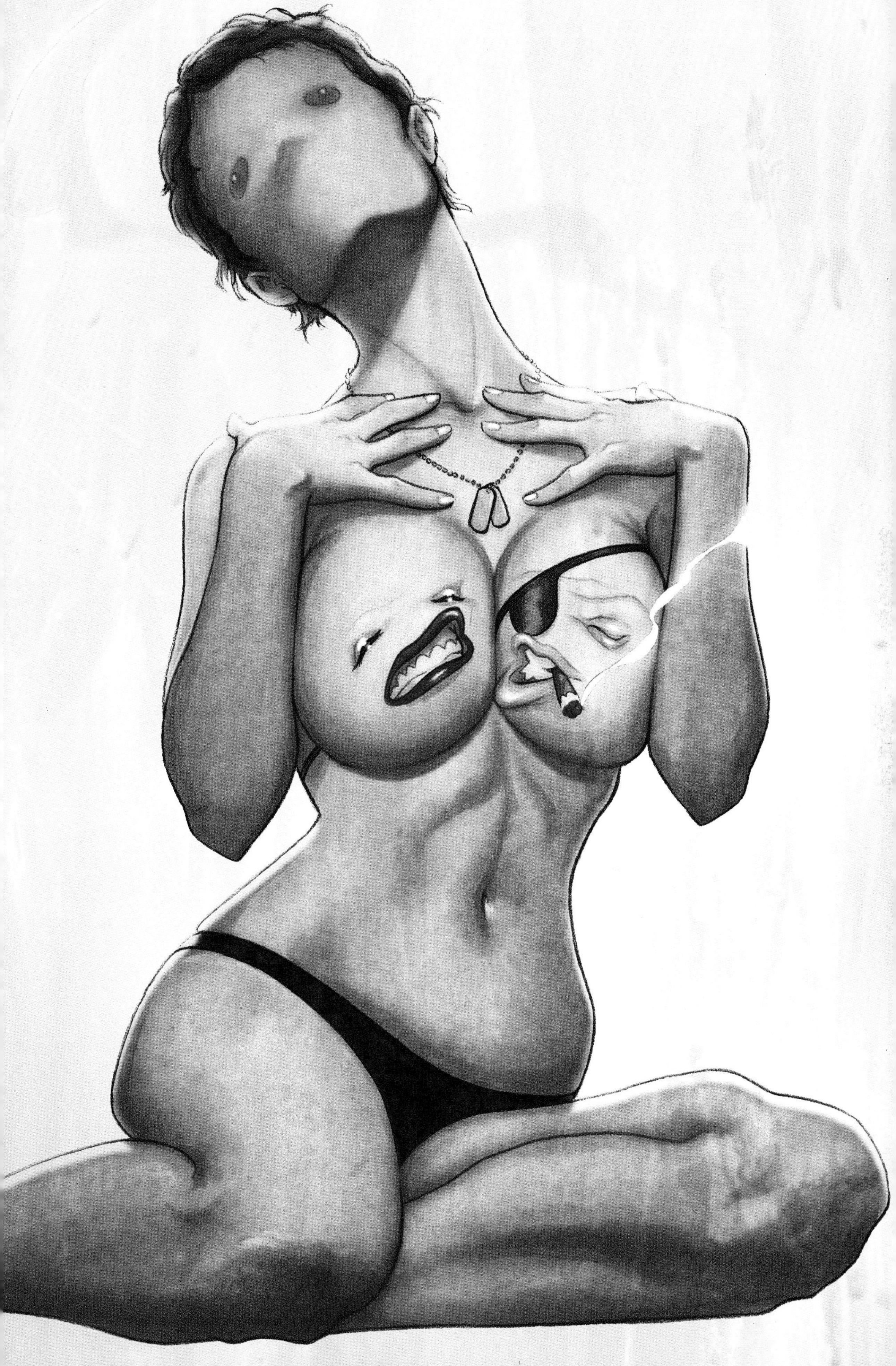

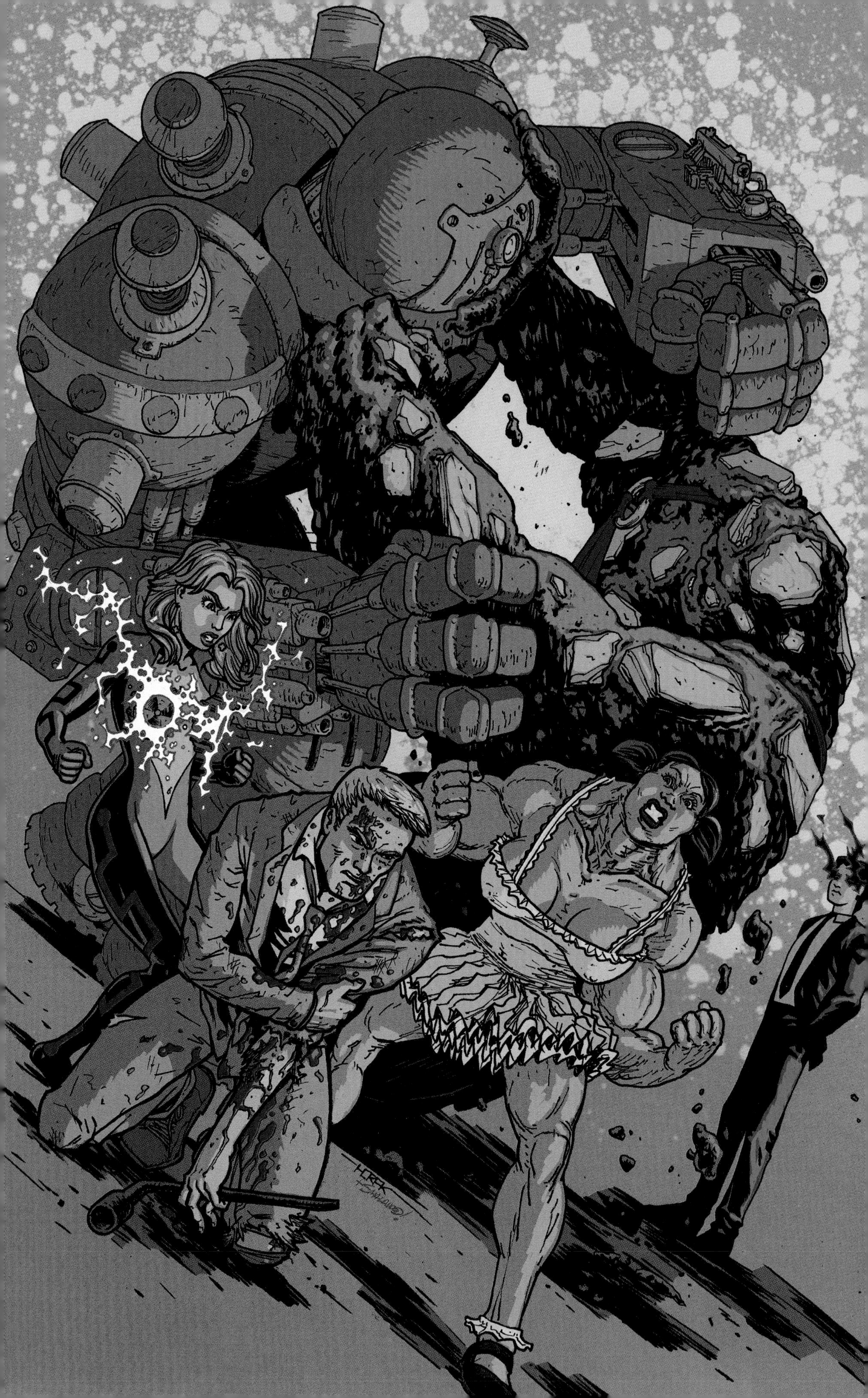

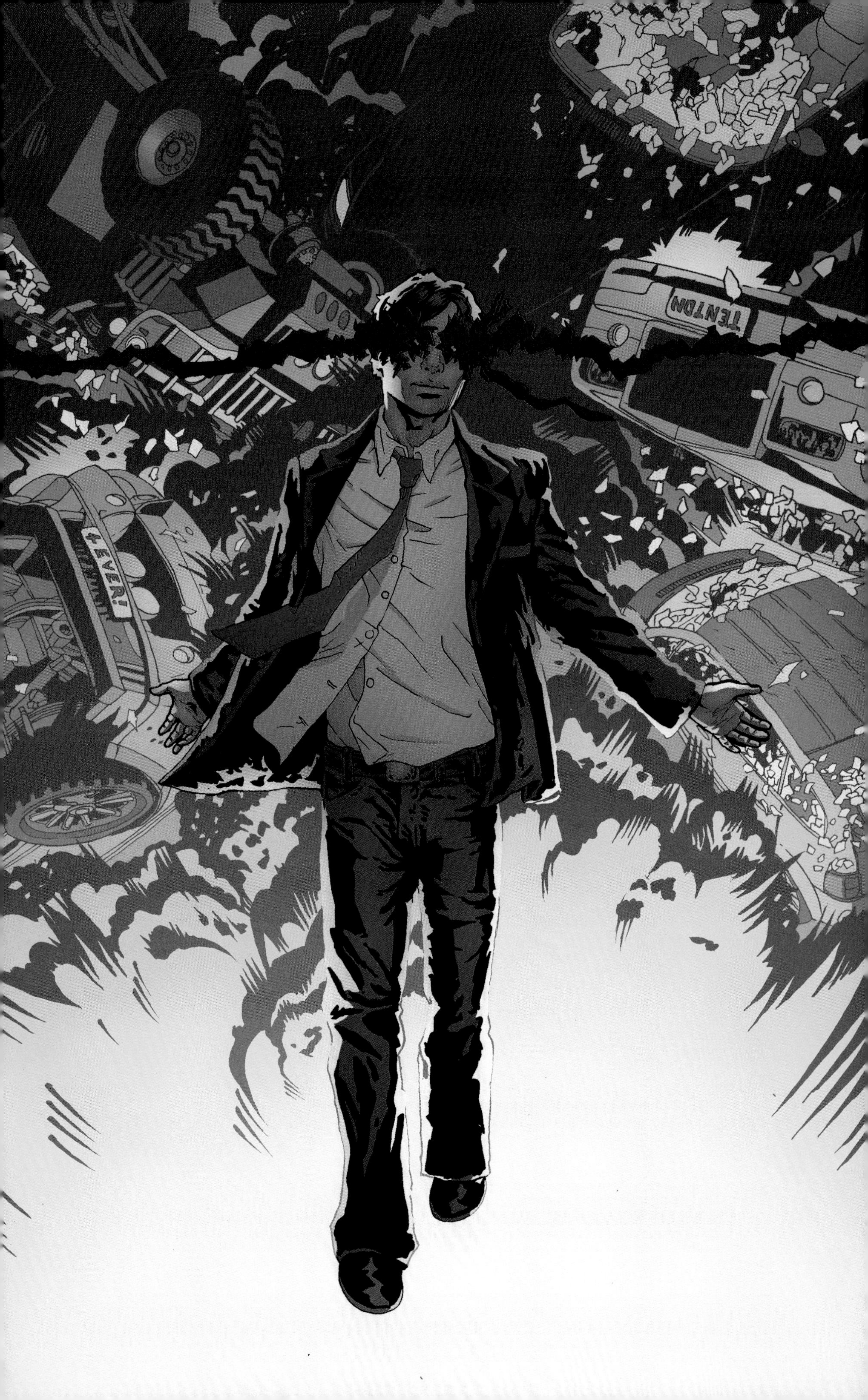
TENTON
4-EVER!

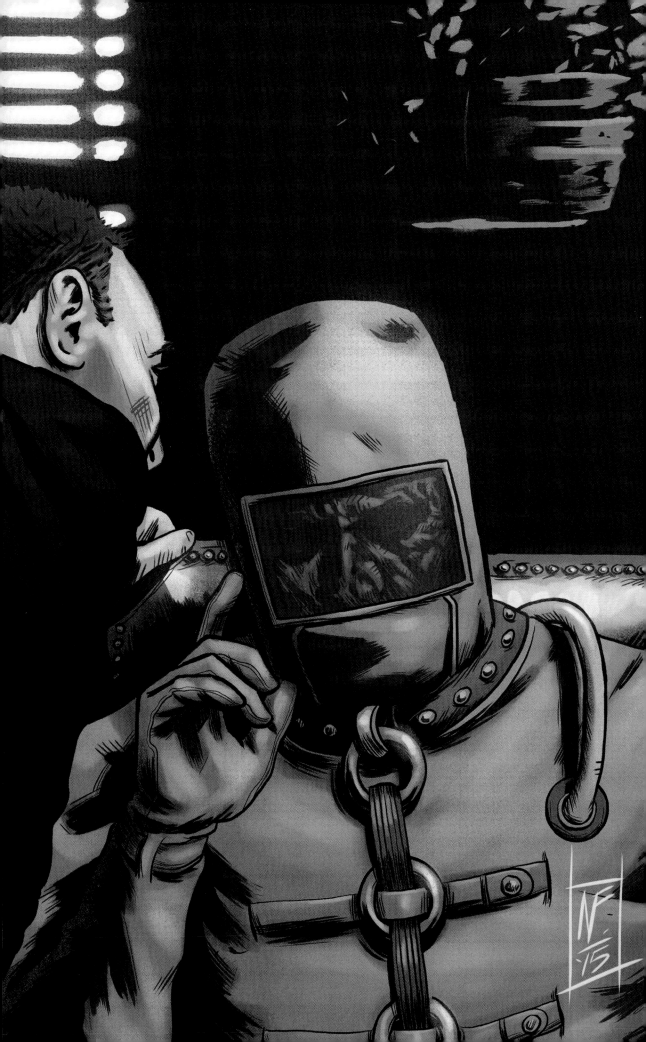

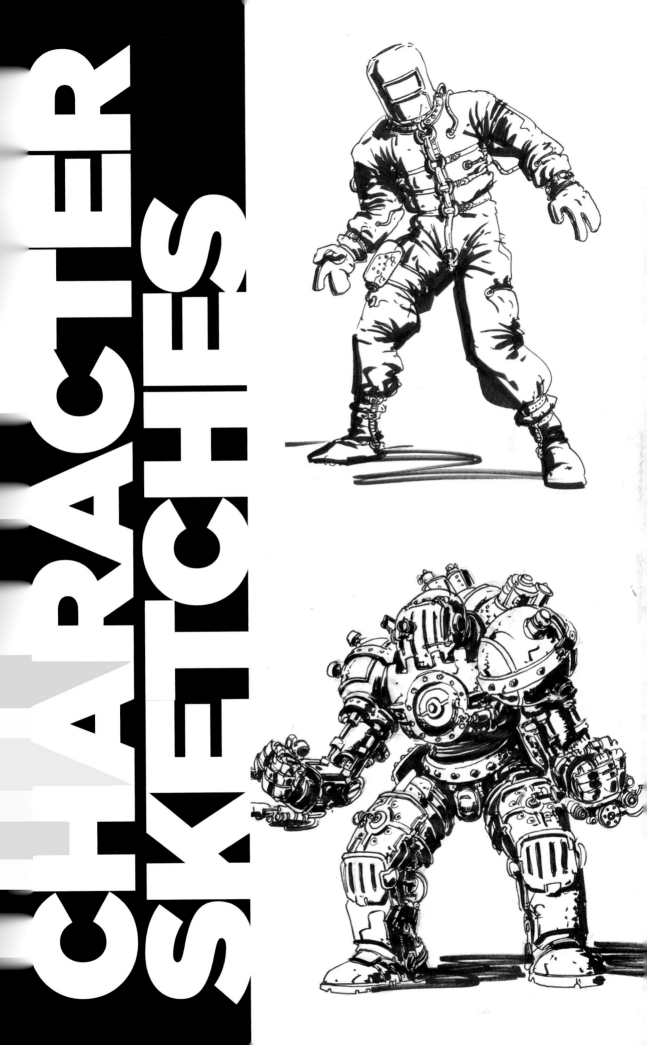

CHARACTER SKETCHES

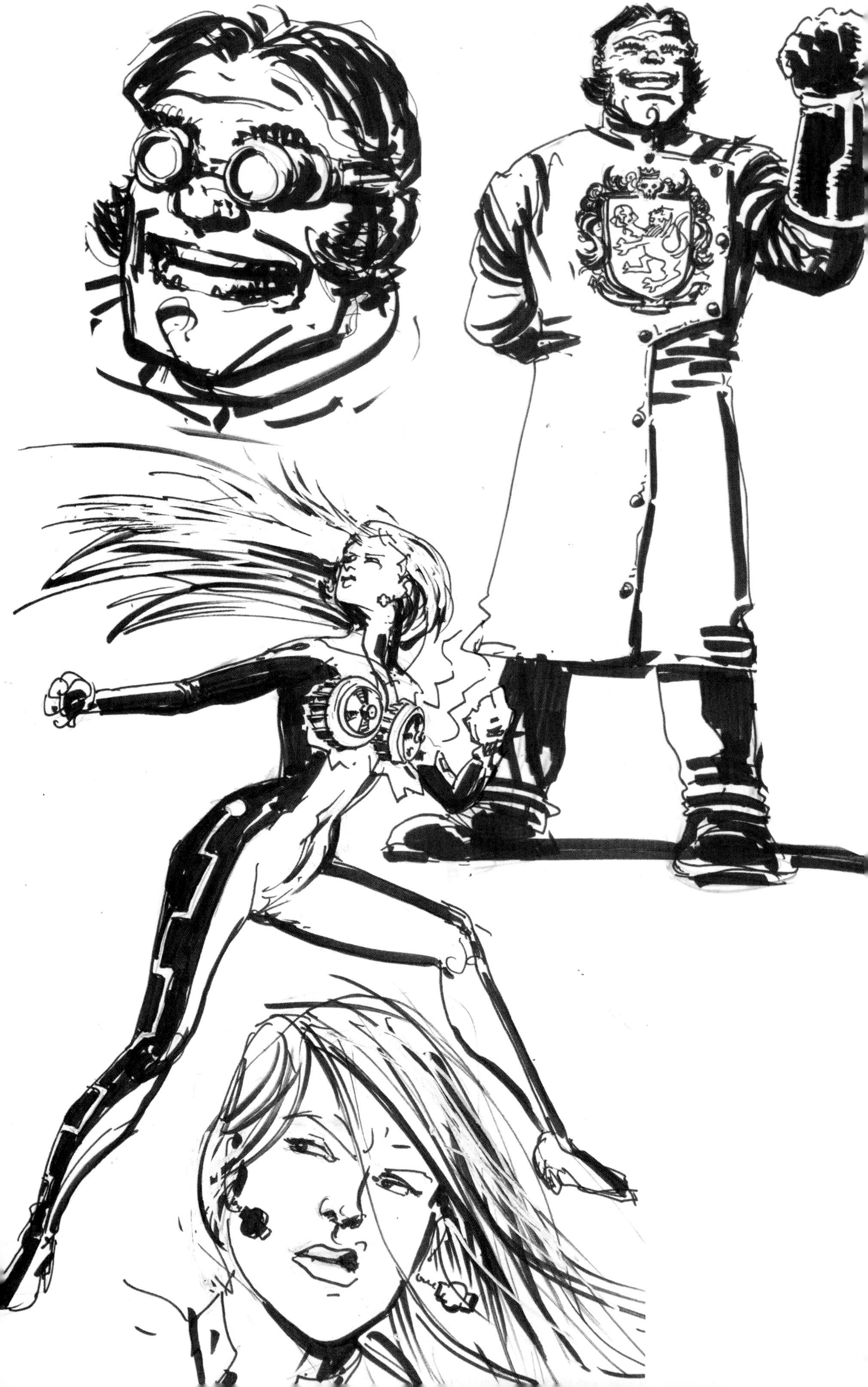

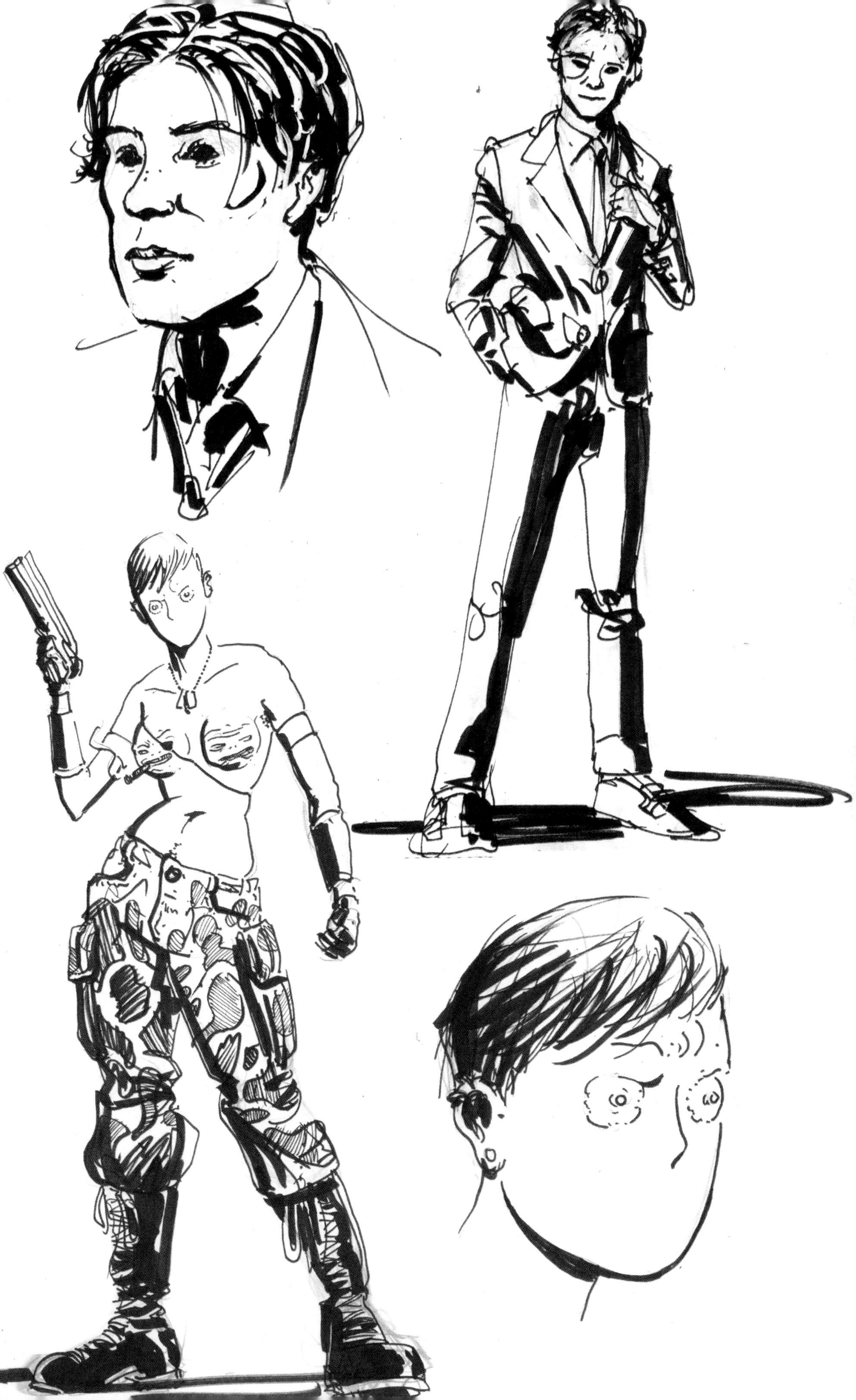

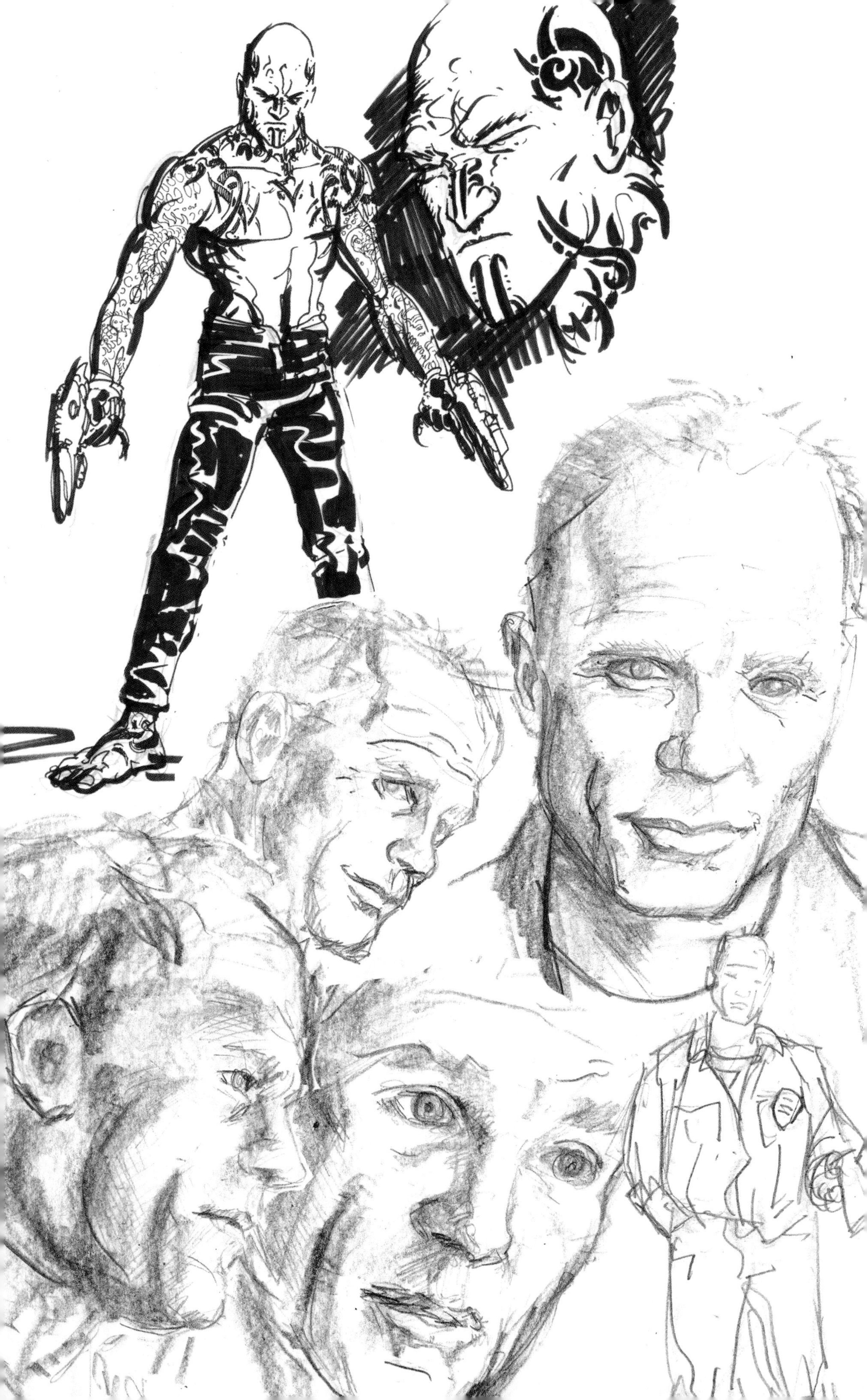

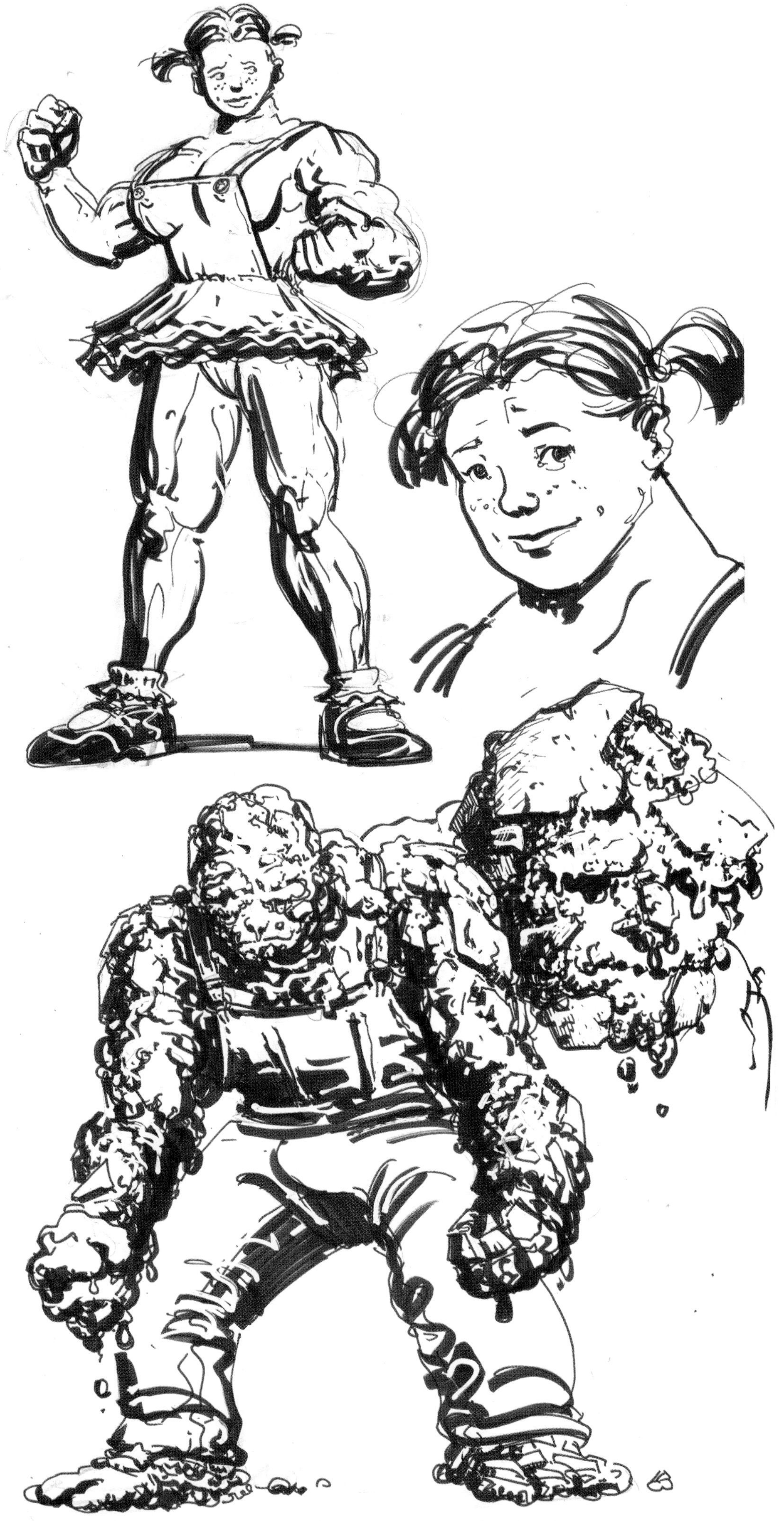

RAW SCANS

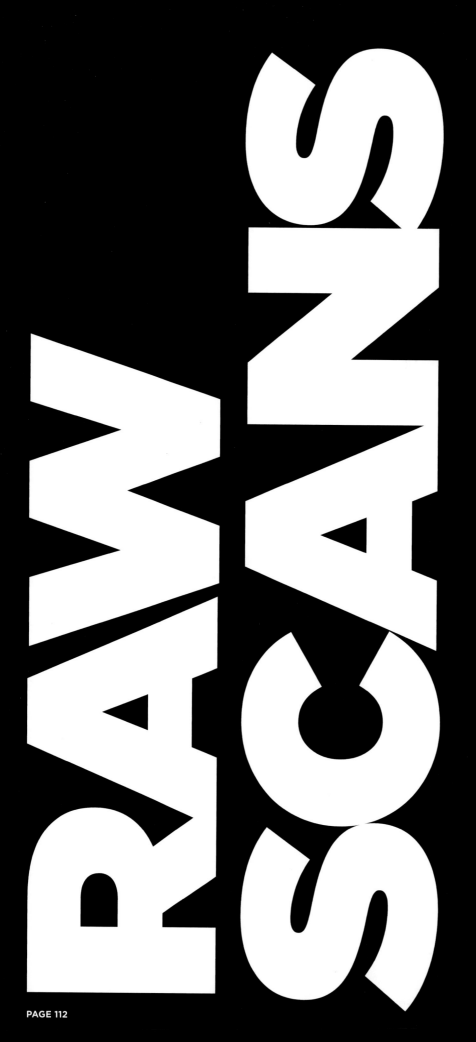

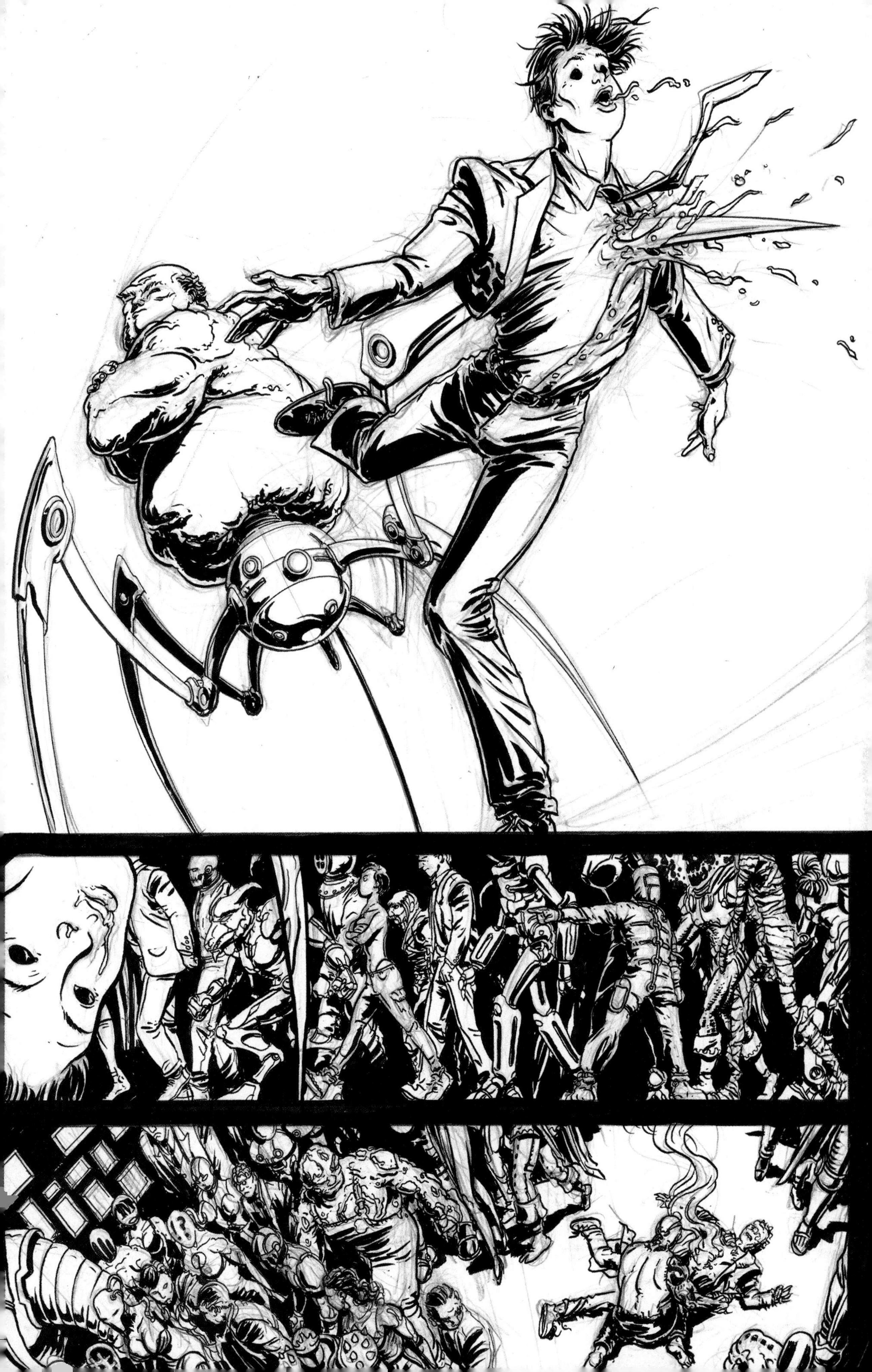

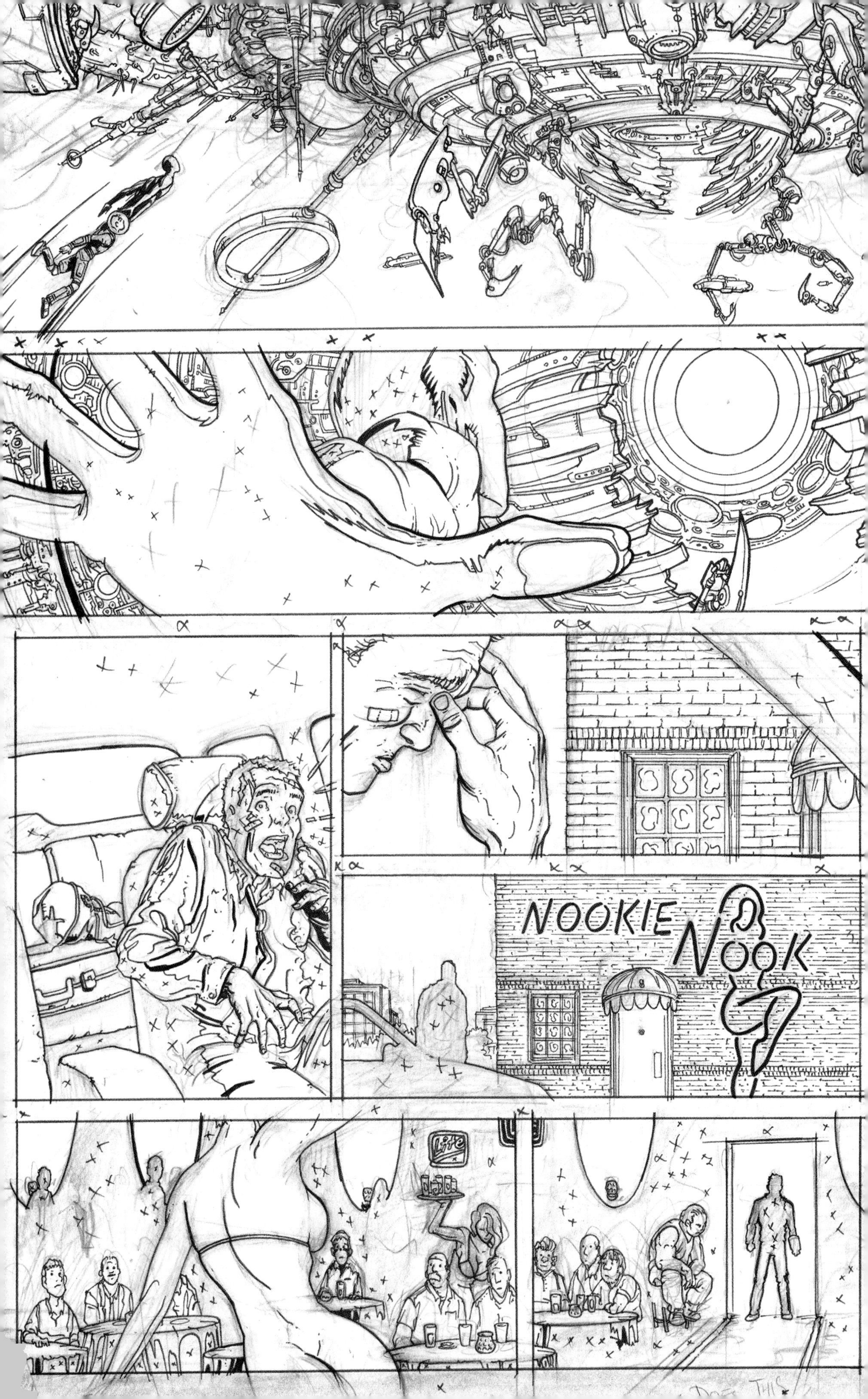

NOOKIE
NOOK
Lite

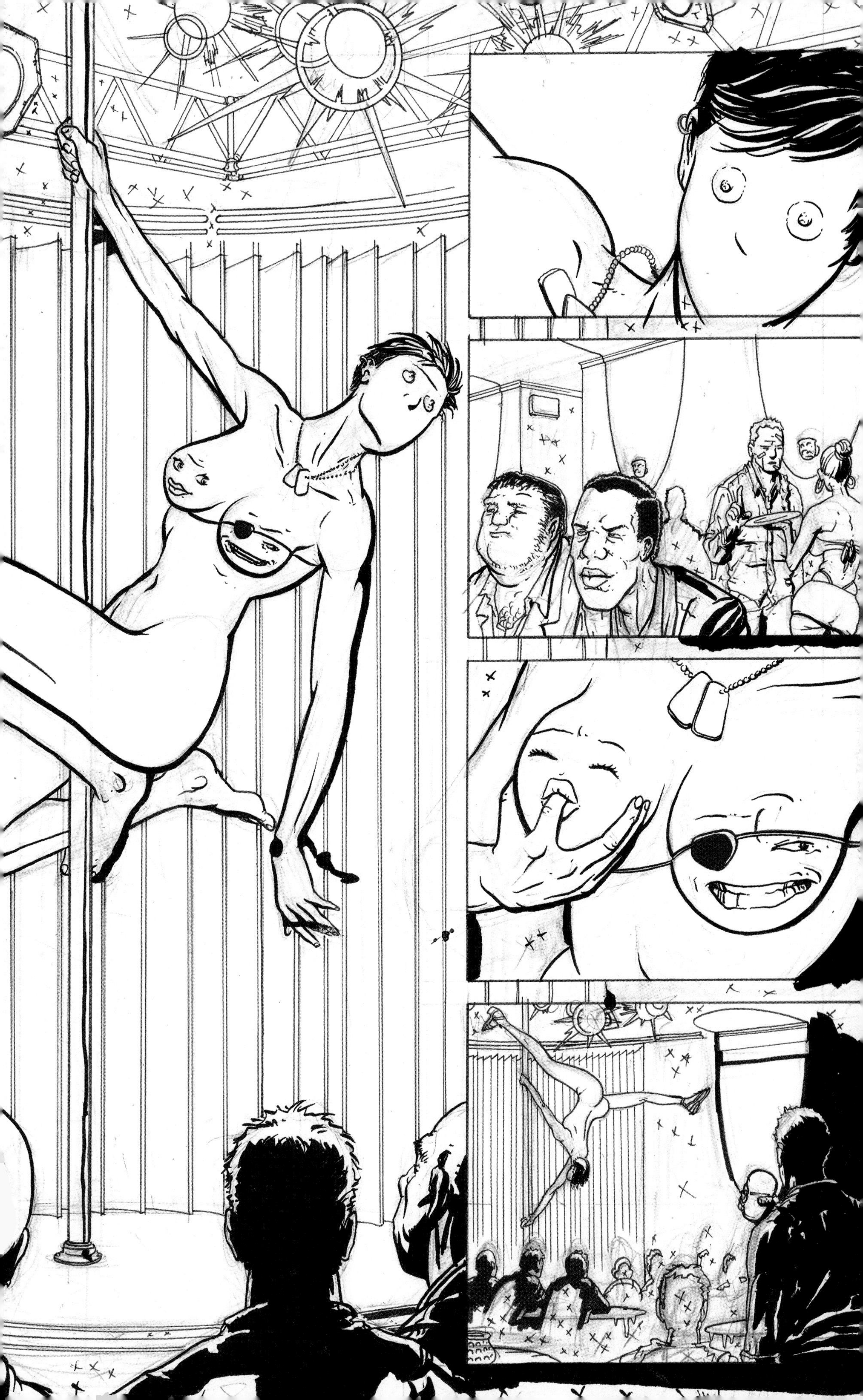

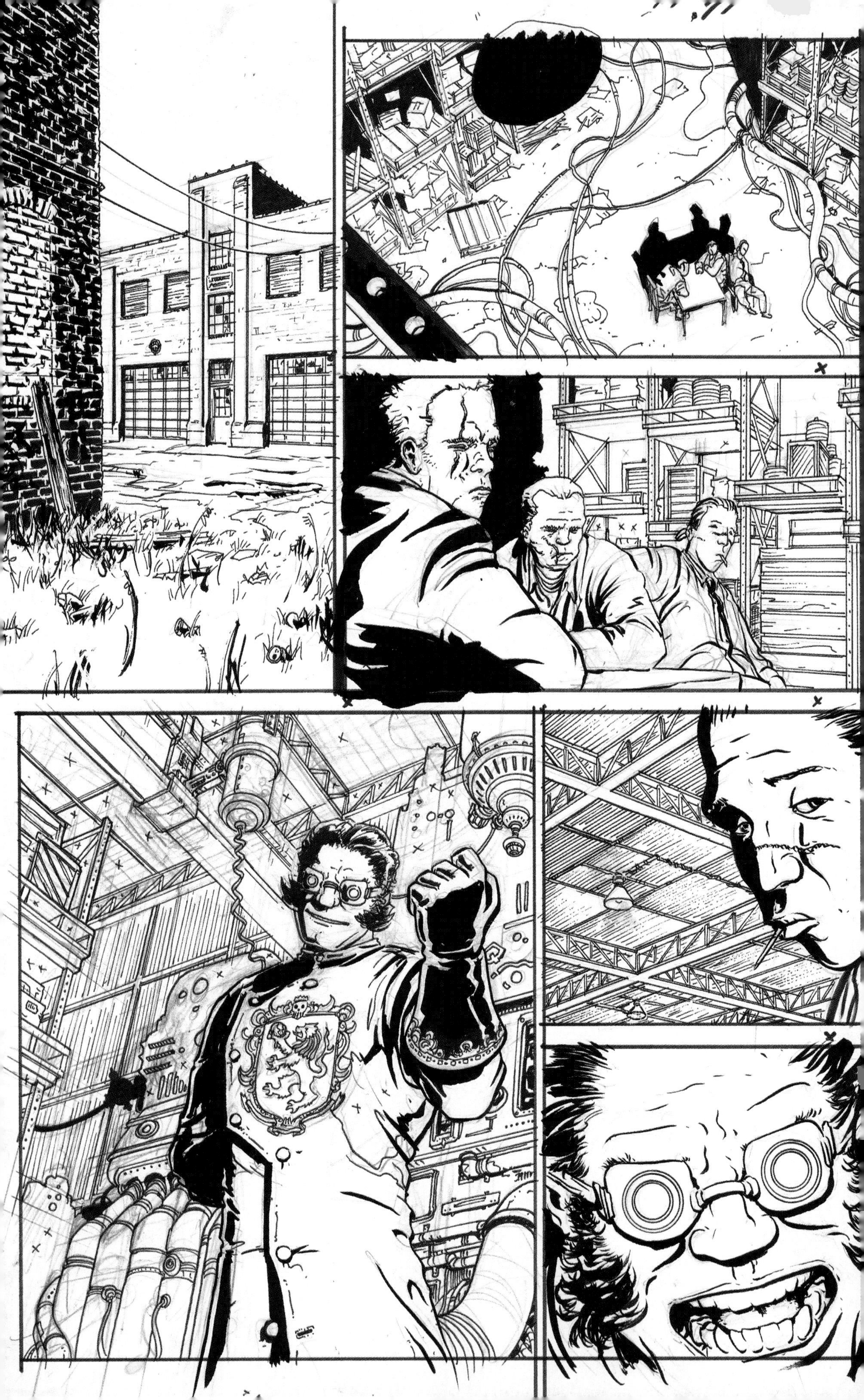

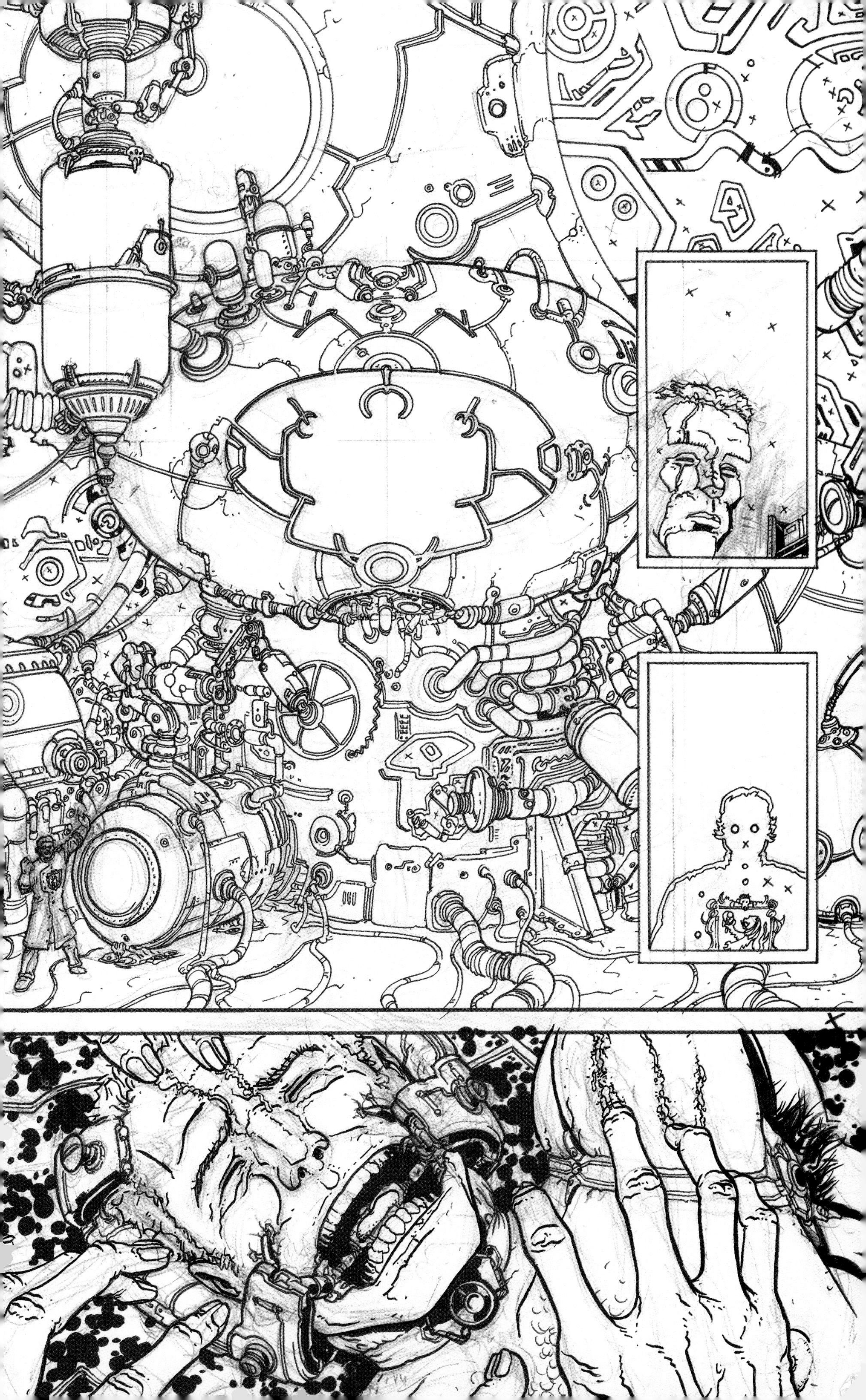

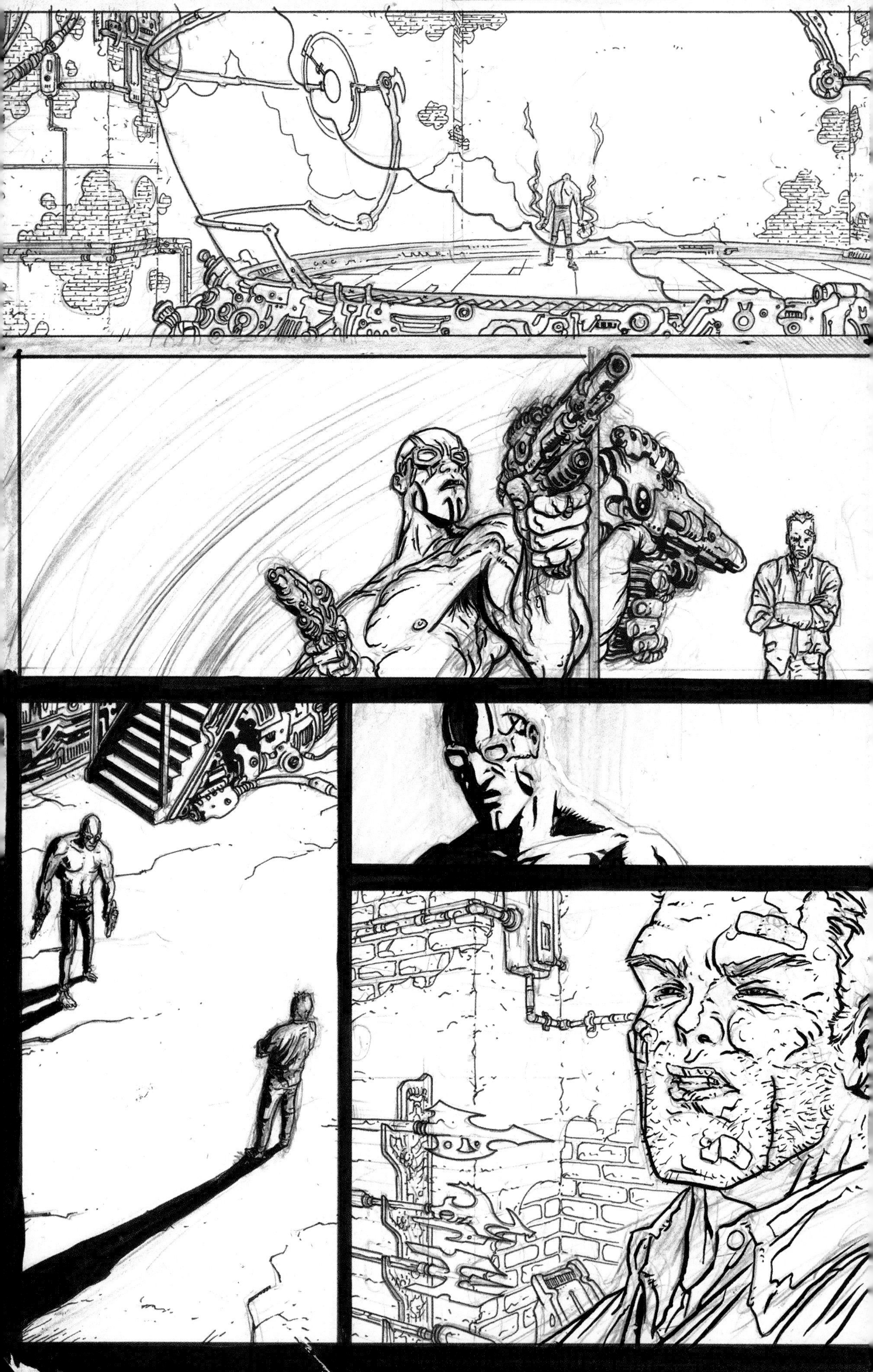

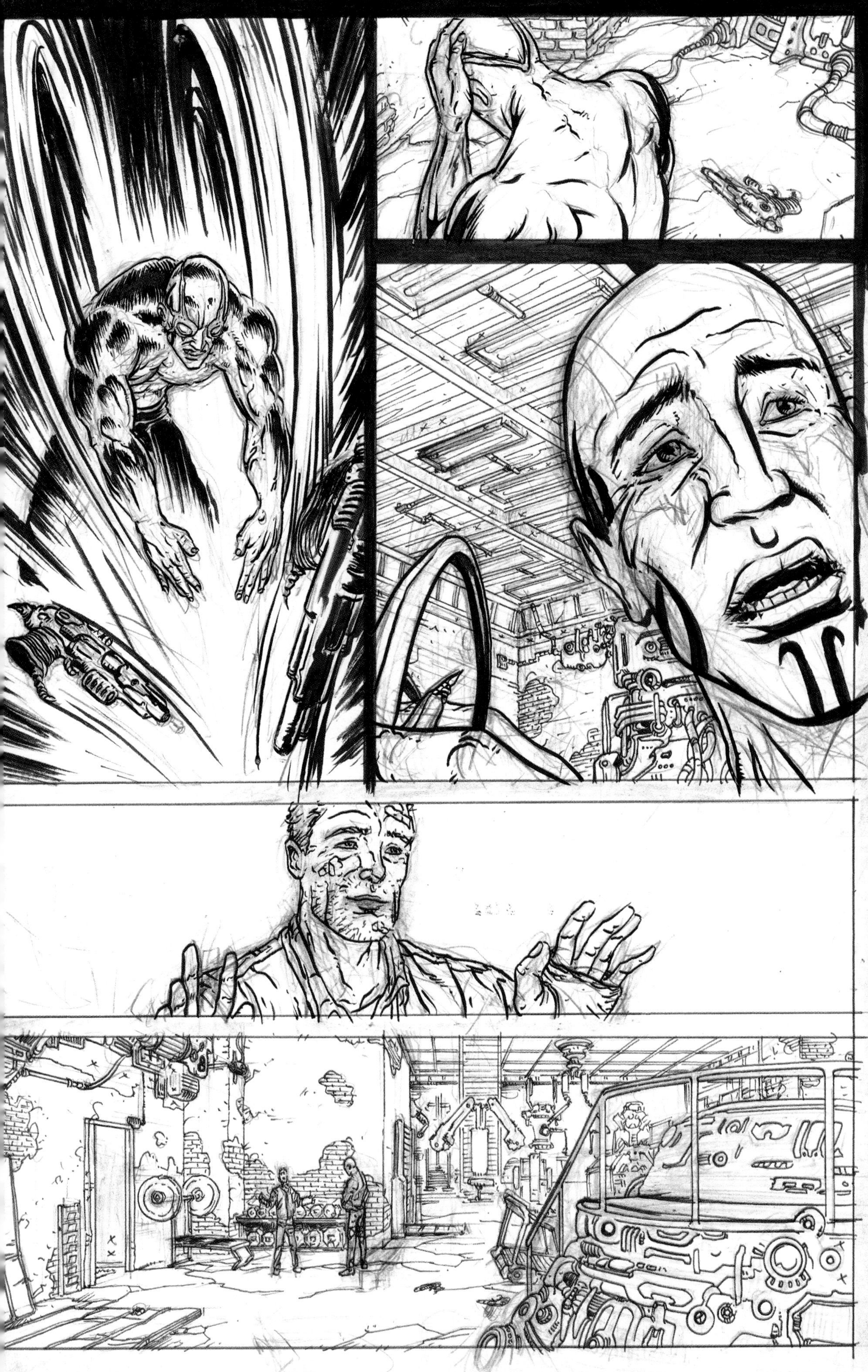

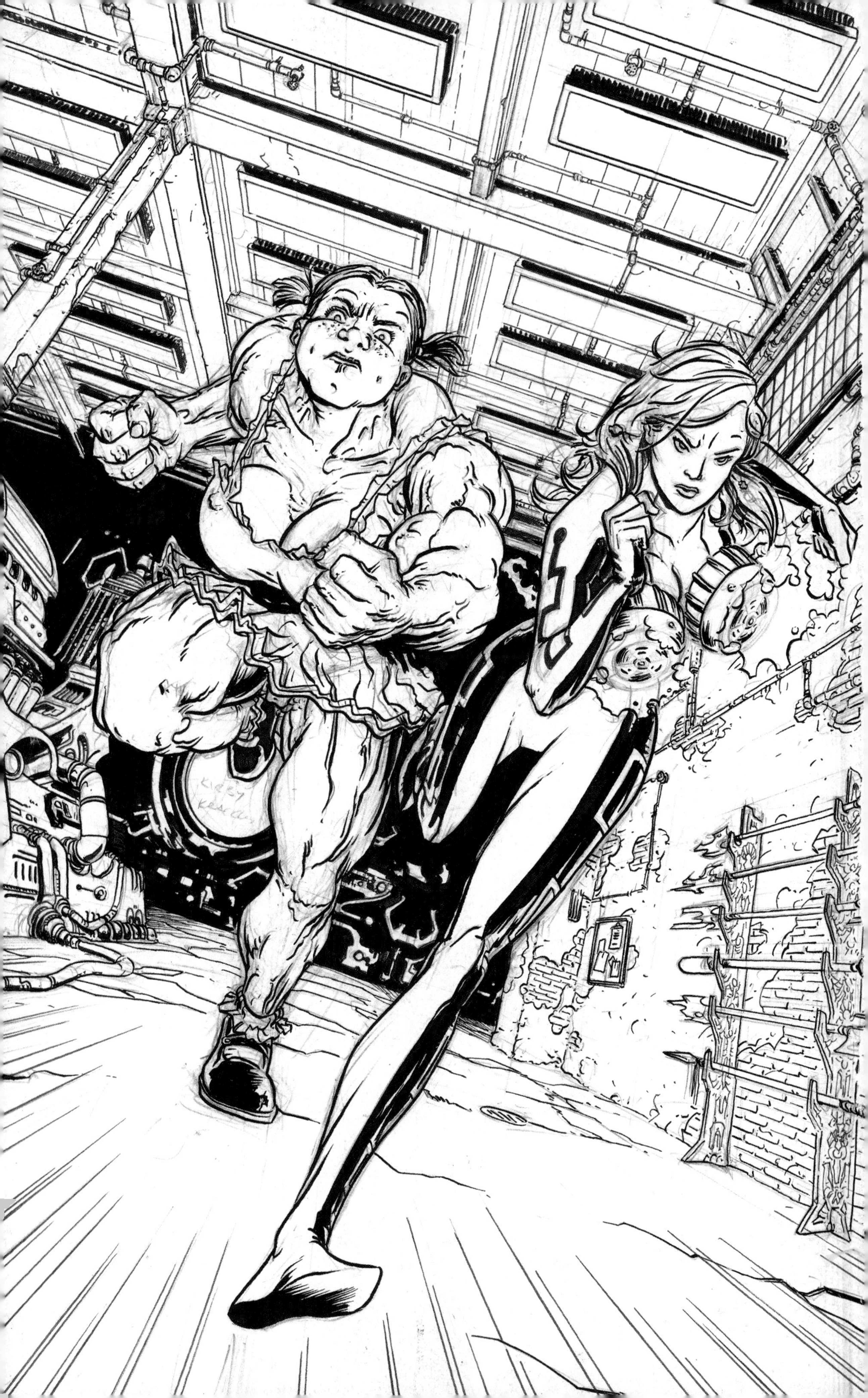

BIOGRAPHIES

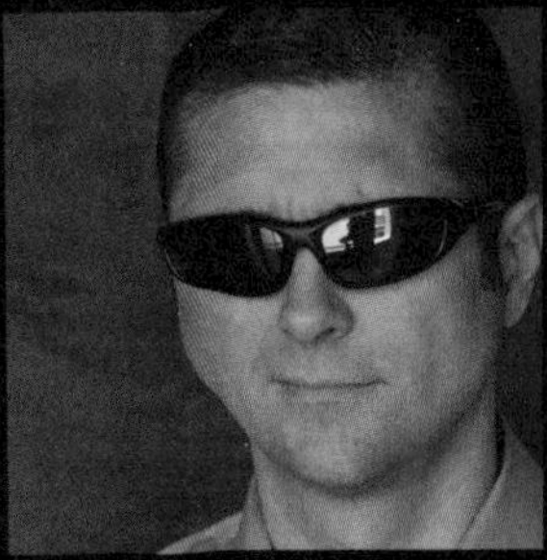

JOE CASEY escaped a childhood filled with nothing but comicbooks, movies and rock n' roll... only to crash headlong into an adulthood filled with nothing but comicbooks, movies and rock n' roll. Along with his bizarre offspring, finding a way to get paid for his interests in all of these was his greatest personal achievement. As a founding partner of *Man of Action Entertainment*, he continues to live, work, write and rock out in Hollywoodland, California.

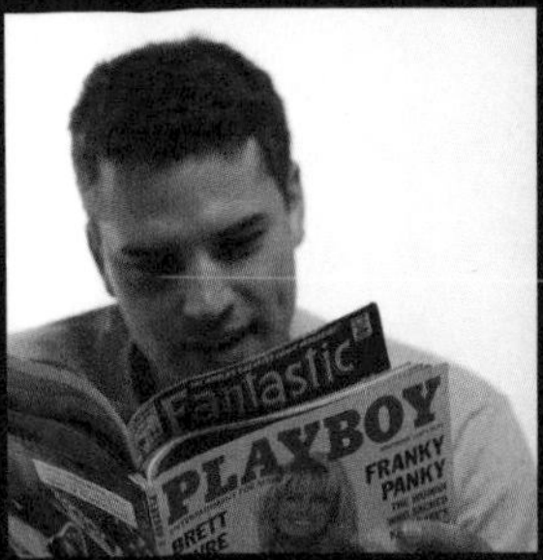
Fantastic
PLAYBOY
FRANKY PANKY

CHRIS BURNHAM is the #1 New York Times Bestselling Artist of Batman Incorporated, and he's almost positive that the success of that book had nothing to do with the fact that it featured Batman or was written by Grant Morrison. Non-bestselling works by Burnham include *X-Men: Manifest Destiny, Elephantmen, The Amory Wars, Fear Agent, Days Missing*, and the *Marvel Mystery 75th Anniversary Special*. His other project with Joe Casey, *OFFICER DOWNE*, is quite possibly the most violent comic book of all time. If you liked this book, you're gonna love that one.

Burnham is currently hard at work on *NAMELESS*, a sci-fi/horror book from Image Comics with writer Grant Morrison and colorist Nathan Fairbairn. You'll love that one, too.

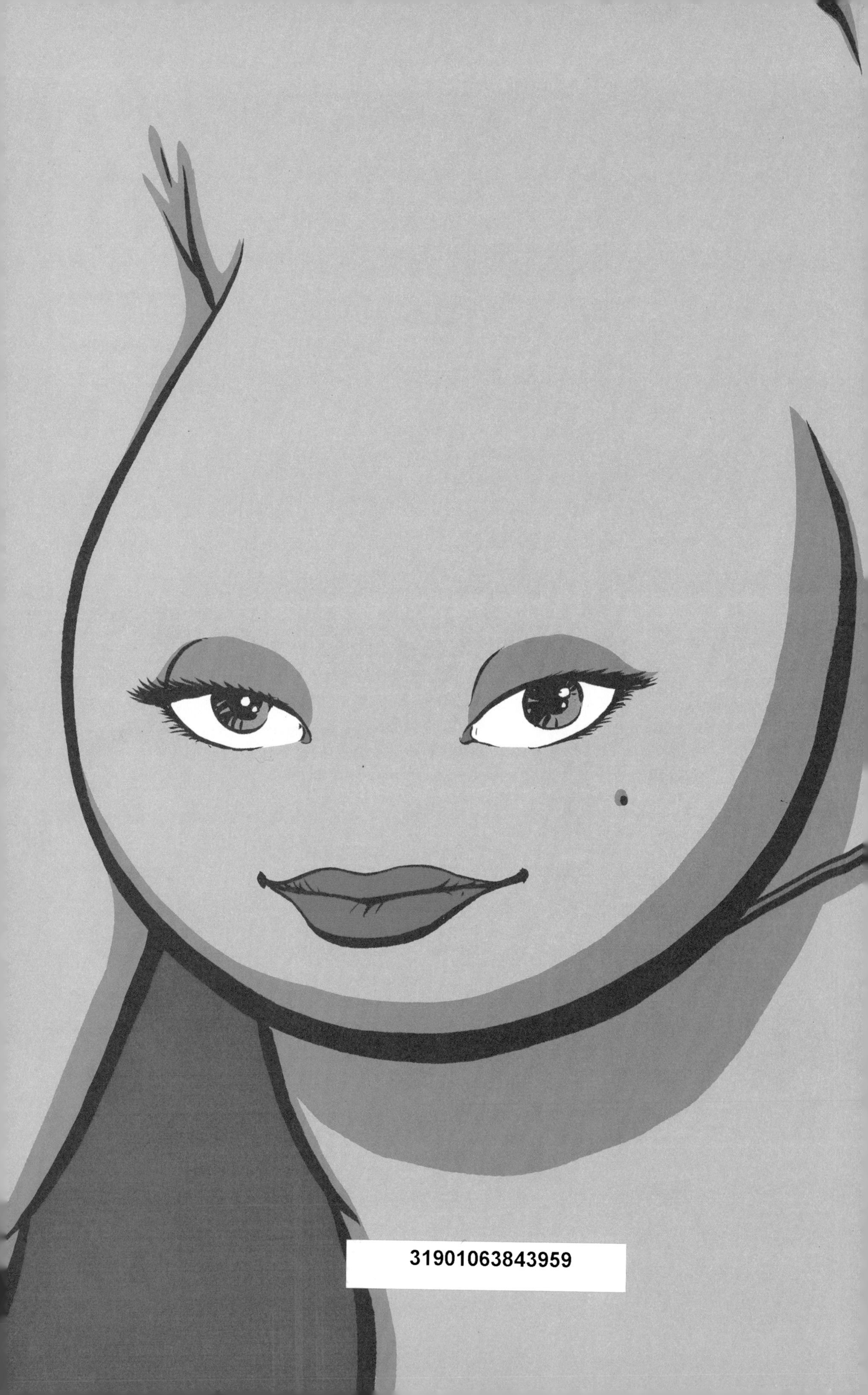